If *You Don't Tell*

If You Don't Tell

A

D.V. Hent novel

Naughty Ink Press

ROM
Hent

This book is a work of fiction. The characters, incidents, and dialogue are drawn from the author's imagination and are not to be construed as real. All locations are either made up or used fictitiously. Any resemblance to actual events or persons, living or dead, is completely coincidental.

ISBN 13: 978-0-9842508-0-6
ISBN 10: 0-9842508-0-8

Acknowledgements

First off, I would like to bow my head before the Alpha and Omega of all things. Thank you God, for without your wisdom, guidance and salvation, I would be nothing. You have given me a gift and I will use it to the best of my ability.

Secondly, I would like to thank my parents. Together, all of you have taught me that education is nothing without the initiative to apply it and the wisdom to use it. I guess that's where my rebellious streak comes from. I know you didn't think I'd be writing erotic novels, well neither did I, but it was one of the most rewarding experiences I've ever had. So next time you see me, please leave the belt at home. Smile!

Third, I would like to send a devilish smile to my muses. The both of you contributed more than anyone will ever know (wink!). You kept me focused and enlightened--which is no small endeavor. Your input will never be forgotten--ever. I would like nothing more than to tell the world who you are, but in doing so, people would believe this book is about you. Little do they know that it isn't about you, but because of your inspiration that made this book possible. Your contributions will forever be in my heart.

Next, I'd like to thank all of my friends and family who brought a third dimension to my characters. Among them: Neesh, Terron, Nela, Mickie, Brandon, Catrina and The Big Man. A lifetime of thanks will never be enough for the laughs you guys have provided.

The final acknowledgement goes to *you*. Without your curiosity, courage and willingness to support the small press, there wouldn't be a point in trying to write something better than the 'literature' that's out there today. Yes, it's a poke, but someone has to stoke the flame, right? Still, I applaud you for making dreams come true--now tell your friends about me so we can get this damn thing rolling!

To everyone else who I didn't get to, love will always be love and I will most certainly get you next time around.

Enjoy!

D.V. Hent

CHAPTER 1

Quinton

"I'm going to kill him."

It wasn't a euphemism. He had about thirty pounds and six inches on me, but no matter how much he fought me, I was going to tightly wrap my hands around Andre's neck and watch as he struggled to cling onto life. A devilish smile crept across my face as the life slowly began to drain...

"Hello Quinton. I didn't realize it was you--bald with a goatee, now. It looks good on you."

Her voice was as seductive as the last time I'd heard it a few years back. She usually wore Brooks Brother's business suits, Versace eyeglasses and Vaneli heels; but tonight she wore a tight, slinky black dress that hugged her sides, exposing her long gorgeous legs. I swallowed hard as I remembered the last time I saw her--how tightly her legs wrapped around me.

I quickly loosened up the tie to the penguin suit I was obligated to wear.

"Hello Val." I managed to mumble.

She makes number five.

1

She took a step towards me and was so close her breasts pressed against the side of my arm. By the smirk on her face, it wasn't done accidentally. "That's all I get after all this time, a 'hello Val'? I thought we meant so much more to each other."

I took a step back. "We don't," I said, still struggling with my tie which seemed to tighten as she drew closer.

Valerie Thomas simply smiled at me, exposing those pretty white teeth that had probably helped her win so many cases. "We had a lot of fun, didn't we?" She whispered into my ear and when I didn't respond, she took a business card and slid inside my pants pocket. "Well just in case you change your mind about...us, take this."

"Is that him?" I heard one of them ask as they headed into the party. "He's really cute!"

"Yes ladies, right there is the mighty Quinton James. Be careful with him, though. He's a tiger in the sack, but he's just a *lamb* when it comes to commitment." Val mocked and the other three began to giggle like school girls as they all continued to leer at my crotch.

Andre has to die.

As I stood next to the professionally decorated, twelve foot tall pine tree and welcomed guests into a home that wasn't mine, I'd always considered myself the prototypical bachelor. I guess prototypical in the sense that I liked clubbing, women and sex, but not necessarily in that order. I enjoyed being single. I relished in my freedom and I loved not having anyone to answer to. Whenever the issue of love came up, I only entertained the notion whenever I felt obligated to do so, but unknown to Val, I'd met someone who had singlehandedly changed my perspective.

After stepping inside the house and looking around the dimly lit room for what seemed like the millionth time that night, I realized that Dre had put together a 'who's who' of my past relationships. So far there were only five, but they never came alone. They *always* brought friends who I'd never seen, but somehow they all knew of me. Whenever any of them passed, and they often did, I'd go as far as acknowledging their existence, but it took a conscious effort for me not to stare.

Even with the influx of holiday alcohol warming my body and lowering my inhibitions, I wasn't naïve enough to believe that I was immune to my old life. Still, that wasn't what I wanted anymore.

I was a changed man.

Unfortunately, not everyone believed in my change and the guest list was a key indication that my best friend, Andre, was back to his old games. As I bit on my lip, thinking about how I'd beat him to death, I remembered the real reason I'd volunteered to do this-- for her.

It was her soft golden complexion and innocent smile that captured me when we met and I was still amazed that even after all this time, I still desired her.

So here we are, three years later, and my fiancée, Laela Booker, was by far the most beautiful woman in the room. When I wasn't forced to play host to past loves, I'd been staring at her for most of the night. Often she'd look in my direction, grin in such a girlish way that even her eyes seemed to smile. Yet, no matter how much I hoped she would visit me, she'd inevitably return her full attention to her best friend, Teniyah.

Usually, I was a guest at Andre's post Christmas-pre New Year's shindig, which he called "The Happy Merry", but this year I was a host at the festivities instead of enjoying them. Though I had no idea that he'd planned on turning this party into a trip down memory lane, this was who he was and to expect anything else meant I'd be fooling myself.

In addition to a few of my partners from the past, he'd invited people from his job at a prestigious investment firm. My hosting position required that I greet the newcomers, laugh with the nearly drunken ones, and whenever possible, parley with his superiors about subject matter I had no clue about. My only reprieve was that before tonight, I'd never realized how awful most drunken people danced. I wasn't exactly sure how anyone could do the robot to 'Jingle Bell Rock', but as I watched several people making a conscious attempt, I was definitely being educated and entertained.

The only problem I had was that during the whole party, all I thought about was walking over to where she was to just be next to her-- to indulge in that sweet scent of hers. I was finally about to renounce my hosting duties when a hand perched itself on my left shoulder and the smartass voice I'd grown used to yelled over the blasting music.

After about an hour listening to Christmas songs blast throughout his mansion, my best friend appeared from the crowd, still dancing, with two glasses of champagne in his free hand.

"Hey cocoa brother, I don't know if you knew, but somewhere in the house-- like pretty much everywhere-- there's a party going on with ass to be conquered! And for your information, the entire collection of reputable ass is in the *opposite* direction of where you are staring. Speaking of which, you suck as a host. There's no liquor in your hand and what the hell are you staring at?"

"I should kick your ass you for what you did tonight!"

"Whatever do you mean?" I glared at him, and he understood that I wasn't joking. "It's not my fault that you've slept with half the women here! Hell, probably with half the women in Houston! And since I've pretty much banged the other half, you make the selection of potential partners decidedly smaller."

"I had a daydream that I was strangling you."

"Was I still sexy in this daydream?"

"Dammit Dre, can't you stop joking? You invited Valerie? That's the fifth girl I've seen. At some point the shit stops being funny, man. At the door, I felt like her and her girlfriends practically eye-raped me."

"I fail to see the problem."

"That's your problem, Dre. You *always* fail to see the problem!"

He leaned over and tightened the tie I'd worked so hard to loosen. "Look, Q, if I knew you were gonna be so bitchy, I wouldn't have done it. I figured it'd be a pre-bachelor, bachelor party. You know--the kind where we take a trip down memory lane."

I yelled, trying to over speak Run-DMC's 'Christmas in Hollis'. "You did all of that, but the future Mrs. James is over there with her best friend!" I grabbed one of the glasses from his hand and quickly washed it down. "At some point, the shit you do stops being funny."

"Look, Q, I'm sorry. Maybe I took it too far. This is a Happy-Merry, so let's just make the best of this." He grabbed me and squeezed until I swore he was about to crush my ribs. "I love you, man." As soon as he let go, he apologetically handed me the other glass of champagne.

"I'm going over to see my fiancée." I tried handing him the glass back, but he folded his arms.

"Damn Quinton, you're at a party where there's a plethora of potentially premier poon, most of it part of your personal repertoire, and all you can do as fantasize about your own girl? There's something seriously wrong here. The Quinton I know would at least dance with that fine piece of ass, known as Valerie, before he retired for the night. Dawg, it's a party! Have some fun and stop acting so damn whipped!"

"I like being whipped," I said. "It keeps me from being *you.*"

"Just imagine this. If you're not concerned with your fine ass exes, think of how Lae's absolutely gorgeous girlfriend, Teniyah, would look naked. Then imagine me and her rolling around in a bed full of Jell-O. That, my friend, is the kind of domestication I could go for. Whatever whipped shit you're on, that shit makes my penis frown."

I raised an eyebrow as I turned towards him, wondering how long it took him to concoct such an elaborate fantasy. I continued walking towards the kitchen, passing a couple who reeked of eggnog. I

4

managed to catch the man as he stumbled, giving each a contrived smile before turning around and facing Dre.

"You know, Franklin just might not like what you're saying about his wife."

Franklin and Teniyah Oliver were the oddest couple I'd ever met. Niya was a model: beautiful, tall and a wild card. Franklin, on the other hand, was about six inches shorter than his wife and reminded me of a geeky version of Al B. Sure.

"Franklin is a pussy. If he heard what I just said, he'd probably cry. The way I see it, she must be putting it on his ass to have that brother whipped the way he is. Hell, I wouldn't mind being on the receiving end of whatever she's got him whipped with." He smirked, hardly taking his attention away from Teniyah.

"Why is it that I'm domesticated for liking where I'm at, but whenever you want to be whipped, you talk about it like it's the best thing in the world? And of all the people you want to be whipped by, you choose another man's wife? You're a goddamn walking contradiction!"

He smiled at me as only Dre could smile: self-assured and sarcastic. "You don't get it, Q. You've made the winning TD, the final basket, the overtime goal. You're safe. You've found that illusive Golden Poon and now you're going to marry it. I will never marry! To me, GP is a mythical beast that women tell us about to get us to commit. You know how much I hate commitment, as much as you used to, which makes banging another man's beautiful wife all the more appealing!"

My throat was beginning to hurt with all the yelling we'd been doing, but bantering was what we did best and tonight wouldn't change that.

"You're a goddamn poet."

"I try."

"So what you're saying is that to find your 'mythical beast', you'd sleep with a married woman?"

He raised an eyebrow. "And you wouldn't?"

"I just can't go along with that. Marriage is supposed to be sacred and I don't have a lot of pity for adulterers. What's the point of getting married if you're going to cheat anyway?"

"Let's not kid ourselves, though. Teniyah is fine as hell. She could talk shit about me, my lifestyle, my deceased parents and even make fun of my five inch love stick and I'd still put in enough work to break her hip. Hell, Franklin could even be in my cheering section. Truth is, I'd sleep with any married woman in this house, in front of her man, and not be remorseful. I'd even go so far as to say that I'd knock the dust of the draws of a fluffy chick-- while you all watched-- if I knew the coochie was good."

I frowned at the prospect of watching him have sex. "You know something, Dre. It took me a while to figure this out, but you're a nasty-ass man."

"Perhaps," he began almost laughing at my commentary, "but before you go down on the last person you'll ever go down on, maybe you should try listening to me for once. Do something else with someone else. Threesomes are pretty trendy and if you were to get down with Lae and Niya, you'd be a god among men. Of course I'm not advocating this adulterous love triangle, but I'd be willing to give you wedding with a 'paid in full' receipt if it ever went down-- just so you know."

Even when I was only a few months from my wedding, Dre was still Dre. I guessed that was why I revered him and was repulsed by him at the same time. Without another word, he shrugged and walked back into the crowd.

I'd almost made it into the kitchen when another shouting voice reawakened the darkest memories from my past. I closed my eyes and hoped that it was just coincidence, but it wasn't. Out of all the people Dre chose to invite, she shouldn't have ever been allowed to step through the door-- number 6.

I accidentally dropped the glass of champagne as she approached me.

"Hey Big Daddy, why are you so hard to catch up with nowadays?" She reached out her arms to embrace me, but I instinctively withdrew, bumping into an older gentleman and spilling his eggnog onto the floor. I excused myself, but the man shrugged his shoulders and continued dancing. She shook her head at my recoil.

"I see you're still a little bitter."

I was so angry that I began to shake. "Don't touch me."

Her name was Leslie Watson and though she was still one of the finest women I'd ever met, she was also one of the worst mistakes I'd ever made. The problem was that her beauty came with a price. She was a sociopath.

I'd met Leslie five years ago when I first began working for Expedited Package Deliveries, EPD. She'd already been there a year and for my first ten months, we worked together. Our days were professional, but during our nights, the sex was as mind-blowing as any I'd ever had. It wasn't until she wanted a monogamous relationship that things suddenly went sour. At first, she began throwing public tantrums at the job, but after I ended our arrangement, she became more deceitful.

6

During the first few months after our falling out, she sent me daily texts messages proclaiming her love and how I'd inevitably 'come around'. When I blocked her number, she began calling my apartment and leaving disturbing messages. From pregnancy to claiming that I gave her Herpes, there wasn't a lie she was afraid to tell. After losing her job and with me finally filing a restraining order, my car became the victim of her wrath. A week later, I found my car on fire.

Instead of jail time, she was ordered to complete therapy sessions and to pay restitution. The last time I saw her was a month before I met Lae and to avoid her altogether, I moved in with Dre to escape the whole ordeal. I was finally off of her radar.

Now, she knew where Dre stayed and since Dre had already known what I'd been through with Leslie, only God could help him if he'd actually invited her.

"Quinton, what's with the hostility? Perhaps I've done some things in the past that I was ashamed of, but I had no idea Andre stayed here. I was invited to a party by one of the ladies in my anger management group and here I am. I've learned to let things go. Tonight, I just happened to see someone from my past who I've wronged and I wanted to apologize. I don't see anything wrong with that. I certainly don't see why I can't even get a hug after not having seen you for the last few years."

I grabbed her arm and without much resistance, pulled her to a corner of the room where I was sure that Lae wouldn't see us speaking.

"What the hell do you want, Leslie? Why the hell are you even here? The restraining order said five hundred feet at all times and you can't get any more specific than that. What the fuck do you want now? Do you want to set fire to me in person or wasn't my car good enough?"

"Quinton," she sighed, "I didn't come here to fight. I honestly didn't even know you were going to be here, but here we are. It's like fate."

"Get the hell away from me," I said through clenched teeth.

"I've already apologized and I really am sorry for those crazy things I did back then." Again she tried to wrap her arms around me and again I backed away from her. "Maybe one day you can forgive me and perhaps we can continue where we left off."

"Left off? What the fuck is wrong with you? Leslie, setting my car on fire was the last straw. I don't ever want to see you, I certainly don't want to fuck you and if I can help it, I don't even want to inhale the same air that you're breathing. There is no goddamn us and there never will be! If you came here *with your friends* like you said you did, then stay

7

with them and get the hell away from me. In fact, don't even acknowledge my existence."

"It's not *always* about you, Quinton. God, I forgot how self-absorbed you can be. I'm here to have fun, just like everyone else and if you don't believe that, maybe I'm not the only one who has to deal with anger issues."

I stormed away from her. The forty months that had passed since the last time I'd seen Leslie had done nothing to curb the malice I'd retained for her.

I can't believe her crazy ass is here! I went looking for Dre, still pissed from what I'd believed was outright betrayal, when I almost knocked Teniyah over as I quickly passed through the kitchen.
Wearing barely enough blouse to cover both breasts and jeans that accentuated her curvaceous frame, she turned around to see who had interrupted her conversation with Laela.

"Excuse you," she said with a little agitation.

"Sorry," I began, "I didn't see you there."

"How could you not see a six foot tall, mind-blowingly fine and carnally adventurous, black woman in a sea of white folks? Clearly Quinton, you wanted a free feel of all of the lusciousness. It's okay to let it out. Talking about your lust for me can be therapeutic." That was typical Teniyah-- always the center of attention.

"Niya, if I really wanted you, asking is the last thing I'd have to do." Lae let out a quick laugh. I looked at the ring I'd given her just a few weeks ago, which helped to ease the tension I was feeling.

Teniyah eyed Lae and mouthed *"traitor"* before she smiled at me and continued whatever conversation she and Lae were having.
"So then this little ass man proceeds to tell me that he can do everything for me that my husband can't do," Teniyah said, raising her eyebrow. I walked by her to pour myself a glass of champagne.

"You're talking about the guy that just left?!?" Lae asked incredulously. "That guy already has a girlfriend! His name is BJ and in fact, doesn't he work with you, Quinton?" She turned around in her chair and smiled at me.

I took a sip from my glass and shrugged my shoulders. BJ was a co-worker of mine and I wasn't about to get anyone in trouble tonight.

They continued with their conversation. "I saw him walking around like he'd just lost his puppy. What did you say to him, Niya, to make him look so sad?"

"Sad is right. That brother was as sad as they come. After he ran off his lines, I stood up and let him stare at my assets for a quick second--

you know, let him lick his chops. I raised my hand just above my head and let him know that to ride this ride-- he has to be this tall." Teniyah said while laughing.

Lae joined in with her, and I smiled just a bit. I liked BJ. Like Leslie, we all worked at the same job, but unlike Leslie, BJ was still employed there. Besides, I'd met BJ's girlfriend and though she wasn't anything to get excited about, even I knew that with Teniyah, he was way over his head and certainly out of his league.

I took a gulp from my glass, nearly finishing it and kissed Lae on her forehead. "So is that all you guys have been doing all night? Talking about the dominant sex?"

"Only dominant thing on y'all is body odor," Niya mumbled under her breath.

"And no matter how much you want to deny it, you love some good dick."

"Ok now, children! I don't want to have to send you two to your corners again." Lae eagerly interjected.

We joked a lot with each other and even though she was too stubborn to admit it, I knew Teniyah liked it. The only reason we pretended to fight was simply for Lae's benefit-- and her attention. So, rather than just get along, we constantly bickered about the most meaningless things. I liked it that way, too. It gave us something to do.

"That's okay, Lae, I feel like dancing anyway." Niya stood up and stretched her arms. As soon as she began bringing her arms back to her side, a drunken party-goer bumped into her and continued through the crowd as if nothing happened. "So what am I, invisible?" She shouted and shook her head.

"Speaking of invisible, where is Franklin?" I asked.

"He's probably learning how to dance from some drunk fool. I think he may be the only black person I've met without rhythm. In fact, most things that need rhythm don't suit him." She winked at Lae, but even I knew what she'd been suggesting by that. She grabbed the champagne glass from my hand and finished it off before pouring herself another glass from the bottle on the table. After winking at me, she disappeared in the direction of the loud, thumping music.

When she was gone, Lae shook her head. "She's such a flirt."

"You noticed that," I added sarcastically.

"I also noticed how you were staring at me the whole night. Is there something you wanted?"

Just as I was about to speak, the voice had found its way back to me.

9

"Well Quinton, who is this lovely lady that has captured all of your attention?"

I turned around to face her, but before I had a chance to speak, Lae extended her hand and introduced herself. "My name's Laela. Quinton is my fiancé."

"So, you're his *fiancée*?" she asked, and then looked at me with genuine surprise. "I guess a leopard can change its spots."

"Go away, Leslie." I said, with my teeth now grinding.

"I never even knew about your engagement! Why can't I meet your beautiful fiancée? After talking to some people here, it seems to me that she's the only woman on the planet who could humble the untamable Quinton James?"

"You know, Leslie, I'm not seeing five hundred feet between us. That is what the court order demanded, right?"

She walked around me and straight to Laela. "You better be careful with this one, he's a beast-- especially in the bed."

"I know. It's a shame you realized that after you lost him."

After looking at Laela up and down, she walked away without another word.

"So, I take it that she was one of your cutty-buddies?" Lae asked, nonchalantly. "I can see why I've never heard of her."

"I never wanted to even think about her again. She was committed for a while after setting fire to my car."

"So are there anymore crazy, dick-whipped women I have to worry about? I don't want to have to be this nice the whole night."

I laughed loudly enough for her to show a smile.

After an hour of dancing to every Christmas song I'd ever heard, I left Lae with Niya and found Dre. He'd found time to change from the dark suit he'd been wearing into some khakis and a tan sweater with mistletoe attached to the collar. He was sitting on his loveseat, sipping on a glass of champagne with a white lady I knew to be his neighbor. As soon as he saw the look on my face, he excused himself and walked with me away from the party.

"You brought crazy ass Leslie here and she confronted me in front of Lae!"

"I saw her, but I didn't invite her. She came with someone I knew. It's a sad case of a friend who knew a friend who brought her crazy ass. That's it. There's no conspiracy here, man."

"So where is she now?"

"She's getting smoked out with my friend and some other friends. Perhaps a little weed in her system may mellow her down."

"You need to kick her ass out! I mean like yesterday! Both her and your friend!"

"Whoa, no can do. She's not burnin' up any of my shit up and this party is for business connections. How good would I look if I just started kicking people out who hadn't done anything wrong? Look man, truth is I really want her friend's draws and if I kick her out they all leave. The way I see it, if I do it your way, it ends badly for me. So I let them get a little high, pacify her for the time being and perhaps I can get a 'job well done' screw."

It was my turn to shake my head. "You know what, your damn happy stick is gonna get the both of us in trouble one day."

"As long as it's not today, I can live with that. Speaking of trouble, there's something I gotta do." He dashed down his spiral staircase and into the dancing crowd downstairs.

I walked over to the loveseat and finally sat down, after hours of smiling and drinking all night. I closed my eyes and relaxed, allowing the champagne that I'd been sipping take its effect. I almost completely drowned out the sounds of the party when the hoots and hollers of the crowd downstairs grabbed my attention.

I looked over the balcony to see that everyone had encircled three people. One of them was Dre, who had taken the mistletoe he'd been wearing earlier and dangled it above two women, a short blond and a brunette. Both girls were extraordinarily beautiful, young and voluptuous, which is why I knew Dre had sought them out. They looked around the room at all the attention they had gathered, and smiled sheepishly at each other as Dre revealed a mischievous grin of his own.

"Ladies, this is mistletoe." Dre displayed the mistletoe for everyone to see. "And tradition dictates that if you are at my 'Happy Merry' and also under this mistletoe, you have to kiss with anyone else under it." Dre once again donned his patented smile and again catcalls reverberated throughout the room. The girls, aware of what was about to happen, turned their looks of awe from each other to the ringleader.

"I, the mistletoe god of Happy Merry, deem you ladies *mistletoed*. You may begin the kissing at your leisure."

The crowd again roared into screams and hollers as the girls leaned towards each other. As if on cue, the entire room grew silent as the lips of two beautiful women approached each other. We were all on the precipice of an explosion, but as the girls lips touched, both pulled back, essentially sucking the air from the entire room.

As quickly as the catcalls had filled the room, boos from all around the room now angrily replaced them, causing both girls to disappear into a different section of the crowd.

"Is there anyone else willing to entertain the masses?" Dre looked around the room, but only one other person raised his hand.

"Only if it's me and you, man!" BJ shouted.

Dre turned back towards the crowd and before he had a chance to speak, he found another hand had risen. It was Teniyah's, but the person she was pulling through the crowd wasn't Franklin, it was Laela.

"Now that's the shit I'm talking about!" Dre shouted excitedly. He looked up at me with a raised eyebrow, then at the girls as they approached him. Life had once again been brought back into the room as the cheering began and everyone moved to allow both women quicker passage.

Once they made it to the foyer where I'd been earlier, Lae looked as mortified as I'd ever seen her, but Teniyah reveled at the attention. She was already as tall as Dre, so she continued to raise her arms, getting the crowd even more excited in anticipation of what we were about to see.

"Since I know the both of these women, I don't need a speech. I'll just hold the mistletoe up here and let you girls do whatever the mistletoe compels you to do."

As Niya leaned over and Lae's eyes closed, I thought about yelling out to Lae, but even I wasn't sure if I was to support her or detract her. So instead, I remained quiet and watched. As soon as their lips touched, my immediate erection ruled out any idea of stopping them.

Niya reached her arms around Lae, grabbing her by the waist and pressed their bodies against each other. It wasn't automatic, but while their mouths discovered a common rhythm, I watched as Lae grew increasingly more relaxed. Not long after the initial kiss, Lae conceded to Niya's tongue and the room watched in unadulterated delight as it finally invaded Lae's mouth. Not yet ready to relinquish the attention she was receiving, Niya slowly withdrew, sucking on Lae's lip as she pulled away.

After Lae finally opened her eyes, the room erupted in cheers. Shouting over the deafening crowd, Dre repeated several times, "That shit was hot! Somebody please tell me that wasn't the hottest shit ever! Holy shit, I think I just exploded in my pants!"

As the crowd helped Niya cheer herself on and a breathless Lae waved to the crowd, for the first time that night, Dre and I were in complete agreement.

That shit *was* hot.

"So what made you go up there with her?" I asked.

I was dead tired when we had finally made it to our apartment on the southwest side of Houston. Instead of jumping in the shower to wash off all the stale, smoke smell I had accumulated, I threw off my shirt and slacks, leaving only my boxers on before I jumped in the bed. Lae insisted on washing up, wearing a long t-shirt with a picture of a pony on the front as she exited the bathroom.

"I didn't want to go, but she just pulled me up there. I thought she was joking about doing it until I could feel her breath inches from my face."

I knew it was on her mind because I couldn't forget about it. "So what made you kiss her back?"

Lae thought for a second and smiled. "I have to get some practice from somewhere, right?" She laughed, I smiled. "Besides, if she would've dragged you up there, what would you have done in front of all those people?"

"I wouldn't have kissed her in front of Franklin, besides, she's married. What would you think of me after I just made out with a married woman?"

She threw one of the pillows from our bed at me, hitting me in the back. "Quinton James, don't you dare sit on this bed a lie to me. If we're supposed to be so open, then why can't you just admit that you would've kissed her too?"

"You know me, Lae, kissing is intimate. I gotta at least like you to kiss you."

"So what you're telling me is that you'd sleep with Niya-- if she wasn't married, but you wouldn't ever kiss her?"

"Her lips would be the only dry thing on her body." This time she slapped me on my bare back. "Damn, that hurt! Don't make me call the abuse hotline on you."

"And men say that women have their priorities messed up?! You are the only man I know who wouldn't sell his nuts for a crack at Niya. Are you saying this just to pacify me?"

13

"Pacify you? My girl just locked lips with another girl and I'm trying to pacify you?"

"Are you upset with me?"

"Was she a good kisser?"

"What you're really asking is, is she a better kisser than you."

"And?"

"You don't have anything to worry about. You have her beat by light years and I'll prove it to you."

"What did kissing her feel like?"

She pulled her stethoscope from off the nightstand and placed it around her neck. "I guess it's like kissing a man without a moustache, but her tongue was so forceful! For a few seconds, I thought hers was about to body slam mine and take it as a trophy."

I laughed at the thought of Niya's tongue beating up on mine, yet I felt a little uneasy. I lied to Lae, but I knew her well enough not to fall prey to a question about Niya. Dre was right about Teniyah, she was too sexy and way to out there for her own damn good. Problem was that if given the chance, I would've probably done it too.

I thought about the kiss the two shared as I allowed Laela to straddle me. Even with my boxers on, I could feel the heat coming from under her shirt and once again my erection returned. With her stethoscope hanging from around her neck, she pressed the cold metal on my naked chest before switching sides and listening to my heart.

"Why Mrs. James, did you find what you were looking for?" I asked softly.

"Mrs. James, you say? Since we're not married yet, perhaps we shouldn't be doing this." She revealed the same devilish smile that I'd grown to love.

I softly brushed my lips against hers. "I won't tell if you don't and for the record, I can't wait for you to be my wife."

"Me either." She slid her stethoscope into my boxers. "Mr. James, I'd like to hear the sounds an erection makes."

"I could tell you the sound a certain nurse makes when she gets too close."

I rolled over, causing her to fall onto the bed. I quickly mounted her and ran my hands along her thighs. When I reached the bottom of her t-shirt, I pulled it up, revealing her neatly trimmed temple and the real reason she'd gone into the bathroom. I bent over and kissed her steeple several times, allowing several verbs to escape her mouth. Not stopping there, I pulled her shirt above her breasts and softly bit the tips before taking her nipples into my mouth.

14

"Going north tonight?" she whispered.

"Shhh, I'm working."

I sat her up and pulled her shirt over her head, softly kissing her. I slowly invaded her mouth with my tongue and soon after, tasting her lips and those of the last person who'd been there. Cherry. She'd worn cherry lip gloss when she'd kissed Laela and now her taste was on my tongue as well.

She dragged her fingernails down my back as we kissed, causing me to pause and deeply inhale. With her hands still on my back, I placed my hand around her neck and pushed her back down to the bed. I ran my cherry flavored tongue around both sides of her neck before stopping, softly nibbling on her left ear.

She dug her fingers deeper into my flesh as more vowels were expelled. Her nipples now fully awakened, I returned to her breasts engulfing the right one in my mouth. I slid my hand down her stomach and parted her thighs. I quickly pulled my erection out from its hiding spot in my boxers and slowly rubbed it against her.

I wanted her so badly that my dick began to throb, but I wasn't ready to enter her.

Not yet.

Even though I had the taste of two women on my tongue, it felt almost as if Niya were next to us and cheering us on. I shook the thought of her from my thoughts and returned my attention to my woman.

Moving from her right breast to her left one, gently sucking her breasts and teasing her nipples, I wrote Q-U-I-N-T-O-N as I dragged my tongue across her belly and worked my way back to where I'd began my journey.

I knelt before her temple, softly kissing her thighs and began skating across her clitoris with my tongue. Using the figure eight as my inspiration and the infinity symbol as my finale, I tasted every inch of the woman I loved. She responded immediately with grateful groans and as her steeple grew in size, her innocently wandering hands quickly became fists that bludgeoned our sheets. Not long after cursing me, I finally tasted her sweetness.

I alternated between my eights and infinities for a few moments afterwards-- until she pushed me away. I fought her, trying to work my way back in between her thighs, but she was adamant. She pulled me close to her and hungrily kissed me. It was filled with such passion that I had no doubt that she'd sampled what I had just savored.

I pulled away from her and with my dick begging for attention, I flipped Lae over and as she lay naked and winded, I slowly entered her

15

from behind. She was warm--so warm that I had to quickly retreat. As I eased in and filled her once more, I pushed her untamed hair to the side and kissed her neck. Then, between her shoulder blades, I finished my autograph. I wrote J-A-M-E-S along her spine as our bodies began the ritual of grinding.

Like always, we made a masterpiece. She was my canvas and with each broad brushstroke, my painting neared completion. I reached under her, cupped her breasts a pushed deeper into her. Amid her masochistic whispers, she urged me to climax for her and soon after, with her.

I softly called to her as I always did before I climaxed and as her warmth overtook me, I went deep one last time before I exploded. The force of my climax was so fierce that for a few seconds afterwards, I'd forgotten to inhale, causing me to fall off of her.

As I lay next to my fiancée, her face resting on my chest and her wild hair tickling my nose, not a single word was spoken. Words weren't ever needed. With heavy eyelids, darkness began to envelope me and only one thought remained.

Damn, that kiss was hot.

CHAPTER 2

Laela

December 31st (Saturday)

The sun had barely met the horizon and I saw him getting ready for work. I didn't want him to go, especially after the shiver down my spine reminded me of last night.

I listened to him complain about being late before he rushed out of the front door, forgetting to kiss me on his way out. I should've been upset, but I was on cloud nine. I'd had multiple orgasms last night and I was still feeling the lingering affects even after I'd gotten some sleep. I staggered from the front door to the bathroom, turned on the shower and let the steam fill the room before I took off my housecoat and stepped in.

I closed my eyes and let the water run down my face. I found myself thinking a great deal about the kiss that Niya and I shared. I couldn't believe that I'd actually gone through with it. As much as I wanted to pass it off as just Niya being Niya, I really enjoyed it—more than I knew I should have. As a small smile crept across my face, I suddenly remembered meeting Leslie. Though I hadn't told Quinton and passed Leslie's words off as indifference, it was a façade. I didn't want to admit it, even to myself, but the truth was that she got under my skin.

17

Admittedly, she was a little off in the mental department, but why hadn't he said anything about her? The added fact that we'd shared a man didn't help with the uneasiness that began to grow from the pit of my stomach.

I'm thinking way too much. A kiss is just a kiss and an ex is still and ex.

I showered for ten minutes before I stepped out, wiped the mist off the glass and sized myself up in the mirror. After remembering how perfect Leslie looked in her skin tight dress, I began to examine how far I'd fallen off the wagon since I'd been in a serious relationship. My butterscotch complexion was a complete contrast to my dark eyes and hair, but I still had my mother's figure; two handfuls of breasts, small hips, and a round ass. I wasn't chubby, but I'd been out of the gym for a while and I was starting to lose my definition. *Solid is what brings them, solid is what was going to keep him.* I patted on my stomach and smacked my ass for good measure. I walked into our bedroom and threw on my royal blue scrubs. I was hoping to leave out a little earlier than normal to avoid the awful Houston traffic, which would most certainly put a damper on my easy-going mood.

I grabbed my stethoscope, which was surprisingly still warm and I smiled as I thought about last night.

I'm certainly going to have to sterilize you when I get to work.

I grabbed my keys off the coffee table and began to walk out the door when the phone rang. I thought about answering it, but not at the risk of enduring even worse traffic than I was already about to run into. I glanced at the caller ID to see that it was Simone. I grabbed my purse and reminded myself to call her on my cell on the way to work.

I pulled out of the parking lot onto the street and turned right, driving my new gold Honda Accord and feeling like a new woman. After about ten minutes of driving south on Highway 6, I jumped on 59 North before I dialed up Simone.

"Girl, I just called you." She sounded busy. Ever since she'd married the *anti*-man, she always sounded rushed, which was due to his lazy ass not helping her out with even the most minor tasks.

"It's Saturday, Monie, why do you sound like it's a weekday?"

"I'm cleaning up around the house."

"And where is Michael? In case you hadn't known, he's your husband and most rumors suggest that it's his house, too." Her husband Michael was one of Quinton's closest friends, though I was in the minority when I told everyone how much of a piece of shit I believed him to be. Simone, on the other hand, was one of my best friends who I'd met

18

in high school. I loved her like a sister and she knew how disappointed I was in some of the choices she made, especially when it came to her rushed marriage to Michael --whom I've always suspected of cheating. I've told her several times about my suspicions, but she always shrugged it off by telling me that there wasn't any proof and a good woman always stands by her man.

"Can we please not do this today, Lae?"

"Fine." I said, a little more agitated than I should have. Between Simone's husband and Quinton's ex, I was a bit snappier than I should have been.

"Anyways," she began, "even though you woke up on the wrong side of the bed today, I just wanted to know what you and future hubby are doing for New Year's."

I thought for a second before answering. "We don't have any plans that I know of. Why?"

"I don't know, I just wanted to get out of the house and do something fun for the New Year."

"We had fun. Remember last night? You were supposed to be at Dre's Happy Merry party. Don't give me any BS excuses about how you forgot because I reminded you yesterday morning."

"I wanted to go, but we couldn't find a baby-sitter," she said unconvincingly.

"Is that just your way of saying that the all important Michael Hall got his way-- again?"

"Look Lae, I didn't call you so that I could be nagged to death about my husband's faults. I just wanted to see what you and Quinton were doing tonight."

"So that's a yes to the 'got his way' question?"

"I hate you."

"I love you, too." I laughed. "So what did you have in mind for New Year's?"

"Why don't we all get a hotel room and just get drunk?"

"That's the same thing you want to do every holiday. At some point you have to stop being so predictably spontaneous."

I didn't mind indulging Simone's idea, but sometimes I'd catch glimpses of her mother in her. Seeing her developing a drinking problem took me back to those years when we walked home together. Because Simone's apartment was on the way to my house we walked together every day. Usually we'd be laughing the whole way, but as soon as we stopped at her building, the laughs would end. Simone would smile sheepishly, then slowly open the front door and send me a quick wave before I continued on my way. Yet, the few times she had allowed me into their place, I could see why she didn't want me there. The house was a complete pigsty and Simone's mother was usually in one of two states. She was either drunk out of her mind, cursing Simone for not having the house spotless or high as a kite and sprawled out on the floor of their apartment. After only a few months of even knowing Simone, I was there to support her after her mother died from an overdose.

I never saw Simone as far gone as her mother, but as soon as she and Michael began having problems, Simone began to disappear more often and her drinking was noticeably heavier. I knew it wasn't my place, but I knew what she'd been through. The truth was that she didn't have anyone else in her corner besides her aunt, whom she despised, so I constantly reminded her of what life would be like for her son, MJ, to grow up without a mother.

I didn't want to always play mother hen with Simone and the role was beginning to wear on me, but she was still my friend and friends were supposed to look out for each other.

"It's New Year's!" She exclaimed. "You don't have to be prudes all the time!"

"I'm not a fish, but somebody has to keep you from gettin' pissy drunk, right?"

"Look, Lae, I need to get out of the house. I need to do something. I'm going crazy and I think Mike has some other plans. He hasn't said anything yet, but I hear him on the phone talking with his boys, telling them that he doesn't have anything to do yet. I would at least like to bring in this year with him. At least if Q is gonna be there, he'll come."

"I hear you. I'll talk to Quinton and see what he wants to do." I knew that I hadn't spent much time with Simone lately, but between Quinton, the job and the wedding, I usually didn't have much time for anything else.

"Thanks girl." She sounded genuinely appreciative.

After we hung up, I searched for my 90's R&B CD. There were a few songs that mellowed me out before work and with a full moon out last night, I was probably going to need it. I popped it in and listened to it for the rest of my morning commute.

I pulled into the Harris County Regional Medical Center around fifteen minutes before my shift began, which was exactly the amount of time I needed to park, walk to the floor, and punch in. Since the garage was right across the street and the labor hall was on the second floor of a seven story building, I didn't have much traveling to do, but I found myself yearning for the breakfast I'd intentionally skipped – all thanks to Leslie and Teniyah.

Damn them and their Coke bottle figures!

When the elevator doors opened to my floor, it appeared as if a bomb had just gone off. The phones behind the nurse's desk were constantly being lit up by physicians who were calling in for reports on their laboring patients, nurses were running around with charts in hand, monitors were beeping out of control and even a few patients were walking up and down the halls, complaining of their unbearable pains. I hated working at a county hospital, but I loved being a labor and delivery nurse. The only thing I loved more than the job was the pay.

I walked past the morning commotion and on my way to the lounge to grab some coffee, bumped into our morning charge nurse, Pat McMahon, on the way to the time clock.

"Put your game face on, Lae." She said. "It is definitely gonna be one of those mornings."

I clocked in, received report from the night shift, and prepared for the onslaught.

After the morning rush trickled into the early afternoon, there wasn't much left to do. I walked down to the nurses' lounge, a room which could barely even been considering a place to lounge to catch a few minutes of rest. With just an old couch, an unusable refrigerator, a television set whose color was slowly fading, and a plastic table with only one available chair, the term lounge was used very loosely for a place where old paint was chipping from the walls.

Still, I could hardly wait to flop down on my most favorite sofa in the world, a furry blue couch we affectionately named 'Cookie'. One of the nurses had named it after the big blue monster that used to be on our favorite childhood show and since no one took offense, the name stuck. My body was already longing for its soft cushions and I still had four more hours left in my day.

It was there that I found Niya, already occupying most of Cookie and watching some talk show whose topic was paternity tests. I hadn't seen her all morning, so I suspected that she had been hiding. With only one laboring patient, she'd gotten off easy, especially seeing as I was stuck with triple the workload. One of them was a nurse's worst nightmare--a whining black woman, in her early twenties, who wasn't even laboring, but cried about every single labor pain. She wasn't anywhere near giving birth, and complained of cramping that never seemed to stay in one place. On more than one occasion I was prepared to throttle her.

Teniyah kept her legs up and laid them across the cushions, daring me to move them. My body ached so badly that I was ready to face her wrath when I pushed them over the edge and sat down.

"You know something? You're so lucky that you're my girl," she warned, "or there would have been some serious drama. Still, with all that work you had to do, I didn't feel like whooping your ass so late in the day." She half-smiled as I raised my eyebrow towards her.

Teniyah had such a sensual voice that she could just charm the pants off of any man she chose, but instead, she usually bullied people whenever they allowed her to. Quinton would joke about the both of us having the voices of phone sex operators, but she would have more men releasing themselves to the sound of hers. She was already a self-proclaimed professional in the art of men, but given the chance, I honestly think she'd try to get paid for sex if she could.

Because I knew her too well to take her threats seriously, I usually received a free pass, but her husband, Franklin wasn't so lucky. On more than one occasion, I witnessed her belittling him in front of random people.

"You're lucky that I don't march straight to the desk and get Pat to give you one of my patients...." I smirked at her.

There was a lot of history between us during the eight years that I'd known Teniyah. We began our friendship in our second year in nursing school and been inseparable ever since. Back in college we were two of about a handful of black people going to the same nursing program so we clicked instantly. Only by chance did we end up in the same dorm room. She was supposed to live with her sorority, but through a mix-up the both of us roomed in the honor's dorm. At first we were complete opposites and everything was awkward, but through our experiences together and as we grew to know each other, we became something more than friends. We were kindred spirits; or rather I lived my crazy side vicariously through her. I was able to tell her some things that I hadn't told anyone before and she'd confess to me the kinky things going down at fraternity parties, always noting when she was the kinky thing. There wasn't anything that we didn't share with each other.

More often than not, when we were dating gorgeous frat men, they called us sisters even though we looked nothing alike. She was more mocha colored, a complete contrast to my lighter complexion, and she towered above me by at least six inches. Her eyes, with their almond shape and similar color, have lured many men in our direction. Even now, the wedding band she wore did nothing to deter their advances. Add in the fact she still had the figure of a high school cheerleader, despite giving birth to my two twin godchildren, DeShawn and Brianna-- five years old, and she was damn near perfect.

I still believe that the only thing that stopped her from marrying some exotic millionaire was she'd gotten pregnant in the last year of school and ended up marrying the man she suspected was the babies' father; but even I knew she did it more out of obligation than love. He loved her, but I still think she wasn't ready to marry and in the end, she'd settled.

Though Niya was my *other* best friend, she and Simone couldn't be more opposite, which is probably why they didn't get along. Teniyah's always been aggressive, confident, even demanding at times. Both Simone and I have always been laid back, moderately stubborn and a little more inhibited than most. It was amazing how little Niya cared for her even though Simone and I were a lot alike.

"Sticks and stones, Lae. Besides, you know what hard work does to me!"

"It makes you lazier?"

"So now you know why I can't have more work. Now that we've gotten that out of the way, what did Quinton think about our kiss last night? Was he upset that I turned his woman out in one night?"

"He thinks you're a mouth rapist." I said, trying not to laugh.

She frowned. "Is that what he seriously thinks?"

"No. Well, not really. He actually thought that it was pretty-- steamy. It just caught him off-guard that you would put the both of us in front of an audience."

"So, what you're saying is that like every other man in the room, he wanted some of this." When she stuck out her long tongue and wriggled it around, I couldn't help but laugh at her crazy ass. She joined in not long after.

"He didn't exactly say that, but he was curious to know how much I enjoyed it."

"And how could you not have? Am I not a kissing goddess?"

"It was-- interesting. I hadn't planned on my best friend slobbing me down in front of a crowd at my fiancé's best friend's house party."

"It doesn't have to end with last night Lae," she whispered. "But you already knew that."

I knew where this was heading and it was time to change the subject. "Why are you even watching this crap?"

She completely ignored my question and began her interrogation. "Lae, have you even thought about the thing we talked about?"

It had been at least a month since I told her about my dream. On several consecutive nights, I dreamt about another woman doing things she shouldn't to me, but I didn't want her to stop. It was so real that when I awoke, my panties were wet.

I struggled with telling Quinton, but when I did, he suggested that we indulge. There was no way I could tell Simone and because of her strict upbringing. I was too embarrassed to tell her because I feared that she'd see me differently.

When I finally told Niya about my dream, she not only embraced the idea of me being with another woman, she offered to be her. Lately she'd even been lobbying the idea of solo test drive before committing to the threesome with Quinton.

"Yes, Niya, I've been thinking about it, but I'm not sure if I'm ready to go there. This was supposed to be a Quinton and I thing. I don't think that making it a 'me' thing is exactly fair."

"So don't tell him."

I thought about asking her if she would do the same thing to Franklin, but before even a syllable left my mouth, I already knew the answer. She never told him anything and I wasn't sure that I wanted that kind of relationship. "Just because you never tell your man anything doesn't mean I have to do the same."

She scooted over next to me and rested her head on my shoulder. "Tell me that you didn't like the way my lips felt when they were pressed up against yours and I'll never bring this up again."

As I reminisced about the kiss we shared just hours ago, I could tell her that I didn't appreciate the way she rammed her tongue into my mouth or I could admit that she'd caught me off-guard, but the one thing that I couldn't say was that I didn't like it. As I remained silent and let the sounds of the television fill the room, I could almost hear her smiling.

"Enough said."

I didn't know why I'd enjoyed her kiss so much, but the spontaneity of all made it more passionate and sexy than most of the kisses I'd shared with men. I'd never been a fan of public affection, but as our lips and tongues became synchronous, it was as if everyone in the room had disappeared and somehow the kiss had me more aroused than any kiss I'd ever had.

The warming of my body and hardening of my nipples was evidence that I needed to change topics. "So, you never answered me when I asked why you were watching this."

As if on cue, she immediately switched from being sex goddess back to being Niya. "Because I like the suspense and it's good TV. These women are out there losing their damn minds, pinning their babies on a man who isn't even the father, and then run off the stage crying because they're nasty."

"Uh-huh," I mocked.

I looked away from Niya, towards the television and took in a deep breath--using it to calm myself and forget about last night. "You're a piece of work, you know that? Like you really know who your babies' daddy is! And like you aren't one of the nasty ones? You should be right beside your girl right on that stage. Maybe you should call up the show and have a secret revealed."

"Well," she smiled sheepishly, "the likelihood that the kids are his is greater than the likelihood that they aren't and that theory doesn't need to be tested, ever." She smiled, letting me know that she herself wasn't sure, and was never planning on finding out.

"Why don't you take him on this show? You know, just to be sure," I mused.

"Now you're talking crazy. Besides, we're semi-comfortable now. And I see no reason to mess that up." She paused before making her next statement. "So, since I know you liked kissing me, have you really thought about my proposition?" Teniyah looked me directly in the eye when she asked, knowing that I wouldn't look away.

In what seemed like an eternity, I stared at the woman I'd known for the last eight years, but words couldn't escape my mouth. Finally, she took her eyes from me and went back to watching TV. I stood up and walked around the room, paranoid that there was some hidden camera or secret spy hidden in the crevices of one of the corners. I finally sat back down after I was sure that no one else was in the room. She laughed at my uneasiness.

"You just won't quit with these questions until I give you an answer, will you?"I asked.

"No, I won't."

"I already gave you an answer. I don't think I can do it without Quinton being there."

"So you're scared."

"Niya, you know me. And you know that I'm a good girl and good girls don't do things like that." I was avoiding her stare, playing with my

25

favorite black pen, a gift she had given me, another reminder of our eight year bond.

She seemed disappointed, but was too stubborn to show any emotion. "Is that a 'no'?"

I didn't want to rush my response, but I did anyway. "It's not a *no*," I paused, "I'm just saying that I'm not sure. Niya, you're like one of my best friends and I don't know about all of this. It's just so sudden. I mean if I said yes, I'd have more questions and even more importantly, I wouldn't know what the hell to do! I don't know how we'd look at each other afterwards. What will you think of me? What'll happen if we both *like* it? I just don't know how either of us will be affected if we-- *go there*."

"C'mon, Lae, it's not like we don't have a history. Besides, there's no reason to worry. You're my best friend. You need to stop thinking so damn much. For once in your life, just do something without knowing what the consequences will be. If you're really going to do this, don't you at least want to go in with a little bit of experience?"

As much as I would've hated to admit it, she had a point. If Quinton and I actually followed through with our fantasy, I didn't want to be the only person in the room who was essentially a virgin to a ménage. All I'd had was a few intense dreams about being with another woman, but in my fantasy, I was never the aggressor. I didn't know how to be. If I had at least some experience of what being with another woman was like, perhaps I could show my husband-to- be that I could be proactive and not just reactive. I stalled for a few seconds, unsure of what I wanted to say next. "Give me until after the New Year and then I'll give you an answer." I bit on my bottom lip before adding, "I promise."

"Why do I have to wait until then? What are you doing tonight?"

"Tonight I'll be spending some time with Quinton, Simone and her husband."

"So you'll be spending time with *her* and not with me? What if Franklin and I wanted to do something tonight? I see how it is now."

By the way she'd said *her*, I knew she wasn't about to call Simone by her first name--no more than I was willing to call Mike by his first name. "You know what, Niya? You're such a baby. I at least promised to give you an answer, but instead of being happy about that, you bust my hump about me spending time with someone else other than you."

"You mean there's someone other than me?"

"God, you sound like Dre! You'll have your answer next year!" She seemed relieved at knowing that the answer was pending and that there was a deadline. "You know, Lae, you don't have to be so secretive.

We aren't spies and no one is taping what we're saying. Truth is, I don't want to scare you away. I just want to know how butter pecan tastes these days." She smiled devilishly and left me in the lounge with her last assertion echoing in my head.

Right after she strutted out of the lounge, I received an announcement over the PA that I had a call waiting. I already knew who it was because our fifty-three year old secretary, Natalie, wouldn't let another call through until I picked up.

"Hello, lover," I said.

"Hey, sexy," he replied. "You don't have too sound like a one nine hundred voice for me, I know what you look like." I giggled, but laughed out loud when he told me that Natalie had already promised him her panties. "So what are you crazy ladies doing today?"

"I was telling everyone who'd listen how I broke your back last night," I said, smiling to myself as I thought about last night and already knowing how Quinton would respond.

"I'm pretty sure that's not the way it happened. You can continue to tell these lies, but the way I remember it, you got broke off and I got a consolation prize."

"Is that what you call it-- a consolation prize? I should kick you in your pancreas, Quinton! Next time you tell me you're about to fire one off, I may have to get up and walk away-- you know, let you finish on your own."

"Fine, I could do it better anyway."

"You must really want to be single." Like Niya, Quinton was good for talking himself up. I never knew how I could stand the both of them, or how they could stand each other, but somehow we all got along. The funny thing is that if Niya were single, I have no doubt that our three-some quest would have ended a long time ago, but Quinton always swore that he would never violate the vow of marriage and that was one of the things I loved most about him.

"I'm just kidding. You were wonderful last night," he whispered.

"I know. You just bring the nasty out in me." I knew he'd give in. If there was one thing he didn't like, it was having his manhood challenged.

"You're very welcome. So what's going on over there?" He asked.

I told him that I talked to Simone, but completely avoided what I had just shared with Teniyah. "I was just talking to Teniyah about one of the patients on the floor-- nothing much going on here."

"Still looking for potential partners?" He spoke as casually as if he'd just asked me the time.

27

Like Simone and Niya, Quinton and I share almost everything. We always manage to keep each other abreast of our friends' "issues", but this particular situation was a bit different. We'd talked about a threesome, but truthfully, the idea of another woman being with him wasn't something that I was sure I could positively handle. If we did a threesome with Niya, I was pretty sure that I wouldn't have any worries because of who she was. Quinton, on the other hand, had so many exes who wanted him back that doing a threesome with any of them was out of the question--especially Leslie. The longer I thought about what Teniyah had said, the more it began to make sense. I might need a test run to see if I could handle being with another woman, but I wasn't willing to share what Teniyah and I talked about with him-- at least not yet.

"I hadn't thought about it, but I could probably find a few willing participants if you want to lax your standards."

I didn't really know why I didn't want to tell him. I loved Quinton, but even replaying the whole conversation with Teniyah in my head gave *me* butterflies, and I certainly didn't want him thinking that Teniyah and I couldn't be trusted around each other.

"You mean Niya, right? Lae, why do we always seem to be coming back to Teniyah?"

"Because she's the only person I know who'd do it without condition and I trust her. I'm sorry I don't have any unmarried friends and before you even say it, I'll answer with a no. I'm certainly not willing or going to trust any of your exes."

"Please don't tell me that this has anything to do with Leslie."

"It has nothing to do with her," I lied, "but finding people who are open to doing something like this with us isn't like picking an apple from a tree. I'm just saying that if you lax your position for one night..."

"Look, you wanted to do this. I don't care whether it happens or not, but I don't want to wreck one marriage or have you going into marriage regretting anything that you never got a chance to do. You're the one who told me about 'the dream' and if you still want to do it, I'll support you. If you don't, then fine, I'll be behind you on that, too."
I shook my head and hoped that I hadn't just started an argument over something that shouldn't even be argued about. "I'm sorry, boo, stressful day and I'm still tired from going to sleep so late."

"It's okay, I understand. I've been a little on edge myself today."

"So, what are we were doing for New Years. Simone called me this morning and asked me, and since I didn't know, I asked you."

"Well, what does she want to do, drink?"

28

"And you got it on your first guess! Then she wants to have a drunken orgy. You and Mike can go at it while she and I watch."

"There is no way in hell I'm goin' to *that* party. Sorry sweetie, but I'd rather watch you and your beloved Mike go at it before I'm ever *violated* by another man."

"What makes you think he wants to be the taker?"

"Because I'll never be the receiver. It's as simple as that."

"I don't know, Quinton. You may permanently do some damage to poor Mike if you're the giver."

"Okay, okay," he conceded, "enough talk about men's asses. Look, we can do whatever, but tell Mike if he wants to get close, he has to at least buy me dinner -- and a couple of flowers. I need to feel like he cares and that this isn't just a sex thing."

"You're a disgusting man."

"Anything for you, baby." He laughed. "You know I should take what I do on the road. I'd call it 'The Aim to Please Tour'."

"I see you've been talking to Dre again and that he lent you some of his narcissism."

"Since you can't prove that, I'm going to evoke my right to counsel. Anyway, about Mike and Simone, tell them we can hang out tonight. That way, I can give you what you need in front of an audience. I like it when a crowd cheers me on."

I liked when he talked dirty and he knew it. As I thought about last night, my body began to warm all over again. "Why settle for a cheering section when you can make them all jealous?" I whispered.

"Be careful what you say. You just might get the full force of Hurricane Quinton tonight."

"I'm glad it's a hurricane. I'm looking forward to getting wet."

"You're innuendo has come a long way, grasshopper."

"I learned from the best." We laughed for a few seconds afterwards before I spoke again. "I love you."

"That's because you can't help yourself. It is me, after all, that you're loving."

"I can't stand you."

"Love you too, baby."

After hanging up with Quinton, I stayed on the line and called Simone to let her know that the plans were a go. I wasn't sure if I'd have time later, so we chatted about all of the specifics before she thanked me, and hung up. I presumed she would take it from there.

I pulled open the door to the lounge to leave when Teniyah lightly grabbed my arm and guided me back in.

"Um, you know one of my patients is probably in labor, right now. If she's already crowning, I'll tell them know that you harassed me in the ladies' room." I joked, as she released me from her grasp.

"She can wait," it was almost a whisper, but it held an undertone of seriousness. "I need to tell you something."

She seemed a little excited, so I figured it was new gossip. Working with an all woman crew, there's always an endless supply. I headed for the couch so that we could talk, but instead Niya quickly pinned me to the door. I looked up to meet her intimidating gaze, but as I was ready to break away from her, the warmth of her hands under my scrubs brought a sensation that left me paralyzed.

I closed my eyes, averting her piercing glare and listened to the sound of my breathing as my nipples began to grow increasingly erect. She gently slid her tongue up and down my ear, hitting all the right spots and seemingly oblivious to the fact that we were at work.

"What are you doing?"

She was still behind me as she softly whispered into my ear. "I just wanted to give you an idea of what it would be like." She placed her hands on my shoulders and continued to nibble on my ears, knowing they were my primary weak spot from our numerous college dorm 'girl talks'.

I suddenly found myself floating away—seemingly on another plane of existence as I watched from above what was happening to me. Yet, I still felt every fingernail she dragged across my torso. Niya had taken me to another world--a world that I'd only visited in my dreams. She delicately slid her fingertips across my nipples, eased both hands inside my scrub pants, down to my pyramid, all while still biting the side of my neck.

I wanted to move, to somehow whisper her name out loud, but I was weak and the words were lodged in my throat, unwilling to break free.

I was already wet as her fingertips gingerly caressed my clit, and I felt it throb with anticipation before she pulled her hands away, turned me around and softly kissed me on my lips. A rush of emotion rolled over me and I returned her kiss with as much passion as she'd given me. It was last night again, but this time I was prepared for her. This time, I knew that I wanted it to happen. I wrapped my hands around her as if she were a man--my man.

The feelings that arose were as intense as any I'd ever had-- reminiscent of the handful of times I'd had sex in my bedroom, with my parents watching television in the next room and with only paper walls separating us. For those few seconds, time seemed to have stopped and we were the only two people in motion.

She quickly pulled back and I was startled by the return of bright fluorescent ceiling lights in the lounge.

"Good girls don't do *that*," she mocked.

I was so horny that I paid no attention to the sarcasm, only to the wind that swept by me as she walked out the room. The kiss lingered on my lips; I licked them, hoping to rekindle the sensation, but it was a little too late. My body craved the feeling she'd left.

Good girls didn't do that, but I *did*, and I'd be damned if I hadn't liked it.

CHAPTER 3

Simone

"I hate my life...and I'm lonely."

By definition, to be lonely means to be without companion; unfrequented by people, and even as a wife and mother, this statement is most likely the truest sentence I've ever uttered.

My aunt Ida tells me that it's the greatest paradox ever told. Seeing as how I have a very needy infant, a nymphomaniac husband, self-righteous friends, gossipy co-workers, and a dysfunctional family, she could be right. But in order to understand me, I guess they'd have to walk a mile-- hell, a few steps-- in my shoes. Lord knows anyone would have a hard time moving in these cinder blocks.

On a visit to my doctor last week, I explained to her how sluggish I'd been feeling lately. I'd hoped she could explain to me how she was in the same situation, or reveal to me a similar story, but as all doctors seem to do nowadays, she prescribed an anti-depressant, thinking that I was suffering from post-partum depression brought on by my only pregnancy. I even let her know that I'd felt this way even before I was pregnant, but I didn't challenge her professional opinion.

As I walked out of her office, prescription in hand, I was almost convinced that she was an automaton, designed by the pharmaceutical company to randomly hand out prescriptions regardless of the diagnosis.

It's the story of my life. I've come to the point where I despise waking up because I find myself trapped in the same situation that I said

I'd never be trapped in, always finding a way to smile, even though I feel like I'm shattered from the inside out. I guess at one time, I felt like I could do anything, but that was so long ago I don't think I can feel that way anymore. I always put on a happy face for others, even when my own world is going to shit in a tidy little hand-basket. I honestly wasn't sure if I could stand it anymore.

Being a black woman, I was raised to believe that I was made to handle struggle. I'm *supposed* to tough it out, let God handle the rest, and that suicide was a coward's option. But the more I thought about it, the more I knew I needed to remain in my drug induced euphoria. I often thought about what turned me into this depressed woman. I used to be vibrant and I wanted to do all of the things that my parents never had a chance to do before they died. I wanted to become something, make a name for myself and be someone recognizable to more than just the people in my neighborhood. But my life was nowhere near my dreams. I was just another statistic for the drug companies. As I walked through the front door of the hospital, I looked at my doctor's handwriting, and couldn't help myself from bursting out into tears.

Is there something wrong with me?

It was the only thought that reverberated through my head while driving home. The skies were cloudless for the last week of the year, and since the sun was out, it didn't feel like the typical winter day. I stopped at a red light before getting on the expressway, and then looked at the doctor's stationary one last time before I balled it up, and buried it at the bottom of my purse. A new year was coming up and it was time for some changes. I wasn't going to let a doctor make an overly zealous patient out of me. Something in me wasn't quite ready to give up just yet.

That was only a week ago.

Now that it's 'New Year's Eve, I'm almost ready to become a post-partum statistic. I had the day off from work, but my head was so full of needless, worthless shit that at this point, I'd readily welcome a drug-induced coma if it saved me from my daily repetition. Ok, not really, but I'd almost consider it just to keep myself from idly repeating the mindless monotony.

In truth, my life is a model of tedious repetition. After just waking up, my morning migraine comes to me right on time, which coincidentally tends to be minutes before I wake my husband, Michael, up and we begin our ritual of uninspired sex. Well, I guess it's only uninspired for me because with all the grunting he usually does, you'd think he was giving birth.

33

As usual, at 6:00 a.m., I nudged him, letting him know that it's time to get up. Then, just like clock-work, he rolls his half-naked 250 lb frame onto my slender, 140 lb one, complete with stank ass morning breath, and grabs the lube that we keep by the bed. It continually amazes me how he moves that humungous gut around, especially when he's only 5'9", yet he still manages to take off his draws and lube up "Mandingo" all in the same motion, without even so much as a "Good morning, love of my life, mother of my child, apple of my eye" to me. Knowing the morning routine by heart, I never wear any panties before going to bed anymore. The lube allows some comfort, not much, but he still pushes inside of me, knowing that I am rarely wet enough for him to enter me without wincing in pain.

"You like that dick, don't you, girl? Tell big daddy you love this shit." The words I despise hearing are usually the first words that come out of his mouth. "You love this shit, dontcha girl? Whose pussy is this?"

The devil in me wants to say the name of some random guy or simply just that 'I'd haven't met the man who owns what you married', but before the mischievous phrase escapes me, I utter a soft, "Yours, baby. It's yours."

I've become such a good liar that I could be a great lawyer. I almost want to laugh, but I don't, knowing that that type of outburst won't go unpunished. He doesn't hit me, he never has, and never will, but Mike had a way of pouting that got on my last damn nerve, and I didn't want to be part of the silent treatment on New Year's. The sad thing is we'd only been married six months and already the sex has become a nuisance.

Altogether we've been together for almost six years. When we met, I wanted to follow him to the ends of the earth. He was my leader, my messiah and I was his faithful follower. He made me happy and nothing on this Earth could bring me down from the heights we shared. Whenever we were out, he'd make me smile, hold my hands, kiss me in public, and then we'd sneak off to the men's room to have sex. Albeit he was never the best, he was adequate and I sincerely loved him which seemed to intensify any sessions we shared.

While he continued his awful grunting, I began to daydream about the times when the sex was warm and loving. I usually helped me to enjoy at least some sex, but today wasn't going to be one of those days. Today Mike was about as gentle as a hole puncher and though he nearly smothered me, I succumb to his needs. I am his wife, he is my husband and a good wife sacrifices her needs for her husband's.

To accelerate his orgasm, I pretend to enjoy it with moans of pleasure and fallacies that no other is his equal. I grab his ass and push him deeper inside of me, hoping that this will finally end my morning torment, and within a few seconds, it's over.

Mission fucking accomplished.

"I love you," he whispers to me as he rises out of bed, but the sentiment is more rehearsed than heartfelt.

"I love you, too." It's my deflated response. The truth is that I do love him and as his love still lingered between my legs, I wondered if he actually realized how much I meant what I said. He never seems to take into consideration that I bathe, feed and clothe our child without his assistance or appreciation, yet when I bring it up, instead of apologies, we fight. He consistently tells me that he's from an old household and feels that it's the woman's responsibility to take care of these things, which incidentally, are the same beliefs that his parents have passed down to him. Tired of constant arguments, I've learned not to bring it up anymore.

After the morning's "exercise", I threw my legs over the side of the bed and picked up my satin purple kimono off the floor. It was this Christmas's gift from my best friend, Laela and somehow it'd already found its way towards the heap of clothes by the bed. I stood up with my back to the hallway so that all my husband can see is my bare ass before he walks into the bathroom and closes the door, and I wrap it around myself on my way to fix breakfast. "Every damn day!" I uttered to myself as I tightly closed my robe to keep myself warm in a house that was practically freezing.

In the kitchen, I cut on the light, grabbed a few headache pills that I'd left on the counter for this particular occasion, and swallowed them without even thinking about getting a glass of water to help wash them down. To keep myself from staring at my sullied reflection in the kitchen mirror, I put my head down and stared at the sink while waiting for the aspirin to work its way down. It hurt like hell without water to help it along, but at least it's not the worst it's ever been. I drudged over to the refrigerator to get breakfast ready for the family.

In the six years of relationship we've shared, Michael and I have one child together, MJ, who just turned six months last week. We were married barely a week before he was born because Mike didn't want his child born out of wedlock. Sometimes I think that's the only reason why he asked me to marry him. I love Michael and MJ is a blessing to have, but I'll be damned if the both of them ain't also a curse. Don't get me wrong, I love them to death, but sometimes they can drive me up a wall.

After everyone ate, I washed MJ, clothed him, and bagged up his daily usage of the breast milk, which I'd already pumped the night before. I placed the diapers, wipes, toys, and extra clothing, in a baby bag for my aunt, who usually did all the babysitting. I wanted MJ in some sort of pre-school, but Mike and I seemed to never have the money and we were basically living from check to check.

I took him downstairs to Michael, who snatched him up, put him in his car seat, backs up out of the driveway, and drives out of sight. No kisses, no goodbyes, no affection whatsoever. *Damn, apparently goodbye kisses are a scarcity these days.*

With the cool breeze reminding me that all I had on was a thin piece of silk cloth, I ran back upstairs to relax. It was the week-end, and I enjoyed my rest from the dead end secretary job I loathed. I believed in getting things done whenever I had the time. Time was a precious commodity that I couldn't afford, amongst other things, and for the last 190 days, I hadn't had a single second for myself.

I still had no idea of what I wanted to do and after eating a bowl of cereal, I headed to the bathroom for a shower. I took off my kimono belt and allowed the rest of the robe to fall casually to the floor before stealing a glance of my reflection. I usually didn't look in the mirror when Mike was around, afraid that he'd again ridicule my stretch marks and my engorged breasts, but with another year on the horizon, I needed to make another resolution concerning my weight.

I pinched my love handles several times before frowning at the baby fat and accumulated weight after the pregnancy. I sized myself up. "I don't think I look that bad. Need to get rid of this tummy, these flabby arms, maybe get a flatter stomach. I don't see anything that a little exercise wouldn't cure."

After hearing myself talk about my reflection like we were two different people, I became a little more self-conscious. My mother always said that too much talking to oneself made a person crazy, but whenever she spoke to me, she was always coked out of her mind and consequently, died from an overdose when I was barely a teenager. Knowing that, I really couldn't remember if she was ever lucid, but I still didn't want to test that theory. So I just smiled. For the longest time, I thought I was an old maid, but looking at myself again through fresh eyes, I wasn't half bad, almost sexy even. Mmmm, *sexy*. I hadn't heard that said about me in a while.

I was still the same mahogany complexion that I was in grade school, with the same slender 'Asian' eyes, and the same bulldog cheeks my momma grabbed when I was younger. At roughly the same height as

Michael, steady at 5'9", it looked much better on me than it did on him. The stretch marks on my breasts and thighs are a little more pronounced, but the addition gives my once stick-figure a lot more depth, a few more curves, with a few more miles to match. My stomach, of course, is still a little soft from the pregnancy, but for the first time in a long time, I wasn't overly critical. After taking in all of my measurements, I winked at myself, put my loose flowing hair up in a pony tail, and turned on the water for a relaxing bath instead of the shower I'd considered earlier.

Not long after I closed my eyes and relaxed, an idea had finally come to me. I quickly jumped out of the bathtub and without the warmth of the bathroom, I almost froze to death in the kitchen. As I silently cursed myself for not drying off before I ran out, he droplets of water on my body were quickly turning to ice cubes on my flesh. Still, I needed to talk to someone before I lost my nerve and my idea would be carted off to "Never-heard-from-again-land".

I dialed in the phone number of my best friend, Laela, hoping that she would pick up on the first ring. Lately she'd been the only person with whom I could talk about the personal things that go on in my life. I'd known her most almost half of my life, and met her when we were only two of the ten black girls in an all-girl Catholic high school. She'd always been a good student and sometimes she'd help me out with my homework when I didn't know what the hell I was doing. Since high school, she'd gone to college and become a nurse with a handsome pre-husband and, though I was a little envious of her and her life, I was also very proud of her, too.

My stomach was churning with anticipation. I wanted her to pick up, but if she didn't maybe I could say it in her voicemail. But as I thought it over, if she didn't pick up, there was no guarantee she'd call me back. I needed her to pick up the phone so I could tell her my idea, but after all the worrying I'd done, she didn't even answer.

Feeling defeated before the day even began, I walked back to my bedroom and put on an old sweat suit and commenced cleaning the house. After a few minutes of dusting, the phone rang; she'd called back.

The nausea from all the anticipation I felt just a few minutes ago came back with a vengeance. I didn't know exactly how I wanted to say things, so I beat around the bush before telling her my idea. Like she always did, she harassed me about my marriage. Not wanting to deal with it, I avoided it and even though she sounded skeptical, Lae still told me that she and Quinton would spend New Years' with Mike and I. It took a few calls, but I found a hotel near the airport for us to party at --

not from where Mike and I stayed. By the time she finally called back to confirm, the day was just about over and Mike would soon be on his way home. I was so happy to hear the good news that I almost hung up the phone prematurely. My day hadn't started off so great so anything positive at this point was good news.

Because I hadn't told Michael about what I'd proposed to Lae, I paced around the house for the next few hours while wondering how I wanted to reveal my plan to him. Even though the house was drafty, I'd intentionally only wore his old football jersey. I knew what it might take to sway him and easy access was probably going to be my only saving grace in this instance. I rehearsed what I was going to say, never uttering a single word out loud, but simply ran all scenarios inside of my head. By the time he made it home, I was exhausted. I figured that I'd let him know about what we had planned right before his shower, but immediately after he got his nut.

As I heard him and MJ walk up the stairs, there was an obvious distinction from the norm: I was actually wet. I was damp to the touch and uncharacteristically aroused.

I opened the door for him, gave him a kiss and watched as he took a napping MJ to his room. As soon as I saw him heading for the bathroom, I threw my shirt on the bed and rushed into the shower with him. After grabbing his bare ass, I immediately pushed my breasts up against his back before he had a chance to turn towards me. When he craned his neck to glance at me, I looked at him like I was a child asking their father for permission to watch the living room TV.

"Hey, babe," I almost swallowed my tongue, but I closed my eyes and finished off my rehearsed lines, "Laela and Q want to know if we're going to kick it with them. They rented a hotel room and wanted us to bring in the New Year with them."

He rolled his head up to the ceiling before bringing it back to down to look at me. I already knew that some excuse was brewing in his head. "Damn. I wish you would've told me earlier. I already made plans to go out drinkin' with Pookie and the fellas."

All the elation and the butterflies left my body in a brief exhale. I'd fallen off of my cloud and had returned to my life. Even though the shower water was pouring over my midsection, I could feel the moisture that was once between my legs dry instantaneously. "Dammit Mike, do it with them next year. Spend this one with me, please." I was almost begging. Hell, I *was* begging; begging for my husband and me to spend our first married New Years together.

"Look, Monie, I made a promise. I gave them my word and going back on that shit ain't cool with me if they asked me first." He was nonchalant, turning the water temperature up as we spoke.

My head began to pound as the lack of chivalry manifested itself from this man and my temper finally boiled over. "I'm your wife, goddammit! Are you Pookie's wife? Do you have a child with him, too? Are you *married* to that pot-smokin' nobody?"

His face quickly contorted from nonchalant to confrontational. "Get outta my face with that bullshit, man. If this shit would've been planned earlier, we wouldn't be having this discussion, but it wasn't, so don't come at me acting like you asked first." He put his face into the water, drowning his ears to avoid listening to me.

"Well then, fuck you!" I screamed. "I'll go by my damn self!" I ran out of the bathroom and stumbled over the clothes he left on the floor on my way towards the bedroom. I tried to hold back my anger and frustration, but I couldn't. As teardrops streamed down my face, it was impossible for me to tell the difference between how much water was from the shower and how much had come from me.

In all our time together, I'd never spoken to Mike like that. If my aunt were here, she'd say that a good wife does as she's told and never disrespects her husband by speaking back, but I intended for tonight to be special. It was ruined and he'd ruined it. If she were here, she'd probably curse me, and no doubt Michael was going to tell her what happened to make sure she would.

I didn't know how long I'd been crying, but when I finally pulled myself away from the security of my pillows, Mike and MJ were gone. As I once again walked passed by the mirrors in the bathroom, I saw that my sullen face had returned. My eyes were swollen and bloodshot, and my features had returned to looking tired. I couldn't believe it. He ruined everything.

When Lae arrived, I felt awful and ugly. Before she picked me up, I threw on a baggy gray sweat suit, some old tennis shoes, and did a quick make up job to hide the tears I'd been shedding. I also remembered to grab my toothbrush, and the new silk lavender Vicky's Secret bra and panty set I'd bought. Whether or not Mike would see me in it, I bought it earlier in the week and I was going to be damned if I wasn't going to get some use out of it.

We arrived at the hotel about three hours before midnight. When I'd called in earlier, I'd been told that we'd gotten room 145, which was on the first floor of a three story building. When we entered the room, it looked like something straight out of a low budget porno. The room had a strong reddish overtone. It contained a bed with red wood that was dressed in a maroon comforter, auburn colored wallpaper, carpet was made of a substance that could only be described as shaggy red wool and the only window we had faced the airport and draped over them were dark red curtains.

"I see we have the Count Dracula suite," Quinton mused, but he was as equally repulsed as me. I was so embarrassed at having been the one to choose the room, but since it was all that was available with the little money I had, I simply nodded in agreement. As we entered the room, all that I could think about was how I'd be spending my first married New Years--alone. With each passing thought of Mike laughing with his friends, I became a little more agitated. I really wanted to take the happy pills, but that would've been suicidal, seeing as I planned on drinking myself into a stupor and I didn't want to scar the few friends I did have for the rest of their lives.

"Nothing left to do but to drink," I said. I learned lately that the sooner we got to drinking, the quicker I could forget.

That's when Laela finally began with her motherly routine. "Monie, I know you're upset, but we're not gonna drink until you pass out. Tonight, we can just talk."

Talk? Talking was the last thing I wanted to do tonight. "Look, Lae, if you guys wanna talk, then fine, but I'm sure as hell not going to be talking with you. If I can't get pissy, I don't even wanna be here."

"Fine, then if you don't want to talk, then we can at least do some truth or dare." Quinton added.

I smiled at Quinton, but looking at him and Lae holding hands reminded me of what I wasn't ever going to have. Lae was so damn lucky and probably didn't even realize it.

What I wouldn't give for one night with Quinton and have her spend one night with Mike.

I smiled at such a mischievous thought, but when I came back to reality, I was just jealous. Still, I wasn't about to do the crazy shit that I was sure they had conspired to get me to do.

"I'll pass." I wasn't in the mood for drinking games.

"Simone, I didn't come way out for you to be spiteful all night. I know Mike can be an ass, but you're with us now. If you want to do something that might make you smile, we can play 'bullshit', but if you're

40

not feeling right or if you just don't feel like being out, I can take you home." Lae said, almost patronizingly.

I wasn't really in the mood for games, but the only other alternative was for me to sit alone in an empty house. When I compared what they were offering to that, I really didn't have much of a choice. I nodded.

"The rules go like this. I tell you a secret and you tell me if it's a truth or bullshit. If you're right, I drink, but if you're wrong, you drink. Got it?"

"I got it." I said dryly. Lae knew most, if not all, of my secrets and I was sure that I knew most of hers. Though I didn't know any of Quinton's, I was sure that Lae knew enough of his to make this game interesting. Even though I nodded, I still wasn't too enthused at having Quinton hear any of my secrets before I got a drink into my system. After I was drunk, I wouldn't mind letting go of a secret or two. That way I could always blame the alcohol. But as usual, they were right. I knew that I shouldn't be bringing my troubles from home, but that didn't stop it from hurting any less.

For about an hour, we told a few truths as we did a great deal more drinking before they realized I was in a better mood. For me, alcohol was always a perfect solution, and sex with alcohol was the best compound. Knowing that I was feeling better with all the shared laughter, we all went crazy and began to drink and laugh uncontrollably. As the night progressed, Quinton questioned me several times about the girl I told them I'd kissed, but I wasn't ready to reveal that much to a man who wasn't mine.

After the game had ended and I'd realized exactly how much I didn't know about either of them, the overwhelming feeling of loneliness began to take hold of me again. I glanced over at Lae and Quinton as they laughed about their secrets and then tenderly kissed each other as if they had when they'd just met. I hated watching them, but who could blame me. They shared the only thing I'd ever desired and even though they were my friends, that didn't lessen my disgust.

I excused myself, walked to the bathroom, turned on the shower and continued where I'd left off at home. I cried like I had when my mother passed. I didn't know how long I'd actually been crying, but by the time I'd stepped into the shower, I was exhausted.

As the water pounded against my flesh, I thought about my marriage and everything that had gone wrong. I thought about what I'd done and wondered if this was my punishment for my betrayal. I wanted to call Mike and plead for him to be here tonight, but I knew he was too

41

stubborn to come and even if he did show, I was too tired for his shit or his "Dingo".

I took my time putting on my t-shirt and when I opened the bathroom door, I quickly realized that out of habit, I'd forgotten to add my underwear to the ensemble. I was about to return to the bathroom when the familiar songs of Lae echoed throughout the room. For the second time that night, my jealousy had gotten the best of me, but instead of walking into the bathroom again, my curiosity demanded that I sneak around the corner.

Hiding at the corner of the barely lit room, I watched Lae slowly rode her fiancé. With Quinton's hands guiding her, she cursed profusely as she repeatedly rocked her hips across his.

Dammit, even their sex is perfect!

As if on cue, Quinton tore away the covers that protected the two and flipped Lae on her side as he quickly mounted her. I pulled away so that they wouldn't notice me, but I'd already briefly seen Quinton's manhood. I held my breath and prayed that they hadn't seen me, but unable to defer, I quickly exhaled and returned my attention to them-- to him. I watched as Quinton relentlessly pounded Lae, both of them on top of the covers, and for a brief moment I imagined that I was Lae.

I closed my eyes and remembered the last time I'd been aroused like this. With Mike, it'd certainly been before we were married, but as Mike's face dissipated from my memory and was replaced by Quinton's, I quickly opened my eyes. It was then I realized that my fingers had wandered under my t-shirt and they were damp from the experience.

What are you doing?

As I watched them, more aroused then I'd probably ever been, my stomach began to turn in knots. Numerous times before, Mike and I shared the same room with them, but in the opaqueness, I'd never actually seen them. Now, I had a front row view. Lae had confided in me a few days before about her quest for a threesome partner and never in my life had I been so tempted to indulge.

But that would be wrong. You're married, remember?

I didn't care about wrong. I still indulged in another Q fantasy, imagining him clutching my throat, slowly asphyxiating me as he relentlessly pounded against my flesh. As the feeling engulfed me, I returned my fingers to their hiding place under my shirt and eased them across my throbbing clitoris. It had been so long since I'd climaxed that I wasn't going to miss an opportunity to do so—not when I was so ready for one.

After Lae's multiple orgasms and what felt like an eternity, Quinton finally admitted to his readiness. He quickly pulled himself out from Lae and as soon as she sat up, he fed her his seed. I watched in shock as Quinton revealed the full extent of his manhood and I stared in awe as Lae accepted him into her mouth, never gagging and swallowing his cum.

Shit!

I began to tremble as my own climax began to overwhelm me. I wanted to cry out, but as my orgasm approached, I clutched my own throat and softly squeezed.

Yes Quinton. Yes baby. Squeeze harder.

I let my throat go as the last possible second before I was ready to pass out and experienced the most incredible orgasm I'd ever had. The intensity of it all was so overpowering that my legs collapsed and I fell against the wall.

"Simone, are you okay?" Lae shouted from around the corner.

I quickly and quietly walked back into the bathroom. I sat on the toilet before yelling back a lie. "Yeah, Lae, I'm just, uh, getting out the shower." The bathroom was my sanctuary. After what I'd just witnessed—what I'd just done, I had no idea how I was going to casually walk out of the bathroom.

"Simone, you can come out now." She chuckled. "We're finished and it's almost midnight. Let's watch the ball drop."

"Okay." I shouted back, but I wasn't finished. Their peep show had ignited me and I had hoped that they'd fall asleep, giving me time to cool myself down.

I walked out of the bathroom hastily with a towel draped around my shoulders to hide my erect nipples. I passed by the happy couple, both smiling and fully clothed, on the way to my bed and plopped down.

As the ball drop in Houston ended the previous year, screams from the television crowd and unintelligible shouts throughout the hotel, filled my ears. Yet, in all the chaos, my attention was focused on solely on Lae and Quinton. As they softly kissed several times, I desperately wanted what they shared. I checked my phone to see if Mike had texted, but I hadn't even received a missed call.

"Happy New Year, Simone!" they shouted in unison.

"Happy New Year," I replied without any of the exuberance they'd shown. Feeling the bitterness of jealousy slowly eat away at me, I laid down without another word. Before I fell asleep, all I could think about was how lucky a woman Lae was. She had a good job, a nice place to live, solid finances, and not to mention a good man with a nice, thick dick, who loved her. All I had was a shaky marriage, a man who only dreamed of having an adequate sized dick and, according to Miss I'm Never Wrong, he was cheating on me. As the reality of my life crept back into my thoughts, I hugged the pillow and fought back more tears.

I awoke to discover him kissing on my neck. He began to bite on it, not painfully, but forceful enough to fully awaken me. I wanted to ask what he was doing, but truthfully I didn't care. After he realized I was awake, he threw away the covers and slid his hands up my thighs and under my kimono.

The belt I wore around my waist to keep my kimono from falling opening was torn off by his teeth, and thrown aside. As he looked at me with the same hunger that I had seen in his eyes before, I pushed him back until he stood straight up and I was kneeling before his throbbing penis.

I pushed down on it, not sure if it was real, but it bobbed back up, tapping me on the nose on the upswing. I cupped his genitals, opened my mouth as far as I could, and placed as much of him inside my mouth as my body would allow.

I wanted him. I wanted everything the he had offered Laela and more. I pushed my mouth as far down him as I could before I began to gag, and then I retreated. Using my hands to massage what I had just lubricated, I sucked on the first two inches, while continually stroking the rest.

"Faster," he demanded in a deep, guttural voice and faster I went. His moans thoroughly aroused me, sending electricity through me and I began to prepare myself for his inevitable plunge into my love. I was his to command tonight. Whatever demand he desired of me, I would most certainly obey.

He pulled me from my knees, disrobed me, and laid me down on my bed before he spoke. "I want to lick it. I want to taste you, baby, from your teacup to your C cup."

I spread my legs for him so that he could sample all of me. He didn't disappoint, gently sliding his tongue from inside me all the way up to my breasts, and then back down again. The feeling was unbearable and within seconds I came for the first time ever onto his lips.

Smiling, he mounted me. He pushed into me so quickly that I shrieked, and arched my back so that I could accept him without pain. He threw my legs around his waist and forced each thrust, dripping sweat as he pounded his thighs against mine. What was once pain was now insurmountable pleasure and I wasn't about to be hushed, not even if it meant waking up Laela. The room was filled with the screams of my abrupt orgasm, combined with the sound of two bodies loudly slapping one another.

After my orgasm, he slowed down and pushed all of himself into me. I was amazed at how much more he had left and even more astonished that I could take it all, but there was a slow subtle rhythm while he stroked in and out of me. He placed his muscular arms on each side of my head and slowly pushed deeper into me. I sensed he was about to climax, but the expressions on his face showed that there was a definite internal struggle.

"Cum inside of me," I whispered. "I want all of it. I want you to cum inside of me. Please, baby," I begged. I glanced over to the next bed to see if Laela was watching, but the darkness around the room prevented me from seeing anything further than two feet away. Even though I secretly hoped she was watching us, the pleasure reverberating through me weakened me, forcing me to fall back onto the bed.

I looked back into Quinton's face to make sure that whatever struggle he had before had left. I felt his fevered thrusting, before he began pulsating inside of me. He was cumming and with his foretold climax, my own was on its way. I threw my legs up higher, and pulled him closer to me; feeling his penis jerking I grabbed onto his back and dug my fingernails into him as my orgasm preceded his.

"Say it, Quinton," I pleaded, "Say my name, baby!"

"Simone!" he screamed. "Simone!"

"Simone. Simone." I awoke to the sound of Quinton calling my name. He was a dark figure standing over me, but through the darkness, I saw his look of concern. "Are you okay? You were talking in your sleep."

I rose up off the bed with sweat pouring from my head and Laela looking concerned in the other bed. I was dreaming, and I hoped that I hadn't been talking. Even more so, I prayed that they hadn't heard anything that was going on in my dream.

A little disoriented, I responded, "I'm okay--just a crazy dream." They both nodded and Q went back to lying down in his bed. As I gathered my bearings, I was in awe of the dream I just had. It was then that I noticed my bottom half was freezing. I peeled back the covers to find that I had a wet spot the size of my lower half underneath me.

Embarrassed, I ran to the bathroom once again to clean myself up. My heart was still racing from the discovery that I had soaked my bed, but whatever happened, I couldn't change it. Since I hadn't brought any other change of clothing to sleep in, I put on my Victoria set, which was only a little damp from earlier, and snuck out of the bathroom. Upon returning to the room, I pulled the comforter off my bed and placed it on the floor while hoping that everyone was asleep so I didn't have to explain why I wasn't sleeping in my bed.

"Are you sure you're okay?" Laela asked.

I wasn't okay, and I knew it. "I think I had too much to drink. I, um, had an accident in my bed," I confessed. I wasn't hoping for sympathy, just for an extra blanket.

"You can sleep with us," she offered. "I'm not going to let you sleep over there. I'm not your husband."

Her comment stung, but after everything that had gone down between me and Mike, I was beginning not to care. As she opened up the covers to allow me to sleep in her bed, I found myself sleeping in between Lae and Q, facing her with my back towards him. I just knew this wasn't the position I wanted to be in and that it was going to be almost impossible to get back to sleep - until I felt an erection creeping up the underside of my leg.

I smiled in the darkness.

I was still desirable.

CHAPTER 4

Quinton

January 1st (Sunday) 10:30 AM

After we woke up and got ready to leave the hotel room, I struggled with the thought of me generating an erection after Simone slept next to me this morning. Lae and I had been entertaining a threesome, but Simone was never the person I'd choose for it. Not only was she Mike's wife, but after having MJ, she was a little 'doughy' for my tastes and she seemed a little repressed. Rather than lament, I just chalked it up to me not being accustomed to another woman being so close to me in bed and pushed it to the back of my mind. It was the best thing for me to do concerning my good friend's wife, especially since I'd most likely be seeing him today anyway at the poker game.

The Fellas Only poker game began six years ago as an annual event between Dre, his boy Coop, and me, but over the years we picked up a few players. Outside of playing poker, it was a chance for a bunch of fellas to talk shit about a range of topics, which usually only consisted of their last year's conquests, and our New Year's Resolution to add more conquests to the list. Occasionally, we had some pretty decent conversations, but I doubted that this would be one of those years, especially with BJ present.

Andre's place had already been designated game central this year, so I jumped into my car, got on I-10, and headed about an hour west, back out to his suburban bachelor pad in Katy.

Traffic was light around Hobby, so I made it to his home in less time than usual, even though I'd made a pit stop at my apartment on the way. He stayed in a gated subdivision, and since I was cool with Martha, the security lady, she let me in without me harassing me--this time.

Five minutes later, I pulled up into the driveway of a practically new Mediterranean style house. I didn't see either of his cars in the driveway, so I assumed either no one was home or he didn't want anyone to know, so I grabbed my things out of my car. I pulled an extra key out of my pocket and walked into the house without some much as a knock.

Dre's house was one of the biggest in the subdivision, which was saying a great deal for a neighborhood like his. His four year old house sat on a three acre lot, with the house spanning an incredulous 5500 square feet. From the outside, his house looked like something from the "Lifestyles of the Rich and Famous". The outside was a beautiful two storied house made of marble colored stucco and lined with golden trim. The lawn was perfectly landscaped with animal shaped hedges and intricately designed flower bed mazes, which I considered an extreme waste of money, complete with the motion-sensor ground effect lighting that preceded every step on my way to the front door. A pool was installed in the back a few months ago when he bought this luxurious estate, but he hardly ever used it, mostly because it was still a little cool during the winter season.

I opened his front door and stopped when I heard voices coming from the back of the house. I walked towards the noise and noticed some of the re-decoration he'd had done recently. Since the party a few nights ago, all of his walls had been painted tan, an upgrade from the eggshell white. Also there was newly laid marble tile, instead of carpet, leading from his front door all the way to the pool in the back of the house.

By the time I finished noticing the new additions and rearranged interior, I'd almost walked past the dining room, which was the second room on my left, where I thought I'd heard some noises before they suddenly stopped. I began to turn around and head back towards the kitchen when I heard girlish giggling and shouted out, "Dre, where you at?"

There were a few seconds of silence and more giggling before he yelled, "Back here."

I followed his voice down the hallway, towards the back of the house and found him relaxing comfortably in the library. He sat on his black leather sofa, pant less, with the same white lady I'd seen him with a few days before. Instead of sitting on his couch and talking, this time I found her between his legs focused on nothing but his pleasure stick, which never vacated her mouth.

I shook my head. "I don't mean to bother you, your highness, but don't we have a game to prepare for?"

He seemed surprised to hear the news, but didn't move from his position. The woman looked at me and smiled before going back to blowing his brains out. "That's today? Well then, I find myself in a little predicament, Quinton. Either I stay here and enjoy my company or I get ready for a bunch of rowdy men to eat all my food and destroy my house. Hmmm."

"You know what then, I'll get it ready." I said, walking away.

"Okay, damn, can a brother get a few minutes?" He looked down at his guest. "You can finish in a couple minutes, can't you baby?"

She winked at me and I walked towards the kitchen, opened up his stainless steel refrigerator, and fixed myself a roast beef sandwich. By the time I'd finished eating, she'd certainly unclogged whatever it was jamming up his pipes-- I could tell by his feminine screeching. Then he jogged out of the library and hugged me as I put my plate in the sink, grinning like a schoolgirl, while his neighbor walked past the kitchen, smiled at me again, waved, and then strolled through the front door without uttering a word.

"I take it she needed some protein," I said smugly.

"Yes sir, and now her belly is full of the most potent protein this side of the Mississippi. That Dre Shake', baby! Mmmmmm yummy! They just can't get enough of this damn shake!"

The thought that he callously talked about his seepage made my stomach turn. "You are a nasty ass Negro."

"Why? Is it because I get down with white chicks? You need to try it, man. Freaking a white girl is almost like being with a virgin all over again! Besides, they're not scared to do some kinky shit on the first date. I love that shit!"

"What the hell are you talking about? You had me walk in on you getting head! I didn't need to see that shit this early in the damn day!"

"We are family, Q. What's mine is yours. But since you wanna be like that, make sure to put this on my headstone: 'He was philandering philanthropist who delivered protein to any woman in need of some.'"

I sat down at the kitchen table, a small, mahogany wooden table hidden in the breakfast nook of his kitchen. "Ugh. You want that on your tombstone?"

"Why shouldn't it be?" He asked, not even batting an eyelash.

"Like I said, you're sick. I mean we're fam and all, but I don't need to see your crooked little weenie-do. Besides, the headstone is bought and paid for already and I damn sure ain't paying for extra words." We both had a good laugh before setting up the card table and getting the snack trays out for the smorgasbord of free food.

There wasn't much I kept from him, so I told what had happened earlier this morning. I went over everything in detail, all the way to the point where I had to wake her up from shouting out my name and then sleeping next to me, but I did conveniently remember to leave out the part of me having an "erectional response".

He walked over and sat in the wooden chair next to me. Like a child waiting to hear another Aesop's fable, his eyes grew as big as saucers, complimenting his devious smirk. "Your dick got hard when she got in the bed with you, didn't it?" he chirped. Like I said, we knew each other too well.

"No. Actually I was pretty cool about the whole thing."
He looked at me like I'd just told him that OJ was guilty.

"Okay, I'm lying. Yeah, I may have been just a little bit excited, but dammit Dre, is that all you think about? I tell you about the craziness that went down and all you focus on is me and Pedro? Why are you always focused on what happens below the belt?"

"Is there something important that goes on above it?"

I smiled because I'd almost forgotten who I was talking to. "I'm just saying that it was a wild night."

"Don't be such a dumbass, Quinton. You know that girl wants to jump your bones."

I walked over to the fridge, grabbed an orange soda and shook my head as I sat down. "You're on crack, right? Have you forgotten that Mike is her husband? You know Mike, Mike Hall. The Mike that fixes your cars so that you don't have to pay a grip to get those super expensive pieces of shit fixed and don't let us forget that small matter of Mike and I being good friends."

"No, I haven't forgotten, but you're on that 'I'm trying to be a good friend' bull. How many times does coochie have to fall out of the sky and onto your lap before you realize there are other women out there who are jones-ing for you? Man, if I had whatever you've gotten a hold of, I'd be the Wilt Chamberlain of the banking world." He leaned back in his chair, balancing on the hind legs, waiting for my response.

Everything was said with a bitter overtone. Not necessarily bitter in a bad sense, but because we'd had this conversation many times. He

50

was getting fed up at the fact that I didn't seem to acknowledge anyone other than Laela, I was upset that he wanted me to.

"What the hell are you talking about-- if you had what I had? I'm insulted that you'd even go there after what I'd just witnessed a few minutes ago. Dre, I came into this house and you were getting your balls licked by someone who didn't care that I was watching! Then after she had your ass crying like a little girl, she smiled, waved at me and left! Like that shit is *normal*! What the hell type of shit is that? She waved! Does she win the good fuckin' neighbor award or what? I mean literally *and* figuratively."

"Yeah, that was kind of nice, wasn't it? You gotta train them early." He looked off as if he were daydreaming about the experience. He tried to hide his smirk, but seeing him smile broke the stone face I'd tried to maintain and he was the first to speak after witnessing my goofy grin. "All I'm saying, Q, is that women are digging you. It may be because you won't notice it, it may be because you have a woman, but don't act like it ain't there when you have two eyes just like me. Denying it only makes the problem grow until the dam bursts and the floodgates open, then you'll be ass out and soaked in a pool of your own bullshit. It's a new year; stop being the same old you."

"Speaking of the same old me, what happened with Leslie the other night? After you put her in the room, she stopped with her usual bull. What did you do, drug her?"

"Well, um, I've been meaning to talk to you about that. I kinda banged her."

"What the hell?" I asked incredulously. I honestly couldn't believe what I'd just heard. I jumped out of the chair and began to pace around the bar before I stopped in front of the refrigerator. I turned to face him.

"Please tell me that this is a New Years' joke and you're full of bull."

"It's no joke, Quinton. I banged her, you know, slept with her. We fornicated with each other. I'm sure you get the gist of what I'm saying by now."

In all the years I'd known Dre, I knew just about everything he was capable of, but this kind of betrayal was something I'd never expected.

"What the *fuck*, Dre?!!"

"Look, Q, I know what you're going to say, but hear me out. First of all, I was slorny as hell, so all the drinking I did that night had me a little edgy. Secondly, it wasn't something that I planned for. I was getting down with her girl, like I said I would, and suddenly she walked into the

51

room and wanted to be a part of it. Thirdly, between the two of them, the sex was so goddamn righteous that even if I wanted to I couldn't say no."

"What the hell is 'slorny'?"

"I was a little sleepy and a little horny. It was one of those nights where I needed a nut to get some good sleep. I'm just the only brother willing to put a name to it."

"Slorny? You actually made up a word for stabbing me in the back?" I left the kitchen and walked into his dining room.

Dre followed me and grabbed my shoulder. I tried to pull away, but his grasp was a little stronger then I'd anticipated. "Quinton, it's not that serious, man. I fucked up. It won't happen again. Okay?"

But it wasn't okay and I wasn't willing to let it go. "Why would you do that shit? You couldn't say no? What kind of friend are you? What type of man are you trying to be, Andre? You know what she's capable of and you know how I felt about it? Did you even once consider that? When you're out doing dirt, do you think about anyone but yourself? What the fuck?"

I couldn't believe that even though I was giving him the third degree, he smiled. "Man, I already apologized, but if you want answers, then fine. To answer your first series of questions, I think about the dirt that I do, but I'm not going to fool myself into thinking that I'm something other than what I am. I like pussy and I will never turn it down. Let me restate that for you, *I will never turn it down*. I don't even actually remember it happening. I remember the sex, but when I woke up, both she and her friend were naked and sleeping on top of me. Since I wasn't sure who got some, I'll just rack it up as a drunken threesome."

I couldn't believe that he was making light of the situation, but this was typical Andre. Though I expected more from him, I knew I shouldn't have. As much as I'd talked to Dre about the sex between Leslie and me, it was almost inevitable that his curiosity would get the best of him. The only problem was that he didn't know what he was getting himself into. He didn't know Leslie like I did.

"Dre, this is the crazy heifer that set my car on fire. You remember her? The same crazy ass girl who stalked me, lied about her being pregnant, and constantly harassed me to the point where I had to get a restraining order! Think about that! A man having to get a restraining order for a woman! All that history and yet you still bang her?"

"Will you get of your goddamn high horse? I know the history, Quinton, and I don't need a rundown. I fuck women--all women. That's what I do! I'm not ashamed of it and I damn sure won't run from it. By the way, the coochie was fucking mag-nif-i-cent, I think. Listen here dawg; you're the one who tries to set this high standard for me when even you know that I won't follow it. I'm not you! You're the marrying type, I'm not. Once you get that shit through your goddamn head, the better off we'll be! Now let's eat goddammit, I'm hungry!"

He marched back to the kitchen, but I just sat down in one of the chairs at his dining table."I already grabbed a sandwich." I said while shaking my head. As much as I hated to admit, he was right. He wasn't me and because Leslie and I had cut our strings a long time ago, the both of them were free to do whatever they wished. But that still didn't stop it from being nasty and for Dre, very dangerous.

"So you like the marble I had put down?" He shouted from the other room, immediately changing the topic and trying to diffuse the tension.

"How did you get it put down so fast? The party was just a few days ago."

"It's been done for a week. I just asked the guys to put some carpet over it because I didn't want people scuffing up the new marble. The shit is nice, right?"

"It's cool, but can we start getting this thing set up?"

With the rest of the gang coming in the next few hours, we began preparing the snacks by opening up every bag of potato chips and pretzels we could find. Since I'd bought some soda on my way over, we were ready for any and all hungry Negroes with their free food appetites.

About an hour later, everyone else arrived. The first was BJ who promptly raided the fridge as soon as he walked in. We greeted the five others as they came in, handshakes and introductions went around as we comforted old friends and welcomed new ones. Among them, Michael, Simone's husband: his friend, Miles "Pookie" Johnson; my friend and another work buddy, Marcus Jackson; Teniyah's husband, Franklin Oliver; and Darryl "Chicken" Cooper, Andre's oldest friend. After looking around in awe at Dre's place, Mike was the first to speak up. "This is the new spot? Me likey the new digs. Damn, Dre, you getting paid out the ass, dawg."

"Yeah, I manage," he replied with a smug smile on his face.

We directed them towards the game room, a massive room located adjacent to his garage, which contained Dre's monogrammed pool table and one of the three walkways to the upstairs. By the time we all sat at the poker table, we were all full, laughing, and talking so much crap that I'd almost forgotten about Dre and his tactless escapade with Leslie-- almost.

I didn't speak to him during most of the game, instead thinking of how I would plot my vindication. My first thought was about dicking down his neighbor, but I couldn't. It would mean going back to who I was and even more importantly, it meant betraying Lae. No matter how spiteful I wanted to be, I refused to stoop to Dre's level.

By the time the game ended several hours later, we'd covered women, sex, sports, and even talked about the best childhood cartoons. Unfortunately, Franklin and Cooper were almost out of cash and I was in a very distant second. Somehow the newcomer, Pookie, had blown us out. Damn beginners luck.

I was ready to take my money and leave, but everyone else had talked themselves up, each hoping for an unlikely comeback. After Franklin and Cooper were eliminated, we all just gave up and took what we had-- which for most of us, was just a little less pride than what we came in with.

While stuffing my pockets with the little change I had left, Mike walked up to me and tapped me on the shoulder. "Hey, Q man, I need to holla at you."

I turned to Mike to see he wore a disturbed look across his face. "That's cool, Mike. What's going on?"

I was a little apprehensive, wondering if Simone told him about my 'erection mishap', but I shook it off. After I put away all my change, he pulled me into the library and closed the door. Rampant thoughts that Simone may have said something gave me a nervous edge about why he'd brought me here. In the few years I'd known Mike, I'd seen him angry a handful of times and I didn't want to be on the receiving end of his wrath.

"Look," he began, "I know you wanna get married, but are you sure that this is the way you wanna go out?"

I sat down on the sofa and sighed. "I know that you and Simone have your issues, but that's not a good enough reason for me to stay single."

"You can't understand how women get until you marry them. I don't go out that much, but every time I do, she's calling me back home to watch MJ! I mean damn, can I get some free time?"

"He's your son, too, right?"

"It don't matter. She's the damn woman and she wanted to have kids, so she should stay at home! Every week it seems like they always on some new bullshit. Like how she's always on me about my job because I don't make enough to support the whole damn household. Shit, she got a job too and we still can't manage to pay the damn bills

54

because she always buyin' shit! You know, dumb shit like that. As soon as you get married, they expect you to do every damn thing while they sit back and don't do shit!"

"Lae's not like that, man. Maybe those are your hang-ups, but we don't have kids and she makes enough money so that we're not struggling. We've already talked about all that shit and I'm still good with my decision."

He began to laugh. "So it don't make no difference to you that she makes more money? I hate to be like this, but it seems like you're the woman in this relationship. I mean Dre told me about all those fine ass chicas at the party and how you got mad that they were there. That don't sound like the Quinton I know."

I shook my head. "That's not who I am anymore. I made a commitment to Lae and I plan on keeping it."

"Commitment is overrated."

For the first time I understood what Mike was saying. "You're screwing around on Simone, aren't you?"

He looked up at the ceiling, then at the floor and shook his head. For as long as I'd known Mike, every time he did the ceiling to floor thing, it was always followed by a blatant lie, but he appeared thoroughly distressed. He looked like he was about to say something to me when he raised his head to the ceiling once more.

"If Simone ain't given it to me how I like it, I gotta get it somehow, right?"

I jumped up and was about a foot away from Mike when I stopped myself. After taking in a deep breath, I asked "Who is she Mike and why stay married if all you're gonna do is screw around?"

"So what am I supposed to do? She's the mother of my child and my family will never let me get a divorce."

"Stop messing around and try to make things right. It's not that damn hard."

"Damn, the way you say it makes it seem like I'm wrong."

"Aren't you?"

"You don't know Simone like I do. I know she's been cheating, too. Even before we got married she was messing around on me and I'm sure as hell about that. I just don't know who it was, but when I find out, they're gonna catch hell."

"So you're saying its okay for you to mess around, but not her?"

He walked away from me and sat on the same couch that I'd gotten up from. "Damn straight it's okay. Women do that shit for love, but for me, Simone just ain't doin' it for me anymore."

"So why tell me now? What's the mystery woman's name? Where did you meet her?"

"Her name is Starr."

"Starr? What is she-- a stripper or something? "

"Yeah, she's something like that, but that shit ain't important. I don't know how much longer I can deal with Simone's ass."

"Okay, and what do you want me to do? You're a newlywed and this shit is wrong, man. I can't be in your corner for this one. If Monie was just your girlfriend, it'd be different. Wait, you're not coming to me because this girl Starr is pregnant, are you?"

"She can't get pregnant. She can't have kids."

"She told you this? How can you trust someone who just says that and be cool with it?"

"Q, she can't have kids, man, and I really prefer it that way. Quiet as it's kept, I didn't want MJ. I told Simone to get the abortion, but she didn't wanna listen to me. Her ass never listens to me."

I sat down on the coffee table, across from him, and sighed. "Look, because we're boys I won't say anything, but you gotta do right by your wife. Are you gonna tell her? You gonna come clean? I mean, damn, man, if you're thinking about leaving Simone why are you telling me and not her?"

"I can't tell her yet. I'm not ready. I'm gonna stop messing with Starr, but only to see if we can make it. I thought about coming out with y'all on New Years, but I had already planned on spending it with Starr. If this thing with me and Simone doesn't pan out, I don't want you left with the feeling that I'm the only bad one in the situation."

"Well, whatever you do is up to you, but I just think that if the both of you are together just for MJ, then you really need to do the right thing and let go. But I think you guys can make it work, man. I really do."

We both walked out of the room as quietly as he'd snuck me in. Not long after leaving, I thanked everyone for contributing to the 'Q needs money for the wedding' fund. Walking out to the car, I suddenly found myself thinking not only about Mike, but also about Leslie.

As much as I cursed Dre for having slept with her, seeing her again brought back lust that I'd long stuffed in the back of my mind. She was by far, the best lay I'd ever had and for a few months after our falling out, I couldn't even climax. Even though a day didn't go by when I thought about the burnt out shell that was my car, I couldn't shake the thought that Leslie was the one that got away—until I met Lae. It was Laela who stopped me from going back and possibly making the biggest mistake of my life and it was Lae who brought the orgasms back.

"I'm out, Q-Dawg." BJ said, as he brushed past me on the way to his old Ford pickup. I waved to everyone and as I started my own car, I had to laugh about all the drama I'd been through in the last twenty-four hours.

When I arrived home, I didn't see Laela's car parked in the usual space and when I entered the apartment, it looked like she hadn't been there all day. After a day like today, I was too tired to care.

CHAPTER 5

Laela

Checkout was half an hour away, but I washed up, threw on a white blouse and some blue jeans before we packed our things up and left.

When we made it to the parking lot, I gave Quinton a kiss before he jumped into his car and pulled away. All through the morning he had been trying to find out the answers to some of the questions we posed last night, but I didn't reveal any secrets and so he left with a slight chip on his shoulder.

With both Quinton and Mike going to play their 'holier than thou' man game at Andre's house, it was left up to me to drop off Simone. As we eased through the light holiday traffic, we hadn't spoken since we'd gotten in the car. I was still a little embarrassed from the previous night, but that could easily be blamed on the liquor. But the bed urination was something entirely different and I knew it was a little more than what I was ready to tackle.

With everything that Simone had been through, I didn't have a right to put Simone out like I did, but to my credit, she fought back just as hard. When I looked at her, she appeared lost in a daydream. I didn't want to awaken her from one of the biggest smiles I'd seen her wear in a while, but someone had to break the deafening silence. There wasn't any good reason I could think of as to why we shouldn't be talking.

"Hey, Monie," she looked over her left shoulder, looking surprised that I'd spoken. "I hope you at least had a little fun last night."

"Yeah, it was cool. Good thing I slept through my hangover. It would have been hell if I hadn't. Besides it was fun to get out of the house and away from the kids. "

I was about to remind her that she only had one kid, but then I figured she was adding Mike. "I feel you, girl. Sometimes you need time off to just deal with yourself. I think that's the reason I'm everybody's God-parent." She hit me when she laughed, just like we did to each other when we were teenagers.

Everything quickly grew tense once more when she asked, "Lae, I know you don't care for Mike that much, but do you really think he's cheating on me?"

I didn't know how I wanted to answer. With this being a new year, I hated reminiscing on last year's problems, but Simone was my friend and I had to be truthful to her. "I'm not saying he is, but I'm certainly not saying he isn't. But look at the facts, Monie. He works a whole lot of overtime, but you guys are always struggling to pay the bills? Not only that, but he bowls enough to be on tour, yet when we play, he barely beats any of us. Monie, you know your routine better than I do, so I can't answer that. But as women, we have an inbred intuition that we have to learn to trust because our intuition is rarely wrong."

She hesitated a little before asking, "How did you know Q was the one?" We had come to a stoplight and she looked me in the eye, waiting for my answer.

"I didn't. I had to groom him to be the respectable man that you all see before you. I had to do a serious overhaul and it paid off." I chuckled. "He's not well off like the man I said I'd always marry--like my parents wanted me to marry, but he has a big heart. Then again, the way he puts it down kinda makes staying mad at him worth the makeup sex."

I smiled at the thought, but Simone fell over from laughter. It was good to see her laughing again. No sooner than we caught our breath, my phone rang. It was Teniyah.

"Happy New Year," she chimed. She was certainly in a good mood and with her husband, Franklin, out playing cards with the rest of the guys I figured she'd be calling sooner or later. With company next to me, I didn't want her asking any questions.

Before she had a chance to ask any, I cut her off. "A Happy New Year to you too, Teniyah! Simone and I were just talking about you." It was the only lie I could think of on such short notice and Simone looked at me as if she had just smelled something foul.

"Oh, so it's a ladies day out. You didn't invite me? Thanks for thinking about me, *Lae*."

"No, it's not a ladies day out. We just left from the hotel." I just shook my head because I knew what was coming.

And as usual, she didn't miss a thing. "Oh. And you spent the night with her, did you? That's so very interesting. Didn't tell me that this was going to be an all night thing, did you? Just handing the goods out to the poor folk when I was the first in line, huh?"

"You are just too funny this morning," I said, trying to play it off like we weren't talking about anything serious. "No, Mrs. Oliver, we were just out kicking it. I figured you married folks were going to bring in the New Year with some screaming and hollering, like you're supposed to do."

"No, I intentionally went to sleep on him. He bores the hell out of me. You know we haven't been intimate in months. God, I'm so horny. Are you horny to, Lae, or did the bag lady take care of you?"

I couldn't help but let out a nervous laugh and then quickly turn lead the conversation down another road. "So what's up? Where are my God-kids?"

"Nothing is up, girl. Like I said before, it's just me today. The kids are with my momma and I'm at the house, bored as usual. I was just gonna see if you wanted to go out and um, eat, but I see you have company." I became instantly flushed.

"So what do you say, Lae? You wanna grab something with me? You can bring a friend if you like. She can eat too. Course, she has to scrounge around the garbage can, but at least it'll be behind a decent restaurant."

"You are an awful person, you know that?" I was holding the phone so tightly against my face that I was scared it would break. I knew one thing though. I had to get her off the phone before she had me saying something that shouldn't have been said, especially with Simone looking at me with her eyebrow raised.

"Let's meet at Chingas, that new Mexican restaurant I told you about. It's not that far from here--over there by I-10 and Highway 6. Besides, I feel like tasting something spicy." She was trying to seduce me with innuendo and I knew it. After being with Quinton for so long, I was practically a master at deciphering all types of innocuous sexual commentary.

"Okay," I told her. "We'll meet you there in half an hour." After she hung up, Simone gave me a strange and confused look.

"Was that 'Raven'?" Raven was Teniyah's sorority name and Simone's sarcastic one.

Once I told Simone her "other" name, it stuck and she never called her anything else but Raven.

"Nevermore," I mused, trying to break the tension, but failing miserably.

"She wants to meet at Chingas. You feel like Mexican?"

"Not with her there. I don't know why you hang out with that stuck-up heifer anyway. Even if I was hungry, I wouldn't eat with her if she had the last hamburger on earth. Besides, I'm broke."

"I'll pay for it." I wasn't ready to make my decision concerning Teniyah yet, so I was going to need Simone to help me avoid the pressure.

"Nah, I'm cool. I gotta pick up my son and we're already out by where I stay. It doesn't make a whole lot of sense for you to drive out to the southwest side and then back over here. Especially when we're only a couple minutes away from the house as it is."

"Okay," I conceded. Maybe it was better this way. Lately it seemed that Teniyah didn't care who was watching--or listening. She was a flirt and when she had your attention, she poured it on, disregarding anyone around.

I dropped Simone off a few minutes later at her house and was right back on the freeway heading west on I-610 five minutes after that. I took 610 to I-10 and with the absence of a heavy traffic flow; I made it to the restaurant thirty minutes later. It was just off the freeway, a quick turn to the right after I'd made it to the Highway 6 exit.

Had I not known where it was, it was still too hard a restaurant to miss. The fluorescent yellow stucco walls and bright orange top made for an interesting décor, but the parking lot was full of trucks, a norm for Texas. I'd been fortunate to pull up when someone else was pulling out, so I didn't have to walk far. I just hoped that Teniyah was here before me or she'd catch hell finding a parking spot. Luckily she hadn't yet arrived, which was typical for her and should've been her New Years' resolution.

The hostess smiled at me when I walked in. She was a young black girl, with long, beautiful hair that flowed down to her lower back. She was obviously mixed with something, but upon closer inspection I couldn't guess what. Looking at her reminded me a lot of myself, a teenager always trying to make some extra money on a holiday.

"Welcome to Chingas. How many are in your party?" she asked.

"Well, I'm waiting on a friend. How long is the wait?"

"Not long. Maybe ten minutes. Would you like to look at a menu while you wait?" I nodded at her suggestion, she handed me a menu the size of a pizza box and went on to greet the people behind me as I sat down on one of the hard wooden benches provided by the door.

I was so engrossed in reading the pages of food that I never saw her come in. She sat next to me, acted like she was about to whisper in my ear and subtly kissed me on the side of the neck as the menu kindly hid her indiscretion.

"Hello, sexy stranger."

I jumped, startled by her advance. "Don't do that!" I whispered to her. "You almost got beat down. I thought you were some guy trying to get on." She removed her shades and with her daunting glare, tried to get me to fall into her cat-like gaze. I refused to look her in the eyes, but nevertheless, she looked amazing. She wore a lacey black blouse that slightly showed her black sports bra, a black mini-skirt to show off her long legs, with black straps from her heels creeping halfway up her calf, and her braided hair pinned up with a black bow tying it all together. I wanted to comment, but thought better of it.

"So, there's a man walking around with the voice of the sexiest woman you know?"

"Stranger things have happened."

"Do tell." She smiled when she said it, and I knew that she had to be talking about last night. "Anyways, you made it here pretty fast. I already called in and had a table set up for us."

"You see this cell phone?" I pulled it out of my purse and held it a few inches from her nose. "You could've called and told me. That would've been nice." I was a little upset after having sat on the bench long enough for my butt to hurt.

"Yeah, but that would've ruined the surprise. Oh, yeah, surprise!"

"Ha. Ha," I said, rolling my eyes. After she spoke to the hostess, a waiter came and guided us to our table. We sat in a booth near the back. It must've been a private booth because there were only two other couples and twenty other tables. The windows were deeply tinted, almost opaque, giving the lighting in our area more a romantic bistro feel. It certainly felt dark for it to be noon outside. The waiter left and came back with two glasses of water with a lemon slice in the corner. After we ordered, he left us to talk.

She raised her right hand and placed it under her chin, letting me know I had her full attention. "So tell me about last night, in detail. I'd like to hear what happened with you, Q, and your plus one." I saw that she was anxious to hear what happened, so I told her most of what I could remember. Before I'd even finished telling her about our night, she blurted out, "You had sex, with Quinton, while she was in the bathroom?" She was in awe. "You are just the nastiest whore!!! I mean, damn, how come I can't ever get that kind of peep show action?"

"Simone didn't see us. She was in the bathroom the whole time."

"Lae, she peeked. That heifer is as nasty as us normal people. Hell, I would've peeked and then I would've molested the both of you for making me peek. So when do I get my own show?"

I ignored her and continued with my story. "Yeah, well, it was a new year and we were feeling it. The fact that she was in the bathroom, right next to us, just added to the excitement. Besides, we could never do that with you and Franklin because he's a square and you're some super freaky voyeur. I refuse to be the cause of the breakup between you two."

"Bullshit! You and I are going to play some strip poker before this year is over. In fact, that's what we're gonna do at the end of this year, I promise you. I'll start getting him ready now so he'll be prepared." She then mimicked giving fellatio with the same hand that she'd used to keep her head up. When I didn't say anything, her hand retreated back under her chin. "Okay, you can finish."

"Are you sure?" I asked. "I don't want to impede your interpretive miming. Is there another viewing coming soon or do I have to add another quarter?" She gave me a sarcastic grin and I finished my recap of our New Year's Eve.

As usual, her first response to Simone was negative. "That heifer peed in her bed? Ewww, that's nasty as hell. It'd be different if she was in labor, but she just pissed all over a hotel room bed."

"Will you stop being so judgmental? First you call her poor like a million times over the phone and now you call her nasty. What do you have against her anyway?"

"Lae, let's get things in perspective. She urinated-- in her bed. Doesn't that say volumes about a person's character? Would you be defending her if she shit all over herself? It's practically the same thing! That's why I don't like her."

"Don't act like you ain't ever peed in somebody's bed."

"And I don't like myself for that either. Besides, like I said, you have to put things in perspective," she sang. "When I did it, I had already told Richard that he was too big and in effect, my bladder was recuperating from the trauma -- while I slept. All that banging he did up in there loosened some things. In fact, I might still be recovering."
This time I couldn't help but laugh. "You always have an excuse."

63

"Not an excuse, a reason." Teniyah rebutted. She then dug in her purse and pulled out a dark colored lipstick that I hadn't seen her wear before. While looking in her purse for her mirror, she dropped the lipstick on the floor, under the table. "Can you do me a favor and grab it?" Already knowing that she was going to ask, I lifted up the tablecloth. In the dimly lit area, under an even darker tablecloth, I saw Niya without any panties on, masturbating. I raised my head, forgetting I was under the table and almost passed out from the pain.

"Do you see it?" I came up from under the table, forgetting her lipstick and breathing heavily.

"Yeah, I saw it. I also saw something else I shouldn't have. Why didn't you warn me?"

"If I did, you wouldn't have gone down there." She took her free hand and tapped me on the nose. "I didn't feel like wearing any panties today. The man wasn't at home, so I figured why bother. I didn't start getting hot until you told me about what happened last night. Not wearing panties only gave me more of an incentive to do it. Don't be mad. I didn't drop it on purpose, but since you were down there, I just figured that now you've seen it, so you can't say no. That's how the fellas do it."

"I'm not a *fella*."

"You could be mine or maybe I could be yours. No, I definitely have to be the man, I'm taller."

"What goes through your head when you do these things?"

"Sex."

I shook my head. "Amazing," I said flatly.

"C'mon Lae, you've seen me naked before. Besides, I already know you want to do something. If you didn't, you would've already told me no." I opened my mouth to speak, but nothing came out. She quickly picked up on my silence. "You don't have to say anything. Your look says enough."

"So you think you know me that well?"

"Better than you know yourself." She smiled at me as only she knew how and I suddenly began to understand why she and Quinton pretended to dislike each other. As much as the bickered they weren't rivals. They were essentially the same person only wrapped in different exteriors.

"If you know me that well, then what will my answer be?"

As soon as I'd asked the question, the waiter began setting up and placed our steaming food in front of us.

"Hold that thought. I'm so freaking hungry." She fiercely bit into one of her chicken enchiladas. After looking at her for a few moments, I had no idea how she stayed so slim. Here she was, tearing apart two large enchiladas while I'd just ordered a salad, trying to start the New Year by losing some weight. As soon as she finished the first one, she smirked at me.

"Because you're Lae, you're going to tell me no. Then you're going to say no because of how it might make you feel, not because you're not genuinely curious."

Damn.

"Why don't we go out tonight? We don't work for the next few days and we haven't had a girls' night out in a while."

Between making love to Quinton and playing mother to Simone, I hadn't gotten much sleep. It was barely after midday and I was already dragging my feet.

"I don't know. It's been kind of a long night."

"So, you can have a sleepover with Simone, but you can't kick it with me?"

"Fine."

After we finished eating and said our goodbyes, I drove home. Finally able to rest, I took a long nap, recuperating from the last few days. As soon as I woke up, I showered and called Niya. When she didn't answer, I opted to go through the closet just in case she decided to call back while standing just outside my apartment door.

I thought about calling Quinton to let him know, but since he had his man-only time, it was only fair that I had my woman-only time, too. After twenty minutes of closest searching, I picked out the cutest beaded halter neck dress. I'd forgotten exactly where I'd gotten it, but that didn't seem to matter. The dress filled out my curves perfectly and the midnight blue color looked really good on me.

I was glad that I'd only eaten a salad earlier and as good as I knew I looked, all I could do was shake my head when Niya finally came knocking at my door an hour later. Naturally, she'd found a way to outdo me, wearing a dress made completely of black lace which barely fell it below her thigh. The dress was practically translucent, with the exception on the black lining from the waist down.

"Oh my God, you are not going to wear that in public! Did Franklin actually see that before you left?" I squealed.

"He's still at his *men-only* game and besides, Lae, its New Years. If there ever was a time to get buck wild, tonight is that night."

"Wild is something I can get with, but pornographic is just out of my range."

"Lae, you need to shush now. You're ruining my sexy high. Fine, I'll put on a bra then." She looked at my chest, then at hers, which was clearly two sizes bigger before smugly saying, "I'll buy one on the way."

I locked the apartment door and as we walked to her red Chevy Cavalier I asked her about her husband. "So what's Franklin going to say to you when you walk in the house wearing your little getup?"

She smiled. "That's already taken care of." As I approached the passenger's side, she opened her door and revealed a conservative looking black silk blouse.

"You are terrible."

"I know."

Teniyah wasn't the only one with naughty thoughts. I'd intentionally allowed Simone to share our bed to see how Quinton would react with a married woman next to him. With neither he nor Simone talking about it, it was hard for me to gauge how either of them felt. I hated using Simone as a test subject, but I knew that using Niya would've brought anything but sleep.

Not much was said as we jumped onto I-10 and headed downtown. After what she'd tricked me into doing in the restaurant, the last thing I wanted to talk about was what happened earlier. Between what I'd done to Simone and what Niya had done to me, I was having mixed feelings about having another woman in my bed. I knew Niya would do a threesome in a heartbeat if I asked, but Quinton was holding steadfast to his "no married women" rule.

Why couldn't he make it easy? Why did he have to be so damn stubborn?

I was so busy in my own thoughts that I'd forgotten to remind Niya to buy a bra, but somehow I knew she'd preferred it that way.

We found a parking spot in the back of a bank, grabbed our purses, and stepped out of the car. Niya walked quickly across the parking lot to the back door of the bank and knocked. Within a few seconds, the door opened a fair skinned woman as tall as Teniyah wrapped her arms around her and they hugged. Then, we were quickly ushered into the building and soon found ourselves being approached by a topless man.

Even in the dim lighting, I could see that he was gorgeous. He was bald, tall and had more muscles than Quinton on his best day. He carefully grabbed Niya and I by the hands, led us down a short hallway and into a room filled with other fine topless men like him.

66

From the black lighting, to the disco ball that dangled above an empty dance floor, the room screamed 'club'. Even with slow songs emanating from several speakers around the room and its purplish glow, things seemed a little more intimate than I was used to. Through the dimness, I could spot several tables set up with purple candles at each one. The room was filled with other handsome men who were dancing near or on women who were wearing less clothing than even Niya, if that was possible.

Our silent "Adonis" continued on as we walked through the main room to a secluded area in the back. Several rooms, which had 'private' placarded on the doors, were already closed and even though I could hear the cries of women emanating through them, I didn't dare stop to ask exactly where we were going. We followed him to an available room and in it we found a round, empty table and a brown leather and suede couch in the corner. As soon as we sat at the table, he disappeared.

"Lae, I want one of him for Christmas," Niya whispered.

"Christmas has already passed!"

"And you still haven't gotten me a present! I want him!"

"Where have you brought me? Is this an orgy?"

"No, just an all-male review for the next hour or two. After that, then this place becomes a club."

"Who was the woman you hugged?"

"She's one of my sorors. She's the one who hooked this thing up and told me about it. Each dance is twenty, but I want one from the guy who brought us in before I even bother with these others."

Before I had a chance to respond, our "Adonis" had returned. While bringing a bottle of champagne and two glasses to our table, it was then that I noticed he wasn't wearing pants and also the bulge in his tight shorts. Niya looked at me, winked and as soon as he arrived at the table, whispered something in his ear.

He placed the bottle and glasses on the table, smiled and slowly began to walk towards me. Immediately, I began blushing like a schoolgirl and turned towards Niya just in time to see her don her devilish grin.

"You liar!" I mimed to her, but that made her grin even wider.

He pulled my chair away from the table and slowly kneeled before me. Without a word, he slipped off my 4-inch heels and placed each one of my toes into his mouth before dragging his tongue up my right thigh and halting at my kneecap.

I was finally allowed to exhale, and after my eyes rolled out from my forehead, I looked down at him. "Um, sir, I don't know if my friend told you, but I'm engaged--to be married."

"She told me," he said in a deep voice, "but I won't do anything to get you in trouble. If you get too hot, just let me know."

With that said and still kneeling in front of me, he pushed up my skirt just enough to kiss me on each side of my thigh. Then he placed each one of my fingers into his mouth and sucked each one with the kind of attention only a pro could give.

I wanted to hate every moment, but as I turned to Niya, I saw her move towards the couch with another sexy muscular dancer. After she sat, her dancer quickly opened her legs, knelt in front of her, but instead of him having control, she had both her legs resting on his shoulders while his head disappeared under her short skirt. Watching her as her head rolled around was just as arousing and even though I tried to stop it, I could feel my underwear dampen.

I shook my head and returned my attention to my "Adonis" as he stood up and with his manhood pulsating directly in front of me, he began to bite my neck. I soon found myself clutching the edges of my chair and felt my stomach tightening, which I knew meant trouble.

"Stop... I'm hot."

Without so much as a struggle he stood up and began to simply dance for me. My body cursed me so badly that I almost regretted that I told him to stop, but as my body began to cool, I was glad I had. A took a few deep breaths, ignored the whispered screams coming from Niya and dug in my purse to pull out a twenty dollar bill for "Adonis" as soon as the song ended for his dance.

When Niya's 'friend' finished with his tongue dance a few minutes later, I watched in horror as he wiped his mouth and she paid him for a job well done. She walked over to me, knees trembling, and sat down at the table.

"I can't believe you brought me here." I whispered as loudly as I could. "You didn't even know that guy! What if he had something?"

"He does have something—Niya on his breath."

"Sometimes I can't believe you!" I said, shaking my head.

"Does Quinton go down on you, Lae?"

"What does that have to do with anything?"

"I'll take that as a yes. And I'll even go so far as to say that you love the feeling of his tongue in between your thighs. Supposed he was to come home one day and say that he won't do that anymore? How long would you wait for him to get through this phase? A month or two?

Maybe six? Try five years, Lae. Since we've been together, Franklin hasn't ever done it and dammit, I needed it. God knows I needed that."

"So you'll get your fix from anyone who'll give it to you?"

"Lae, I'm sorry. It was weird making you watch, but I *need* to be needed sometimes. I'm not used to rejection. First it was Franklin who rejected me. Then Quinton rejected me and earlier you did it."

She moved the candle to the side and grabbed my free hand that rested on the table. "I didn't come here expecting this, but I needed to be catered to instead of me having to be so damn hard all the damn time. I'm weak and dammit, I needed to feel human again." She sighed and closed her eyes, letting her head fall back. "You think I'm happy with the way things turned out, but I needed to be grabbed. I needed to hold onto someone and feel like a woman."

I knew Niya was risqué, but I'd never known her to do something as bold as being ate out in a club. I also knew I had the bad habit of being a matron and judging, but this was a new year and even I knew that I needed to stop putting everyone in a box.

"Look, Niya, I didn't mean to judge you. It's just you never told me about you and Franklin's, um, problem. And what do you mean by we reject you? I've never rejected you and you've never said anything about it before tonight."

She poured herself a glass of champagne and downed it before pouring herself another. She rested it on her lips and continued.

"Franklin doesn't want to mouth fuck me. Quinton thinks I'm somehow tainted and would never do a threesome with someone like me, even though I'm clearly the most qualified and willing person you know. And then we come to you." She signed and then looked down at the table. "I don't know, Lae. I just thought that when it came to something like a threesome, I'd always be your first-- your only choice. I thought you'd lobby for me or something. You know, do something crazy like tell Quinton that if you couldn't do the threesome with me, then y'all wouldn't do it. Hell, if Franklin was any kind of man and he wanted a threesome, I'd sure as hell tell him that if it you weren't the third, we wouldn't do it." As soon as she finished speaking, she quickly poured the second glass down her throat.

As images of Franklin and I flooded my brain, I poured myself another glass of champagne and quickly emptied it.

By the time the male review had ended, so had our bottle supply of champagne. Feeling a little light-headed, I closed my eyes and tried to stop the world from spinning, but when I reopened them, another full bottle had reappeared.

69

"I hope you're not trying to get me drunk so that I'll put out easier."

She smiled. "The thought never crossed my mind."

It took about half an hour for the club crowd to finally filter in, and less than fifteen minutes after that before the room was filled with laser lights and smoke, but we still didn't move from our table. As the slow music died down and was replaced by hip-hop, we were approached by random men to dance.

Instead of saying no, like I usually did, I stood up and danced with the third guy who had asked me. He was in no way as attractive as my "Adonis", but I was drunk and even more importantly, I came out with Niya to have fun. Several times I saw her dancing and sometimes we'd dance with each other, but as the night went on and the drinks continued to flow our dancing moves toward each other grew more suggestive.

On the last song of the night, I found Niya casually flirting with a man with enough diamond studded teeth to resolve Houston's homeless problem. Instead of waiting for her to finish, I grabbed her hand and pulled her onto the dance floor with me. Without much of a fight, she followed me.

As I placed my head on her chest, all I could think about was how loyal a friend she'd been to me. I thought back to college and how she took me under her wing, even though I was a tight-assed introvert, with my head buried in my books. College became so much more fun after I'd met her. We'd been through so much…she was my guardian angel. She was my truest friend. Shit, maybe I could learn some things from her.

Whoa, slow down there girlie. You're drunk.

I didn't care if I was drunk, she was right. It was a new year, and I needed to start taking some chances, trying new things. My stomach tightened. I at least owed her that much.

"Niya, you're my girl. I just want you to know that I love you."

"I love you, too," she whispered.

I'd always found Niya attractive, but I'd never before crossed the line towards being attracted to her, or any woman-- at least not outside of my dreams. Yet, here I was, dancing with her in the middle of a crowded club, hiding amongst the other grinding bodies on the dance floor, and nothing else seemed to matter. Whether it was the alcohol or simply the lingering effects from what 'Adonis' had done, I looked up into Niya's eyes and realized how truly beautiful she was. Since she'd propositioned me, there rarely went a day when I didn't think about Quinton fucking her while her tongue explored me…

I shuddered on the dance floor as the images of the three of us once again dominated my thoughts.

"Are you okay, Lae?"

"Yeah, I just felt a cool chill," I lied. I wasn't alright. With each passing night, my fantasy grew more vivid and infinitely more detailed. Honestly, I wanted to get the whole "vetting" thing over with so it'd stop consuming so much of my sleep, but it was Quinton and his high morals that excluded most everyone I knew.

Perhaps Niya wasn't so wrong to suggest that I test the waters before we did it.

When the song ended, the same man with the mouth full of diamonds ran up to Niya.

"Oh shit! Y'all go both ways?"

"What if we do?" Niya asked, slyly winking at me.

"Well then I can be that freak that brings yo' ass back from the dark side, girl." He looked at me. "You and yo' fine ass friend."

"Sorry," I said. "Tonight is ladies night."

We walked out of the club, hand in hand and I looked back at the shiny-toothed man as he shook his head and mimed, "Call me".

"Niya?"

"Yeah, Lae?"

"I'm not ready... to go home yet."

"I think I can help you with that."

The world was still spinning, but I managed to take the engagement ring that Quinton had given me and place it on the nightstand by the bed.

Teniyah did the same with her wedding band, laying it on top of mine. Then she walked to the side of the bed and turned off the lamp that shared the same nightstand as our rings. Wasting no time, she unbuttoned her dress, letting it fall to the floor and exposing her statuesque silhouette. She was so beautiful and for a brief moment, I envied her. She'd been a mother to twins, yet I could barely spot a flaw on her body.

Lying next to each other on the hotel room bed, I'd never been so nervous. For several minutes, we just looked into each other's eyes-- staring at one another...neither of us knowing exactly what to do and afraid to make the first move.

"So what do we do now?" I asked.

"I was kind of hoping that you'd know what to do. What were you going to do during the threesome you and Quinton are supposed to have?"

I shrugged. "I thought that was why we came here--to help me get comfortable being with another woman."

"Well, why don't you tell me what you want me to do and then I'll do it," she whispered.

"It's not sexy if I have to ask you to do it, Niya."

"It is for me."

I began to cover up, so she took the initiative. Pulling me off of the bed and slowly undressing me. She ran her hands across my breasts, leaned over and softly pressed her lips against mine. The tingle I'd felt days before had returned and rested at the tips of my lips.

She pushed me down on the bed, mounting me and quickly filled my mouth with her tongue. A rush of excitement enveloped me as we fell back together, still passionately engaged and neither of us willing to come up for air.

With Niya on top of me, the shivers I felt from our kissing were replaced with heat, and soon the warmth from her body began to invade my own. As our affair continued, the warmth that she had transferred to me, now seemingly alive, began to migrate.

Whether it was the alcohol guiding me or simply my curiosity with what was happening, I didn't want her to stop. With her tongue in my mouth and my body betraying whatever little resolve I had, I relaxed and allowed her to explore me.

She was relentless in her pursuit of my climax-- slowly working her way down to my breasts, then my thighs and kissing me directly under my navel. I thought about pushing her head down further, but the more I thought about it, the less comfortable I felt doing it. Even though I was comforted by the touch of her fingernails running along my sides and her lips brushing against my flesh, too much too fast would ruin the fantasy. Not long after I dismissed the idea of guiding her, a piercing pain arose from my left nipple.

"Ouch!" I loudly whispered. "Dammit! Teniyah that hurt." She smiled mischievously as she looked at me, letting me know that it hadn't been an accident.

"I didn't know you were so damn fragile!" she whispered back.

My nipple throbbed with pain and this time, her smile wasn't going to save her. "Well I am! Do you want me biting on your tits?"

"Hell yes! I like a little pain with my pleasure."

"Well I'm not you!"

"I'm sorry, Lae. Can I make it up to you?"

I was ready to answer when she moved herself past my waist, removed my last vestige of clothing and tasted me. I was caught off guard and as she swirled her tongue around, all doubts were silenced.

Apology accepted.

After about ten minutes of her rogue tongue, I finally spoke. Honestly, I didn't want to talk, but if I hadn't, I knew there wasn't a chance in hell that I'd ever climax. My body wanted this and I was going to get it even if I had to force myself.

Talking to her was strange, but not as strange as guiding my best friend around my clit. Between commands of "Softer", "Faster", and "Slower", she took some artistic license, but she took direction even better. I could feel my clitoris throbbing and by the look on her face, I knew she felt it swelling on her tongue.

Oh, God, I'm about to explode.

With the exception of the anticipation that was building in my stomach, I was tensed and numb. As her tongue slid across my most private areas, she dug her nails into my thigh, adding pain to my pleasure and finally taking me to the precipice of my orgasm.

Not even a few minutes after I took command, I peaked. I grabbed her by the sides of her head and let out a scream that awakened every sensation in my body all at once. I couldn't see what I'd done to her face as she pulled away, but I could feel the warmth as cum ran down her chin and onto my stomach. I pulled her up next to me, and did something even I hadn't expected. I kissed her. I tasted myself on her lips and sucked my essence from her tongue.

As my body calmed and my head cleared, I returned to Laela--fiancée, nurse, and best friend. I wanted to feel guilty for what we'd done, but the feelings never came. I lay naked for several minutes, trying to remember the last time I'd cum with such fierce intensity.

That's easy, you haven't.

As we began to put on our clothes, I lobbied for my turn.

"Teniyah Oliver," I stood on the tips of my toes, moved her hair from the side of her neck and softly kissed her several times, "will you just let me try? A few minutes are all I need." Through her lace dress, I could feel her nipples growing erect, but she was stern with her rejections.

"Laela, tonight was for me. This is something I wanted to do and I did it. Whenever you're ready to take that leap, you know I'm only a phone call away."

"Don't be like that." I grabbed her hand, practically begging her not to leave. "I'd at least like you to feel what it's like."

She smiled just wide enough to give me false hope. "I never thought that you'd be the one pressing me like I did to you. But even though I like this side of you, we can't. The sun will be up in an hour or two and our men will be pretty curious to know what happened. Do you have a story to tell them?" I shrugged. "I didn't think so. Like I said, Lae, if you want to finish this, it'll be our little secret.

Without another word, we left the hotel room, which was only a few minutes of driving from home. As soon as I pulled into the parking lot of my apartment, I could see the night sky beginning to give way to the sun. I waved to Teniyah and headed up the stairs. Walking into the apartment, I found Quinton in the bedroom, hugging the pillow like he was somehow holding me. I kissed him on his head and cuddled up next to him, moving the pillow.

I wanted to wake him and tell him what I'd done for us, but I knew better. I hadn't done *anything* for us, I did it for me. I liked the way that Niya felt against me: her touch against my flesh and her tongue against my breasts. In truth, I knew that I wanted to do it again--without Quinton.

This was just the first time and if it was only going to get better, I could certainly make the time for another rendezvous with my best friend.

You should hate yourself for feeling this way.
But I didn't.

CHAPTER 6

Quinton

<u>January 5th (Thursday)</u>

It wasn't even noon yet and it was hot as hell for January.

BJ and I backed up into one of the few open parking spots at the station a few minutes before noon. I'd gone with him on his route, but without any A/C in his truck, we were hot and tempers flared. Before I had a chance to apologize, BJ grabbed his stuff and jumped out of the truck. I wasn't far behind him. I grabbed my clipboard and paperwork and rushed into the building towards the cool breeze in my office.

The worst thing about sweating all day is that when I arrived in my new, centrally air-conditioned office, all of the sweat droplets on my body instantly froze. In the time frame of a few milliseconds, I went from being drenched in my own sweat to being bathed in mini-icicles, neither one at all providing any comfort. I longed to sit in my chair, but that would've meant having my sweat soaked pants, now starched by air-conditioning, touching everything below my belt. So I remained standing, stuffing loose paper towels into my pants to absorb the extra moisture.

I slowly leaned back in my chair when BJ stuck his head into my office. "It looks like you got a weenie-do. That's when yo belly sticks out further than yo weenie-do."

I thought about smiling just to try it, but it didn't work. "BJ, I wanted to apologize about some of the things that were said in the truck. It was hot and it's been a long day."

"I ain't worried about that, man. We cool, so apology accepted, but I ain't come in here for your apology."

"Well then what do you want?" I asked, beginning to shuffle through the mountain of paperwork on my desk.

"So what's up with Leslie, man? I know she crazy as shit, but she was lookin' fine as hell at that party. I know you miss hittin' that. That hoe is righteous."

"That ship sailed a long time ago, BJ. I'm a happily engaged man now and no matter how fine she may be, I don't see her like that anymore."

"Q, I don't care how crazy she is, fine is fine. You may not like her, but I watched when you peeped her loony ass and you looked like you were still diggin' her—before y'all started arguing. If I was single, she could set my body on fire after she let me hit. For real, I'd bite that hoe on the booty cheek, twice. " He laughed, but I didn't.

Had he really seen the way I looked at her?

"BJ, let's understand something. Leslie and I aren't friends. We will never be friends. I never want to see that woman again and in fact, when I saw her, I felt nothing."

"You can spit out all the BS you want, she's still fine as hell. Even my dick says the only reason you put up with all that drama was because she was fine and the pooty was good."

This time, I laughed. "No comment."

"So what would you do if she came in here and kissed you?"

"I'm not about to answer a hypothetical question about kissing a woman I don't have anymore interest in."

"Just answer the damn questions, man! Alright then, what if she came in and started sucking on ya balls?" he said with slightly more agitation.

"Then she'd better finish because that is some wonderful shit."

We both laughed, but BJ's observation of me and Leslie left me a little uneasy.

After probably the longest working day ever, I was driving home when my cell phone rang. Usually Laela called to see how my day was and I welcomed the interruption. "Hello?"

"You know I've been trying to reach you for that last couple of days. Why are you avoiding me?" It was my father.

"I'm not avoiding you, pop. I've just had a lot to do in the last week," I replied.

"So much to do that you can't talk to your family, huh? Sorry, I didn't think it took that long to dial a couple of numbers. Forgive me for being so insensitive to your rheumatism."

"I'm sorry. I meant to call you back, but things just keep happening and I'd just forget."

"Ain't that much stuff to do in the world that you can't return calls from your family. That should always be top on your priority list. You never know when you might get the last call. You understand me, boy?"

"Yes, sir." I knew what was coming, especially after I'd just done something wrong. He might as well have sent me a text message that read 'enter lecture here' before he called.

"So what happened to you all at church on Sunday? Your mother was really looking forward to seeing you. Even set aside space in a crowded church, turning people away because she said her son was coming. You really hurt her, boy. What happened?"

He knew how to get to me, but the last thing I was about to tell my father was that I'd been drinking and somehow ended up in one bed with two women—one of them married. After hearing that, my father might've had that heart attack he was always talking about. On the other hand, I couldn't lie to my father either, so I had to be vague. "Lae planned something for us to do. I didn't know it was going to be an all night thing."

"So, what you're telling me is that you fornicated when you should have been thanking the Lord for another year of life."

He didn't beat around the bush and like I said, I couldn't lie to the man. "Yes, sir."

He was silent for a few seconds and then let out a long sigh. "Quinton, take a second and look at your life. At what point in your life are you going to make the hard decisions. You done spent so long walking away from struggle that it's become a part of who you are. Take it from me, people don't care what you've almost done; they only care about what's tangible, like a degree. When you gone learn that lesson?"

"I like what I do. You may not be proud of it, but I am," I interrupted.

"Look, Dad, I love you, but I'm not going to live for you. Either you're proud of me or not. Lae's proud of me and really, that's all that matters right now."

"Is it?" He said in a slightly condescending tone. "Laela's a great woman, and she may love you, but what happens if you all don't make it? Cuz I sure as hell ain't letting you live back here. Can you support yourself? Will you ask for alimony because of what you're 'accustomed' to with her around?

"At what point do you get your shit together? At what point do you realize that if you keep giving up, people will give up on you? At what point do you stand for and apply the lessons your momma and I taught to you? We both know that since you're black, you have to work twice as hard just to be considered half as equal. We both know that because we are people of color that we are born into the curse which makes it so much harder to succeed in life, but that much more rewarding when we do."

He took in a deep breath and I remained silent as he spoke. If I knew one thing about my father it was to never interrupt him when he had his speech going, so I remained quiet.

"As black folk, we love to blame someone else, because it's easier than admitting our own downfalls. There is no 'white man' keeping us down. The system is screwed, yes, but in truth we're doing that well enough on our own. You're becoming a statistic, Quinton. You have every opportunity and you still squander it because you don't know what it's like to truly struggle. Barely keeping ya head above water, but that's okay to your generation. You like to see others swim by you, take what you should have, so then you have a reason to rob them. Let's look at Dre, for instance. Now, he wasn't the smartest man I've ever met, he has struggled and now look at him, making at least six figures a year, a gorgeous house in the suburbs, and a good head on his shoulders. Though I believe fornicating is probably a routine thing for him, he's at least got his business mind right. But I'm sure his mama is looking down on him and is proud of what he's become. You could be making the same, if not more than he does, but you gotta learn how to stick with your plan."

"Yes, sir."

"This isn't a comparison between you and him because I got on his ass earlier about not showing up--but throughout the years, all you've gotten is praise from people. Now look at you, just a cog in the system, when you could've created your own network. I'm proud of you boy, but just so damn disappointed that you're letting your potential go to the crapper. Wake up before you find out that life has passed you by and you're greeting people at a supermarket when you're sixty-five, just to make ends meet. You understand?"

When he finally finished, all that I could respond with was another, "Yes, sir."

"So what are you going to do about it?"

I was ready to listen, but I was unprepared for the Q & A session. I honestly didn't know what I was going to do. "I can probably pick up a few classes after work."

"See that you do. You're my only biological child and I love you, but don't think that I settle because you do. So can I expect to see you at church this Sunday?"

"Yes, sir." And with that he hung up. I remained on the phone and held it to my ear for another minute afterwards as I recalled his words.

It was dusk when I arrived home. The house was silent and though Lae's car was outside I couldn't find her anywhere. After a day like today, I needed to vent. It seemed like the whole world was riding me. My employees, my boss, even my family had a turn at getting on my nerves today and I needed to relax.

Sometimes, when Lae was here, she'd calm me down by teasing my release valve, but no such luck today. I wanted to crash on the couch, but my stomach knew better. I dropped all the paperwork I'd carried into the house on the kitchen table and made me a grilled cheese sandwich before calling Dre.

"Hello?"

"What's going on, man? I just had the day from hell." I said while falling onto my couch and turning on the TV.

"You think you had a bad day, one of my clients just lost damn near half-a-mil investing in shit that I told him he had no business investing in. Now he threatening to leave, but he's not going anywhere. I made him too much moolah for him to go anywhere. Some people are such dumbasses. They never listen until it's too late. But that's enough about me. Let me hear of your woes."

I explained everything that happened during my day and he silently listened. I guess that's what I liked most about Dre; he was an asshole most of the time, but when you asked him to shut the hell up, he did.

"Damn. You know how to alleviate all this bad crap you're going through?"

"How do I do that, oh wise one?" I asked.

"Get a new job. A new job would stop everybody's griping and you could live in peace. You know me, Q. I don't say it unless it needs to be said. Besides you got enough time to change shit around. I mean it ain't like you got anybody pregnant yet and you're not dying of some terminal illness, so there is time left."

He was beginning to sound like my father. "Well, dad, why don't you get me a job at your firm?"

"Why? Because I don't want to see your ass in the mailroom-- especially not when all the righteous tail is walking around the third floor."

"So either I'd sort mail or I'd be obligated to chase skirts." I paused for a brief second before speaking again. "I think I'll pass."

"I know you're proud, but if you want to pick up some extra classes and you need money, holla at me. I got money for you, for school if you wanna do it. We're brothers and that's what brothers do."

It was all starting to make sense now. Dre never talked about school.

"You talked to my father."

Even though he laughed, I could almost hear the guilt behind it. "It wasn't even ten minutes ago. His advice was that I should be convincing. Personally, I think I should get an Oscar for that performance. Still, if he asks, I was intimidating."

"Indeed, you were intimidating," I mused. "I was thoroughly impressed by how much thought you put into the presentation. The changes in inflection were so masterfully done that I would have never known it was rehearsed. I was moved. Can I cry now?"

"Crying is for sissies."

"It takes a big man to cry."

"It takes a bigger man not to," Dre countered.

"Did he say anything else?"

"That was it, but anyway," he said changing topics like only Dre could, "let me tell you about this new girl I got lined up for tomorrow. Man, her ass is so nice. And her titties sit up like a couple of 'A' students and-"

"And if she lets you get it in the first night, you're gonna throw her back in the gulf, just like all the rest." I said, while flipping through channels.

"Well, we can't all be like you, Q. The man who has wives and maidens alike fawning all over him. Don't think I forgot about the Simone thing. You know Mike called me and told me he's fooling around. I mean turnabout is fair play and Simone does look pretty nice for a married chick that just had a kid."

"Would you please get the damn Simone thing out of your head?"

"Dawg, I'd hit it if she let me, even with Mike watching. That's *your* boy. But I don't see them lasting too much longer, either. You can tell they're not happy. It's not like that's a well kept secret. Besides, as men, we're bound to fuck up--it's genetic, baby. Men were made to spread their seed. See, that's why we don't need to be married; we just screw it up for everyone."

"You truly are the pimp of pessimistic prognostication."

"See, that's what I'm talking about. You say shit like that and I know for a fact that you'd be better off with some sheepskin nailed to your wall. I'm for real, man. You could be the best at whatever you chose to do. I mean, Q, you are the smartest idiot I've ever met. Well, at least the smartest one without a degree."

I smiled as I thought about how hard he was trying to get me back into school. "So you're saying that there are people you know, who have a degree, who are smarter than me?"

"Truthfully, I don't know anyone smarter than my brilliant ass at the job, but I'm pretty sure they exist. So, by default, if they're smarter than me, then they gotta be smarter than you."

"If I remember correctly, you copied off of my homework and my tests. It's a shame how soon we forget."

"That wasn't cheating, it was educational synchronization. I was just making sure your answers were correct by comparing them against mine. I try to help you out and this is how you turn on me? That hurts me deeply, Q."

"You're an ass."

"Well then I guess that makes you the hole."

We spoke for a few more minutes about his love life until Laela walked in looking exhausted. I got off the phone to help her out. "Are you okay?"

"Yeah, I was with Teniyah and she tired me out."

"What? Y'all went shopping again?" She leaned against me and looked as if she'd just finished running a marathon.

"Yeah and then we went to the gym. That girl has incredible stamina." She kissed me on the forehead. "Thanks for the help, but I need to take a shower."

"I'll jump in with you," I suggested.

"No, that's okay. I smell funky and I don't want you commenting on how manly I smell."

I gave her a reluctant, "Okay," and watched from the couch as she dragged herself into the bathroom.

Damn, Teniyah, what have you been doing to my baby to keep her so tired lately?

CHAPTER 7

Simone

<u>January 8th (Sunday)</u>

The headaches that were plaguing me were becoming almost unbearable. My head constantly pounded and I needed at least three aspirin to make them go away. Ever since the night I spent with Q and Lae in the hotel, I had butterflies in my stomach almost as often as I had migraines.

It'd been a week since the New Year's argument and it was still uneasy in the house. I didn't give Mike any sex and he didn't ask. We walked around the house, rarely speaking, barely coexisting. I continued to fulfill my wifely obligations by taking care of the house, while he usually went out 'bowling' immediately after coming home from work and wouldn't come back until late in the night. When he wasn't around, and after I put MJ to sleep, I'd sit on my bed and cry. I never thought that in such a short time we'd be more like roommates than soul mates.

The only time we actually spent together was during church, but we drove separate cars and today wasn't any different. During service, I sat right next to Mike with MJ on my lap, but I felt no warmth towards him or from him. The preacher spoke of miracles, but I was in such a daze that I only caught the sermon in spurts.

After benediction, I began to greet everyone I knew--even some that I didn't care too much about--all while donning my phony smile. It was a welcome release to finally have interpersonal contact again, but when I looked around for Michael, he'd already left. During my exit, some of the ushers I grew up with asked where he was. I lied and told them that he had to go to work. I felt awful for lying, but I didn't want to share the details of my life, especially not with church folks.

On the drive home, I considered calling Laela, but I didn't feel like hearing her chastisement, so I rode home in silence, with MJ in his car seat, sleeping. Not hearing him cry all day was a blessing in itself. I guess it's true that children do sense when something's wrong.

When I returned to the house, it was exactly as we left it, quiet. I put MJ in his crib and felt the migraine working its way to the front of my skull. I took three more aspirin and after I let my brain relax, I was in a significantly better place to begin cooking Sunday dinner.

My aunt always said that no matter how mad you are at your husband, it's a wife's duty to keep food in his belly. I hated how traditional she was, but even though I was mad as hell, I was still a wife-- his wife.

I couldn't understand him. *How could he do that to me--to us? All he had to do was be there for our first New Year together.* My brow furrowed the more I thought about it and my head began to ache again.

Okay Simone, stay cool. There's no reason to undo the affects of the aspirin.

As I began making Sunday dinner, I noticed how eerily silent the house was. I felt the tears coming, but decided that I'd rather be listening to Laela's verbal abuse rather than not have anyone to talk to. I called Lae, but instead, Q picked up.

"Hello?"

"Hey Q, is Laela there?"

"No, Monie, she just left. Niya picked her up and they're gone."

"That figures. If I didn't know any better, I'd swear she liked the Raven more than me. Is that her new best friend? Have I been replaced?" He laughed. It was good to hear especially when there wasn't any laughter in this house. "Teniyah has special needs --like she needs to be away from Franklin and I think Lae is her only escape. I don't think you have too much to be worried about, but have you tried calling her on her cell?"

"No." I paused, thinking carefully about what I wanted to say. "Quinton, I want to ask you some questions and I'd appreciate the truth."

This time he was silent for a few seconds.

"Is Mike cheating on me?"

I could hear the sounds of him exhaling before he spoke. "I'm sorry, Monie..."

"Quinton," I interrupted, "please don't lie to me. I get enough of that from him. Maybe I can have one friend around me who can be honest."

"Look Monie, I'm not going to be the cause of a riff between you and Mike. I think this is something that y'all need to talk about."

"So you know who she is, but you won't tell me? You know, Quinton, I figured you to be the type of man to respect a marriage, but I'm beginning to see you're just like all men. You know the thing that hurts the most, is that I really liked you."

I hung up the phone and was ready to throw it across the room when it rang. It was Quinton.

"Hello."

"Look, Monie, we all have our allegiances and my allegiance is to Mike. But simply because I can't tell you something I don't know anything about doesn't diminish the love I have for you. If you want the truth about Mike's infidelity, the maybe you should talk to him."

"Let me ask *you*, Quinton. If Lae were cheating on you and I knew about it, would you want me to tell you?"

"Sometimes ignorance is bliss."

"I'll remember that."

I had been exercising for about any hour before Michael came home. I hadn't planned on working out, but the prospect of being single again gave me the motivation to get off my ass.

Mike walked into the bedroom and without even a greeting asked, "How long has he been sleep?"

"Why--the hell--do you care?" I snapped, barely able to breathe due to the fatigue. "You weren't around--to help put his ass-- to sleep! Dinner is in the kitchen."

"It smells more like it's on the pot." He smiled. I'd fallen asleep after talking to Quinton, accidentally burning dinner, but his attempt at humor didn't crack the stone face I was giving him. "Look, I'm sorry I'm home so late. I had to take care of some things."

"Was it just *something or someone*, Mike?" He looked at me like a deer caught in headlights. "You know what Michael? Could you at least be honest for once in your life?"

"So you think I'm cheating? Is that what it is?" He walked up to me and stood so closely that I swore he was ready to hit me. "I just need to get out of this fucking house sometimes! I need to get away from all the crying and goddamn complaining!"

"Everybody knows but me, Mike! Everyone fucking knows! You don't spend New Years' with me, you're always either bowling or fixing cars and for the last week, you've never even touched me! Then you want to try and blame your son for you leaving? At least be a man and come clean! If you don't want to be with me, then say it and stop dragging us along, dammit!"

He looked up at the ceiling, then back to the floor, his usual lie pose. "You want the truth? The truth is that I've found someone else, Monie. We haven't done anything, but I've been so tempted. All I ever hear around here and from your friends is what I can't do and what I don't do. I'm sick of hearing that shit! You knew how I was when you married me and yet you can't stick up for me when your friends are clownin' me? You know how that makes me feel? You let Lae talk about me like a dog—a goddamn dog Simone and all you can say is that he's my husband and I love him? Do you want to know why I went looking for someone else? It's because the woman I got doesn't respect me!" He stormed out of the room.

"You want my respect?" I shouted and ran after him, catching up to him in the kitchen. "Well, prove to me that you want to change. Prove to me that you want to be a husband and not just be here because you fucked up and had a son with me! I look like a fool to everyone I know for staying with you this long because I do love you. I want us to make it, but not at the expense of my sanity."

"I want us to work, but not at the expense of my pride," he said quietly.

We both sat down at the kitchen table and he grabbed my hand. "I was raised to believe that women should take care of the house and men should take care of the bills. Maybe if I had some college like Quinton or Dre, we could be better off and you wouldn't have to work, but I can't be them. I wish the both of us didn't have to work, but we do. If you want me to be a better husband, talk to me instead of nagging me." He paused and for a few seconds, not a sound could be heard anywhere in the house. "What could I do better?"

Sex! My brain screamed. *Sex! Sex! Sex! SEX! Tell him about the lousy sex!* But the thoughts never congealed into words and the words never made it to my mouth. "No. Nothing I can think of. Just keep the vows you made."

86

He came over and kissed me on the lips, the same lips I imagined him kissing the other woman with. A shudder ran through me knowing that his mouth had been on another woman, but the truth is, had he known what went down on New Years', I'd be the one kissing his ass. "I really am sorry and I'd like to make it up to you." He thought hard about what he was going to say next. "How about we go out to eat?"

"MJ's still sleeping."

"Okay, then. How about we take the baby to your aunt's, and I take care of you?"

"You want make up sex?"

"No, how about I just take care of you."

Now we were getting somewhere. I couldn't even remember the last time he pampered me and I smiled while thinking about what he had in store.

It didn't take us long to call my aunt to make the arrangements and get the baby ready to go. Thinking about that night had my stomach in bunches and after a week hiatus, my body was as ready as it'd ever been.

For the first time in what seemed like forever, we shared the same car. On the way to my aunt's house, which was only a five minute drive, we talked about some of the things going on at our jobs, a rarity between us. It seemed as if he was really trying to turn over a new leaf and I desperately wanted him to.

After dropping off MJ, we rushed back home, tearing away at each other's clothes after we shut the front door.

"Let's take a bath together," he suggested.

We made it all the way to the bathroom with his hand cupping my breast. His lips were working my neck when I asked. "What's her name?"

"Aw, c'mon, Simone--why do we have to do this shit now? I told you I was sorry. I told you that it won't happen again. What the hell do you want from me?" When I didn't concede to his pouting, he continued.

"Okay, fine, goddammit. Her name is Starr."

"Is she pretty?"

His uneasiness showed on his face. "Not really. She was just someone to talk to."

I wanted to have sex so badly it hurt, but I needed to know the answers. "If she wasn't pretty, then why wouldn't you just talk to me about it? Why take a step down from what you already have? Why go somewhere else? Why kiss someone else?"

"Simone, I don't know. Sometimes when you feel alone, it helps to have someone to talk to that's not the same sex. You think Pookie or Quinton would understand what I'm feeling? The only other woman I know is Laela, and since she doesn't like me that much anyway, talking to her wouldn't be a very good idea. I just had all this shit inside me that was eating me up and it felt good to not think about it."

I grabbed his chin and made him look me in the eyes. "We are married, Michael. Shouldn't I have been the first person you came to? Aren't we the ones who are married? Is there something wrong with me?"

"It's me. I don't know how many times I can tell you that. I just don't know how to think about other people's feeling. Yes, we're married and, yes, I shoulda come to you, but it's easier to say that in hindsight. If you remember, you weren't saying much to me either. How do you talk to someone who you know doesn't want to talk back? I'm sorry, Mo. If I could do it all again and do it right, I would. But we have to deal with what's happened and not what should have happened. Can we move on from here, please? I don't feel like doing this shit tonight. All I know is that I want to make this work. You are the one I married and I want to try to make things right."

"You didn't answer my last question. Is there something wrong with me?" I didn't want to hear that there was, but deep inside I knew it was me. *Why else would he go somewhere else if it wasn't me?*

"Yes. There is something wrong with you."

Hearing him actually admit it was more than I could bear. I sat down on the edge of the bathtub and stared at the tile on the opposite wall. My mouth quickly dried up and at the same time my eyes began to well up with tears. I could see my husband's mouth moving, but I was vaguely listening.

"There's something wrong with the both of us," he continued, "but I should've trusted that we could work through it. I love you because of all the good things you're about. I love you because of all the bad things I see. I love you as a whole and not as a part."

"What?" I asked, slowly returning to reality from my daze.

"I said I love you, Mo. Were you listening?" When I didn't immediately answer, he spoke up. "Well, aren't you going to say something?"

"I love you, too." I managed to say and then let out a short chuckle. Then, the tears began to flow uncontrollably. He leaned over, tenderly kissed me on my lips and picked each rogue tear away from my face with another kiss.

"Let's get in the tub," he suggested.

I finished getting undressed and listened to my husband. Though it wasn't as romantic as I would've liked it to be--no music, candles, or even bubbles, I wasn't alone. Even if what we had only lasted for tonight, I looked into his dark brown eyes and saw the love I'd always wanted.

I relaxed in between his legs, feeling Dingo repeatedly tap me on the back as if he were trying to pass me a message in Morse code. We sat silently in the hot water, letting it drain us of any energy we had left and watching the steam disappear as it rose from the water.

We held each other for a while as we reminisced about the times before we were married. Laughing was so natural then and even though I enjoyed Mike's company now, there was a long way before we made it back to those days. Still, it felt good to be married again.

Not long after the steam left, the heat followed suit. Michael stood up, went to the linen closet and grabbed two towels for us to dry off in. Instead of me toweling myself, he wrapped it around me like a blanket and carried me to our room.

He laid me down on the bed, grabbed the baby oil from our dresser, opened up my towel and began massaging my shoulders. With his rough hands, it felt more like he was tenderizing me than massaging me, but I learned a long time ago to never look a gift horse in the mouth. I winced occasionally, but never long enough for him to see anything but pleasure.

He worked his calloused hands from my shoulders down to my calves, never missing a spot, before flipping me over. Then he did something he hadn't done since our wedding night, he parted my thighs and tasted me. I was caught so off-guard that I gasped and accidentally clasped my thighs around his head. He looked up at me, smiled and guided my legs towards his shoulders. With my legs resting on his back, he returned his full attention to the only thing on the menu--me.

He still had a lot to learn about eating, but he was still my husband, and I loved him for trying. I laid my head on the pillow, relaxed, focused on what he was doing. The orgasm came quicker than I had anticipated.

Wiping me from his lips and ready for his orgasm, he mounted me. After what he'd done for me, I was ready for him to have one. I was still shivering from excitement as he penetrated me. Still sensitive and damp from the oral sex, my body received him without hesitation or pain. And as I climaxed again a few minutes later, this time we came together.

We lay breathless on the bed, no words spoken during the entire ordeal. Our escapade had only taken twenty minutes, but it seemed much longer. My body felt as light as a cloud as I lay still shuddering from the best sex I'd had from him in a while.

"I love you," he said.

"I love you, too." I wanted to say more, to release my soul to him. I needed to confess about how lonely I'd been feeling and how much he contributed towards it. I even wanted to share the conversation I'd had with Quinton, but I was too fatigued to even speak. As sleep began to take hold of me, I was glad that my husband remembered how to treat his wife.

CHAPTER 8

Quinton

In my opinion, the management training class I was obligated to attend was a complete waste of time. Everything we had done to this point seemed to be aimed at the dumbest of people and most of us had been invited along to join the ride.

For the last week, we all sat in a cramped, sterile classroom, on the 27th floor of the Edison Building in downtown Houston. With no pictures anywhere in the room and a dull off-white paint job that tried to lull us into a false sense of security, it felt more like prison--which I guessed was the point. As if that weren't already bad enough, we all had been forced to endure horrific morning traffic, sit through 8 ½ hours of lecture, class work, and listen to the most awful business humor known to man. All of this while wearing black pants, white shirts, and dark ties per the tight-assed corporate dress code.

Our proctor was a man named Pete Stottlemeyer, a heavy set, balding white man. Every day he faithfully wore three things: black floods, a red tie no matter what color the shirt, and his thick ass, "I-fry-bugs-on-the-sidewalk-with-my-coke-bottle-sized", glasses. Numerous jokes went around, but all of them I was sure he'd heard. Hell, he would've had to.

91

In no way was he funny, nor was he very interesting--which begged the question of how he got stuck with this job. I personally believed he was put here to either give us inclination to stand up and quit or to bore us until we died. He was nearly successful in the latter as I banged my head several times on my table while falling asleep. Yet as bad as the class was, there was nothing more gratifying than knowing that seven other souls were trapped with me. Had I been alone, I wouldn't have hesitated to plunge the remaining twenty-six stories to my death.

With today being the final day, we all slouched lazily in our chairs, desperately wanting to leave downtown and get our weekends started. It was almost noon when Peter left the room for a phone call and we'd all began chattering amongst ourselves.

"So what are you going to do this weekend, Q?" Steve whispered, breaking up my delusions of suicide.

"Well, I'm going to hang out with some of my friends, maybe see some tits wiggle in my face and then I'll do lots and lots of nothing. Which translates to: I'll probably end up playing video games and eating lots of artery clogging foods. What about you?"

"Well, unlike you lazy black folks, I have loads of work to do. I'll probably be stuck in the bachelor pad. It's starting to look like hell."

During my week sitting next to Steve, I came to the conclusion that he was probably one of the most hip-hop knowledgeable, non-black guys I'd ever met. There was almost nothing that we disagreed on when it came to black people.

The thing I enjoyed most about him was that he didn't take anything too seriously. We were able to poke fun at one another without offending each other. Although, if some of the other people in the class would've overheard him, I'd be scraping his 140 lb frame off of their new and nicely polished Stacey Adams.

"I can't imagine you being dirty! I thought you Asian folk kept a clean house." I retorted.

"I would keep it clean, but my American side makes me lazy and stupid."

I covered my mouth to prevent everyone from hearing me laugh. "So, I guess you're going to make that big pot of rice and whittle chopsticks by hand from the sacred bamboo tree, too?"

"You know where I'm from; black people aren't allowed to speak like that. If they do, they's be catchin' a beatin' with the whippin' stick and have all their fried chicken and red-flavored Kool-Aid privileges revoked."

"Ouch. I guess since I can't get any fried chicken, I'll just have to call your sister and reschedule my Toyota tune-up. And while she's there, maybe I can get her to make me some beef fried rice, right before my happy ending and directly after 'loving me long time'."

He laughed so loudly that everyone in the classroom turned see what the disruption was. "I'm Chinese. Toyota is a Japanese company, you bastard. But I have to admit that you got me on that one, dog. That was actually pretty funny-- almost as funny as your lopsided fade."

"See. You were cool when you talked about me, but now you done gone and started talking about my hair. That's war."
No sooner than we had finished our culturally biased rant, Peter hurried back into the room and made an announcement to the class.

"Um, class. I'm sorry, but I have to leave for a family emergency. As far as your tests go, another proctor will be here after you come back from lunch to administer the exam. Since I won't see most of you again, I wish you luck. You're free to go to lunch." And with that he darted out of the room.

Lunch was uneventful. As usual, Dante, Keisha, Cliff—the other black people who were stuck with me—ate lunch with Steve and I. As we sat around the plastic table, we all speculated as to why Pete had to leave so early.

"Before I left the building, some of the other people in the office said that Pete's mother fell down some stairs," whispered Keisha.

"Damn, that's messed up. So, I wonder who's going to give us the test, and most importantly, will they let us cheat." Cliff looked around the table at us seeing who'd be the culprit to help him pass.

"Clifford J. Sampson," scolded Keisha, "is that all you think about? Cheating? See, that's the problem with men now, always cheatin'. Just can't get it out of your heads--either one."

Dante put his hand over his face and rolled his neck. "You got nerve. Women are all about drama. It's like you need some kind of drama to help you get through the day. I swear that if drama were cookies, all women would croak from diabetes."

"So, is that why you prefer men?" asked Keisha. Everybody looked at Dante and put their head down. It wasn't a secret that Dante was gay, but we just never said it aloud. "You think all the women in the world are just going to drop and die from drama induced diabetes?"

"Don't act like you didn't know, Boo. Add to that--women don't have the equipment I like." Dante retorted.

"Okay!" I shouted. "That's just too much damn information! I ain't trying to hear about man-on-man while I'm eating. Dookie surprise is not on the damn menu."

Steve smiled, but as he looked around the table, no one else was laughing.

"Oh, but you'll listen to a conversation about two women," Dante said, while raising an eyebrow towards me.

I thought it was a rhetorical question until he looked at me like I owed him a response. "Yes. The idea of two women is more aesthetically pleasing to my fantasy. Forgive my erection for preferring that. There could be two ugly chicks kissing in front of us right now and I'd prefer it. Hearing about man-on-man makes my wiener frown."

This time Steve joined in as the other girls laughed and Dante rolled his eyes once more, but I didn't care. He knew that I was indifferent about him being gay, but I certainly didn't want a mental picture of it while I ate.

Lunch was ending and there were only five minutes left for us to get back to class. We quickly left the restaurant and ran across Texas Street to get back into the building. Unfortunately, it seemed the whole building had also chosen to come back from lunch at the same time. When we finally made it back to the classroom, we were just a few minutes late. With all of the other students still talking, we sat down and waited for the new proctor to arrive.

"So if the teacher doesn't show up for 15 minutes after class starts, does that mean we get to go home?" Everyone looked at Cliff and shook their heads.

"Yes, Cliff. That means we get to go home and you can be the first to leave," Keisha mused.

We all stood around the classroom, talking and laughing, waiting for the last day of our class to end. On the outside we all appeared calm, but I knew that underneath it all, everyone's stomach was probably doing the same twists and turns as mine.

When the classroom door opened, we all turned our heads to the back of the room to see her come in. The room fell eerily silent as she strode past us towards the front, only focusing on the chalkboard, never turning her gaze towards anyone in the class.

If there was a word to describe how beautiful she was, I didn't know it. She walked past our table, carrying herself with all the grace of a dancer and the poise of royalty.

When Steve and I looked at each other, we could tell that we were thinking the exact same thing.

94

Damn.

Her deep auburn colored hair was tied in a bun, leaving her golden hoop earrings to sway freely about her neck and the dark blue dress she wore hugged every curve on her small frame. Where her dress ended, the spaghetti straps on her black leather heels began-- wrapped around supremely defined calves and practically screaming 'fuck me'.

She had already settled down at the desk in the front of the room, but the scent lingering around me was as powerful as if she were standing next to me.

"Good afternoon, class. I am *Mrs.* Cheyenne Glenn and I'll be the instructor giving you your test." I could almost hear the whole room exhale after she said her name and not a single word was uttered. "Some of you may have already heard, but Mr. Stottlemeyer had to tend to a personal emergency, and I am filling in for him. Some rules before we begin. No talking, walking, or peeing while the test is in progress. If you have to go, go now or forfeit your privileges. Do we understand each other?"

She passed out our tests and for the next hour, not even so much as a yawn was heard in the classroom.

I was the first to finish my test, not only relieved that this class would forever be behind me, but also happy that I'd be the first to speak to her. But when I reached the desk I was speechless. I tried to say hello, but the only thing that managed to come out was an exhale. I handed her my test and started walking back towards my seat when she spoke.

"So you're Mr. James?" She asked, looking over my test.

"Yes," I barely managed to whisper back. "Is there something wrong?"

She smiled. "No, but I've heard about you. Carmen Lowell. You know her, right? She's a good friend of mine."

Shit. Shit. Shit. I figured there had to be something wrong. If she and Carmen were friends, she would most certainly fail me, just to keep me from being a regular pain in Carmen's ass. The worst part about it was that I was going to have to take this godforsaken class again.

"I see it on your face--what you're thinking, but she actually likes you. She just enjoys busting your chops from time to time."

"And she does it so well."

She covered her mouth when she laughed, but just seeing her smile made my heart skip a beat. "She can be pretty rough on you guys, but if you want to know how you did, I can grade you now."

"I can wait," I replied. I couldn't go through the whole weekend without knowing if I had to return. Perhaps if I knew she was teaching it, I could intentionally fail, but there weren't any guarantees. So I quietly watched her as she pulled out her red marker, began scratching out incorrect answers and then writing little notes on my test.

When she finished, she looked up at me, extended her manicured hand, and was the first to welcome me as an EPD Certified Manager. "Congratulations," she said. "I'm very happy for you."

"Thank you." I lightly grasped her hand and followed her lead.

"Well, now that you're a part of the family, allow me to give you this." She reached inside her purse, pulled out a tan card, wrote on the back of it, and handed it to me. As I looked at the business card side, I saw just about all of her contact information. "Call me anytime. Maybe I can help you with something or just get Carmen off your back."

"It'll be more than worth a call if I could see that happen."

She smiled at me again and I this time, I smiled back. I briefly said my goodbyes to the other guys I'd spent the week getting to know and walked to the elevator. I put the card she'd given me into my breast pocket, but on the way to the car, I remembered that she'd written on the back. I turned it to the back and saw her home number, followed by an invitation to call her. Instead of throwing the card away like I typically did, I tucked it back into my pocket.

What's the harm in having a friend?

I arrived home to find that the house was empty for the fifth time in six days. I didn't mind my solitude for brief periods, but coming home and being welcomed by my echo was becoming a little more agitating with each passing day. I'd probably be upset if Dre hadn't called me earlier in the week and asked me to come out with him and a few of the guys tonight.

In truth, I missed seeing my fiancée. I missed being able to go to her and complain when my day was bad, talking about how good we had it when our friends' lives were in such disarray; the sound of our bodies slapping against each other when she wanted it rough--but it was going on two weeks and I'd barely seen her at the apartment. I didn't want her thinking that she had to stay home with me all the time, but I certainly didn't put that nice sized rock on her finger to be lonely, either.

After making sure that I was alone, I took Mrs. Glenn's card out of my pocket and programmed the number into my phone before throwing the card in the garbage. I didn't want to have to explain to Laela-- whenever she came in, why "Call me!" was on the back, even if she was my teacher and my superior.

It had been another unseasonably warm day outside, and sitting in all that traffic on the way home made me want to take a long shower and concentrate on just trying to kick it with the fellas tonight. With sordid thoughts of Laela and Mrs. Cheyenne floating through my head I intentionally turned the water cold to rid myself of my forbidden thoughts and my stiff traitor.

After the shower and a few minutes of searching, I found some black slacks to go with my red silk shirt and black shoes. I didn't know what kind of club Dre was supposed to take us to, but I figured I'd rather be overdressed. I threw my clothes on the bed and sat down to watch some TV before I called Dre to tell him about my day.

"You must be shittin me, right? My boy, the ex-playboy, is digging some old and dusty puss? With all that young ass following you around, I figured that you'd at least mess around with someone in your age bracket." He sounded surprised.

"I don't usually go for anyone, but dammit Dre, if you could've seen her. She has the fattest ass, too! I'll tell you one thing though, if our circumstances were different, I'd probably try to screw her brains out."

"Still not trying to bang a wife, huh?"

"Why do you even ask?"

"It doesn't matter. Q is back, baby! See, even you can break the shackles of the whipped and join the rest of us lookers."

"You just don't quit do you?" I said, as I began looking for my keys.

"Is there a good enough reason too?"

"Okay, let's forget the fact that I'm with Lae and cheating is not something I'm willing to do. The boulder she wears says 'I have a husband' and you know how I feel about moving in on married women. No matter what, she's off limits."

"How many times do I have to repeat this to you? Rich, married women, who are as fine as the one you met today, are a real player's sole ambition. They're the ones who have the biggest freak in them and like doing the nastiest shit. You want her to swallow your load after you titty fuck her? Just ask. You want her to lick your balls and then your poo-poo shoot? Consider it done. You want her to get her other rich friend and let you nut all over their bellies while they lie on wonderful, Egyptian cotton? Say the word!"

I stopped looking for my keys and just thought about what he'd just said.

"What the hell is wrong with you?"

"Nothing, but my dick is hard just thinking about the shit. Yours should be, too. Now I gotta tuck this thing in my waistband to keep it from poking out."

"Has anyone ever told you how often you go overboard?"

"You do all the time, but sometimes I act like I care." I could almost hear him smiling. "See Quinton, a husband ain't nothin' but a boyfriend with rules. And we all know rules are made to be broken, just like wives are meant to be broken into." He laughed at his own joke even though he knew I didn't share the same sentiment.

"You always seem have some colorful anecdote--some forbidden philosophy for any given situation. I could write a book full of the crap that comes out your mouth."

"Just break me off my ten percent and we could be in business."

"Anyway, she gave me her card with 'call me' on the back of it. I thought about calling her, but I just don't want her husband thinking I'm trying to get down on his wife."

"You are trying to get down on his wife! Don't get it twisted and don't lie to yourself! If she gave you the chance, you'd hit it, old pussy and all. Knock the dust off that junk. You need to call her ass, Negro. You ain't married--yet. I mean truthfully, how much damage can one conversation do? What was her name again? Hell, it doesn't matter. You need to get on that, real quick. Remind me again, how fine did you say she was?"

I figured telling Dre would be a bad idea, but I didn't have anyone else to tell it to. Truth was, I didn't really have many male friends that I could confide in and I knew Dre for most of my life. Unfortunately, his advice usually ended up being a bad thing for me.

"There's something else I want to talk about."

"Shoot." he said.

"Why Leslie, man? Out of all the girls who were there that night, why her?" As much as I'd tried to get her out of my mind, I couldn't. There was so much history and so much bad blood between us. After everything that had happened between us, I'd told Dre everything and for him to sleep with her knowing what I'd been through seemed like betrayal. I needed an answer.

He sighed on the other side of the phone. "Look, Quinton, obviously you still have a thing for her. I'm not exactly sure whether you love to hate her or hate to love her, but you need to let that shit go. I apologized and that's all I'm willing to say about it."

"Fine, I'll let it go, but just to set the record straight, I can't stand that heifer."

"Now that we're done with that order of business, you're still coming out with us tonight, right?"

"Just let me know where to meet you."

"There's a new place that opened up downtown called 'The Spot'. Yeah, it's a dumbass name, but one of my clients opened it up and we're VIP. I don't know about you, but you could put me on the VIP at a gay club and I'd be there every night. There are a few things you gotta know to get in. The first, remember the password. Secondly, the bouncer's name is Block, don't forget that either. Thirdly, don't wait in line. Go straight to Block. And finally, Quinton, don't be late."

I was late.

It wasn't intentional, but shit happens. After bad shit happens, then I'm forced to contend with Murphy's Law and also Houston's traffic.

The Spot was a newly opened 25-and-over downtown club, but trying to locate it caused me to be half an hour later than I'd planned. The main entrance didn't face the street, but instead was in an alley that I'd passed by a few times. I'd seen the crowd by the door, but since crowds were everywhere, I tried looking for signage that I later found out didn't exist.

I walked past the mile long line and straight up to the entrance. People glared and shouted as I walked in between them, but I didn't particularly care. I was already an hour late and it wasn't often I was treated like a VIP-- especially not lately at home.

The bouncer that stood at the front entrance had to be Block. He was quite possibly a ton of black man and he probably earned the nickname due to the amount of city space he engulfed. I walked up to him, called him by his name and recited the password I'd been instructed to remember.

"Out of the night that covers me--" I whispered in his ear. I felt odd about whispering in another man's ear, but in a way I almost felt like James Bond.

Block gripped my hand, gave me a faux hug, and pointed to the place in the club where I'd probably find Dre. As I walked through the entrance, the music became louder and the second set of security walked up to me.

"He's cool," Block yelled. "He's with Kootie." One of the security guards gave me a head nod, pointed towards an area in the back of the club and told me I'd find the guys in VIP. I walked past the second guard, who was considerably smaller than Block, and into the club.

The Spot was virtually dark everywhere but the bartender's table, with black lights illuminating the dance floor and walls around the room. It had more of a warehouse feel than a club with its high ceilings and stone floor, but I guess the addition of the disco ball in the middle of the room qualified it for club status.

I couldn't really see most of the patrons, but I did notice there were significantly more women than men. The boldest women walked around the floor half-naked, probably to garner attention from potential piggy banks. Most of the women were either dancing or flirting, but a vast majority of the men were drinking, smoking, holding up the wall or doing some combination of the three.

"Kootie?" I mumbled under my breath as I walked through the crowds of people, most of whom had a drink in their hand. "What kind of man names himself Kootie?"

The answer became very apparent a few moments later, when I saw everyone I knew sitting at a table near the back of the club.

It was a very big man who names himself Kootie. What Block measured in girth, Kootie was in stature. Looking at his monstrous height and size, he had to have been a professional body builder at one time, but wasn't without style. For such a large man, the suit he wore was a silky dark blue and tailor perfect. He had jewelry hanging all over his tall frame, including a ring on every finger which boasted diamonds in the form of letters. What they spelled I couldn't exactly see, but I could tell that if he ever threw a connecting punch, that poor soul would have a tattoo somewhere on his mangled frame.

I extended my hands towards Kootie's and as we shook, his hand enveloped mine. Even his grip made him seem like a man not to be trifled with. After he released my hand, which he'd virtually crushed, I simply waved at the other guys at the table. With two empty bottle of Platinum Patron on the table, I wasn't surprised that nobody waved back, so I sat in the small opening left at the end of the booth.
The Spot, with its warehouse feel, somehow managed to maintain the relaxed atmosphere of a laid back lounge. Even with R&B flowing from the speakers, most people were simply talking and smiling.

With all the expensive liquor that had been passed around at the table, I knew it would only be a matter of time before we were approached. I was barely settled when a small group of Latino women

100

walked over to us. A beautiful brunette parked herself right in front of me, making sure to rest her sweet smelling breasts in my face. As if completely forgetting that it was *my* face that she'd plowed her tits in front of, I remained unnoticed as she began to flirt with Dre--who just happened to be pissy drunk.

"Hey, Papi, how you doin' tonight?" she asked innocently.

With nearly every man at the table fixated at her wealth of cleavage, I just shook my head and wondered how much further she could lean before they popped out.

He wasted no time leering at her breasts. Like the rest of us, he completely bypassed her face in the process. "Damn, girl, you got some big ole titties. Can you pop out one so that I can what we're working with here?"

When everyone began to smirk, she looked around the table and probably thought about it, but eventually declined. "No thank you, papi, I no roll like that. I not from Missouri." Her accent was sexy.

"Is that right?" Dre asked conspicuously, which meant that he was about to say something incredibly asinine.

"I don't get down like that." she said, her breasts still inches away from my face.

"Well now, I guess you gone have to Missouri some Arizona, Oklahoma, or you might catch an Ohio and be like North Carolina."

She looked around the table to see if we understood, but mostly everyone was too drunk to care. "I no understand. What does that mean?" She finally asked, puzzled.

"I said that you gone have to Show Me some Grand Canyon, Sooner, or you might catch a Buckeye and be the First in Flight."

Everyone fell over in drunken laughter and her group stormed away after giving him the finger and the dirtiest look I'd ever seen.

"Did you see how mad the heifer was?" Dre laughed, clearly more enthused with himself than anyone else.

"Hey, dumbass," I said, "North Carolina is the Tar Heel State, not First in Flight."

"Well if she would've known that shit, she might've gotten the lay of her life!"

"I didn't think you could be a bigger asshole until you just proved me wrong." I said while taking a shot glass from his hand. "Perhaps you should slow down a little."

As I sipped from the glass I took from Dre, Michael offered me a drink, but seeing how messed up everyone else was, I declined. I figured someone had to drive us home and I trusted me more than I trusted anyone else here. Besides, if it got too bad, I'd be dropping everyone off at Dre's house.

Dre turned towards me. I raised my eyebrow, anticipating him to say something, but for a while he didn't say a thing. Finally, after several minutes of focusing on the space behind me, he said, "So, you gone call that nice ass teacher of yours?"

"Probably, but not tonight. Why?"

"Cuz, I just want to make sure my bro keeps all of his options open. It's too early in life to be focused on what might be. I love you, Q. You're my only family and I hate for you to pass up life for what ain't promised. Who's going to tell? Me? Not me. We ride like soldiers! I love you, man! Carpe diem! Seize the day!" He shouted everything he said, his words slurred, and he could barely keep his eyes open.

I tried to keep my distance from him, but somehow he managed to breathe directly into my face. "Damn it, Dre, you're drunk! You need a tic-tac."

"It's too late for me, man! Save yourself!" He shouted. The table was once again engulfed with laughter, but this time I didn't crack a smile.

I hated seeing everyone so drunk. I didn't mind a buzz from time to time, but I hated seeing my friends drink themselves into a stupor, so I stood up to leave when Dre grabbed my hand.

"Hey, man, I'm sorry. I was just playing. I was just messin' with you. Can I use your phone? I wanna call someone to come pick me up." I gave him my phone, but not before asking who he intended to call. "I'm going to call a cab, man. Damn, are you my mother or something?"

"You can be such an asshole when you're drunk."

"This is very true."

With a little trepidation, I left him my phone and headed to the dance floor. I needed a release. I needed to get Lae, Dre and even the job out of my head and I figured dancing might help, but by the time I made it to the dance floor, the DJ began playing songs for couples only. Defeated by Murphy's Law, yet again, I turned around to go outside and get some air when I felt a tug on my hand.

I turned back to find that I'd been detained by a stunning dark-skinned woman with a beautiful smile. She was wearing a silver dress that barely covered the top of her thighs and her hair fell midway down her back. She was gorgeous and almost as tall as me, but it was her smoke grey eyes that made me take notice.

"Are you going to dance with me tonight or will I have to continue admiring you from across the room?" she asked, smiling as she sized me up.

I laughed. "Why should you do it from across the room when you can just admire me up close?" It was a Dre line and I knew it, but I liked the attention. I stepped closer and whispered into her ear. "I'd be honored if the most beautiful woman in here dances with me."

"Thank you." She mimed, and rested her head on my chest as we began to dance.

During the slow dance, we exchanged our names, jobs, and who we'd come with that night. Not only was she was beautiful, but also extremely intelligent, and very single—the three things I typically avoided since becoming engaged.

Yet, here I was.

For three songs, we strolled around the floor, dancing and grinding like we were a couple of teenagers. Even when she moved my hands to where they were just above her skirt, I didn't retract them. I enjoyed the contact and the intimacy we shared so easily. After it was all over, she kissed me on the cheek and pulled me towards the front doors of the club, where the music wasn't playing as loudly.

"I had a lot of fun with you, Quinton, even though you're too nice of a guy for the likes of me to be around. You didn't even try to grab my ass."

"Why try? Trying would've undermined your dominance."

"That's exactly what I'm talking about. You could've taken a handful and I wouldn't have even slapped you--hard. Seriously, you're supposed to be a man and you didn't even let them wander a little."

"You sound upset," I said.

"I am!" she exclaimed. "I was hoping that, you know, you got a feel so that I might be able to get one too!"

We both laughed. It felt good to laugh with her--to be noticed. "I had fun with you too, Anelle." That was her name. I'd found out near the end of the second song, which ironically, was last thing I found out about her.

She took out a pen and began writing on my hand as she spoke. "I'm not one to beat around the bush, so here goes. I know you have a woman—you have to... and don't disrespect me by telling me you don't either." She continued to scribble on my hand. "But anytime you'd like to talk, I'd like to be the one you speak to. You don't have to worry about me taking you from your woman or even trying, because I'm not that kind of girl, but I do get a vibe from you that I haven't really felt before.

So, before I invite you over to my house and get shot down, I'm leaving my number on your hand. You can wash it off, let it fade, or put it where you feel it should be, but hopefully this won't be the last time we speak." Without waiting for a response, she turned around and disappeared into the crowd.

I walked back to my table, stunned, but invigorated. If we had met under different circumstances who knows what would've happened, but my circumstances hadn't changed and I knew better. When I got back, I found everyone in the same position as when I left: glass on the lips, with the exception of Dre, who was confessing his love to whoever was on the other end of my phone.

"Damn, girl. Your voice is so damn sexy that I think I love you. Can't you feel it too? I love you, girl. I want to be with you, and only you." He licked my phone and continued as everyone at the table burst into laughter.

"They don't know what we have. They're just jealous. You make me cry, girl. Can I sing you a song?"

I snatched my phone away from Dre before he embarrassed himself any further. "What the hell are you doing, man? You need to act a damn fool on *your* free night and weekends." He looked upset that I didn't let him sing, but the frown faded and he came back to what was left of his senses.

I put my ear to the phone to find out who Dre was confessing his love to, when I heard a familiar voice--her voice. "Hello? Excuse me, sir, are you still there?" she said.

"One second, please," I said, disguising my voice. I suddenly found myself in shock, but no matter how hard I tried to convince myself otherwise, I knew it was her, her voice was unmistakable. I walked away from the table and quickly found my way to the bathroom.

"Hello?"

"And hello to you, too. With whom am I speaking this time?"

"Mrs. Glenn, this is Quinton. Wait, before you say anything, I just want to apologize for my drunken, idiot friend."

"There's no reason to apologize, Quinton, I did get to laugh a few times. Also, he seemed to know who I was, so I'm guessing that you two have had a conversation about me. Am I right?" I blushed, but before I had a chance to speak, she continued. "I bet it went something like this: 'Man, today I met this sister with the fattest ass!' Let me know if I'm warm."

I had to cover my mouth to keep from laughing--especially when I realized where I was. I thought about the conversation I had with Dre before I told her a bold-faced lie. "Nope, never spoke about it. I hadn't even noticed."

"Quinton, I already know the real answer. I know I have a nice behind and I'm not ashamed of it. Therefore, you shouldn't be ashamed to tell me that you were talking about it."

Caught in my lie, it was just easier to at least tell a partial truth. "Perhaps it went something like that, but not as bad as you made it sound. It sounds so sexist when you say it."

She laughed, causing me to blush for the second time. "So you say, Mr. James. Well anyway, your friend was about to serenade me. For the life of me, I don't know why you didn't you let him finish? It's been a long time since I've had a man confess his love for me."

"Andre doesn't confess his love, he spills it wherever you let him, but I'll be sure to let him know this. It'll probably be right after I kill him, though. Can you at least let Mr. Glenn know that this was a prank call? Tell him that it was just a bunch of drunken fraternity guys who dialed the wrong number."

"Quinton, it's alright. Mr. Glenn is out of town working, and I was having a hard time sleeping anyway. Your friend's call was a good laugh. It was just what I needed."

"In all honesty, Mrs. Glenn, I'm really sorry, for my friend. I just don't understand why you stayed on the phone if you knew that it wasn't me doing all that talking?"

"Caller ID. Your name came up. I thought you called to ask me why I left that note on the back of my card. But when you--or rather your friend, started confessing his love for me and talking about my sexual prowess, I thought it would be wise to listen." I wanted to laugh with her, but I was still too embarrassed.

"Hopefully he didn't offend you too much. Did I mention how sorry I was?"

"Don't worry about it, Quinton. Perhaps I'll think of a way that you can make it up to me."

My heart skipped a beat as I thought about what she meant. "And how do I make it up to you?" I asked, trying not to sound as nervous as I was.

"You can buy me lunch?"

Relieved that she was talking about food, I agreed. "Why are you still up this late?"

"Well, I was reading a book, but I guess I'm just enjoying my solitude."

"If you don't mind me asking, why do you enjoy being alone?"

"Well," she whispered into the phone, "you just never know when someone will come along and demand your attention."

"Indeed," I whispered back.

"But it's late, Mr. James. I hope we can continue our conversation at another time. At that time, maybe we'll both be in the type of setting that permits a more--intimate conversation. Your friend, Andre, gave me a few good laughs and maybe we can talk about him for a while."

"Perhaps we can, Mrs. Glenn."

"Call me Cheyenne. We're co-workers now, Mr. James. Now that I have your number, we'll certainly be talking later." And without waiting for me to say goodnight, she hung up.

Cheyenne. I didn't know if this was going to benefit me or end up disastrously, but one thing did make me nervous. I was already looking forward to our next conversation.

I left the bathroom and headed back to the table. When I found the guys again, Dre grabbed my wrist and leaned on me. I didn't know if he was too drunk to stand, but he stunk of alcohol.

Without much of an argument from anyone, I took everyone's car keys and called for five taxis, one for each one of them. I didn't know who'd driven here, but that didn't seem as important as getting them home safely. They could pick up their keys later.

The taxis all arrived at the same time. I took the "just in case" five hundred dollars out of Andre's wallet and dispersed about a third of it amongst the taxi drivers. I helped Dre into the back of my car and with his head facing the back of the passenger's seat, I hoped he wouldn't choke on his own vomit.

I drove as smoothly as I could on the way to his house and it paid off. Instead of vomiting all over my back seat, it wasn't long before his cries of liquor regret turned to drunken drivel and finally, to snores. When I finally pulled into his driveway, he was dead to the world. I dragged him up out of the car, lugged him through his front door, turned off his alarm, and continued carrying him towards his bed. I laid him on his stomach, making sure to get as much of him on the bed as I could. After making sure he was secure, I walked into the living room, crashed on his couch, grabbed one of the remotes and turned on the TV.

If I were single, there wasn't a doubt in my mind that I would've been all over Anelle, but as I looked at my hand and read her number, there wasn't a doubt in my mind what she wanted. She certainly didn't want friendship, but that's all I was willing to offer. Cheyenne, on the other hand, was something entirely different. No matter how much I didn't want to think about her, the truth was that I *wanted* her.

106

From the scent she wore in class, to the way she walked and talked, she was my embodiment of sexy. Before today, I'd really never desired *any* married woman, but Cheyenne had not only piqued my curiosity, simply mentioning her to Dre aroused Pedro. I closed my eyes and laughed at the thought of us together, but the longer I entertained it, the more I anticipated our next meeting.

What is so wrong about wanting a married woman? Even *Lae* wants to bring Niya into our bedroom...

One thing was for certain, though. I missed my baby. The last time we had sex was before New Years, and I was horny. I chose Laela because I was tired of the games. I was done jugglin' women around. But lately, it seems like every woman I meet wants *something* from me. Yet at home, I barely received any notice from my fiancée-- and she was *always* willing to please me. Now, the only time I see her ass is on the way out of the front door.

Dre was right. I was starting to feel like a devil named Temptation was quickly eroding my dam of restraint and I didn't have anyone to help me hold back the levee.

CHAPTER 9

Laela

<u>January 15th (Sunday)</u>

There were two things that I hated more than anything in the world: a slow shift and a long night. I was having a long night and unfortunately, it was impossible to have one without the other. With hardly any laboring patients, the floor was so quiet that I could hear the punch-in clock ticking.

Ordinarily I hated day/night shift rotation scheduling, but knowing that Niya and a few of the other nurses were suffering with me made my burden seem a little less heavy to carry.

When we all arrived at around 7:00 p.m., the floor was chaotic as usual. Even though the board was moderately heavy, reading only 12 patients on the floor, with four more coming during the night, most of the nurses were ready to give report and leave. I received report from Sandra, a nurse I knew from days, and began writing down all the things I needed for my two patients and began my shift.

Before midnight had arrived, half of the patients had gone to postpartum, and with two out of the four incoming being redirected to others hospitals, we were left with six working nurses to take care of the six remaining patients. As fate would have it, neither of my patients were delivered, but Shanti Patel, the night charge nurse, gave one of them to Michelle Harris, one of the three black nurses working tonight who was lucky enough to have delivered both her patients.

By 2:30 a.m., the last of the triage patients were discharged, and with the rest of them sleeping, the only sounds that could be heard were those of the sanitation crew mopping the floor. With the night being so slow, Shanti allowed us to chat around the nurses' desk, which was typically frowned upon; especially with the things we talked about.

As always when she was around, Michelle started it off. Just a few years older than me, she'd done more explicit things than I could ever dream of doing and usually had pictures to prove it. She didn't have the ideal shape, looking more like a pear each time I saw her, but she was full of life and lust, which I believed offset any physical beauty she lacked. Whenever we listened to her stories, she always tried to whisper, but she was as boisterous as they came, which usually made her stories all that more interesting. Like children at a campfire, we'd hang onto every word she spoke. With the luxury of being single and the only one of the floor who openly admitted bisexuality, her escapades were usually raunchy and recent.

"-- so he went down on me, right, and I was lovin' it, right. This man ate pussy like it was the last scrap of food on the planet. I mean I'm a big girl, but that boy put me in the fetal position several times. So now I'm hot and bothered, I want some dick. I tell him to take off his pants and when he does, out plops the smallest thing I've ever seen!" Michelle admitted in her typical energetic fashion. We all erupted in laughter, but Shanti looked over to let us know that she wouldn't tolerate anymore outbursts. However, Michelle continued like she either hadn't seen or didn't care. "So I'm like what you gone do with that? That little thing ain't even large enough to freshen up my breath!"

"You did not tell him that! That is so hurtful!" Dawn exclaimed. She was one of the two white nurses in the group and was also very single. From her long blond hair and green eyes, to her country accent and her inability to talk about sex like we did, she carried her own personal halo. To me, she was the embodiment of the wholesome southern belle, but when it came to sex, she listened more fervidly than the rest of us.

"I sure as hell did. Told him he could eat this, but he couldn't beat this. Not tonight." She snapped her fingers and started us up all over again. We all snickered, trying to hold back the laughter. I wasn't sure I could hold back, so I bit on my finger.

"He knows what it is. There ain't nothin' less than the lucky number seven that can satisfy all this."

"I know what you mean, girl." Teniyah interjected. "I had the same thing happen to me in college. He was cute as hell and I really liked the guy, but when I saw how small it was I was pissed. All that fine mixed with all that disappointment. I mean he put so much effort into it that I tried to cum, but all he really did was tickle the outside."

"So you married him," I blurted out and fell over, quietly laughing on my way to the floor. The other girls covered their mouths, but most laughed just as hard as I did.

"Aw, see. Why you gotta go there? Now I'm gonna have to go get my box cutter. I didn't want to cutcha, but now I have to. And my hubby is not small! You know what? I'll be telling Franklin what you said when I get home. We're gonna cut yo' ass up together, do it family style."

"That's funny. I always heard black guys had humongous thingies. Is that true or just a stereotype?" Terra said. Like Dawn, she was snowflake white, but she was far from single and within a few months of working here, found herself a doctor. They were engaged six months after they met, and with the size of the rock she had on her finger, I was surprised she didn't always come to work wearing a sling.

Michelle chuckled. "Let me tell you something, sweetie. I've slept with men all over the spectrum. Usually, black men have most of them beaten, but that don't mean nothin'. I could say that based on my experiences that Hawaiian guys have them all beat. The only Hawaiian guy that I'd ever been with had a dick so big and thick that I think he broke both of my fallopian tubes and maybe cracked an ovary, okay? But I won't say that because then I'd be stereotyping. I love my black men, but GOD didn't bless everyone just because of their skin color."

Kim Huang, our only Asian nurse, finally spoke up in her perfectly annunciated English, "I have only been with one person in my life and that is my husband. In my country, being with anyone outside your race is usually considered disrespectful, but being in this country has made me a little curious to what is out there."

"Wow," I said. "The only man you've ever been with is your husband? I don't think I like those odds." We all looked around and agreed, even Dawn, who I swore was a virgin.

"Aw, Poo-Poo," Michelle said. Poo-poo was Michelle's nickname for Kim, though I don't know where on earth she got it from. "Do you want to know what it's like to be with a black man? Miss Michelle is gonna hook you up." She got up from the desk and grabbed her oversized bag and pulled out a portable DVD player. After placing it on the desk, she smiled and pushed play. As soon as the movie began, all of us watched in awe as a man whose erect penis stood halfway up his abdomen began punishing the poor black girl underneath him. She cried in ecstasy or pain, I'm not sure which, at his constant barrage of dick missiles.

I looked over at Dawn, who looked longingly at the screen, then at Kim who seemed completely mortified, but Michelle was enjoying every moment of it, practically clapping to the soundtrack of the movie.

"Hey, girls, I was just wondering what you were--" Shanti never finished the sentence as she came to the desk and saw what we'd all been watching. She stood staring at the DVD screen a few moments before speaking. "Oh my goodness! Oh, dear. Um, Terra, I, uh, just wanted you to know your patient needs help ambulating to the bathroom. Um, can you help her-- her to the, uh, bathroom?" But at no time did Shanti take her eyes away from the screen. After Terra left, the room was once again filled with the sounds of two bodies slapping forcefully together, porn influenced music, and the occasional grunts and moans that movies like this provided.

Twenty-one minutes later, the movie ended. We stopped it short of "our hero" expelling his unborn children all over her, but everyone already understood what was about to happen.

Shanti was the first to walk away, looking a little flustered as she breezed by me. She was so red that I'd swear it was sunburn if it weren't almost four in the morning.

Teniyah was the first to speak up. "Are you always that horny that you need to keep a flick nearby?"

"No, but I did a fun party earlier today and you've gotta have visuals," Michelle responded.

Next, it was Kim's turn to speak. "So, are all black guys that-- large?"

"Only the blessed ones," Michelle chirped.

"It ain't lucky to have a dick that big. I tell you what, if my man was that big, he wouldn't be hittin' this." Terra said.

"It was very interesting," said Dawn. "I think it's time for me to go on break." And she rushed off.

Kim turned to Michelle. "Thank you for showing me. I now realize how much safer I am with my husband."

Michelle laughed. "Sex Ed 101 has now concluded. Ladies, it's been a pleasure." Then, like Dawn, she decided to go on break.

"Why are looking at me like that?" I whispered to Teniyah. I felt like she could see through my scrubs as she smiled at me.

111

"I'm horny," she whispered back into my ear. "I want you to meet me somewhere. We're going to take our break together."

The butterflies were back.

Forty-five minutes later, we were taking our break in an available room.

We'd entered the room, kept the lights off, locked the door and the kissing began immediately after that. We kissed all the way to the electric bed, which was raised to its highest level, per hospital rules.

With the exception of New Year's, I'd only had sex with Teniyah twice and since one of them was spur of the moment, it didn't really count. We'd go shopping and somehow we'd end up at another hotel. I wanted to plan these escapades out, but Niya was too spontaneous and I was enjoying the sex more than I'd led her to believe.

"If we--get caught--, we'll--lose our--jobs." I managed to get out the whole sentence between our lips smashing against each other's face. "I like--this--job."

She pulled back. "We won't get caught if you learn to be quiet."

"I'll let the bed down." I was breathing heavily with anticipation and pulled my lips away from her invading tongue to let her know what I wanted to do.

"Don't waste your time." She hoisted me up onto the bed and yanked my scrub pants down to my ankles. "No panties?" She looked at me and I smiled shyly.

"Needed to wash my thongs," I admitted, but that didn't stop her from pulling my bound legs up over the bed and dining on my nectar. Between the first time we'd been together and this one, she's gotten supremely better. She made no mistakes, rhythmically fingering me, and continuing her sampling of Lae. I wanted to scream, to shout to the world how much I loved what she was doing to me, but I was forced into complete silence until I began grabbing the covers off the bed and whispered, "Niya, I love it. I love it-- Here I cum, dammit. Here--I--Cum!"

I tried to keep silent, but the pressure was too unbearable. As my temple throbbed to release my torment, she quickly moved her tongue from my clitoris to pushing it inside of me. What was once torment soon became an eruption of curses.

My head curled up to my knees and a lion's roar was released from the depths of my body. "Fuck!" I screamed. "Fuck me!" I couldn't hold back. The stunt she pulled increased my orgasm what seemed like tenfold and I couldn't control what came out of my mouth. I pulled in as much air as I could after having expelled so much so quickly.

"You like?" she asked.

"Where did you learn that?" I was still trying to catch my breath. "Where the hell did you learn that from?"

She smiled. "I'm not telling. Okay, pull your pants up. After a scream like that, security might be coming."

I pulled my pants up and as we snuck out the room, we saw and heard no one. "I don't see anything, do you?"

"Nope," she responded.

We snuck out of the room and walked into our break room. I collapsed on Cookie while Niya began to pace around the room.

I lifted up my head from the couch. "What's wrong?"

"There's something that I didn't want to happen and it happened anyway?"

"Okay, so what's up?"

She paused. "I don't know. I've really enjoyed the time we've spent together lately. I mean other than the sex. I just wanted to thank you for, you know, going this far with me. I never figured that it'd turn into this, and Lae, all of it has been such a rush." She gave me a hug, which brought back the butterflies all over again.

"It's been intense, but if the guys found out, I don't think they'd approve." I tried to laugh, but the only thing that came out was a half baked chortle. "But it's a trial. If it hadn't been for you, I might've never found out some of the things about myself that I know now."

"Yeah, I feel the same way, too."

"So this is our learning experience, our self-education class."

Then, she kissed me on my forehead. "Thanks for going down on your girl last week!" We both laughed, but I knew that she wasn't just joking. After everything I'd learned from her, she came a great deal quicker than I had. "But seriously, Lae, I'm glad you did this with me."

"Niya, don't get all mushy on me now. You're helping me practice for you know, the thing with Quinton. We have fun and we get back to our lives."

She frowned as she looked at me. "You make this sound kind of dirty. Is that what you think? Do you really think I'm your secret affair?"

"It's not that and you know it. I just don't want us to get too far ahead of ourselves," I lied.

Ever since the first time, all I could think about was the next time we'd be together. I wasn't exactly sure if it was the thrill of something different or simply the sex, but I didn't like the way sex with Niya dominated my thoughts.

"Truth is Lae, that I think I might be bi."

For a brief second, I involuntarily held my breath, waiting to hear the punchline, but it never came.

"You're serious, aren't you?"

"Yes."

She'd said the "bi" word, but that was Niya. I wasn't sure what I'd been feeling, but I knew it wasn't that I was bi. I couldn't be, *could I?*

"So are you going to say something to Franklin?"

"Why would I do that?" She asked, looking at me strangely.

She walked over and sat down on Cookie, right next to my head. She put my head on her lap and began to run her fingers through my hair.

For a brief second, I wanted to tell her everything. I could've told her how awful I felt about leaving Quinton out, but how exhilarating the rush of sex was. I could've told her how our intimacy brought out all of these feelings that didn't yet have names. I could've told her that I didn't know what the hell I was feeling and that I was more confused about myself with her revelation. I could've told her that maybe it was time for us to stop, but instead I smiled... and said nothing.

CHAPTER 10

Simone

For the last two weeks, my life was like a dream. Michael became the husband I always wanted him to be. He called my job daily to tell me how much he loved me, helped me more around the house, and even remembered what foreplay was before we had sex. With all of the good things that happened lately, my orgasms had returned and my migraines had disappeared.

Everyone knew about the changes. I told everyone who'd listen about how perfect my husband was much to the dismay of Laela. She was the only person who still believed the change was temporary, but since I didn't want her raining on my parade, I chose to avoid her negativity. Part of my recovery and growth meant that I had to get away from all the pessimism and all of the harmful influences that surrounded me. Especially my aunt, who constantly reminded me of what I was doing wrong as a wife. Even if it was only temporary, I deserved to have a few days of joy in my life without someone bringing me down.

I didn't know how long my joy would last, but I was happy. I woke up headache free and for once I was able to keep the resolution I had to work out. I managed to lose a few pounds of baby fat and I was starting to get my pre-pregnancy body back.

Whenever I went to work or came home, it was always with a smile. One of the security guards at my job told me earlier in the day that I was a completely different woman and I was inclined to agree with him.

115

When Friday arrived, my boss, Mr. Dawes, let me off for half the day. I phoned my husband before I left to see if he wanted to have lunch together, but his boss picked up and told me that he had to take care of some personal business. Since Mike hadn't called me, I knew it couldn't be anything wrong with MJ, but I called my aunt just to make sure.

As soon as she answered, I asked her how MJ was doing and that's when she began her rant. "Child, this boy is fine. He eats too damn much if you ask me. If you were a good momma, you'd--." Before she finished, I hung up. The last thing I wanted to hear was a lecture on how much of a bad parent I was.

It was a beautiful, breezy day, without a cloud in the sky. At first I was nervous about what might have happened, but the weather was so nice that I put any paranoid thoughts I had to the back of my brain. I walked out to my car, took two deep breaths before I opened the door, and calmed myself before I sat down. After the anxiety was gone, I started up the car and began driving home.

Traffic was heavy on I-45. Since lunch time was typically light, there had to be an accident of some sort up ahead. My dark colored car plus the sun beaming down was beginning to turn my car into a sauna. To keep from passing out, I rolled up my windows and blasted the AC. Since I wasn't going to be moving anytime soon, I began to look at other people's license plates, trying to make words out of the letters I saw.

A black Trans Am with tinted windows pulled up next to me. A man, who had previously been hidden behind the tint, pulled up to my left, rolled down his windows and honked at me. I only rolled down my window when I saw him waving at me. I didn't know who he was, but I was hoping that he wasn't about to tell me that I had a flat or some other bad news.

The man was absolutely hideous, and when he smiled, I could see that he wasn't into oral hygiene either. His ragged hair looked like it hadn't seen a comb in a few years, his face was covered with several scars. His top row of gold teeth couldn't deter me from his bottom ones, which looked like he'd just smeared a whole candy bar all over them. I quietly prayed that he wouldn't say anything was wrong with my car.

"Hey girl," he said.

"Is there something wrong?" I asked, afraid of what he might say.

"Naw girl, I just wanted to tell you how fine yo ass is."

Even though he was ugly and dirty lookin, it was still a nice gesture and I was flattered by it.

"Thank you," I said, but I made sure to show him my ring. "I'm married."

"That's cool, but how would you feel if I just ate you out. We ain't even gotta do shit."

Horrified, I immediately rolled up my window and prayed that one of our lanes would move. Looking for a way out, I saw an opening in the lane to my right. I jumped in front of the slower cars, stayed with the moving traffic and within a few minutes I'd gotten past the accident and was on my way home.

When I pulled into the driveway of the duplex, Mike's car was already there and I was surprised to see it there so early in the day. I figured I'd surprise him and make our half day together memorable. I grabbed my purse out of the car and looked for my keys on the way up the back stairs.

With the bottom door lock being broken for the second week in a row, I walked up and through the hallway, bumping into the landlord as he opened his door and tried to take out the trash. With all the noise he made, I half expected Mike to come out and ruin my surprise, but he didn't. I took my heels off and crept up the stairs, careful to miss the stairs I knew would creak.

By the time I made it to the top, I pulled out my keys and was about to open the door when I heard him walk into the kitchen, talking to someone on either the house phone or his cell. He sounded upset and I stopped to listen why. I couldn't hear the other person, but I could hear his responses to whatever they were saying:

"Why you on that bullshit again? I told you that I'd take care of it!" He paused. "Look, like I said, she don't know shit and she ain't gone know shit. You keep yo' goddamn mouth shut and we won't have problems. I don't want to hear shit about you callin' here no more. This is my house. My family lives here and I don't bring this shit into my home. If you still want *this*, respect my rules." There was another pause.

"What? You sorry? Yeah, you sorry alright. Aw, there you go again. I already told you. What? You want me to say it again?" I began to chew on my nails, something I hadn't done since I was a child, hoping this conversation wasn't what I thought it was. I closed my eyes and sent him mental messages I prayed he received, but he didn't. The next words he spoke tore through my soul and ripped my heart apart.

"Okay, I'll say it again. I love you and that shit was good. Are you happy now? I gotta go. I don't like talkin' about this shit on the phone."

I gagged, ready to throw up all over the back hallway. But instead I covered my mouth and tip-toed my way back down the stairs as quietly as I went up. I ran back to my car, shoeless and emotionally destroyed.

I scratched all over the driver's side door of my Oldsmobile 88, tearing away the blue paint as I tried to get the key into the door. After finally getting in, I angrily turned the key, causing a scratching sound in the engine. I took two breaths, closed my eyes, started the car again, and pulled out of my driveway.

I didn't know where I was driving, nor did I care. I just wanted to be away from him-- away from that house. I needed to distance myself from all the lies and betrayals. Tears streamed down my face, partially blinding me, but I didn't care. I drove like an angry woman, possessed by despair, barely dodging traffic, and considering whether Mike deserved to live.

Maybe that would end the pain. Perhaps it was time I stopped hurting myself and begin to let others feel what it was like to be me. That's what I'll do. Everyone else would finally feel the pain I was going through.

Memories from when Mike and I met started to fill my head. I began to dwell on how we met in the Galleria during one of the hottest summers in recent memory and all the conversations we'd shared since. We'd talk for hours and I felt I could tell him anything. I could remember laughing at his jokes, our first kiss, even sneaking into his parent's house to have sex when they weren't home. Two weeks into knowing each other, we'd slept together for the first time. It wasn't the mind-blowing sex he'd promised, but the passion behind it was just what I'd needed.

After five years of dating, he proposed, but I knew it was only because I'd gotten pregnant. We didn't even have a wedding; we just went downtown and were married by a judge who had a long list of potentially happy couples behind us. It was after the wedding that I noticed dramatic changes in his personality. Once upon a time he was gentle, funny, even spontaneous, but now--nothing but contempt. He became just as cold and indifferent as the men I'd dated in my youth and I hated him for it.

The sound of a blaring horn brought me back to the present. I turned left onto 610, heading west towards the Galleria—back where it all began. As I pushed harder on the gas pedal, I ravaged through my purse, hoping to find a stray pill, but I couldn't find anything that I'd been using. Since we'd gotten married, I'd gotten used to the anger and frustration that came with it. So much so that even though I knew now was the perfect time for it, I felt almost nothing-- nothing but loathing.

Then it became clear. It wasn't Mike I hated, I hated myself. I allowed myself to become what I said I'd never be. I got pregnant and destroyed the Michael I loved. I was the one who drove him to cheating. I'd done this to us.

The tears continued to fall from my eyes. A voice in my head began whispering to me and it grew louder and louder until it became a megaphone in my head.

Maybe it's time for you to go. DO IT! DO IT! I don't want you here! I don't give a shit about you! I'd rather fuck her anyway! The voice in my head was no longer anonymous. I knew whose voice it was now, telling me to end it. It was Michael's.

I didn't want to admit it to myself, but maybe he was right. I'd forever be at peace and these thoughts would finally disappear. No one could boss me around anymore! They will miss me when I'm gone, all of them! I would finally be away from the mountain of shit that was falling down on me!

I began swerving through cars, thinking of the quickest way to end it all. I knew the only way to make the pain go away was to be on a completely different level of existence.

I veered off onto the Westheimer exit and turned around so that I could return home. If I was going to end this misery I was trapped in, everything I needed was at the house. If Mike was still there, maybe I could start by taking him with me. After all, we were married.

Till death...

I pressed on the gas until I couldn't push it down any further and sped towards the passing lane, ahead of the truck. I tore down the expressway at speeds I have never even dreamed of going, swerving in and out of traffic. I came close to hitting several cars, but I swerved out of the way just in time to step on the gas a little further and push the engine just a little harder.

I didn't take my time getting home. I parked my car behind Mike's, but this time, I leapt from the car, not even bothering to close my door.

I marched up the stairs, stomping on each step so that Michael knew I was coming. The sorrow I felt earlier turned to rage. With each step upward, I grew angrier and still more determined to end our lives.

MJ deserves better than us. MJ deserves better than us.

The chant continued to run through my head until I reached the top of the stairs.

I grabbed the doorknob with such ferocity that the door rattled, causing a few woodchips to fall from the decrepit doorway arch and into my hair. Blinded by my tears, I could barely see the lock in which I was trying to jam the key into. After finally forcing the key into the lock, I turned as fast as I could.

119

Once I pushed the door open, I half expected to see Mike on the other side, but the place was silent. I grabbed the first objects on the counter that I could attack him with, and small silver fork and a half drunken bottle of Tequila, and went looking for him. I searched each room, but I didn't find Michael anywhere in the house.

Filled with hate, vengeance and remorse, I ran towards our bedroom and fell on the bed. I squeezed the fork as hard as I could, trying to equal the same pain I felt inside, but I couldn't. Instead, I threw the Tequila on the bed and repeatedly stabbed the bed as many times as I could, wishing that my mattress was Mike.

Laying on my back, breathless, the tears flowed like a fountain and I replayed everything in my head. From the point where I stood outside the door to his confession of love, I watched it replay as if I were there all over again. But this time it was different. This time I couldn't move, I couldn't speak and as his voice approached the door he began to whisper something to me.

At first I couldn't hear it, but the closer he moved towards the door, the louder the whispering became.

It's time for you to go.

He was right.

It was my time to go.

I sat up from the bed, reached over towards my dresser and grabbed the pills my doctor had given me weeks earlier. The same pills I'd shoved into the bottom of my purse, the same pills I swore I'd never take again and emptied them into my hand. I grabbed the bottle of Tequila from off the sheets, swallowed as much as I needed to wet my mouth, and then took two pills.

With each mouthful of liquor, I ingested two more pills. Once the Tequila bottle had been emptied, I threw the rest of the pills on the floor and collapsed onto my bed. The only thing left to do now was let go.

I'd always told my friends that I wanted to know how I was going to die and here I was, getting exactly what I wanted. I never imagined that I would die the same way my mother had, but I could finally understand why she'd done it. All my life I called her a coward for leaving me alone, but she was tired of living with the same pain every day, tired of this cursed life.

"Forgive me, mommy," I said, barely allowing it to escape through my lips.

A cold chill began to run through me, but I didn't move. I pulled a pillow over my face and quietly prayed that it would all be over.

I closed my eyes and whispered, "Forgive me, Lord." Almost instantly, flashes of my life blurred through my mind, until the reel ended and the last picture in my mind was in full view for me to see. It was my mother holding a picture of a smiling MJ.

She handed the picture of MJ to me and mouthed one word: *Don't.*

My eyes shot open and moving faster than I ever had in my life, I ran to the bathroom and shoved my fingers down my throat. I didn't take long before I was spewing all of the contents of my stomach into the toilet.

When I finished, I wasn't even sure that I'd gotten it all, but I cried nonetheless. I tried to stop the tears, but I needed this and it felt good to finally release everything. I cried because of what I was about to do, because of what could happen to MJ without his mother around and I cried because of how I felt when I lost my mother. Wiping the saliva from my mouth, I slowly got up from hugging the toilet, walked to my bedroom and called the only person I knew wouldn't judge me.

I called the cell phone and even though I knew he was at work, I needed him. I was relieved when he picked up.

"Quinton, I did something bad."

"Monie, what happened? Are you okay? You sound sick."

"I caught Mike cheating--and I was about to take some pills to take away the pain, but I'm okay now."

"I'm on my way! Don't you go to sleep! I'll be right there!"

He was actually coming to see me and a warm feeling enveloped me. He did care. He actually wanted to come over to make sure I was okay. Mike wouldn't ever come home for me, but he'd bang his slut when she wanted him to.

"Quinton, I'm okay. I never took any of the pills," I lied. "I just wanted someone to talk to."

"I'll always be here for you, Monie, but are you sure you don't need me to take you to a hospital? I'll be there in a few minutes if you want me to. If you say you're okay then I'll stay here."

"Thanks Quinton, I appreciate you just being a voice for me."

"Call me in a few hours so that I know you're okay, but if you need anything at all, you call me."

"I will."

And with that we hung up, but I couldn't get over one thing he'd said.

Even though I still felt awful from what I'd just done, knowing that Quinton would always be around overwhelmed me with more emotion.

For an hour I walked around, making sure that there weren't any lingering effects of the pills and liquor—fighting any urges to sleep. I thought about Quinton and how perfect of a man he was. When I was sure that I'd be okay, I laid on my bed, closed my eyes and thought about my best friend's man until I fell asleep.

Mike nudged me when he found me on the bed. "When did you get here?"

"I've got a better question. Why the hell weren't you at work today?"

"Something came up with Pookie's car. I dropped the car off and he came here to get me. What's with the twenty questions and why the hell does your face look like that? It looks all swollen. Are your allergies acting up?"

"I'm fine," I answered. I stood up and walked past him like he didn't exist. "I need to speak with you about something."

"About what?" he asked.

I walked into the kitchen before I answered. "I want you and your shit to get the fuck up out my house."

Caught off guard by my snapping, he instantly became defensive. "Huh? What the hell is wrong with you and what the hell are you talking about? This is my shit and I swear to God that if someone is leaving this bitch, it's gonna be you."

I reached into my kitchen drawer and picked out the biggest knife I could find. I wasn't going to use it, but if he put his hands on me, I'd be forced to cut him. I was as serious as I'd ever been. "So, Mike. Who do you love, besides me? And really, who are you fucking? Since you can lie to me with a straight face, try lying to Mr. Knife." I aimed the knife at him and wagged it several times. He backed away from me, looking mortified. It was the first time I'd seen a black man turn snow white.

"Don't lie to me, Mike. Please don't do it. I came home earlier and heard you. Now, you can talk and lie, or you can take your shit and get the fuck out!"

The yell seemed to snap him back into reality. "I'm going dammit! At least for now, but when you calm down, we can talk." He walked back to the living room and I followed.

He made me laugh. "Mike, I am calm. This is my calm look." I frowned at him as he sat on the couch and stopped moving. "I don't see you leaving." He put on his shoes, threw on his jacket, and grabbed his keys.

"No." I said to him as he picked up his keys. "I pay for it, I keep it."

"What about my goddamn house keys? I'm going to need to get my stuff."

"Call me after I get home tomorrow. I mean you weren't at work very long today, so I'm sure they won't notice that you're wearing the same thing."

He gave me a nasty look and walked out the house without saying another word, but made sure to slam the door upon his exit.

After I heard the bottom door slam, I locked the top door, dropped the knife, collapsed on my couch and let the tears roll down my face.

I was awakened by the sound of my phone ringing. At first I thought it was a dream, but when it didn't stop, I knew that it had to be my aunt.

"Hello?" I was still half sleep.

"Lord have mercy, girl! What is your problem? Mike done called me crying and told me you done kicked him out! And you was waving around a knife! Haven't I taught you better than that? What's wrong with you? I should call the police, but I don't want MJ without no mother! You need a man in yo' house and your husband is that man!"

"Aunt Ida, I'm tired and I don't feel like hearing this now. While you're taking his side, did he tell you that he's been sleeping with someone else?"

"Well, a man wouldn't have to go nowhere if his woman was taking care of him at home! That's yo' fault! Waving knives around like you--like you crazy! Y'all need to talk and get past this. Marriage is forever!"

"Auntie, you'll never understand. You're still stuck in that old world thinking where it's okay for your man to be a man, as long as he comes home. I want respect. I want to be treated like a woman, not a slave. Is that so wrong? Why do I have to be less than I am, just so that he can feel like a man? If he wants to run this house, he needs to act like a man. He should take care of his responsibilities. He doesn't pay for anything in this house, but he always has money to spend on drinking, bowling and his whore! I don't ask for much, but I'll be damned if I get treated like crap everyday for the rest of my life." Before she had a chance to say anything else, I told her that I'd be by in ten minutes to pick up MJ and I hung up.

Fifteen minutes later I was at my aunt's house. I left the Olds at the house feeling that riding in Mike's car would help me to feel independent, but it didn't. At least not like I thought it would.

My aunt was already sitting on the porch of her forty year old house, a brown and white colonial style home, which she'd owned for thirty out of its forty years of existence. It was the same house I'd been raised in since I was 15, right after my mother died.

My aunt was an older woman, sixty-seven and counting. She was my father's eldest sister and she was the only family I had left on this side of the Mississippi after both my parents died, so I was left to her care. Growing up, she was the strictest woman I'd ever met and as I grew older, the person I came to resent the most.

She was from another age and we lived in two different worlds. Whenever I was in grade school, she made sure I left the house in a skirt that reached well past my ankles, but when the school closed, she immediately sent me to a Catholic school. Since we had uniforms, fashion wasn't a concern, but when I wanted to go to a movie, my aunt made sure that the long skirts went with me. Luckily, when I met Lae in high school, she and I were the same size. Whenever we went out together, she always brought me another set of her clothes or else I might have never dated.

After high school, my aunt wanted to enroll me in college, but I could never focus on doing the schoolwork, so I dropped out, much to her dismay. I got a temp job as a secretary, which lead me to office manager, but that still wasn't enough for her. So when I met Mike, we quickly moved in together after only six months of dating. Being with Mike was the only time she seemed to be okay with I was doing with my life. Catering to a man for the rest of my life was fine with her.

I walked up the stairs and past my aunt who, under her breath, gave me a "Humph." I opened her front door, grabbed all of MJ's bags that were sitting by the television, and picked him up out of the playpen where he'd been sleeping.

I didn't see my older brother anywhere in the house so I walked out the same door I came in, loaded the car with the baby bags, put MJ in his car seat and drove off without so much as a 'thank you'.

I felt good about what I'd done. He was gone and I could do whatever I wanted, whenever I wanted, without his supervision. I thought about calling Lae, but I didn't feel like hearing her congratulate me, nor did I need a lecture.

"I'll call her tomorrow," I said to myself and continued heading home.

After cooking dinner and finally putting a teething MJ to sleep, it was almost midnight. I found it funny that I could be tired earlier when I'd gotten home, but restless now that it was time to sleep. So instead, I sat on my bed and watched a late night movie.

January 21st (Saturday)

At 3:30 a.m., I was still awake. No matter how dark the room became, I couldn't sleep and I knew why--I was alone again.

The bed seemed so much bigger now that I laid in it by myself. There was no Michael to nudge me to the end, no snoring, and no grunting; no anything. Every time I closed my eyes, I'd see Michael. He was smiling in my head, seemingly oblivious to what he'd done to us.

I wondered what he was doing. I figured he'd probably called his parents, turned them against me too, and was sleeping in their house for the night. Perhaps, he was in her bed. In the bed of the mystery woman who loved him and his damn "Dingo". I could see him making love to her, with him rubbing her, touching her, feeling her. He probably said the same things to her that he said to me when he came. She was probably some 5'7", 130 pound, big-tittied, long-legged tease, who moonlighted as a porn star. That whore! How could she do this to me?

How could *he?*

My stomach twisted around in knots. I knew I wouldn't be able to sleep, so I turned the TV back on, tried to watch the 10 o'clock news reruns, trying to accept the fact that I was going at it alone.

After a long night without any sleep, I jumped in the shower, making sure to run mostly cold water. I left the bathroom door open to hear if MJ was crying while I washed up and brushed my teeth. After getting him ready and throwing on blue jeans and a red blouse for myself, I made breakfast for the both of us and drove MJ to my aunt.

After being forced to listen about how to treat a man, I knew I needed a day to myself. I walked to my car and thought about calling Lae. I figure we could go shopping together, but I still wasn't ready for "I told you he was no good." Besides, I was pretty sure I'd been replaced by 'Raven' and the thought of that made me sick. So I just drove aimlessly around downtown, hoping that I could figure out what the hell I wanted to do with myself.

I wanted to be a good wife, but somehow I knew that I'd brought this all on myself.

I'd secretly fantasized about my best friend's man. *Check.*

I tried to take my husband's life. *Check.*

I was going to leave MJ motherless, like me. *Check.*

I could only think of one reason why my life was going to hell, I was being tested.

No, you're being punished.

After sitting in the Galleria parking lot for a few minutes, I started the car and returned home. I slowly drove back to the place where I'd threatened my husband not more than sixteen hours ago. I walked up the stairs and entering the kitchen, I knew what I had to do to save my sanity.

I dialed the number and then put in his extension. I didn't know what I was going to say when he answered, but I figured the words would come to me.

"Electronics, this is Mike Hall speaking, may I help you?" I froze up. "Hello? Is anybody there?"

"Mike," I whispered into the phone, "this is Simone."
I could hear the agitation in his voice once he heard who it was. "Man, what the hell do you want? Forget it, I already know. I'll be by the house at six to pick up my shit."

"That isn't why I called. I just wanted to talk. If you're busy, we can just talk later."

"I ain't got time for this. What? What do you want, Simone?"

"I just wanted to know how you were doing. Are you okay? Where did you sleep last night?"

"I slept at my parent's house if that's what you wanted to know. I'm not dumb, Monie. I know what you're getting at. Why don't you just cut the bullshit and say what it is you wanna say?"

"I--I want you to come back." When he didn't immediately answer, I decided to explain. "We're married Michael. MJ deserves a father and I deserve a husband. What you did was wrong, but we can make this work. I can be a better wife." I couldn't hold back the tears any longer and began sobbing uncontrollably. "We can make it work. I know we can."

"I don't know if I want to come back," he said smugly. "You got some things you really need to deal with and I don't have the time to mess around with you, Monie. I have a wife who acts like a child and then swings around a goddamn knife when she gets mad. I know things ain't been great between us, but the last few weeks were good, right? I was doing what I was supposed to, but you couldn't help but to mess it all up, huh?"

I didn't care if he blamed the whole thing on me. I didn't want to be alone and I wanted him back where he belonged. "Yes, and I'm sorry. What do I need to do to make it better?"

"How bout we move on from there? I don't want to hear about none of this shit no more. Maybe I'll be by tomorrow or something and we can talk, but I gotta work right now."

"Okay. Tomorrow? You said tomorrow, right?"

"Yeah, tomorrow."

"I love you, Mike."

"Yup." He hung up without returning my declaration, but it was something I was already used to.

I looked around the kitchen, mentally making a list of things to cook for dinner. I needed my husband home with me. As I stood up from the table, everything somehow seemed surreal. It was as if everything that had occurred during the last couple of days was just a dream. Any minute now I'd wake up and laugh at how insane this nightmare was, but when I pinched myself, nothing changed.

If Laela knew what had transpired between Mike and me, she would've killed me after she found out that I welcomed him back. But how could she possibly know what it was like? She was Miss Perfect. She was born with a silver spoon in her mouth and nothing ever went wrong for her. My life, on the other hand, was a constant struggle. I wasn't a strong woman and I didn't pretend to be, but regardless of it all, I'd gotten him. My man was coming back home where he belonged.

CHAPTER 11

Laela

<u>January 31st (Tuesday) 11:00 A.M.</u>

"I love you, Lae."
I love you, too, Quinton.
It was practically an automated response to any statement about love, but it hadn't come from Quinton. It came from my best friend. I was unsure of exactly how I felt or how I was supposed to feel, but one thing was certain, Teniyah didn't know me like she thought she did. In the last few days, things were said that shouldn't have been and our experiments were becoming less random and more frequent. Between Quinton's constant bickering about our sex life, or lack thereof, and Niya's completely over-the-top sex drive, I found myself needing space from the both of them. I was so stressed that I was ready to pull my hair out.

Opening my eyes, I was relieved that I wasn't with either. I'd just landed in Cleveland, OH, and after only three hours of rest, most of them interrupted by my loudly snoring neighbor, I was still fatigued and very agitated. When I looked through the windows of the plane, everything for as far as I could see was covered with a blanket of snow. The sky was so gray and cloudy that it reminded me of my mood and I'd wished my parents stayed closer to home, where it was sunny and warm.

When I stepped off the plane, a blast of cold air was ready to greet me in the gateway. I pulled my coat out of my carry-on bag and put it on as I marched up the jet way from the plane to the terminal, bypassing the growing mass of people who congregated at the top to make sure they had all of their belongings.

"Remember to pick your bags up at carousel eight!" shouted one of our overly excited flight attendants and I began looking for signs that would lead me to baggage claim.

I walked through Cleveland's Hopkins Airport, seeing signs everywhere welcoming me to Cleveland. After finding signs that pointed downstairs towards our carousel, I found my way towards baggage claim. Compared to Bush Intercontinental, the airport was considerably smaller and much easier to navigate. I took the escalator downstairs and found carousel eight directly to my right, with my mother already standing beside it, waiting for me.

"How's my baby?" she shouted in a nearly silent airport, hugging me around the neck and almost cutting off all circulation.

"Can't--breathe!" I exclaimed, hoping that she'd lighten her grip around my neck.

"I'm glad you called to let us know you were coming, but a little more notice would've been appreciated. Your father almost had a heart attack when you called so early in the morning. He thought that something had gone wrong so you know that he was ready to drive back to Houston if necessary. But he was more than happy to buy the tickets for his little girl to come see him." She looked at me suspiciously before placing her arm around my neck. "I may be old, but I'm not naïve, Laela. Your father and I have paid too much money for this wedding for y'all to be unsure!"

"Ma..." I began, but Lashae Booker would not be interrupted.

"We've already taken care of the cake, the caterers, and did you know that the reception hall cost us as much as your first year of tuition! Not only that, but do you know how much food I've sacrificed to fit into that tight little number at the house? And I will fit into it!? I pray to God that things are good with you and Quinton, but if it isn't, we still have enough time to get most of our money back!"

"Ma," I shouted a little louder than I should have, "we're doing fine." I tried to smile, but I was so tired from my restless journey that I only managed a grimace. "Yes, mommy, everything is okay between us. I just missed you guys. I just wanted to get out of warm Houston for a little while and see what the big deal is about snow and ice."

"Uh-huh. It'd *better* be." My mother was not one to usually fall for my brand of bull and I didn't expect her to now, but I was too tired to come up with a better lie. Even after all these years, I still couldn't lie to her and get away with it. "Well, we'll talk later, the conveyer belt is about to move."

After fifty years of life, Lashae Booker still had the radiance of a miniature sun when she smiled. My mother still looked younger than her age would suggest and she was still as beautiful as I'd remembered. I was especially glad to see that the cold weather didn't do anything to take away from her natural glow. She was still the golden complexioned queen I'd grown up with and though we shared a lot of the same features, I hoped that I would look as good as she did at her age, especially after having to deal with me and my little brother. In the last few years, either she'd shrunk or I'd finally grown taller than her, but she still stood with her head up and shoulders back; my mother-- the runway model.

"It's nice to know that the cold weather isn't treating you too badly. With all this snow around, I thought you'd probably be frowning more often," I said.

"Actually it's better for me than the burning sun being out all day and melting my face away." We laughed. "Besides I love snow. Maybe it's because of the newness of seeing it all the time, but I still enjoy seeing it."

"So how is it up here? How are the people? Are they as nice as the people back home?"

"Well, we really don't have that many neighbors. In Houston, everything was a subdivision, but here there's farmland everywhere. The people are pretty nice and we don't have to deal with that awful Houston traffic."

"Houston traffic builds character."

I didn't care too much for the snow or the city so far. I grabbed my garment bag and suitcase from the carousel and we walked over to short term parking. We took the escalator up to the second floor where she took out her keys, pushed on the alarm button and a shiny red, BMW Z3 Roadster lit up. "I see daddy bought you another car."

"You know how your father is about cars. He sold the other two cars and replaced them with three new ones. He says they're for business, but you know your father; as soon as a new model comes out, he's drooling all over it."

"What about David? Did daddy buy him a car?"

David was my younger brother, only three years my junior, but he'd lived with my parents for all twenty-four years of his life. He was a complete opposite from the rest of us, lazy and usually unemployed. For as long as I could remember my father wanted to kick him out, but my mother would always protect him.

"Is he still making him work at the flower shop?" I asked.

She raised her eyebrow. "Think about that one, Laela. Has it been that long since you've been around your father? Do you even remember your father's philosophy; the one he's had since before even he could work?"

"Yes, mommy, I remember. The old, 'if me no work, then me no eats' speech."

She giggled, revealing her smile all over again. "It's always funnier when you say it, but your father is now requiring that he pay rent."

I loved my brother, but it was too obvious how much they still catered to him. "It's about time. You need to stop babying David or else he'll always cling onto you guys. I still can't believe it, though. You guys are actually forcing David to become an adult. This is a big step for you, ma. What's next? Are you going to stop cutting his waffles into teddy bear shapes?"

"You're not too old for me to take my belt off, young lady!"

"See, you guys are harsh on me, but when was the last time Tank got a good whippin?"

"Why do you still call him Tank? You're the only one that says that like it's a term of endearment."

When my brother was younger, he had a problem with bed wetting, so my cousins and I gave him the nickname of 'Tinkle King'. As he grew older, and the peeing in the bed grew further apart, the name shortened and he just became 'Tink'. Once he got to junior high, we called him Tink so often that when his friends overheard us call him Tink; they thought we had said 'Tank' and the name stuck.

I didn't answer my mother's question, but instead I just looked out the window at the new whiteness that covered ground. The roads were so full of salt that they looked almost as colorless as the snow covered ground. I began to follow the highway signs so that I could remember how to return to the airport if anyone was too busy to bring me back. We took I-480 East all the way to the Solon exit. After a few turns we were on Aurora Road, heading towards the country. According to my mother, the drive usually took twenty-five minutes, but due to the foul weather, it ended up being almost twice as long.

When we arrived at the driveway of my parent's new house, it was a little after five o'clock, and the sun had already begun to set. With the view that I had from the passenger's seat, the sun seemed more like it was hiding behind my parent's home than saying goodnight.

The house was a great deal bigger than the one my parent's shared in Houston, though not as quite as large as Dre's mansion. It looked like an old farmhouse, minus the silo and my father's company had the house built to my father's specifications. The whole house was made of red brick, with the exception of the porch and the patio, which were both enclosed and both were made of wood. The backyard went on as far as I could see and when the garage door opened I saw the two other new cars my mother had told me about, the brand new silver Cadillac Escalade and a pine green Mercedes S-500, all recently polished.

"I see what you mean about his cars. It's like an auto show in here."

"Well, now that your father has the money, he really indulges. Cars are his only vice, but they're very expensive vices. He took the Hummer to work. It's like his third child, but I still think it costs more than both you and your brother's childhood put together."

"So if all the new cars are here, Tank must be here too."

"No, your brother catches the bus to work. And then after work, he has his new girlfriend bring him home." She turned to me and shared the same look she always wore when she had some new gossip to tell.

"About your brother's girlfriend, I kinda like this one; she's a big step up from what's-her-face."

"You mean Lisa, ma. I didn't like her too much, either. This new girl, she's been the tenth one since he's been here?"

"Probably, but I'll let him tell you about it. He seems to really like this one." We exited the car at the same time and the trunk automatically opened. "We have your room already set up," my mother said as she walked towards the trunk. We took my belongings in to find the house empty.

"I'm going to start dinner. I figured you'd want to see your brother, especially since he doesn't know you're here, so I mapped out the directions for you. Just go upstairs to the right."

The inside of the house certainly had a country kitchen appeal to it. The floor, the walls, and even the staircase were all made from wood. I walked upstairs to my room and found that my parents had it designed in the exact way I'd had it before I went to college; from the canopy bed, to the old Bell Biv Devoe poster, everything was in the same place it'd been in my old room with the exception of a brand new computer on my desk.

"You guys just don't quit!" I yelled to my mom. I heard her laughing all the way from downstairs and just as she'd said the directions to my brother's job were lying on the bed.

"There's a lot of snow on the ground so take the truck when you go to see your brother!"

I hung up all of the clothes in my garment bag before heading to the kitchen, grabbing the keys from my mother, kissing her on the cheek and jogging out to the garage. Since the garage was attached to the house, I was thankful that I didn't have to brave the cold weather with the sun going down and jumped into my dad's shiny black Escalade.

I punched in the address on the car's GPS and as soon as it came to life, I pulled out of the driveway and onto the snow covered road. I drove as slowly as I could so that I didn't end up in a ditch and after some slow turns and a few miles, I found myself back on Aurora Road. The GPS directed me northward and I headed towards the flower shop where I'd find my little brother.

I was on the border of Bedford Heights by the time I saw Mr. Johns' Exotic Flowers for Showers Etc. It took me a few tries, but I managed to maneuver the large truck into the small parking area that was on the side of the building and quickly ran from the truck into the store. I opened the door to find a short, elderly, black man spraying flowers down with a bottle of something that had his shop smelling wonderfully.

The chime at the front door alerted him to my presence and he slowly turned around. "Hello!" He sized me up and I could almost read his dirty thoughts. "It's not often I get such beautiful customers. How may I help you?"

"I'm here to see David Booker." I said, trying not to be offended that he was paying more attention to my well-covered breasts than my face.

The old man frowned instantly upon hearing my brother's name. "Oh, you want him. Why you young ladies ogle over that nothing of a man confounds me." He turned away from me and walked to the back of his shop. "David! I done told you about having these young women come to my shop, even when they're cute! I'll tell you this, young lady, if his father wasn't one of my best patrons, David would be very much unemployed. If that's what you're looking for in a man, you've found the perfect candidate. Why is it that all you young girls want these so called thugs and such?"

I wanted to laugh, but I pinched my lips. A few seconds later, my brother came out wearing a smock covered in fertilizer.

"Lae!" he shouted and ran to hug me, forgetting he smelled like a barn.

"Three feet please!" I shouted, slowing his pace.

"I forgot I was wearing this." He took off his outer garment and tightly squeezed me. "How are you, sis? Why are you here? How's it going back home? Why hasn't Quinton been online to get his butt kicked in Madden?"

"Why do you and mommy try to squeeze the life out of people when you hug?" I managed to get out before I knew the pain would begin. He let go, but the old man didn't seem too happy to see such affection. "I'm okay, I just missed you guys." I hit him in his stomach as payback for the hug.

"Ha! You still hit like a girl!" he shouted, but he made sure to cover up the rest of his chest. "Hey, Mr. John, this is my sister from Houston, Laela Booker; nurse extraordinaire and the fiancée of my boy Quinton--just so you don't get any ideas."

"A nurse? That's a good job to have. It's a good thing too, because you're making my heart beat real fast." He smiled and then disappeared into the back of the shop.

My brother leaned over and whispered softly into my ear, "Don't mind him. He's a dirty old man." I'd already figured that much out by myself. "Anyway, so you're here and you left Quinton behind? Sounds like trouble in Happyville to me."

"You're starting to sound like mom. What's with your conspiracy theories anyway?"

He shrugged his shoulders and the small pout he made reminded me of us as children. His lip pout was always so funny that we affectionately termed it the 'big hangey'. "I'm just saying that it never looks good when people start taking vacations alone-- that's all I'm saying."

"I'll tell you just like I told momma, we're fine," I said in a tone of finality. I didn't want my family to keep bringing up Quinton, especially when he hadn't done anything wrong. I was the bad one, and being reminded of my infidelities wasn't why I came home.

"Anyway, how's my boy Quinton? I haven't had a chance to really talk to him since we moved."

"Quinton is cool. He's taking on some extra responsibility at work, so he's not online as much anymore. But according to him, he's tired of kicking your ass anyway."

134

"Damn! The blows just keep coming! Anyway, he got me when I was still green, but I'm ready for him now. I gotta test my skills out on someone good. These Cleveland folks ain't really no competition for me!"

"Who do you play that's no competition?"

"My girlfriend, but that's beside the point. She represents Cleveland, so if I beat her, it's like beating Cleveland."

I shook my head. "Speaking of which, I hear you got this new girl bringing you home. Poor Tank," I began scolding him, "Why are you still running the same old games? Why don't you get your money together and buy a car instead of preying on these helpless girls?"

"It's too far to walk home and its fucking cold up here to keeping waiting on the bus. I practically freeze my ass off just waiting on the damn RTA. By the time I get my money together and buy a car, mom and dad will have already died and what would be the point? Did they tell you they're making me pay rent and they make me pay for every meal I eat? It's like living in a damn hotel! They're sadists, Lae, pure and simple. And for your information, big sis, I don't prey on women, they offer things and I don't have a problem accepting. I'm not using them if they offer it, right?"

"Wrong. Using is using regardless of what pretty face you put on it. Do you even like this girl or are you just using this one too?"

The room fell silent. My brother smirked at me and said, "Lae, I haven't felt this way about another woman, ever. Every time I'm around her I get butterflies in my stomach. Truth is, I already bought her ticket so that she could come to the wedding with me and I bought it with my own money!"

I intentionally stumbled back. "You paid for someone to come to Houston? And you're doing it with your own money? Tink, you're finally becoming a responsible man! I'm so proud!"

He blushed, turning as red as the roses he was standing next to. "So anyway, now that you're here, I can take the rest of the day off and introduce you to my new girlfriend."

"I take it back. You're still not that responsible yet."

Tank stuck out his tongue at me, pulled out his cell phone and dialed the phone number for the shop. The phone rang several times until Mr. Johns picked it up. "John's Flowers for Showers, how may I help you?"

"Hey, Mr. John, my sister doesn't know how to get back home so I'm going to leave a couple of minutes early. I just wanted to let you know."

Since my brother put him on speaker phone, I could hear everything the old man said back. "Whatever. You couldn't just walk ten feet and tell me? You lazy ass, good for nothing, sorry son-of-a-" He hung up before finishing the rest of his rant.

"Let's go!" My brother exclaimed and grabbed his coat.

"What's her name?" I asked as we ran to the car. I used the remote to unlock the doors and we both jumped in and furiously rubbed our hands together to bring back the warmth.

"It's Janette, Janette Booker. We've already eloped" I punched him in the stomach for the second time in the short span since I'd seen him. "I'm just kidding! It's Janette Jordan."

Janette lived in Euclid, another suburb of Cleveland. With Tank directing me, we took I-271 North to I-90 West and got off on E.260th.
"She lives all the way over here? This is a long way to go to pick you up from work and then turn around and drive home. You'd better not be doing her wrong because this girl has to love your crazy ass to do this every day."

"What can I say? I'm lovable." He pulled his cell phone out of his pocket and dialed another number. "I'm outside," he said, and hung up.

We made a right at the bottom of the off ramp and drove all the way down until we saw Lakeshore Boulevard. After a few more left turns, we pulled into the driveway of a small green and white house. Before we left the warmth of the car, the front door to the house opened and my brother quickly ran up the stone steps into the house.

Looking down the street, I saw that the neighborhood was made up of only single storied houses. I was a little worried about leaving my father's Escalade unattended, but there were several Cadillac trucks parked on the street, already covered with snow, which helped to calm my nerves. I got out of the car, set the alarm, and inched my way up the frozen steps.

By the time I made it into the house, Janette and my brother were already kissing. "I didn't mean to interrupt," I said, covering my eyes.

She pulled away from him. "I'm sorry. He attacked me. It's nice to finally meet you, Laela. I've heard a lot of good things about you." She came over and hugged me while Tank disappeared into the kitchen.

"You heard good things about me--from Tank? Wow, will wonders never cease?"

She laughed. "You'd be surprised. All he ever talks about is his big sister, the super nurse."

"Nurse, yes. Super, occasionally." We both giggled like school girls.

As I looked over the house, I frowned at the green carpet and saw that none of the walls were decorated with any pictures. With only one picture of a rainbow colored butterfly resting in the corner and the only furniture being a plastic covered couch which faced a nineteen inch television, I wondered how long she'd been here.

Janette saw me looking around. "I've been here for about a month and haven't really had the time to get things set up."

I smiled. "I completely understand."

"I can hang your coat up if you want me to. It gets really warm in here."

I nodded. As she walked towards me, I had a chance to really see her. Her beautiful brown sugar complexion, though, was completely opposite of my brother who was high yellow. She wasn't very tall, about three to four inches shorter than I was and wore micro-braids that looked really nice on her. She wore a large green sweater with blue jeans and open toed house slippers that revealed a nicely done pedicure on some cute toes. I was jealous of how nice her feet looked.

"I don't know if your brother told you, but I'm in nursing school. This is my last semester and I'm getting my clinicals out the way now. Right now they have me doing rotating in onco/gyno, but I've already fallen in love with L & D."

I was impressed. Usually, my brother went for the pretty girl with no brains, but Janette actually had some substance. "So, my brother has finally found someone with a plan. I'm so proud of you Tank!" I shouted into the kitchen.

"Bite me!" he yelled back.

I turned back to Janette. "Well, I'm L & D too. If you ever need some help, call me. I can help you get ready for your NCLEX. It's been a few years since I've taken it, but experience really counts."

While Tank stayed in the kitchen, probably stuffing his face, Janette and I sat in her living room conversing about the joys and pains of being a nurse. She was easy to talk to and I knew why my brother had been so infatuated with her. Already in her last year of school, which meant eighteen hours of class and thirty hour weeks for clinicals, I didn't know how she found the time to do anything else. I wondered how she was able to pick up and drop off my brother and pay for the house, but since it was none of my business I didn't ask.

"I just finished up one of my eight-hour clinical shifts and it was hell. I emptied more JP drains and colostomy bags than I care to

137

remember. Not only that, but we had to lift and ambulate a 500 pound lady who was wasting away with pressure ulcers, Stage three and four. It was pretty horrific to look at. I can't imagine it being that hard all the time. After all these years of being a nurse, do you still feel the same?"

"Well," I began, "there are some days that you're happy to be there and other days you just want to stab everyone. But more than anything, it's the people you work with that determine how much you'll love your job. If you have a good crew, then you won't mind."

"Well, enough about that. How long are you here and what do you plan on doing while visiting our lovely city?"

"The truth is I have a lot on my mind and I planned on lounging. Lately I've been torn in so many directions that I just wanted to give my mind a chance to relax."

Tank reappeared out of this kitchen with a mustard stain on his shirt. "And you won't get a chance to do it here. I want you guys to get a chance to know each other. I don't know the next time Laela will visit us up here, so I want you two to have some fun. Since Janette doesn't have school tomorrow, why don't you ladies go down to the Flats or something?"

"I don't know, David. What if your sister wants to relax?"

"She can relax tomorrow. I mean nothing really goes down on Wednesday. I would go, but I have to be at the flower shop at eight o'clock, so that means I have to catch the 6:55 bus. Lae, that's cool with you, right?"

I was tired as hell, but I didn't have the heart to say no. "Yeah, I'll go if Janette goes."

"I need to do something besides school and work or my head will explode," she said. "Let me grab some clothes from my room. I already know what we can do tonight."

When she vanished into her bedroom, Tank loudly whispered, "I had to get away from all that damn nurse-talk, but isn't she great?"

"I don't think she's your type. She has a future."

"You sound like your father."

"Well, you make it so easy. Janette's really nice and I would hate to see you stick it to her." There was something definitely familiar about Janette. She reminded me a lot of myself--before I met Teniyah.

We arrived back home an hour later, with Janette driving her blue Ford Contour behind us. Driving home in the dark with snow all over the ground wasn't my forte, so Tank drove. We entered the garage as slowly as we could, hoping that our father wouldn't come out to greet us. If my father would've seen Tank driving his precious truck, we'd be writing our epitaphs.

Relieved that no one had seen us, we snuck into the house and standing by the door was my father.

"So why was David driving my truck?" he asked.

Instead of trying to create a lie, I yelled, "Daddy!" and ran over to hug him.

"How's my little girl?" His cold glare turned into a smiling face and he returned my hug. "It's good to see you, little lady. Kinda spur of the moment calling here and telling me you're coming, don't you think?"

"Yes, but I missed you guys. Houston is a big place to live in with no family."

"Yes, it is." He lifted his head and saw that we had company. "Hello, Janette. How's school?"

"Everything's going well, Mr. Booker. School is fine." He glanced at my brother who was sneaking up the stairs.

"Boy!" he bellowed. "Don't think I forgot about you. Rent is due this week."

"I know," he said and continued moving up the stairs with Janette covering her mouth and trying not to laugh.

"I still don't see how this girl got hooked up with that boy." He said, shaking his head. "Anyway sweetie, how was the flight and how's your husband-to-be?"

"The flight was fine and he told me to tell the both of you hello. Before you ask, daddy, I just want you to know that we're doing fine. I would love to stay and talk, but I need to jump in the shower. It's been a long day and I'm supposed to be going out with Janette tonight."

"Already?" My mother asked.

"Well, you know how Tank, um David is. He's trying to get me comfortable with this one." Whispering in my father's ear, I told him, "David says that there's potential with this one."

My father shook his head and I ran upstairs. My parents were good at reading me and I wanted them to focus on Tank's relationship instead of mine. Truth was that I loved Quinton, but with the complicated relationship Niya and I shared, even I wasn't exactly sure how things were going.

In the room, I disrobed and threw my clothes on the floor, put on my bathrobe and walked into the bathroom. I thought about Quinton

139

and Niya as I showered, hoping to come to some epiphany, but the more I dwelled on it, the more confused I became.

Was it possible that I loved Niya more than I was supposed to or Quinton any less? Could I even love a woman the way that I'd learned to love a man? Why didn't I want to stop my rendezvous with Niya even with Quinton telling me that he needed me?

I stepped out from the shower more confused than when I had gone in. After drying myself off, I walked out of the bathroom and threw the towel on my bed. I walked around the room several times before I took in a deep breath, sat on the bed and replayed the conversation that Niya and I had the night before I left:

"I love you, Lae."

I pretended not to hear her, but I knew that she'd repeat herself. She'd been saying a lot of things lately that I wasn't comfortable with hearing.

"Didn't you hear me, Lae? I said that I loved you."

"I heard you Niya, but I think you're taking this a little too seriously. We're intimate because we want to get better, not because we're in love. This is just us experimenting, that's all it is." I was unsure whether I was lying or not, but she didn't have to know.

"Lae, this stopped being an experiment a few weeks back. God...If you're going to lie about what this is, then at least you could be more convincing."

"I wish you'd stop saying that! I'm not gay! We did all of this for fun, remember? This is our experiment--that's what we said, right? Why are you trying to make this more than it is? It's practice for me and Quinton's threesome. Don't get mad at me because he doesn't want it to be with you!"

"That's a low blow, Lae." She sat up in our hotel bed and pulled the spread over her. "Fine, you can tell yourself whatever you want, but it's not a goddamn experiment, Laela. I'm just the only one here woman enough to tell the truth about what it is. You like pussy."

I attempted to pull the comforter away from her, but she held her grip. "You don't speak for me! I have a fiancé that I love. I did this shit because you wanted me to do it! I did it because you begged me to do it and you wouldn't leave me alone about it! You said that I should at least try a woman before I did a threesome and I did! I didn't want to sneak around behind Quinton's back and I sure as hell ain't gay!"

"Lae, we've been fucking for almost a month!" She said incredulously. "If Quinton was sleeping with another woman for a month, you would kick his ass out. You've been doing it, but it's okay because

you're experimenting. Why are the rules so different for you? In all the time we've been sleeping together, you never complained about where my tongue went and you certainly knew where I wanted yours. Where was this almighty indignation when you were lying to Quinton late at night to be with me? Where was it when you went out of your way to find a different hotel room for us to be in? You didn't just lick me between my legs because you felt like you owed me, Lae. You did it because you enjoyed making another woman climax! You like being with a woman and it's so goddamn hard for you to just say it! You wanted all of this, as much as I did. The only difference is that I'm comfortable telling you what I feel!"

"You don't know shit!"

I walked out. I left the hotel room and didn't turn back.

Once again, I was left without an answer for the problems that surrounded me. There was no question how much I loved Quinton, but I couldn't understand why I needed to be with and around Niya so damn much. Even here in Cleveland, I tried not to think about either of them, but they invaded my every thought.

A knock at my bedroom door brought me back to reality, but as soon as I sat up, the door opened. "Laela, are you ready?" Janette walked into my room unannounced and saw me sitting naked at the edge of my bed.

I grabbed the comforter from the bed and I tried to cover as best I could.

She closed the door behind her. "Sorry, girl!" She put her hand over her eyes. "Is there anything special that you wanted to do?"

I quickly wrapped the towel around myself and tried to smile, but I only managed a stupid grin. "Wherever you go, I'll follow."

"Well, I'm ready when you are, just holler for me. I'll be downstairs."

I nodded. *Why does this shit keep happening to me?*

After Janette having seen me naked, I hurried and threw on some clothes before Tank was next to burst through my door. I'd left Houston because one too many people had seen me naked and here in Cleveland, I'd simply picked up where I'd left off.

My mind and body ached for rest. I took a deep breath, shaking off the impulsive thoughts I had of calling the whole night off. But, I'd come here to get away from my problems. I stood up and went through the clothing my mother had hung up for me in the closet. After rifling through several dozen tops, I finally picked out a pair of brown jeans, a tan turtleneck with a matching sweater. I then put on my brown boots and went downstairs to find Janette.

My parents had already gone to their room for the evening and I found Janette sitting on the couch in my parent's downstairs living room. I was so focused on covering myself before that I hadn't noticed how completely different she looked from earlier in the day. When we'd first met, she'd worn clothes that seemed oversized for her small frame. But as she stood up to see me, I saw that she wore black dress pants, and a matching vest over a short sleeved shirt the cut off just above her belly button. The outfit she wore made her breasts appear slightly larger than mine, and flaunted the muscular contours she had in her arms and flattened stomach.

"What on earth are you wearing? It's like two degrees outside and won't you freeze in that?"

She smiled. "I'm used to the weather." She stood up and was began walking towards the front door before turning around. "And I wanted to apologize again for bursting into your room. I should've knocked, but you know how easy it is to bring hospital etiquette back home. It wasn't my intent to see you naked, but now that we've gotten that out the way, we won't feel awkward if I ever deliver your baby."

"It's okay," I lied. "I should've locked the door. What's done is done."

She put on a leather coat that was as long as she was tall then pulled her keys out of her purse. As we began walking to the car, my father stepped out of his room and called out to me.

"Laela, come here for a sec!"

Janette turned around to come with me, but I suggested that she warm up the car and I walked over to see my father. "Yes daddy?"

"I just wanted to give you this, just in case." He handed me his platinum MasterCard. "If anything goes wrong, just use this. Don't tell your mom." He kissed me on the cheek.

"Thank you!" I loudly whispered. He turned, smirked and walked into his room.

After twenty minutes of random turns and continuous chatting, I decided to ask her where we were going.

"A friend of mine suggested we go to the all male review down at Candie's. Usually it's a women's strip club, but once a week, they bring out Candies' Canes. I thought that since we're two ladies, who happen to like canes, we should go."

"That's not a bad idea. I went to one earlier this year in Houston and there's nothing like some stranger's long, sticky, and glistening candy dancing in our faces to help us relax."

She smiled at me and within a few minutes, we were in downtown Cleveland. We stopped at an ATM, took out some cash and found a parking spot. It didn't take long for us to get into the club and even though it was cold as hell outside, mostly nude and exquisitely defined men were bobbing their dicks all over the room.

Janette was next to me, waving her money like a wild woman and her exuberance was contagious. I soon found myself screaming at the top of my lungs as random men came to the stage and visually seduced us.

"You know, my fiancé Quinton could be good at this if he ever quit his job."

"Your brother wouldn't make the cut here."

I laughed at the expression she gave me after she spoke, but I was surprised at her nonchalant demeanor.

A dancer named Sir Dicks-A-Plenty approached our table and began to dance for me. He wasn't as good as my Adonis in Houston, but he was certainly my favorite here. He was by far the most defined and reminded me a little of Quinton - if Quinton had put on twenty pounds of muscle and shaved himself bald. I looked over at Janette having a good time, but I wasn't too overly concerned about her shoving a wad of money down a strange man's g-string. Knowing Tank, I was sure that he'd done it a few dozen times since he'd been here.

In the midst of all the partying, Janette tapped me on the shoulder, breathless from all her screaming. "I think it's time for me to go! I'm on a stipend and I used up my whole wad on Taj's whole wad. Besides, I think I'm suffering from penis envy."

"Nurse Janette," I asked with a hint of sarcasm, "How do you know when you're suffering from penis envy? Have you had it before? What are the symptoms of PE?"

"The symptoms include wanting to whip one out and play with it. Men can play with theirs all the time and as a woman, I don't have one to pull out and start fiddling with it. I've never done it before, but it looks like it could be so much fun!"

"Well, hopefully you're not out there playing with random men's penises when you get the urge."

"Well, between work and clinicals, it's not like I have too many to choose from. The only guys I see regularly are the sanitation engineers and a few homeless guys. Somehow I don't see myself sticking money in their pants."

She had a sense of humor. I liked her already.

Though I agreed to leave, I was still slightly disappointed. For the first time since I'd been in Cleveland, I'd forgotten about all of my problems. Niya and Quinton were whispers in the wind and I was actually enjoying myself. But I didn't want Janette to feel left out with all of her money gone, so I waved good bye to 'S-DAP', as the DJ had called him, and he returned the favor, without even using his hands.

"Where do we go from here?" I asked, as we exited the club and ran to the car. The wind had picked up and the breeze was much cooler downtown than it was at the house. "Damn, the chill has picked up."

"That's the lake effect. The closer you get to Erie, the worse the chill gets. It's a pain in the ass on winter nights, but that's not going to stop you from going to the Flats. It'll be nice to relax after such lively entertainment."

I nodded in agreement, knowing that I needed a strong drink to curb the anxiety that was returning. The last time I went to a club like this, I allowed Niya to seduce me and the feelings of wanting to be with her were returning. At this point, I didn't just want to kill the thoughts of her; I wanted to completely annihilate them.

"Let's go," I said.

The Flats were less than a five minute drive away from the club. It was a series of bars and nightclubs that sat under a bridge on the Cuyahoga River. Though lively enough for an early Wednesday morning, I didn't care about the people or the atmosphere. All I cared about was getting something stronger than water in my system. We settled on a sports bar and walked in.

"Wow, a sports bar that plays R&B? I guess I'm just so used to country playing." There were several basketball games playing on the large LCD screen TV's, but there were also a few people dancing. The bar was extremely warm so we took off our coats and placed them on the back of our chairs.

Not long after we sat down, a handsome white guy, with dark brown hair and a pretty smile, came over to our table.

"Hello, I'm Matt and I'll be your server. What are you lovely ladies having tonight?"

144

I looked at Janette and read her 'I'll have a Matt-to-go' face and we both laughed like we'd been thinking the same thing. Matt never got the joke, but then again, he wasn't supposed to.

"I'll have a VD."

"Make that two," I added.

"Two VD's coming up," Matt repeated and walked away.

"What the hell is a VD?" I asked. "Well, let me rephrase that. As a nurse, I know what a VD is, but I've never thought about drinking one."

"VD means Virgin Daiquiri. We both ordered an alcohol free drink."

"Alcohol free? I want to change my order." Upset that I hadn't updated my alcohol lingo in a few years, I elbowed Janette in her side. We laughed, but I wasn't about to drink kiddie drinks all night. "Look, this is the *ladies'* night out. It's just you and me. Whatever we do, our men don't have to know about, unless of course we tell them. When Matt comes back, we're drinking Tequilas--the official drink of Houston, TX and everything fun."

When Matt returned, we thanked him for the drinks and then requested a round of Tequila shots and a double of Sex on the Beach.

"You must be a heavy drinker," Janette looked worried.

"Nope, I hardly drink at all. But tonight is a night to let go. I'm out of town, I want to try something new and--" I whipped out my daddy's platinum card, "-- I have one of these!"

Her eyes lit up like a child on Christmas day. "It's so shiny! Can I touch it? Better yet, can I have one?!"

"I'm sorry my sister, you must get your own." We both laughed like it was the funniest thing we'd heard.

"You're right. It's just I can get a little crazy when I drink. I tend to talk too much and sometimes I can't shut up."

"Don't worry about it. If you start to talk too much, I'll just get you a muzzle." She smiled, and we drank our VD's until Matt came back with the good stuff.

He wasn't gone too long when he brought our two glasses of SOTB, four Tequila shot glasses, four lime wedges, and two salt shakers. I had to educate Janette on how to take a Tequila shot, something Teniyah had taught me in college.

"Okay, first you lick a spot between your forefinger and thumb, and then you dash salt on that wet spot. After that you lick the salt up, pour the drink down your throat and suck on the lime, got it?"

"And why do you suck on the lime?"

"Stop asking so many questions! You just do! Got it?"

"I think so." She set everything up just like I'd instructed her. We looked at each other, smiled, and took our shots.

"Wow!" Janette exclaimed. "That's some strong stuff and it burns all the way down." Her face was balled up like a little kid who didn't want to eat their vegetables.

"Are you ready for the second one?" I asked. She nodded and we repeated the process several more times.

After the first three, the world began to tip slowly sideways for me and poor Janette just went into an uncontrollable rant about her life. She kept talking about how someone named Nicole was just a bad friend. I tried to get her to change subjects, but Nicole became the central figure of her conversation. The fourth went down pretty hard for me, causing me to squint and went from burning my throat to burning my stomach as well; even Janette was affected by the extra alcohol, her speech began slurring and she began holding and rubbing my hand.

By the fifth, I could barely hang onto the table and I decided to slow down before I passed out, but Janette's eyelids were getting heavy and instead of ranting, the conversation began to get very interesting.

"You--know--Laela, I--I care for your--your um, brother--but he just--doesn't know--anything--not one thing about--me. You know what--you know what I'm--what I'm saying--Laela. Jeez, you are--you are so--fucking sexy. Has anyone--ever--told you that? If they haven't, they should. I've--dammit, I've wanted to--don't laugh--I wanted to with--you. You're so pretty. Forget about--um--Nicole. She wasn't any good for--me. I don't love her--no--no more."

I began to laugh and though the world was swirling I closed my eyes. "You're too--too--too late," I stuttered out. "I already have--a--um-a girlfriend." I couldn't control my laughing nor did I care to. "You should've--been there. I slept with her last night and it was so--so-nice, but I made her stop. I don't love her, dammit! I can't! I'm-- I'm not gay, dammit!" I shouted, trying less and less to whisper.

"You have a girlfriend?" She began to rub her eyebrows. "I do too! That's crazy! But see," she began while staring at my chin, "I'm not--confused. I like a little pussy--in moderation. I mean, if I drink a little-- a little alcohol every now and then, I'm not an alcoholic. People always gotta give us these labels. I just like--I like to um--to ah--sleep with women--sometimes. I guess you could say that I'm bi--bipolar." She fell out of her chair, laughing hysterically.

While she picked herself up off the floor, I continued with the questioning. "So, you've been with another woman, too? But did Nicole seduce you and then try to blame you for how she felt? Did Nicole ever suggest that you have a relationship behind your fiancé's back when you're supposed to be married in--a few months? Did she ever make you so mad, then made you feel so bad and kiss you so tenderly you're your toes curled up? Did she Janette?"

"You had sex-- with Nicole, too! That bitch! I knew she couldn't be mahoganous!"

I laughed hysterically. "You mean monogamous?"

"Why, did she do that, too?" "You're a little too drunk, Janette. No, I didn't have sex with--with Nicole." I smiled at Janette. We were going through the same things and it felt good that someone else understood me.

She leveled her hands like they were scales and moved them from side to side. "Pussy or dick or dick and pussy. They both balance out nice." She snickered. "Well, I haven't ever eaten pussy. At least not since--the last time!" She started giggling uncontrollably but kept on. "Not since I met--your brother. But before--before I met--him--I was in--in an exclusive--relationship with another woman. I loved her. I-I-really really did. But no more about--um-Nicole! She's a tramp and a whore!" Janette shouted, flinging her arm in the air. "I hate her!"

"You, woman, are drunk. I'm drunk, you're drunk. It's time--time for us to go."

She grabbed my hand. "I'm sorry--Laela. I'm just a little off. The world--it's spinning. I'll drive us home."

"That's a bad idea. Why don't we just sit here for a little while? We can talk until we sober up."

"I'd love to keep talking to you, Lae, but the bar's about to close."

Even though the world through my eyes was on a vertical axis, I could see that the bartender was putting the stools on top of the counter.

"So what are we going to do, Lae? I don't want to leave my car downtown."

I thought about our situations and then I remembered the credit card my father had given to me earlier. "Is there a hotel where we can crash for the night?" She shrugged, but just as she had, Matt had returned to deliver our bill. I asked him the same question I'd asked the clearly drunken Janette.

"Well I don't live too far from here if you guys are looking for some hot white guy in-his-first-ménage type of action."

Janette folded her arms across the table and buried her face while I laughed so loudly that I could see Matt turn a bright red. He was bold, but not even I was that drunk.

147

"You're a very handsome man--Matt," I smiled, trying not to make him feel too badly, "but you couldn't handle either of us--certainly not both of us. And I'm engaged."

"Yeah sure, there's a nice one down Euclid. Would you like me to call you guys a cab?"

"You're such a sweetie. If she wasn't taken," I pointed at the collapsed Janette, "I think she'd really consider your request."

He smiled and disappeared behind wooden double doors. Five minutes later, we were being helped into a taxi that took us to a posh downtown hotel.

When our cab ride ended, I shoved Janette, who had already fallen asleep and helped get her out of the car. She was still half asleep when we walked into the hotel, slumping on me for support even though my legs were about to give out.

We paid the driver and not long after the bellhop helped us up the first set of stairs we were in a dual occupancy on the first floor. Janette had a little time to let the alcohol work its way through her system and as she became a little more alert of her surroundings, she was finally able to stand using me as her crutch.

We made it to the room without falling on the hotel floor, but once we were inside we cut on the lights and the both of us collapsed onto our beds.

"The light's too bright," Janette loudly whispered.

I wanted to move, but with my head still swimming, I couldn't. Since Janette's bed was closer to the light switch, I figured it'd be easier for her to cut it off than it would be for me.

"Hey, Janette, are you still alive?"

"I'm sick. My tummy hurts."

"Damn, you shouldn't have drunk all that liquor without some food."

"Hot wings are food."

"You mean the hot wings from the strip club? You trust wings made and served by naked men?"

"You don't?"

Clearly, that was enough of that line of questioning. "So can you turn off the light?"

She groaned for several seconds, attempting to sit up long enough to cut the light off. "I can't do it on my own. I need your help."

I reached over, grabbed the ice bucket off the nightstand and threw it on her bed. "There you go, just in case you feel the need."

"Why don't you do it? You're the one who got me drunk with the 'official drink of Texas'. If anyone should cut off the light, it's you."

I slowly picked myself off from the bed and dragged myself towards the light switch. As I stumbled past her bed, the world began to spin a great deal faster than it was supposed to. As I looked for something to grab hold of, I thought of Janette's neck, but she was right. I hated that she was right. I also hated that I didn't know whether to curse Janette from making me cut off the light or myself for feeling guilty enough to do it. Once the light was out and my migraine began to subside, I knew I wouldn't be able to make the return trip to my bed and fell on Janette's.

"Laela, are you okay?"

"I will be when the room stops spinning. If I throw up, at least it'll be on your bed." I rolled over and suddenly I found myself face to face with her. We were so close that I could feel her breath on my lips and see that her eyes were closed. Even in the dimness of the room, I could see her smiling at me.

"That's okay. If you need me, I'll be there to pull back your hair." This time it was my turn to smile. "You'd do that for me?"

"You're my hero. You're everything I want to be: professional, fun to be around, and-- sexy as hell."

For the first time in a while, I blushed. "Thank you, Janette."

"I just--tell the truth."

I watched as her lips began to move towards me, yet I did nothing to halt her advance. When our lips touched, an intense bolt of lust shot down my spine and suddenly I found myself returning her kiss with the same fervor I'd shared with only one other woman.

CHAPTER 12

Quinton

<u>February 3rd (Friday)</u>

"So she just up and left without any forewarning? Wow, dawg, you know she might do this when y'all are married. As soon as she gets upset, she's flying back home to see her folks."

"She didn't seem all that upset when she left. Well, I can't say that, but I know for a fact that she wasn't mad at me. She was going on about some stuff going down at work. She seemed more frustrated than anything."

It'd just hit noon when Andre called. Ordinarily I'd be out delivering with CJ, but luckily I'd stayed in the office to catch up on the overwhelming amount of paperwork. Lae left on Sunday and I hadn't spoken with another soul outside of work since she left. I ignored several calls I received earlier, but because all the paperwork was becoming monotonous, Dre called me at the perfect time.

"The bottom line is that she left you here--alone. The way I see it, she's practically begging you to get up in some new booty." Ever since I'd told him Laela left, it was only a matter of time before I was going to hear it.

"Dre, you need to cut that shit out. Lae is about to be my wife and the last thing I need is my best man talking about new ass all the time."

"Hey, until you jump the broom, I can't let it go. I mean just imagine it. Lae will be the last person you will ever bang. Let me re-emphasize that. Laela Booker will be the *last* person you will ever bang.

That whole threesome idea that you guys are throwing around, it'll never happen before you guys get married this summer."

"Oh thou, who has slept with the spawn of Hell, how did I know you'd say that?"

"You just can't let that shit go, huh?"

"I tried."

"I think you're still hung up on the whole Leslie thing because you want to screw her one last time. If she hadn't done you so badly, you'd give her one last ride before the end came."

"You're joking, right? I spent three years trying to stay away from her and now that I've seen her, I'm supposed to drop everything for her? You couldn't be more wrong."

"Well if you're going to hound me for the rest of our lives about this shit, then at least the coochie was good. I'd probably feel bad if it was shitty, but it wasn't."

"You're a piece of work, you know that? I don't think I've ever met a bigger asshole."

"Quinton, you're a lost cause. The only reason why you hate me so much is because deep down, you wish you could be like me. Right now, you're going through pussy withdrawal and you're agitated-- easily upset. What's wrong with going out there and getting a hand job? Maybe I can convince my neighbor, Jennifer, to give you a titty-fuck? Whatever your hidden fetish is, get it out of your system so that you won't be so damn uptight."

"And now this conversation is over." I hung up on Dre before he had a chance to say another word.

I was about to get back to work when the blinking red light on the phone reminded me that someone had called earlier.

"Good afternoon, Quinton. Sorry, we haven't spoken in a while, but I've been so busy holding things together over here. I'd love to hear how things are going over there and especially how Carmen's treating you. How about we meet up for lunch? Call me."

At the first syllable I knew who'd left the message. It was Cheyenne. As I listened to it, I felt my heart pounding in my chest, but when I looked at the clock, I almost panicked. It was already after noon and I hadn't called.

I grabbed my cell phone from out of my desk and quickly dialed her number.

She picked up on the first ring. "Hello, Cheyenne?"

"Hello, Quinton. It's nice to finally hear from you."

151

As she spoke my name, I immediately noticed my growing arousal and the lies I'd just rehearsed became moot as the truth began to fumble out of my mouth. "I'm so sorry. I ignored your call even though I was here and I would love the chance to -- eat you-- eat with you."

She laughed. "Slow your roll, Quinton. I know what you mean, but I think I heard a couple of Freudian slips in there. I'd love to eat--I mean go out to eat with you too and I don't have a problem fitting in around your schedule."

I was so embarrassed that I actually felt my body begin to warm. I took in a deep breath and started over. "I, Quinton James, am not busy after work. If you aren't busy, then maybe we could grab an early dinner?"

"That's fine, but I hope Mrs. Quinton won't be mad at me for eating dinner with you."

"Somehow I doubt that. *Miss* Quinton has been out of town this week."

"I understand. Well then, I'll see you after work."

"So with your wife-to-be gone, are you lonely?"

We'd been at the restaurant for about ten minutes and spent most of it talking. She looked as beautiful as the first time I'd seen her, choosing this time to wear a loose turtleneck sweater and blue jeans. To complement her ensemble, she wore the same perfume that I loved the first time we'd met. Because I came straight from work and had to fight through Houston rush hour traffic, I didn't have the time to change. In my work clothes, I felt overdressed and subconsciously believed I smelled like a garage, but I didn't sense that she noticed as she seemed to hang onto my every word. It'd been a while since I'd gotten this kind of attention from Lae and it felt good.

"I guess. I have so much work to do to keep me busy, but when I get home it's a lot quieter than it usually is. For now, it's just me and the TV."

"I understand what you mean. Believe me when I tell you I know all about being alone. I've been by myself for almost fifteen years now. My husband hasn't really been around after my kids hit their teenage years. The more he worked, the more I grew used to the idea that my husband and I had become strangers living in the same house. I used to think that the only reason we stayed together was for the kids, but now they're grown, he's always gone and I still act like an old maid--always stuck in the house with nothing or no one to do."

"So what do you do for fun?" I asked, not exactly knowing how a woman as attractive as her could be neglected the way she'd claimed.

"I have dinner with handsome, random strangers."

I smiled. "So this is something you do regularly?"

"The start of a trend."

I liked her wit. "Well then I'm sure there isn't a shortage of men knocking down your door."

"Even if that were true, I don't have time to deal with boys posing as men. I like men who are confident, secure and who are able to articulate their thoughts with a great deal of intelligence. Those are the traits I find most desirable."

"I'm not so-- *discerning.*"

"I see you're one of those men who like a big butt and a smile."

"Is that so wrong?" *Oh God, I'm beginning to sound like Dre.*

"It eventually wears thin. I thought you had more substance than that. Perhaps I was wrong about you. Maybe the accidental call I received was more in line with what you're about than I wanted to believe."

"I'm a simple man who likes simple pleasures. If she can offer more, I welcome that, but I will never be the type of man who bypasses a woman simply because she doesn't fit perfectly inside of an impossible little box."

"Well said." She smiled and once again I could hear my heartbeat.

"Indeed, I was the one who said it." My nerves were calming and the swagger was returning. It's been years since I've been out with another woman and I was a little hesitant. Luckily, her characterization of me brought about my pride.

"Touché, Mr. James."

For the rest of dinner, we spent our time talking about our lives, jobs and even our fantasies. I looked at my watch periodically to see what time it was, but time was moving so swiftly that I knew our night would inevitably end. In the few hours that we'd spent together, I finally felt like someone understood me and could relate to the loneliness I was feeling. I didn't want to stop talking and laughing with her. I didn't want her to leave.

When the busboy returned to our table for the third time in ten minutes, she stood up and grabbed her handbag from the table. "So, Quinton, is there anything else you wanted to do tonight?"

I could almost hear Pedro screaming from inside my pants, but I couldn't listen to him anymore than I would listen to Dre. I'd never wanted another woman as badly as I wanted Cheyenne, but I wouldn't give in to my urges. "I didn't have anything planned. Since no one's at home, I just figured I'd watch a movie and call it a night."

"That sounds like a great idea. I'd like to watch that movie with you, if you don't mind."

Aren't you tired of being lonely? It's just a movie.

"I don't mind at all."

As she followed me to the apartment that Laela and I shared, all I could focus on was not doing the one thing I desperately wanted to do with her. I tried to bury the most salacious thoughts, but the one that continued to haunt me was the belief that I would have brought Cheyenne to my home--even if Lae wasn't out of town with her parents.

When I finally opened the front door and walked in, she quickly rushed past me and into the opaque apartment.

"It's darker than I thought it'd be. Which way do I go to use the powder room?" she asked.

Damn. I hadn't cleaned a thing since Lae's been gone. I turned on the lights, revealing my unkempt bachelor pad. Between the open pizza boxes, condiment filled wrappers, empty soda containers and loose work clothing; I didn't even know where to begin.

Sensing my embarrassment, she quickly took the lead and began picking up the clutter. "I know how it is to miss a woman's touch. Why don't you just grab your clothes and I'll take care of the rest."

While she picked up the garbage I'd neglected for the week, I cursed my laziness and placed the clothes in the hamper in my bedroom. As soon as I'd finished pushing the clothes as low as they could possibly go, I looked up and saw her standing in the doorway.

"So this is the place where the magic happens?" she asked smiling, taunting me with her curious glare.

"It's probably one of the least used places in the house."

"That's such a shame. How can that even be when your bed looks so comfortable?" She walked over to the bed, sat down and fell back with her arms spread outward. "And it smells so nice, like perfume. I think I've smelled this fragrance before, too. It smells like someone with some taste has been here recently."

I'd forgotten that I sprayed one of Lae's shirts with her perfume earlier this morning, but with Cheyenne here, I hadn't smelled a thing.

"Sometimes I spray her perfume when I feel like I'm alone. It helps to remind me of her."

Who the hell is 'her'? Why aren't you saying Lae's name, Quinton? Is it because you don't want to remind yourself that you are engaged?

"So, you are a romantic," she whispered.

Clearly, it was time to change the subject. "So, what kind of movies do you like to watch?" I turned towards the living room, but Cheyenne called me back.

"Quinton, why don't you lay next to me?"

The thoughts I'd had in the car returned and even though every rational thought in my head screamed for me to run, I slowly walked towards Cheyenne. I sat next to her while my stomach felt like it was tying itself into a knot, but I remained as cool as I possibly could.

She rose from the bed and sat on her knees behind me. She began to unbutton my shirt, rubbing one hand across my chest while the other worked its way up after releasing each button. After the top button was opened, she threw my shirt on the floor and began to kiss me, starting at my right shoulder and carefully moving to my left.

"It's okay, baby, you can breathe."

I wanted to breathe, but I was afraid that if I had, she'd stop. I looked away from her, trying to compose myself, but my erection and my dirty thoughts had already betrayed me:

You're such a fucking coward. Stop acting like a goddamn virgin and screw her goddamn brains out! She wants it, you want it, and Lae isn't here-- to ignore you.

I didn't want to believe what I'd told myself, but it was true. No matter how much I wanted to disguise it, the most beautiful woman I'd ever met was with me, running her tongue down my spine, while my fiancée was everywhere but here.

As she tenderly kissed the nape of my neck, I turned to Cheyenne and pressed my lips to hers, tasting her tongue and finally succumbing to every fantasy I'd had about her.

With my hands exploring her body, she was as perfect as I'd imagined she'd be. From the softness of her lips, to the tenderness of her kisses, the passion between us was unmistakable. I'd never in my life felt such lust for another human being and even though she was here with me, I wanted more.

I leaned on top of her, pushing her onto the bed and ran my hands under her sweater. I eased past her flat stomach and instinctively guided my way up her stomach towards her breasts. When I reached them, I ran my hands along the border, teased the tips of her nipples and with a twist of my fingers, unsnapped her bra, tossing it to the side. Soft moans escaped from her mouth as I slowly lifted her sweater and took each nipple into my mouth.

"Quinton--," she managed to say, "I want you in the shower."

I took her legs and wrapped them around my waist. "Hold on tight."

She did as she was told and I lifted the both of us from my bed. Still kissing, I walked us into the bathroom and turned on the shower. Once I sat her on the marble counter, she released her legs from around my hips and we quickly began to tear away at each other's pants.

Hastily kicking our pants to the side, we were left in only my blue boxers and her purple satin panties. It took me a few seconds to absorb exactly how beautiful she really was. Her breasts were as taut as those of someone half her age and though I searched for any sign of imperfection, I couldn't find one. Without waiting for me to pick her up, she jumped up and again wrapped her legs around my waist, sliding herself onto my manhood as I carried the both of us into the shower.

I pinned her against the wall and we kissed like two people starved of affection. Every time she ran her tongue along my neck, a large chunk of all of the pent up animosity I had towards Lae seemed to slip away.

As the hot water ran down my back, I eased her off of me and released her from my grasp. I lifted up her right leg, pressed her against the back wall of the shower and entered her. She dug her fingers into my shoulders and winced until I was completely inside of her.

Our music was perfect. With every withdrawal, she pushed me back in, begging me to return. I adored the way she felt on me and loved even more the way I felt inside of her. I wanted to feel bad for what we were doing, but I couldn't think of a time when Lae had ever felt this good.

With her free leg stabilizing her, I grabbed her hips and pressed her further down onto me.

"Shit, Quinton."

It's was the first time I'd heard her curse and it gave me more incentive not to stop. I drew closer to her, grabbed her ass with both hands and pulled her towards me and I pushed deeper inside of her.

"Oh--oh--oh." With each lunge into her, she released another vowel.

As steam crept up the bathroom walls, she wrapped her hands around my neck and pulled me in for a kiss. But instead of kissing me, she placed her lips on top of mine, heavily exhaled, and screamed into my mouth.

Feeling her beginning to collapse, I took her free leg and wrapped it around my waist. To steady herself, she held onto the shower rod and our symphony played on.

Ordinarily, I could tell when a woman climaxed, but whether Cheyenne had one or was fighting me, I didn't know. All I knew was that my resolve was weakening and I was pleasantly surprised that I'd lasted this long with her. Whether she had read my eyes or my thoughts, she slowly pulled me out of her, walked around me so that the stream of water now ran along her flawless frame and bent halfway over. As she guided me inside of her, the ass I'd daydreamed about from the first day we'd met was now mine to control.

Using the wall under the showerhead for better balance, she spread her legs as far as they could go. With so much of her ass facing me, I closed my eyes and tried to imagine something other than a beautiful woman acquiescing. I started off slowly, but with her warmth engulfing me and the softness of her behind brushing against my skin made me want to open my eyes.

With her pushing herself onto me as I forced myself into her; she was daring me. With our bodies now clapping against one another and the water running from her back onto my manhood, I knew that I couldn't hold back any longer.

"Shit, I'm about to--."

"Cum inside of me, daddy."

My perfect woman.

With more force than I'd ever had, I held onto both sides of Cheyenne and climaxed. As I pulled out of her, stunned and dazed, she turned around. Without any warning she placed my limp member inside of her mouth and removed anything that was left.

My perfect woman.

When I was a bachelor, I usually didn't allow women to spend the night. Now that I was engaged to be married, it was an even worse idea, but that didn't stop me from allowing Cheyenne to share my bed.

I felt remorseful, but I knew it was more out of obligation than sincerity and that's what scared me. I loved Lae, but if Cheyenne could do this to me, I knew it wasn't long before I'd get myself in more trouble. But I didn't want to think about the future--at least for now.

I just wanted to spend the night with *my perfect woman.*

<u>February 4th (Saturday)</u>

When I awoke, the apartment was as silent as it had ever been and when I reached over to wake Cheyenne, I saw the room was with one less occupant. Still naked, I searched through the apartment to find her, but I knew she'd already gone. She had a family and what we had was simply an affair-- nothing more.

"I'll never sleep with a married woman. Marriage is sacred to me and I would never do something like that".

In a nutshell, that's what I told Dre and I found myself shitting on the virtue I believed in most. I thought about confessing what I'd done, but who was around? Sure, I could tell Dre what had happened and listen to him praise me for my indiscretion, but I didn't feel much like celebrating. If I called Cheyenne, I knew we'd just end up re-living last night. It wasn't a terrible idea and the more I thought about it, the less self-destructive it sounded. The problem was that I'd probably end up asking her to return here tonight and Lae would be coming home to me tomorrow. Besides, I wasn't exactly sure what I'd say to the woman who'd just blown away every other lover I'd ever had-- including Leslie.

With Lae's plane landing tomorrow afternoon, I had plenty of time to clean up and get my head straight. Other than cleaning, I didn't have a single thing planned for today, but I needed to get out of the house.

After my shower, I thought about Simone and Mike. Since Mike was going through the same struggle, I figured that perhaps he could provide some perspective. I dialed their number, but I didn't feel like talking to him over the phone. I needed to get out and the drive over to his house would do me some good.

I threw on some jeans and a long sleeved t-shirt, jumped into my gray Camry and rode West Airport down all the way onto the on ramp for 59 North. After about twenty minutes on 59, I followed 610 South to 610 East and immediately before the signs directing cars towards Hobby Airport appeared, I exited.

Traffic was light for a Saturday morning, but it gave me a chance to think. I knew I couldn't ever come clean to Lae, but what if Cheyenne wanted to do something else? Could I reject her? Would I even want to?

158

I pulled up to their duplex forty minutes after I'd left the house, but Mike's brick colored Maxima was gone. I got out of the car and knocked on the front door just in case it was in the shop.

The chains and locks on the door rattled and Simone poked her head through the door. "Hey, Quinton, long time no see!" She gave me a half smile, but I knew something was wrong. Ordinarily she was a pretty girl, but today she looked completely worn out. The black rings forming under her eyes made her look tired, and her small frame appeared a great deal more withered since the last time I'd seen her.

I kissed her on her eyebrow. "Are you okay? You look like you haven't eaten in days."

"I'm okay, just so, so tired. I've been doing a lot with the baby and keeping the house clean. I really don't have time for anything else anymore. I work and then I come home to do more work. You know how it is. Besides, Mike's been--um--busy too."

"Is that why we haven't heard from you since New Years? It's like you guys have fallen off the face of the planet. Is something wrong?"

"No, nothing's wrong." She tried to smile, but I could see it was strained. "If you're looking for Mike, he's not here. He went to help someone with their car. You know how he loves to tinker with them."

I looked over her Olds which was falling apart. He likes to tinker alright. I returned my attention to her face, which appeared to grow even more miserable since I'd looked away. "Well, alright then Monie, tell Mike I stopped by."

She grabbed my arm and pulled me into the house. Her exaggerated front began falling to pieces as she hugged me and cried on my shoulder. I held her and let her cry before helping her back up the stairs to her apartment.

I closed the door and directed her towards the couch where she collapsed. "I'm so sorry for breaking down like this. I just don't know how much more I can take, Quinton. I don't know how much longer I can do this!"

"Do what?" I knew exactly what she was talking about but, as a man and one of Mike's friends, it was my responsibility to play dumb so that she wouldn't suspect that I knew anything.

"Quinton, I admire your loyalty, but I already know about Starr. I know that he's probably with her right now. I know that he's slept with her--on several occasions." She sobbed. "I even know that he probably doesn't really love me and the only reason he even comes home is to see MJ."

I sat down on the couch next to her and I told her everything I knew. I told her that I'd known about Mike and Starr for about a month, but since he hadn't said anything recently, I thought it was over. I also told her about what I told him about family being his priority. I wanted to stop talking, but Simone seemed to hang onto every word that came out of my mouth.

"I'm sorry I didn't tell you, but he asked me not to. It's like Lae confiding something in you and asking you not to tell me. I wanted to tell you, but I couldn't. It wasn't anything against you. He told me that it was a one-time thing and it wasn't going to happen anymore. I mean he's my boy and I believed him. I'm sorry, Simone. I really am."

"I know, Quinton. I know how honorable of a person you are and I was hoping that you'd rub off on him somehow. I know Mike is a good man, very deep down, but I honestly don't know where we went wrong." She leaned on my shoulder and I allowed her to weep. "I'm sorry, Quinton, but I'm glad you are here. I thought I was going to go crazy. I thought about calling Lae for the last week, but I didn't want feel like hearing her say 'I toldja so'. Can you please just sit here with me for a while?" I nodded. She wiped the tears from her face and as soon as she finally calmed down, as if on cue, the baby began to cry.

"I think you should go grab MJ." When she walked away, I began to feel awful as I thought about her saying how honorable I was. Coming clean on Mike was one thing, he'd already told her most of it, but because he'd told her first, I didn't think of it as confessing is secret, it was more like re-affirming.

When she returned, she was bouncing MJ on her right arm as he studied my face.

"I don't think he recognizes me," I told Simone as MJ continued staring at me.

"Say hello to your God-daddy, MJ. Say 'hi, God-daddy'." She waved his hand at me and I waved back. "Quinton, can you hold him while I fix him a bottle?"

I held my arms out and she placed him on my lap, then she turned back around and went into the kitchen. I blew on MJ's belly and tickled his sides causing him to giggle uncontrollably. "Simone, how old is he now?"

"He's seven months but he'll be eight later this month," she hollered back.

"Oh, you're the big seven," I said to MJ, still tickling him as I spoke. When Simone returned from the kitchen, I didn't see a bottle in her hand. "Where's the bottle?"

"I can't find any formula. It looks like we're all out." She sat on the couch next to me and pulled up her t-shirt and bra and exposed her right breast before placing it in MJ's mouth.

"Whoa! Put that thing away!" I shouted. "You could've given me at least some warning!"

"You act like you've never seen a nipple before. Grow up, Quinton; it's a part of life."

"Yeah, just not the part of life I'm ready to deal with now. Do you see me with any kids? I don't even want to think about children right now! Can you imagine what people will think if they find out I saw your tits?"

"You only saw one, Quinton. You worry too much about what people will think of you. Who cares what they'll say. It's natural. Besides, why would you tell anyone? If you want to get used to it, I've got another one if you're hungry," she mused.

"No thanks, I prefer my milk homogenized and from a multi-tittied cow."

"So you'll suck on a cow's nipples before you'll suck on a mother's?"

"Do they sell women's breast milk at the supermarket now? No thanks, I'll pass."

"Well, then, can you do me a favor? Can you take me to the store so that I can pick up some formula and some other things for the baby?"
"No problem, just as long as you keep those things out of my view." I said, pointing at her exposed breast.

She laughed and the withered look on her face seemed to let up for only a brief moment. "It's hard since they seem have a mind of their own, but I'll see what I can do."

Whose body didn't have a mind of its own these days?

After Simone washed her face and got the baby ready, I went down to my car to clean it up. She took the car seat out of her Olds and put it into my Altima. Since the store was only right down the street, it was a shorter drive than I'd expected.

We shopped for ten minutes, making sure the baby had everything he'd need. By the time we'd gotten to the register; I'd volunteered to pay for everything. The cashier, a young black girl, looked at MJ, then Simone, and finally me before letting us know how cute the baby was and how MJ looked just like me. I smiled and as much as I wanted to let her know MJ wasn't mine, the happy look on Simone's face kept me quiet.

I grabbed the bags with the baby's groceries and took them out to the car. On the way to the parking lot, Simone and I laughed about the cashier and her lousy powers of perception.

We made it back to the house a few minutes that. Immediately, Simone took MJ's car seat back to her Olds, while I grabbed MJ and the groceries and headed upstairs through the unlocked front door.

I made it to the kitchen before my arms gave out and I dropped the baby's stuff all over the floor. I heard Simone trudging up the stairs behind me and handed MJ to her when she reached the top.

She took him from me and kissed me on the cheek.

"What was that for?" I asked.

"It was because you're a good friend. Thank you." She walked past me and sat down on the couch. I closed the outside door and sat next to her with the baby in between us.

"You're welcome." I said, still a little confused.

"So how's Lae? I haven't called in a while, but neither has she."

"She went home to be with her parents. She's homesick, but in a warped way. She went up north to be with her family, even though it's nice and warm down here--go figure."

"Yeah, that's your fiancée: stranger than strange. How are you guys doing? She didn't leave to get away from you, did she?"

"Probably, but that's just my way of thinking. Since we spent the night in the hotel, I've hardly seen her. We haven't gone anywhere, we haven't done anything and I honestly don't think that there's been more than two nights in a row that we've spent together."

"Do you think she's cheating on you?"

I'd thought about it, but I always dismissed it as me being paranoid. Hearing it from Simone made it sound like an actual possibility. I briefly thought back to last night and what I'd done. "I don't think so. She spends so much time with Niya that I doubt she'd have time for it. I know Niya's ass is way out there, but they're just girls being girls."

"I'm beginning to think that the Raven has replaced me entirely. I thought it was just me getting the shaft, but now that I know it's not just me, I feel a little better."

"I appreciate the concern," I said.

"Maybe you need to get out more and be a little less dependent on your woman. While she's gone, you should have some fun for yourself."

If only you knew.

"But know this," she continued, "she's about to be married and even though we're not supposed to fear marriage, our friends feel like they're going to lose us, too. It's all part of being us. There are still times when we are scared that we have to lose a part of our identity to be happy. You should try being a black woman sometimes."

"And on that note, I'll be leaving." I stood up from the couch and began walking towards the door when Simone called my name.

"I just wanted to thank you for everything you did today. If you ever need anything from me, no matter what it is, just ask."

I wasn't sure if I was just being hypersensitive, but it almost sounded as if Simone were being suggestive. Perhaps I was letting what Dre said get into my head-- especially after last night.

I just nodded and left the apartment.

I made it back to the house at six o'clock after having visited Simone, then BJ, and finally Marcus. All BJ and I did was play each other in Madden while his girl complained about the amount of time grown men can spend playing games instead of taking care of things around the house. Marcus's apartment had a lot less drama, but also a lot less room with his three hundred and five pound chubby buddy visiting from out of state, so I stayed for dinner.

The way his hefty friend cooked, I could definitely see why she was as thick as she was. The food was absolutely amazing, a complete contrast to Lae's futile attempts at cooking. Even though she made enough lasagna for a small army, I only took a small plate with me when I left.

I arrived home to an apartment exactly as I had left it, cluttered and quiet. I put down the paper plate and began picking up where Cheyenne left off. I threw all the trash into a giant garbage bag, removed all of my work clothes from the floor and I washed all the sheets on my bed from last night-- twice.

By the time I finished restoring the apartment to its pre- cheating form, the sun was beginning to set and I was ready to sit down and relax. Usually I played music to pass the time, but I was so preoccupied by what had happened last night that I hadn't noticed how quiet the apartment was until I'd finished.

Bored out of my skull, I turned on the flat-screen in the living room and called Dre. As I listened to his phone ring, I didn't know what I was going to say to him or how I'd confess, but I needed someone to talk

163

to--someone to tell. When his voicemail answered, I simply hung up and laughed. It figured that the one time I called to tell him I'd done something he'd encouraged, he wouldn't answer.

I was ready to toss the phone to the other side of the sofa when a name from my address book caught my attention: Anelle.

Do you think it's a good idea after last night?

"It's just talking and it beats the hell out of doing nothing," I said aloud.

It weighed on my mind for several minutes before I picked up the phone and called her.

"Hello?" She sounded exactly as I remembered her.

"Hello, may I speak to uh, Anelle?"

"This is she. May I ask whose calling?" So she hadn't remembered me. I was almost glad that she hadn't. It proved that Dre's theory wrong. Every woman that I met didn't always remember me.

"It's nobody." I sighed. "Take care."

I was ready to hang up before she asked, "Is this Quinton?"

Surprised that she'd remembered me and a little upset that Dre had proven me wrong, I replied. "Yes, this is Quinton. I'm surprised you remember, but I appreciate that you did." I was flirting with her, and I liked the feeling it brought.

"Of course I remember you, Quinton. We met at The Spot. We danced to a couple of songs, you didn't grope me, I gave you my number and here we are."

"You must have a photographic memory."

"Well that and I can't forget a sexy voice like yours--not even if I tried. Besides, you were good people. I didn't think you were going to call."

The truth was that I hadn't planned on calling. I wanted her to be just a memory of faces past, but without anyone here, I didn't feel like being alone. Between Lae, Dre and Cheyenne, no one seemed to know how to pick up a phone.

So here I was, talking to a stranger who knew me by voice.

"I didn't think I was going to call either, but you were honest and I liked that." I sighed into the phone. "It's been a long week and right now I don't feel like being alone. I'm glad you picked up."

"See, you're making a brown skinned girl blush. Sure, you can't really see it, but at least you know I'm doing it. Be careful though, Quinton, too much and I might like it."

"Is there anything you don't like?"

"I'll let you know if it happens. If you're so alone, where's the little lady?"

"She's out of town. Actually she's been gone the whole week."

"And you're just now calling? Where have you been? I know we all have our jobs, but I've always been here. You could have called earlier. We could've been getting to know each other. One thing though, I can't do anything for you if you're horny. I play second fiddle to no one. I mean, you're cute and all, but I can't just let anyone get some booty."

"You don't have to worry about me. I'm on a booty-free diet."

"That's too bad. Would you be persuaded if I told you that my ass comes with a shake and a smile?"

"Yeah, I already noticed that. I don't mind the shake, but I'll have to pass on the ass."

"Damn, too bad!" She began laughing. "Just don't take me too seriously, Mr. Quinton, I like to joke. If there's one thing you'll learn about me, it's that I like to be a kidder."

I smiled. Being on the phone with her was a lot like Lae when we first began dating. She was fun to talk to and we laughed out loud several times. We connected like old friends who hadn't spoken in years and I wished that I had called her earlier in the week.

We'd been on the phone for a couple of hours before we realized how late it was. "I hope I didn't hold up any plans you had tonight," I said.

"Well, the truth is it's just me and Mr. TV. I don't know what happened to Saturday night line-ups, but this crap on the television is pretty awful. What happened to the quality Saturday shows?"

"They left with the nineties. All these TV companies now have movie companies and they force you to go watch a movie by putting on crappy programming."

"That makes a lot of sense. So why don't we give in to the subliminal messaging? Why don't we take in a movie? You're not doing anything and I'm not either. Swing by and take me to a midnight show. To sweeten the deal, I'll pay."

"That sounds good, but after everything you told me tonight, how can I trust you to behave?"

"Scouts honor?"

"Were you even a scout?"

"Hell no."

"That's not reassuring."

"Quinton, I don't bite and even though I'm single, I can handle your all-consuming attraction towards me. All I was suggesting was that

165

we get out of the house, talk dirty to each other, and maybe tip a cow or two. Then I'll seduce you, and after you bend to my whims, I'll sex you and throw you out for premature ejaculation. Since you'll inevitably fall in love with me, I'll have to get my play-boyfriend to beat you up so that you stop calling me. The end."

"That's pretty elaborate, but why am I bending to your whims?"

"All men inevitably bend to the will of women. What is your woman teaching you? We're going to have to take Men's Independence Studies off of your curriculum."

"Still, I don't see myself bending to anyone's whims."

"Well Sir, pick me up in twenty minutes and don't be late. The movie theatre is a fifteen minute drive and if you're late, we'll miss it. I stay at Bellaire and Highway 6, in Sugar Land."

She was right down the street from me. That figured. "Really? Well I'm not that far from you, but I don't think that a late movie is such a good idea."

Ignoring what I said about the bad idea, she continued making plans. "Well, then there's no reason you should be late. I look forward to seeing you in twenty minutes."

"You don't give people a chance to say no, do you?"

By the time I left my apartment and walked to my car, my twenty minute window had almost passed. But with her living only five minutes away, I wasn't about to rush. She may have gotten me out, but I wasn't about to "bend to her will".

On a cool and windy night like tonight, I was glad that I wore my long-sleeved shirt with jeans. I threw on my black leather jacket when I walked out of the apartment, but I brought an extra one and laid it on my back seat. I always had the misfortune of meeting women who were notorious for leaving behind jackets and other pieces of necessary clothing. I liked Anelle, but I'd be damned if I froze my ass off for chivalry.

I called her on my cell phone when I left my apartment and I still had her on the phone when I pulled in front of her apartment complex.

"I'm outside your building. Are you ready yet?"

"I told you to pick me up in *twenty* minutes. It's only been eighteen! You're getting here early just messes up my procrastination."

"I don't do CP time. Are you ready?"

"Yeah--well, almost. I'm leaving the door open for you, apartment 107. Just make sure that you come to the right apartment. I'd hate to have to explain to the police why you were shot thirty times."

"You instill me with such confidence."

"Yeah, and I'd still leave nice flowers on your casket, too."

She didn't live in a gated community, but it was still well taken care of. The sidewalk was clean, the grass was cut recently and free of litter, and the willow trees that stood next to the buildings had some of their lower braches removed.

As I walked through Anelle's complex, I could barely see the numbers on the doors, instead relying on the numbers on the side of the building to help guide me.

All of the buildings were two stories and her apartment was the first one to the right in an 'L' shaped building, almost hidden by one of the willow trees. Her door had a wreath on it, but the 107 was still visible through it. I walked up to the door and was about to knock when I saw the mat in front of her door read *James Gang*.

She opened the door before I had a chance to knock and welcomed me in. She had on jeans and a t-shirt, but she still looked the same as she had when I first saw her. She smiled with her grey eyes that were as intriguing as the first time we'd met.

"So are you gonna stand in the doorway or will you come in?" she asked.

"You know vampires have to be invited in."

"If that were true, you would've already tried to seduce me. Vampires are good for that; salutations, seductions, and exsanguinations. Speaking of which, if you want something to drink, grab a juice from the fridge." She disappeared into the back and I was left alone in the living room to admire her girlish decorations.

The whole house smelled like vanilla and almost everywhere I looked, there were plants and pictures in fluorescent colored frames. I sat down on her tan colored couch, and grabbed a Jet magazine off of her coffee table. I was just getting comfortable, when she appeared behind me.

"Looking for the Jet beauty?"

"Of course not, I read it for the articles."

"I take it that you mean the articles with the tits showing, right?" She peeked over my shoulder and found that I was actually reading the articles. She raised her eyebrow and smirked. "Are you ready?" I looked her over and noticed that she had changed from jeans and a t-shirt to a black, spaghetti strapped cocktail dress with black heels that helped accentuate her legs and her backside. I tried grasping for words when her grandfather clock began chiming. "Well, it's time for us to go."

While we walked to the car, I finally choked out what I wanted to say. "You look very--very nice, but aren't you a bit overdressed? I mean all I have on is jeans and a shirt."

"Like I said, I don't get a chance to go out that often, so when I do, I wear the new stuff. I ordered this for myself. It was a Christmas gift, but this is the first time I've gotten to wear it."

"It looks really, really nice."

"I bought it online. Yeah, I found this nice little store on eBay. I even liked the name. It was pretty catchy; Sinofmen."

"You bought a half-a-dress from a place called Sinofmen?" I laughed out. "It's amazing what people will do these days to grab your attention."

Once we arrived at the car, I opened her door as she continued on about the selection at her new favorite online store. I didn't particularly care, but as revealing as the dress was, I was glad I brought an extra jacket.

We bought the tickets and slipped into the theatre with a bucket full of popcorn and with the previews glaring above our heads. I looked around to see that there weren't many people sitting watching the movie. We climbed up the stairs to the last row and sat down in the middle, right under the projector.

"Thanks for the extra jacket. The movie theatre is freezing!" she whispered.

"I always come prepared." I whispered back. In truth, the temptation to touch her was a lot less great when she was covered up. She wrapped the jacket around her a little tighter and laid her head on my shoulder. I looked her over once again and shook my head.

Damn, she even smells good.

Hey, Quinton, what's your last name?"

"James. Quinton James."

"It's a small world. My last name is James!" She began laughing and I smiled at her. "I knew there was some sort of a connection between us."

"As long as it's not the long lost family kind of connection, I'm cool."

"Why should you mind if we're family? We haven't done anything worth regretting." She didn't look at me, but the way she ended her sentence, I knew that she'd held off on adding the 'yet'. She took a handful of popcorn out of the bucket she held between her legs, while her head never moved from my shoulder. "You don't mind, do you?"

"I just want to make sure you're comfortable." But I did mind. My heart was racing and I slowly took in some deep breaths to try and calm myself.

When the movie began, she slipped her fingers in between mine and whispered into my ear. "It keeps them from wandering." With her head on my shoulder and her fingers intertwined with mine, the lump in my pants became a bulge. I hoped that Anelle hadn't seen it and after a few minutes of receiving no attention, the bulge receded back into its hiding place.

"Don't think I didn't see that."

"See what?"

"You know what I'm talking about, but I have something that's going to take your mind off of sex." She lifted up the divider between our two chairs and began sucking on my neck, then went to nibbling on my ears. I tried to move either of my hands, but my free one didn't want to budge and the one she held onto she grabbed tighter.

"How is this supposed to help me forget?" I asked.

"Did I say forget? I meant remember. But don't worry; this is where it will end. I just wanted to see what would happen if I did it and now I know." She withdrew herself from my neck, put the divider back down.

"That demands some kind of retribution." I lifted up the divider and proceeded to do to her what she'd done to me. After a few minutes, I put the divider back down and focused all of my attention on the movie.

"You are a devil, Quinton James. If you weren't such a good boy and I wasn't a good girl, I would lift my dress up right here and really give these people something to watch."

I swallowed, almost choking as I tried to speak before I completely finished. "I already know you're lying. Besides, there are two problems. The first is that other people will see us. The second is that I know you're wearing panties."

"I have an answer for both those problems. The first is that people won't pay attention to what we're doing because they're too busy looking forward. Secondly, who told you I was wearing panties?"

"I saw them already. You said they came with a shake and a smile. I had to make sure I was getting my money's worth."

"How can you get your money's worth when I'm paying for everything?" she asked, giving me the same raised eyebrow that she had in the apartment.

"Free is still a dollar value."

She gently petted my pants where the bulge had earlier appeared. "I can certainly hook you up with a freebie that you won't ever forget."

My erection stayed awake long enough to almost watch the whole movie with us.

When the movie ended, we debated for several minutes about whether or not we liked the movie and how the director could've made it better.

"Okay, I'm hungry now. Where are we going to eat at?" she asked.

"Well, since you're paying, there's this Mexican restaurant on Westheimer that's still open."

Twenty minutes later, we pulled into the parking lot of Chacho's to find the line out the door. I looked at her and she shook her head. "You know what; let's go back to my place. I'll whip us up something." I turned my car around and drove us back to her apartment.

We made it back in near record time. It'd gotten much cooler since we'd first left her place, but Anelle left my jacket in the car and walked to her apartment just as she had walked out of it--half-naked.
Entering her apartment, I welcomed the warmth. She walked to the back of her apartment and I sat myself on her couch.

"It's okay for you to turn on the TV. I'm just getting changed. It's hard to cook in a party dress," she shouted from her room.

I grabbed the remote and began clicking through the channels. Before I'd even found a channel to settle on, she whizzed past me wearing a black lace tank and matching female boxers with the word JUICY across her ass. The hump I'd seen earlier on her backside was clearly more pronounced and now infinitely more accessible.

I returned my focus towards the TV, refusing to be seduced by her rear. "You get comfortable with people really quickly." I said.

"I don't have anything to fear, do I? I know your first and last name. I know your license plate number. I'm pretty sure that you won't do anything worthy of calling the police for."

"If you have all that information, I might as well just chop you up. I'd been planning on it, but now that you're onto me, I might have to find someone else tonight."

"That's fine, but for now, you eat." She smiled at me and continued cooking. "I know that look, Quinton." She laughed. "I promise I won't bite."

I was a little uneasy, but I didn't know that I was broadcasting it. "Maybe I'm just trying not to openly stare at your near nakedness."

"I'm pretty sure you've seen what women look like. I mean, you have seen your woman naked, right?"

"How comfortable would you be with me walking naked around your apartment?"

"Why don't we test that theory?"

"What happened to not wanting another woman's man?" I asked, trying to derail our conversation about nudity.

"You said naked, you never said anything about having naked sex. The two aren't mutually exclusive, and one doesn't necessarily dictate the other."

"So then, what if I was naked and wanted to be inside of you-- then what?"

"Well, you're man enough to hold back those awful, primal instincts. I'm making burgers. You're not a vegetarian, are you?"

"No."

"Good. Are fries okay too?"

"That depends. Do they come with that shake you promised?" I asked.

She wiggled her behind just long enough for the both of us to burst into laughter. I was really beginning to like Anelle, or rather I was becoming extremely aroused because of her. I thought about standing up and leaving, but I couldn't. I didn't want to leave. I knew I'd be picking up Lae in about twelve hours, and I liked the company and attention I had now.

As soon as we were able to take a breath from laughing, I spoke. "I loved that perfume you wore tonight. What was it?"

"Why? Would you like to buy some for your girl?"

She had a way of grinding the reality back into any situation. Ordinarily I would've minded, but I knew that this is exactly what I needed to keep myself from seducing her. "Not particularly. I moonlight as a cross-dressing prostitute and wondered if it would bring in more business if I wore it, too."

"You'd make an ugly hooker. That goatee you're wearing is horrible for a woman to have and your muscles are too big. You'd probably scare off most of the men who were even thinking about it. But then again, you might attract some brothas that might be willing to pay for some prime ass."

"I take it you know from experience?"

"Yeah, I hang out with the cross-dressing kind all the time. We were supposed to have a fun party tonight, but you ruined it. You should close the shades just in case they're spying, though. If they see you here, they may find your street corner and kick your ass."

I laughed harder than I had all week. "You're pretty good. I see you can keep up with me."

She walked out of the kitchen and looked at me with one hand on her hip and the other with a flailing spatula. "You'd be surprised how I can work my mouthpiece. I'm no rookie."

"Yeah, you talk a lot of shit. Has anyone ever told you that?"

"Nope, they usually say I flirt too much."

"Same thing," I spouted as she walked back into the kitchen to finish cooking. I continued flipping through the channels.

She brought both of our plates out, setting them on her coffee table. She went back into the kitchen and brought out two wine coolers. We sat by each other as we ate, talking about high school, our friends and lovers. After we finished, she took our plates into the kitchen, grabbed our empty bottles and walked back out a few moments later.

"Ready for some dessert?" she asked.

"I don't think I can eat any more. I'm stuffed." She came to where I sat, straddled me and began nibbling on my neck.

"So," I whispered, "Was this dessert?"

"No, it's improvisation. If you want some dessert, I might give you some apple pie. All you have to do is want it." My leg began to tremble at the prospect of being inside what I knew was her pie.

I want it.

Rather than openly committing, I said nothing and allowed her to take control.

"How about this?" she whispered into my ear. "You don't have to ask, I'm not going to sleep with you, but I'll give you something that you can leave with and feel better about." She started grinding on me and I could feel her heat through my pants.

"What are my options?" I whispered back. My brain screamed *Stop!* But as my dick bobbed up and down inside of my pants, his argument was too damn convincing.

"I can either ride you with your clothes on, or I can give you a hand job." She whispered as she sucked on my earlobe. Leaning over, she opened a drawer on her coffee table and pulled out a bottle of lube. "Or I can do both."

She began tugging at my pants, releasing their grip on my hips and the most carnal side of me wanted to be old Quinton. I had Anelle exactly like I had all those that came before her--begging me to fuck her.

172

I wanted to say the same thing was true about Cheyenne, but that'd be a lie. With her, sex was surreal. It was almost as if I were watching myself in an intense fantasy. But with Anelle, there was no such illusion. Sex with her would be about opportunity and even coming here I knew I had the chance to slide myself into the back of her throat.

I looked up at Anelle and I was suddenly repulsed by what I was about to do. I knew I didn't want her and punishing Lae for ignoring me wasn't who I wanted to be. I'd told everyone that I'd reformed, but I really hadn't. I just managed to cover it up until no one was looking.

Laela was going to be my wife in a few months and I was being selfish and deceptive. I loved Laela and that meant completely breaking away from my past and focusing on our future. Grabbing Anelle by her waist, I lifted her off of my lap, ignoring my throbbing erection and quickly stood up.

"I've got to go."

"Did I do something wrong?" she asked, looking at me like a wounded puppy.

"No, but I was about to."

As I walked out of her apartment, Anelle began chasing me, but wearing only a t-shirt stopped her at the front door. I walked non-stop to my car and even though I knew that as badly as I wanted to give in to her tonight, I was happy to know that I could turn down sex.

Through the rearview mirror, I watched Anelle's apartment disappear as I headed back onto Hwy 6. Instinctively, I called Lae and got her voice mail.

"I just want to apologize for hounding you these last few weeks for sex. I was wrong and I apologize if my nagging drove you home to see your family. Lae, I really love you and I'm sorry for doing you wrong."

It wasn't entirely a confession, but becoming the old Quinton wasn't doing me any favors.

"So let me get this straight, in the last two days, you could've slept with two different women, both of whom you met on the same damn day?"

"I didn't think about it like that, but yeah, I did."

"See, that's that shit I'm talking about! My dawg finally broke out his shell and is on the prowl for some new pussy! I knew this day would come. I think I'm gonna shed a tear."

"I didn't call for your praises, Dre. I fucked up and I needed to vent." I'd just made it back to the apartment and Dre was the only person I knew who'd keep my secret.

"Look, Quinton, whatever you need from me, I'm there. But I do have one stipulation. There are just some formalities I'd like to get out of the way."

"What is it?"

"Was the pussy good? What did it smell like? Was it soft and wet? Did the pussy feel like it was hugging your dick? Was Cheyenne's as sweet as I imagined older coochie would be? I need some damn details man!"

"You're a sick man. What the hell is wrong with you?"

"You somehow always find the living, breathing, A-1 pussy. A brother like me, I get the coochie that feels like it's on life support. Shit, you know me man, I'm a five and a half inch monster, but it's always like some dude with a monster dick got there the night before me."

"Look man, I just needed to vent. That's all. I just poked my teacher, not the girl from the club."

"Dawg, a fantasy is a fantasy and it doesn't count on the cheat-o-meter. Anytime you fulfill a fantasy, it's not cheating; it's just something on your list for you to cross off."

"And how do you rationalize that statement?"

He cleared his throat as if he were about to give an important speech. "Well, you have to look at it like this. If Denzel's car broke down in front of your apartment building and Lae was at home alone, would she sleep with him?"

"Probably, but..."

"But nothing. That, my friend, is a fantasy fuck. And what did I say before, fantasy sex doesn't count. Who didn't want to bang one of their teachers at one time? That's all fantasy, baby."

He was so self-assured that I was certain that nothing I'd say could bring him down from his cloud. "Fine."

"You know what's funny though? I figured this would happen-- not the whole running away from pussy thing--but the pussy before the wedding thing. That's why I wanted you to get it out of the way. Don't you feel better about it now?"

"Do I feel better? I was about to fuck some random woman when I suddenly became sick to my stomach. I'm just ready to have this damn wedding over man-- before something else goes wrong."

"Quinton let me tell you something about yourself. You're a victim of your own fame. You get a girl, lay down the thunder dick and she's all goo goo-goo eyed for you. When that shit fades, and you don't feel like you're number one anymore, you move onto the next girl. As much as you might want to be with Lae, you always have to feel like you're the center of her universe. It's always been like that with every girl you've met. When all the focus is on you, you're the perfect partner, but when her attention wanders, it's inevitable that you're going to seek out that attention from someone else. I know you, dawg, and I've been seeing what's going on with you and Lae."

I laughed. "So you're trying to analyze me? You're the one who told me to get some new coochie in my diet!" I said incredulously. "This is your goddamn fault!"

"How is it my fault? Ever heard of this thing called personal responsibility? And since when have you started listening to me? That right there tells me something ain't right!" "So now what," I asked sarcastically. "You're telling me fantasy sex doesn't count, but then you want to talk about how I treat women? You--of all people?"

"Look, I really want it to work out with you and Laela, but sometimes you need to hear about yourself, Quinton. Take that pride, shove it up your ass and get your mind right. Lae's a cool girl and now that you've gotten the chip off your shoulder, we can get down to business."

"And what business is that?"

"You need to hook me up with the girl you left hangin'."

CHAPTER 13

Simone

February 10th (Friday)

"Where are you going?"

"I told you already, Mike. Lae and I are just going out to eat. I haven't seen her since New Year's and we're gonna do girl stuff."

"Why didn't you ask Quinton to come? That way we can bring the baby and all of us could go out to eat."

He was doing it again and I was becoming more agitated with every word that came out of his mouth. Whenever he went out, I was expected to sit at home, watch the baby and to never question where he went. Yet when I wanted to go out with my friends, he always wanted a detailed description of who, what, when, where and how.

"Look, Mike, whenever you go out, I never say anything. Can't I go out this once without having to find a babysitter when MJ has a father? It's only going to be me and Lae--no one else. Besides, it's not like I'm going to fix a goddamn car for the rest of the damn day." I knew he'd say something about the last wisecrack, but lately I found myself not caring about what Mike thought.

"You know what, Monie, what-the-fuck-ever. Just be back home early enough so that me and Pook can go out."

"Whatever. I'll be back as soon as I can." I left the house wearing a thick wool sweater and loose fitting jeans, but the way he sneered at me on the way out, you'd think I walked out the house naked, with a "please fuck me" sign attached to my back.

I got in the car and as I pulled out the driveway, I saw that Mike was watching me leave. I let him see me drive towards 610 before I made a quick u-turn and went to visit my brother over at my aunt's house.

It was a little after six in the evening and Lae and I weren't supposed to meet until seven, which gave me a little time to do whatever I wanted. I needed the time to get away from Mike and be alone, so I decided to see how my older brother, Anthony, was doing. With my aunt at her weekly bingo match, it was the perfect time for me to avoid her and still visit him.

Out of all the family members we had, my aunt and I were the only ones to call my brother Tony. The rest of the family called him 'N'shit'. He earned the name by being locked up twice, both times for possession, and because he had the uncanny ability to put the phrase 'n-shit' after everything he said. He was still a great uncle to MJ but, when it came to me asking him to do a favor; he never came through and always had an excuse for every mistake he made.

My brother was also a walking contradiction. He always said that he wanted to be married one day, but the last time we spoke he confessed to me that monogamy was unnatural, while his girlfriend sat next to him. To him, there was simply too much pussy out there to belong to just one man. With Michael's infidelities becoming less covert, I figured I'd be better off talking to a professional to see what I could be doing differently to help keep what little civility we shared at least manageable. Well, at least until one of us could afford a divorce. Since Tony was the most habitual cheater I'd ever met, I hoped he had some insight to share, if he wasn't too high.

I pulled into my aunt's empty driveway and stared at the older house, catching flashbacks from a terrible childhood and a worse adulthood. It took me a few minutes to compose myself and I walked up the front stairs and banged on the door so that Tony could hear me. Since he lived in my aunt's attic I knew that if I didn't bang hard enough, I had just wasted a trip over here.

After ten seconds of furious banging on the oak door, a gruff, half-sleepy voice shouted at the door, "What!?!"

"It's me, Simone!" I shouted, hoping that he wasn't so high that he couldn't comprehend what I was saying.

He opened the door, looked me over and walked back into the house. "I'll be damned. What's goin' on 'n' shit, lil' sis?"

Ladies and gentlemen, N'shit is in the building. It wasn't hard to smell the weed on him. Instead of cursing him, I just shook my head.

"Nothing much, Tony. Found a job yet?"

He turned around and looked at me with one eyebrow raised. It was the same disgusted look he gave my aunt. "I'm a two-time felon. Ain't nobody tryin' to hire my black ass. It's just the man's way of getting us back in jail."

"But you got money for weed?"

"We all gotta hustle, right?" he said, turning back up the stairs.

"Sorry I asked. Anyways, I need to ask you some things right quick."

"You didn't come here to lecture me about getting a job 'n' shit, did you? 'Cuz you can fly that shit elsewhere."

"No, Tony, I didn't. I need your advice on something."

"You need *my* fuckin advice? You must be in some deep shit to come over this way for my advice, but whatever. Tell me what's going on 'n' shit."

"Mike is cheating on me."

"So what, you want me to kick his ass or something? You know auntie loves that punk, but you know I ain't liked him since day one, n' shit. Just point the way."

"The truth is, I don't care about him anymore. I'm really thinking about getting a divorce."

He fell down onto our aunt's couch and began to laugh. "So you're finally starting to see the light. Monogamy is wrong, man. That shit is so wrong."

"Tony, I don't want to hear your monogamy lecture. I just wanna know why men cheat."

"That's easy, Monie. Pussy is why men cheat. For a straight man, pussy is the one thing worth risking everything else for. But even though we fuck up, we can still separate what we feel from how we feel n' shit."

"So what you're trying to say that Mike cheats on me because I don't satisfy him, but he still loves me?"

He laughed again. "You're getting' it. For a man who's always horny, the hardest thing in the world to do is turn down new pussy. Hell, for any man it's hard to turn down new pussy n' shit. That's like asking a starving man to watch you cook, but then you tell him he can't eat n' shit. Men need to feel like men and once that man don't feel that way, he might still love you, but he's gonna go feel like a man somewhere else n' shit."

My brother was six years older than I was, but even with the extra verbiage, I actually understood what he was saying and I had never heard him make more sense that I had just now. "Tony, you just made more sense today than you have in your thirty-something years of life. Thanks for coming through this time. I really needed to hear that."

"I always got you, lil' sis. You my goddamn sister and even though I be fuckin' up a lot 'n' shit, I got mad wisdom. I would love for us to carry on this lovely conversation, but I hear a car pulling up. That means yo ass needs to go because I'm about to get blazed as fuck, 'n' shit."

I gave my brother a hug, something I rarely do, and walked back out the front door to see an old brown Firebird with smoke billowing out the windows, parked behind me. I jumped in my car, let the other car pull out of the driveway and was on my way to go see Lae.

I arrived at the Italian restaurant fifteen minutes before we were supposed to meet. With Lae not arriving for a few minutes, I walked up to the bar and asked for a glass of water. While I waited it gave me time to think about the conversation with my brother.

"Hey there, stranger!"

I turned to find Lae behind me wearing a tan dress, with a matching sun hat and a smile that could've been in toothpaste commercials. "Hey there, yourself! Where have you been hiding? I even heard you ran out of town to get away from us. Are we that bad?"

She extended her arms and we gave each other the type of hug that you give people you hadn't seen or wouldn't see for a while. It was long, warm and full of love.

We finally let go of each other, leaving some of the men in the restaurant full of imaginative stares. "Yes, you guys are that bad." She answered. "So why are you here so early? You're usually the late one."

"You just don't know how bad I wanted to get out of the house. Mike is wearing down my last bit of sanity." I wanted to say more, but then I noticed a waiter standing behind Lae and nodded to her to let her know someone was standing behind her.

The waiter, wearing a white tuxedo, greeted us and walked us to a table in the middle of the Italian bistro. He pulled out both of our chairs, seated us, and then gave us the wine list and menus before disappearing among the sea of other white tuxedos.

"Like I was telling you, Lae," I continued, "Mike is driving me crazy. I don't see us making it too much longer."

"You're married now, girl. You have two options: either make it work or don't make it work. Whatever you choose that's up to you. I'm not into telling you how I knew Mike was a bad choice, but now that it's almost finished you can walk away with your head up." She began to look over the wine list. "You know our final dress fitting is in a few weeks. You're the Matron of Honor and everyone already has theirs in. Please make sure you get in all the right measurements this time, Monie."

I hated it when she antagonized me. "Fine, I'll get them in, but it may take a few weeks, I'm trying to lose weight."

"Is that the New Years' resolution again?" she moaned. "We pledge that every year and we still manage to weigh more the next year. I'm so tired of trying. I'd rather just eat right."

"Well, I've made some changes."

"Good for you!" She was still antagonizing me and I could hear it in her voice. "So what brought on these changes?"

I wanted to say Quinton, but that wasn't entirely true. I enjoyed the morning that he spent with MJ and me, but I wanted the type of relationship that he and Lae shared.

I'd also forgotten that I hadn't told Laela about Mike's infidelity. I always assumed Quinton would tell her, but now that I knew he hadn't, it reaffirmed my belief on how honorable a man he was. "Mike's been cheating on me, Lae. He's been with someone named Starr. I know for a fact he has; he's openly admitted it."

The look of incredulity that spread across her face had me re-thinking about what I should've told her. "He cheated and you're still there! You're still in the same house with that man?" She glared at me and with her teeth clenched; it helped to mask her volume, but not her anger.

"Lae, I knew you were going to say that, but it's been taken care of. I have a family to think of first, not second or third, but first. I didn't agree with it and we talked, but it's not like he's the only guilty one! If you remember, I messed around on him while we were together. You knew about it and at what point did you coerce me into telling him the truth! We all make mistakes, but I have to handle this the best way I know how."

"That was before you were even married! That doesn't count!"

"Would you feel the same way if Quinton told you that after he cheated?"

180

The anger on her face softened, replaced by an apologetic look. "You're right, Simone. We've all done something that we aren't proud of and have hidden away. I have too many secrets to name myself. I'm sorry for going overboard, but you know how I feel about him."

"Yeah, I know, but you have to let me do this on my own. I want to turn my life around. I even went to see Tony today."

The mention of my brother's name brought a big smile. "Wait a minute. You went to see your brother, Mr. N'shit himself? I'd love to hear how that conversation went 'n' shit. Was it good 'n' shit or bad 'n' shit? I mean let me know--'n' shit." She dropped her head and put her thumb to her nose like she was some sort of drunk boxer, but her imitation of my brother was so perfect that I had to laugh.

"You need to stop picking on my brother." It was a weak threat, but he was still my brother.

"He needs to stop making it so easy. Does that boy have a job yet?"

I gave her the same look my brother gave me when I asked the same question. "This is my brother we're talking about. He wouldn't know what a job was if it jumped up, bit him on the ass and gave him a paycheck."

"Some things never change." she sighed.

"What was the sigh all about?" I asked.

"My brother has changed. It's due more to the woman he's with, but I actually saw him in love."

"Your brother is in love? What is this world coming to when the leopards start changing their spots?"

"I don't know, but it's time we ordered. I haven't eaten all day and I'm hungry."

We were both pretty famished, but since she was footing the bill, I decided to order some lobster after she ordered steak. We continued talking while we waited for our food, touching on her Cleveland trip, my work life, and our relationships.

By the time the food came, she was telling me all about Janette, her brother's new girlfriend. Apparently Janette made quite an impression on Lae. All she talked about was how interesting Janette was and how she's going to be a nurse also in a few months. I listened quietly as Lae went on, noticing how often she smiled when she spoke about her.

"So was the vacation all about your brother and Janette or did you actually see your parents?" Suddenly Lae was quieter than she'd been the whole night. "Lae, is everything okay?"

"Monie, can I trust you to keep a secret about something?"

With a mouth full of lobster claw, I nodded.

"I did something I shouldn't have."

"Like what? Did your brother ask you to run interference while he snuck off with another girl?" I joked. As long as I'd known Lae she'd never had any real secret--at least not like the kind of secrets I had. Her secrets always had to do with something someone else told her.

"It's about me." She said never taking her eyes away from mine.

"Did you sleep with another man behind Quinton's back?" I mused. "What kind of dirt could you possibly do? You're Laela: good girl extraordinaire."

"Dammit, Monie, will you just stop talking. I'm trying to tell you something serious."

Instead of waiting for her to tell me some inane secret from some other person, I put my fork down and gave Lae my full attention. "What's going on, Lae?"

"I've done something-- with another woman."

"You did *what!*" I was livid. Not because of what Lae had done, but mostly because of what it would mean to Quinton.

"Quinton and I were talking about a threesome, so I wanted to know what it was like to you know--be with a woman. I want to tell Quinton, but things have changed and I don't know how I want to tell him."

"You slept with fucking Raven, didn't you?"

She nodded her head. "Yeah, I did."

"What the hell, Lae? How could you do that?"

"It was just a crazy night. We went to a strip club, then went drinking and ended up in a hotel room. I don't know why it happened Monie, but it was just a stupid mistake."

I looked at her with the same disbelief she'd always shared with me when she didn't believe what I'd just said. "Lae, you're talking to a woman who has drowned more than her share of problems with a bottle. You may not always remember what you did, but you certainly remember why you did them."

"I was just curious. Quinton wouldn't let me pick her--even though she was the only willing person and I just wanted to get the shit out of the way," she whispered.

I remained silent for a few minutes, absorbing what Lae had just told me.

"I'm not sure if I can keep all of this quiet. Teniyah wants to do it again and Simone, I really liked it."

"Are you saying that you're *gay*?"

"I think I like girls, too."

My stomach began twisting in knots, as I thought about how Quinton would take this. He was a good man, but I didn't think he needed to know this. "So would you choose her--Raven over Quinton?"

"Monie, I'm engaged. But if circumstances were different, honestly, I'm not sure."

We left the restaurant together a little after 8:45. It was a half an hour drive home and I knew Mike would be mad, but I really didn't care. Lae offered to walk me to my car, but I knew that would spur another conversation, so I declined and waved goodbye as I drove off.

On the way home all I could think about was Quinton. Laela was destroying a perfect relationship and she didn't even care. I tried not to think of how much it angered me to see him treated like this, but Quinton told me that if Lae was cheating, he wouldn't want to know.

"What the hell, man? It's almost 9:15 and I asked you to be here before nine."

"Mike, I had a good evening and I don't feel like hearing your shit. Be happy that I got here when I did. All you need to do is throw on some dirty ass jeans, a decent shirt and go! How hard is that?"

"I'm about sick of you. You need to turn that attitude down or--"

"Or what, Michael? Are you gonna hit me? You would really hit a woman--your wife of all people, the mother of your child?" He turned away from me and stormed into the bathroom to get himself ready while MJ just sat on the couch looking curiously at me. I sat down on the couch next to him. "Promise me that you'll never get stuck in a situation like mommy has, MJ. Treat the women you meet with dignity and respect, okay, little man?"

"Da!" he shouted. I wanted to turn to grab Mike and let him know that MJ had finally called for him, but it seemed appropriate that he would miss out.

"That's my pookie. Don't be like your daddy." I stood up in time to see Mike sneak out the back door without a hug or kiss goodbye. He didn't even take the time to tell me when he'd be back; something that was more of a demand than request whenever I left the house.

I sat down on the couch when the phone rang. I didn't feel like moving, but I picked MJ up, pulled myself off of the couch and answered it.

"Hello?" I asked.

"Is Mike there?" It wasn't a voice that was familiar to me. Usually whenever Mike's friends called, they greeted me and then asked for Mike. This particular person, whoever he was, either wasn't a friend or just didn't have any fuckin' manners.

"No, he isn't. May I ask--" Before I had a chance to ask who was calling, he hung up. The prevailing thought in my head was that this jackass had better not call here again or he was going to get cursed out.

A half an hour of news had MJ's head looking for a comfortable spot on my chest as he tried to fall asleep. I changed his diaper and carried him to his crib where I laid him down. He looked so peaceful when he slept and amidst all this negativity that surrounded us, I was glad that he couldn't understand it all.

"You're such a good baby," I whispered to him as I pulled his blanket over his tiny frame. "Your smile lights up my day, did you know that? I love you, MJ." I kissed him on his cheek and walked out of his room into the bathroom.

I thought about calling Quinton, but there'd be enough time for that. Besides, I had no doubt that he and Laela were still making up for the week they missed.

I turned on the hot water and let it fill the tub. I brushed my teeth while the tub filled, taking notes of how tired I looked in my bathroom mirror reflection. After the steaming water was where I wanted it to be, I sat down in the heat, letting all the steam carry away all of the headaches and worries that plagued me. With my whole body relaxed, I did something that I had neglected to do for weeks; I touched myself. Closing my eyes and letting my fingers do the walking, I relived the fantasy I had of Quinton on New Year's Day.

CHAPTER 14

Happy Valentine's Day

Simone

9:00 a.m.

"I'm late! Dammit!"

The LCD display on my alarm clock was blinking 12:00; no doubt from our increasingly problematic power outages.

With every curse word I could imagine pouring out of my mouth, I parted the curtain in my bedroom to see exactly where the sun was before I began looking for my watch. I wasn't any good at reading a sun dial, but as high up in the sky as the sun was, I knew I was late.

I began screaming at Michael, damning him for allowing me to sleep so late, but when I couldn't find him, it finally dawned on me that he hadn't been home in the last two days.

Fuck him. He can stay gone.

It hurt me that he chose to run rather than to work it out, but I guess we were both supposed to be moving onto better things. Still, we had history—a family, and he'd chosen someone else over us. Some part of me wanted to make it right, my body even began to crave the nauseating morning ritual of sex we had, but I didn't have time to sit around and sulk. I had to get to work.

I ran to MJ's room and found him sleeping as peacefully as always. I hated to irritate him, but I needed to get him ready and get to work as soon as possible. I knew they'd be calling any minute, if they hadn't already, to tell me that a no call-no show was grounds for termination. With the future I'd been planning, the last thing I needed to do was lose my job.

Without any time for amenities, I pulled my hair into a bun, pulled a generic blouse and skirt from of the hangers in my closet, soaked my shirt with as much body spray as it could hold and ran out the door with MJ screaming like he was dying.

With a little luck and some careless driving, I'd gotten to my aunt's house in record time. As soon as she opened the door, I threw him into her arms and ran off the porch so that she couldn't hold me up.

With 610 already flooded with cars, I had to take the back roads to work. I hoped that the streets weren't as bad as the expressway and I began silently praying when I found out that they weren't. Fifteen minutes later I pulled into the Main Street parking garage and ran to work. I was late, but still not as late as I could've been.

No one spoke when I walked in, but I hadn't expected them to. It had been hell dealing with me the last few weeks, especially the days after Mike and I had our fights. We argued so much that it went from a daily routine into an hourly one and I was growing physically sick from all the stress.

I walked to my desk, took my purse off of my shoulder and after looking around the office a few times to see who noticed I was late, I began sorting through all of the paperwork.

After a half an hour of work, my solitude was interrupted by a voice I really didn't want to hear. "Hey, Simone, is everything okay? I just wanted you to know you look really--bad." Chris shyly whispered as he walked by.

Chris Moore was the new security guard the company hired after a string of workplace assaults began occurring around the city, but he was the least intimidating looking security guard I'd ever met. He was a young white guy; sandy brown hair, a little chubby, not too bright and probably not too strong seeing as he always had problems lifting some of the boxes I regularly lift. Whenever he saw me, he made it a point to speak, and when I saw him, I made it a point to run.

"Thanks, Chris," I mumbled only loud enough for him to hear. "You know, when you say things like that, it really completes my fucking day. The more you open your mouth, the more I feel like ramming your teeth down your throat. Fuck you very much for your insight into the obvious."

He began looking at the floor and pulled his security cap a little further down on his head. "I mean not bad, but sad. You look really sad. I know you don't like me very much, but would you like me to bring you something. I could if you wanted me to."

"No thanks, Chris. I know you're trying to be nice, but I don't want anything right now."

"Okay, Simone, I'm sorry to bother you." He smiled at me and walked out of the office.

I felt bad that I'd treated him the way I did after I watched him leave. He was a nice guy and didn't deserve my malice. I hated the person I was becoming.

1:00 PM

I had been working for a few hours before I looked up at the clock and realized that I had already worked an hour past my 12:00 lunch. It was a little after one in the afternoon when I grabbed my purse and caught the elevator down to the lobby. I bought myself some chips and a drink from the bodega next to the guards' desk area and sat at a table alone while I ate. I usually ran to the coffee shop at the end of the street, but I was so behind with work that I just needed a quick sugar boost to help me finish the rest of my day.

I thought about skipping the rest of the day, but I couldn't. I didn't have any place to go but home. I thought about Lae and even more about Quinton, but today was Valentine's Day and I didn't want to be reminded of what I should be doing. During the last few days with Mike gone, I'd been too tired to do anything except sulk, moping around. I didn't know why I was thinking so much about my marriage, but the more I glanced at all the smiling couples passing by, the more I just wanted to go home and cry.

By the time I returned to my desk, I was ready to grab my work and go, but something on my desk caught my attention. There were three chocolate chip cookies wrapped in a yellow napkin, twelve yellow roses, and a yellow card that read: *"Even during the darkest days the sun is still up there."*

I looked around the office to see if anyone was noticeably guilty, but no one even stopped to notice me noticing them. Excited just to have a secret admirer, I called Lae.

"Hello?"

"Lae, you'll never guess what just happened to me!" I was almost too excited to talk.

"Well, if I have to guess: Mike died and there was a million dollar policy in your name?"

"No." At the mention of Mike's name, I came to the realization that I might not have a secret admirer. It might've just been Mike trying to get back into my good graces.

"Why should I guess when I'm not going to get it right? Just tell me already!"

"Someone just left a dozen beautiful roses on my desk."

"That's really nice for someone to do." Her exclamation sounded a little deflated.

"You know, Lae, I'd just been having the shittiest day until this. I wish I could find out who sent the roses--."

As if whatever I'd just said hadn't interested her in the least, she cut me off. "Hey, Monie, can I call you back; Niya is calling me on the other line."

Clearly your fuck-buddy is more important than your real friend!

"Yeah, okay. I'll just talk to you later then." As soon as she hung up, I kept my face against the phone long enough to hear the dial tone.

I can't believe her! She didn't even stay on long enough for me to tell her that Mike hadn't come home in the last few days, but then again she was never available for me. Her time belonged to her new lover, Raven.

I hung up the phone and pushed the roses to the far side of my desk while I shoved the cookies into my mouth. *That's okay, Monie. Calm down. She'll get hers one day.*

"It's a good thing these cookies are good," I mumbled as cookie crumbs tumbled from my mouth onto the desk.

"Fuckin' Laela--always does this to me. I don't even know why I was surprised. Hell, I don't even know why I called. I should've known she never had any time for me." I thought that my grumbling was barely audible, but it wasn't.

"Simone, you're talking to yourself."

Chris returned for his afternoon rounds and after looking at his smile for a few seconds, it finally dawned on me that it might've been Chris, not Mike that left the flowers. As much as I wanted it to be my husband, he'd never done anything like this before and I didn't think he'd be the type to start now. The only person it could be was Chris and in some small way, that depressed me even more.

"Hey, Chris, did you leave something on my desk?"

His eyes lit up. "Why? Did you like it?"

"Yes, I did and it was very pretty." He began to blush. "I just want to be sure that no one took anything off my desk. What exactly did you leave?"

"Um...I left flowers and...umm..." By the way he was looking around my desk I could tell that he was searching for something, other than the flowers, to lie about.

I was about to stand up and slap the white off of him for lying, but instead I stayed calmly seated in my chair. "Chris, why are you lying to me?"

He started frowning. "I'm sorry, Simone. You just liked me a whole lot more when you thought it was me. I won't lie to you no more. I didn't send you the flowers."

"Thank you for telling the truth, Chris." As he walked away, I thought of stabbing him in the back with a mechanical pencil, but I was too engulfed in curiosity to warrant prison time. I took the blooming yellow rose out of the vase, smelling it. and smiled. The only person left was Mike.

4:00 PM

Maybe he's trying to tell me he's sorry.

I'd been fixated on the idea for the whole second half of my day, but it didn't seem like Mike. Yet there wasn't another person on the planet that would do something like this for me, so it had to be him. As much as I wanted to hate Mike for the things he'd done, I looked over the flowers and I knew I was ready to forgive him.

I ran all the way to the parking garage. As soon as I saw my car, I pulled out my cell phone and called my aunt as I was unlocking my door. I started the car and sped around the corners, narrowly avoiding several cars on the way down the ramp. I was already out of the parking lot and turning down my first side street by the time she picked up. "Auntie, I know I'm calling late, but I'm planning something tonight. Is it okay if MJ stays the night? He already has some extra clothes, diapers, and formula in his bag."

"Is it with your husband?" I found myself blushing and beaming as I spoke. "Yes, auntie, it is."

"Well, it's about time y'all did something together. St. Valentine's Day is a good time to kiss and make-up. I'll watch MJ, but don't be bringing no more great nieces and nephews over here in nine months."
I laughed. "I promise. Thank you."

"You have a good evening, baby."

I rushed home, running upstairs to begin cleaning. I placed the flowers in a vase filled with lukewarm water and since the house didn't look too bad I didn't have to do too much. With all the rushing I had done this morning I still needed to pick up a few things.

As soon as I finished straightening up, I threw off my work clothes and relaxed in a hot bath. I closed my eyes and began to think about how Lae had been treating me lately, but I wanted to push all negative thoughts from my mind. Even if Mike and I weren't going to last, tonight would be about my husband and me at least spending Valentine's Day together.

It took a while for me to force myself out the tub, but when I did, I walked to the kitchen and grabbed the phone. I wanted to make sure that I wouldn't miss his call and when I returned to the warming confines of the tub, I washed myself up with Mike's favorite body scrub-- Vanilla and Black Cherry.

I left the bathroom with so many butterflies in my stomach that I felt like I did when I was about to lose my virginity. I dried myself off and took what was left of the body spray I'd used that morning and finished it off, making sure to cover as much body as I could before it ran out.

I slipped on my silk kimono before walking to the kitchen and grabbing as many candles as I could find, placing them around the house. I was almost finished when I heard a car pull up in the driveway. Too excited to look, I rushed and lit the remaining candles and laid on the couch with my legs spread.

After a few minutes of repositioning, I grew a little worried when he didn't come in.

The bastard chickened out.

I was about to look outside when I heard a soft knock at the back door. *After everything I've done tonight, he'd better be carrying something worth taking him back for.*

I walked to the back door and before I opened it, I held my kimono back far enough so that he could see that I was completely shaved.

I took a deep breath, smiled, and opened the door.

"Welcome home, daddy."

Laela

It wasn't tradition, but I awoke early so that I could make Quinton breakfast for Valentine's Day.

The sun hadn't yet come up and though I couldn't see my hand in front of my face, I'd lived in the apartment long enough to know my way around and walked to the kitchen without incident.

I cut on the light, opened the fridge and took out all the ingredients I'd need. I grabbed the wheat bread, a few eggs, and four strips of bacon from the refrigerator door. I wasn't a great chef, but I knew how to take care of the basics. Five minutes after I began, the food was almost ready and I felt a kiss on top of my right shoulder.

"You're up early." I turned and kissed him softly on the lips.

"I had to make sure it was you making breakfast. I know how hard you try to test your culinary skills and I wanted to make sure that ice cubes and hot dogs weren't on the menu."

"Ice cubes and hot dogs? Is that all you think I can make?"

"No, you make a pretty mean salad too." He smacked me on the ass and left the kitchen to sit on the couch to watch sports highlights.

"I can cook!" I screamed out to him, insulted by his insinuations.

"I believe you!" he shouted back.

Since I'd been back from Cleveland, I made it a point to avoid Niya and spent every moment with Quinton that I possibly could. I loved him more than anything and being with my parents reminded me of how much I'd been neglecting him.

When I arrived home, he greeted with the most passionate kiss we'd ever shared and I realized how much I truly missed being with my man. He made love to me with as much ferocity as a man who'd just made parole. I liked this side of him and that night I made a promise to him and I intended to keep it. Every day this week we'd gone out either to eat or just hang out and every night, I'd remind him of why he'd put a ring on my finger.

This morning, I wanted to expand my culinary skills so that we wouldn't always have to go out. I was never the homemaker type, but I learned from my mother that I didn't have to be submissive to learn how to cook for my man. I took her advice and his breakfast was ready only a few minutes after he sat down on the couch. I fixed his plate, walked to the living room and sat on his lap as I fed him what I'd made.

When I finished serving him his breakfast, he kissed me on the cheek. "Thanks for breakfast, but I really gotta get to work. I'd love to shower with you, but I know where that would end up."

"Sure you don't just want a hand job?"

He smiled. "It sounds tempting, but I can't be late today."

"I'm going back to sleep anyway," I said. "It's too early to be up and I feel bad for people who actually have to be at work at this hour."

"We all can't be nurses. But really, Lae, I need to get up." I stood up and watched him walk to the bathroom before I walked back to the comfort of my bedroom, collapsed onto my bed and went right back to sleep.

11:00 AM

"Hello, Happy Valentine's Day!"

My eyes were still closed as a vaguely familiar voice filled my bedroom. I had no idea who was calling this early in the morning, but the last thing I wanted to hear was a joyous introduction. In the effort of trying to push the voice mail button on the base of my phone, I'd accidentally pushed speakerphone. "Huh?" I mumbled into the phone, still unaware of who the hell I was talking to.

"I'm so sorry! Are you still sleeping? I thought you guys were only an hour behind us and its noon here. I am so sorry; you must've worked last night!"

"Janette?!?" I rolled over onto my side and strained to look at the clock above the TV. With the curtains tightly closed, it was impossible to read it.

"Hello, Laela. How are things in the Lone Star State?"

"Girl, do you know what time it is? Why are you calling so early?" Since Quinton had unplugged the alarm clock, I rubbed my eyes and strained at the clock once more so that I could get a better view without having to actually get out of bed.

"Early? Laela, do you know it's just after noon here. That means that it's a short time past 11 o'clock there. Early was over two hours ago for you."

I cut on the TV and turned to a random news station to find out she was right. "Hey, girl," I yawned, "what's been going on in C-town?"

"Nothing much. I just hadn't heard from you since you've been home. I guess you forgot about us Cleveland folk as soon as you got back to the warm weather."

"It's not that. I've just been busy playing catch up with Quinton. You know how it is."

"Uh-huh. Well, anyway... I guess you worked last night and I didn't want to wake you. I just wanted to you know, say Happy V-day and I wanted to thank you for the time we spent-- together."

I knew what she meant by together and though I couldn't deny it any longer, I didn't want it hanging over my head forever either. "Look, Janette, I'm glad we did what we did. It gave me perspective, but that's not who I am. You are my brother's girlfriend and I am engaged to a very wonderful man. I can't be that girl. I won't be that girl."

"Lae, you helped me to realize who I am. I'm a woman still attached to someone else, even though I care for your brother. We're a lot more alike than you think. Look, I love that we got to know each other. I had more fun that night than I'd had in a while. But I do know a little something about being bi-sexual-- having had a girlfriend for the last couple of years and all. You can only deny it for so long before it begins to eat at you. Whether it's an experiment or not, you should really come to grips with the person inside of you."

She sounds exactly like Teniyah. Am I that transparent?

"So does that mean that you're telling my brother what happened?"

"Nothing happened."

"Happy Valentine's Day, Janette." I heard the click on her end and the dial tone before I pushed the speaker button for the second time.

I stepped out of my bed and realized I needed to get moving. Having slept through almost all of the morning, I knew it was time for me to get out of the house and buy what I needed to for today. Usually, I bought a card a couple of weeks in advance, but spending all of my free time with Niya had me procrastinating, something I didn't usually do.

I showered briefly before throwing on some jeans, one of Quinton's blue t-shirts, and my Nike Shox. While putting on my shoes I noticed that my toes needed another coat of polish and I needed a serious pedicure. "'You're *seriously* slacking," I admitted to myself, but I could take care of that later. I had a lot to buy and only a little time to buy it if I planned on having everything ready by the time Quinton came home. I wrapped my hair around into a pony-tail and jogged out of the house.

On the way to my car I noticed how good the late morning sun felt against my skin. Houston winters had me so spoiled. It wasn't even comparable to what I knew my parents were going through in Cleveland.

I drove to the card shop that I usually frequented for holidays, which was down the street from our apartment. As I entered, I waved to the elderly white lady behind the counter and headed straight for the fluorescent pink section marked 'Valentine's Day Cards'. It didn't take me long to find what I was looking for, a colorfully sentimental card to give Quinton. The front was decorated with roses, highlighted by glitter and in the inside was more of the same.

As I walked to the front counter to pay for the card, I thought of calling Niya, but I wasn't sure what I wanted to say. The last time we spoke, she confessed her love and I left the hotel room upset and confused.

"Hello, how are you doing?" I asked the lady at the counter. I had no idea what her name was, but she was sweet and every time I bought a card we would small talk.

"I'm doing well, enjoying each day as it comes. Is this one for the hubby?"

"Yes, it is." I smiled. After she rung the card up, I paid for it with cash and waved again as I left the little store.

I was halfway home when my cell rang with Niya's ringtone. I debated on whether to answer it and ignoring her wasn't going to make the problem magically disappear.

"I see you're answering your phone now."

"Look, Niya, we need to talk."

"I already know what you want to say, Lae. We haven't talked ever since I told you how I feel and now you're just avoiding me. I never asked you to feel the same way. I just asked you to understand me and it seems like you can't even do that."

She was right and that much I couldn't deny. "I just don't think that what I'm doing is right. Either we tell Quinton about this or we just end it. I can't be two people. I can't love two people. It's not fair that he's the man I'm supposed to be marrying, but we're sharing a bed every other night."

"So I guess that this is it."

"I guess so."

"Look, I'm gonna be busy for a while. I'll call you back when I get the chance." She hung up without saying goodbye or even waiting for my response.

I closed my phone, turned the volume off and threw it onto the passenger's seat. Then as soon as I made it back to the parking lot of my apartment, I placed both hands on my steering wheel and banged my head on the horn four times, repeating a different curse word each time my head hit. I got out of the car and stared at my apartment through the darkened bedroom window before sitting back down in the car and driving off. The way my day seemed to be going, home was the last place I wanted to be.

How could I be in love with two people and how in the hell do I handle this?

I had been driving around the city for a little more than an hour trying to figure out how I wanted to sort this mess out, but it always came down to the most basic solution: I *had* to stop sleeping with Teniyah. But knowing what I had to do was easy, actually following through was what worried me the most.

Quinton was the type of man I'd always imagined myself marrying; intelligent, dedicated, he had a great sense of humor and the sex was unbelievable. I loved him and I knew he felt the same way about me, but even though we connected physically, it was Niya with whom I'd connected with in ways I had never dreamed of. During the last month, our intimacy only strengthened that bond.

She was the dark knight to Quinton's white one. I loved her spontaneity and her boldness. Sex with her was as passionate as it was with Quinton, yet she was also my best friend. I could share everything with her without fear of her judging me, but she didn't trust that I could do the same. Her only flaw was that she wasn't Quinton--she couldn't be my man.

Yet, more than anything in the world, I still wanted to be Quinton's wife. In all my life, I'd never met anyone who I knew I needed and who wanted me as much as he had. He was loving, hard-working, and most importantly faithful. In our time together, he had earned the right to marry me. What right did Teniyah have to demand that I give that up?

I'd stopped at a red light and on my way back to the apartment when out of the corner of my eye I saw my cell phone light up. I reached over to answer it when my hand seemed to go numb and I withdrew it.
"I can do this." I took in a deep breath then exhaled before I reached over and flipped up the phone.
"Hello?"
"Lae, you'll never guess what just happened to me!" It was Simone and she sounded like she was in one of her manic moods. She didn't know that I knew, but after she had MJ, she was always either extremely happy or obnoxiously depressed.

I knew I'd never be able to guess, but I took a stab at it anyway. "Well, if I have to guess: Mike died and there was a million dollar policy in your name?"

"No."

"Why should I guess when I'm not going to get it right? Just tell me already!" I didn't really want to play guessing games and I was slightly disappointed that it was her and not Niya. As much as I tried to mask it, I didn't feel like speaking with her right now. She was having a good day, I was not, but I certainly didn't want to hear anymore about hers than I had to.

"Someone just left a dozen beautiful roses on my desk."

I tried not to sound too uninterested, but I knew I failed miserably. "That's really nice for someone to do."

"You know, Lae, I'd just been having the shittiest day until this. I wish I could find out who sent the roses--."

She was halfway into her next statement when my phone beeped and I saw that Niya was on the other end. My heart fell into my stomach, but I just knew that I had to speak to her. Somehow I had made things awkward and I had to set them right. "Hey, Monie, can I call you back; Niya is calling me on the other line."

"Yeah, okay. I'll just talk to you later then."

I clicked over just in time to catch her. "Hello? Hello?" I shouted into the phone.

"Lae, I'm sorry. I know I can get a little bitchy sometimes, but I like what we had. To me, it's like someone took away the one thing I wanted. Maybe it's my ego, but I just don't like finishing second."

"You know how I feel about you."

"Well then, say it. You always put me off to do the right thing, but what was so wrong about what we did? I loved it. You loved it and don't say you didn't. If you could stop being so damn politically correct all the time, then maybe we could really have something."

"I'm not you! I can't be gay for you and be straight for him! I just can't do it! Everyone always thinks they know what the right thing for me to do is, but I have to figure this out on my own. Dammit! Why can't you just let it go, Teniyah? Why do you have to do this?"

"I can't let go because I love you Lae." She paused. "I mean--I really love you."

"This is you, *Niya*. You always want what you can't have and how do I know that I'm not just next on the list? What promises do I have from you?" I don't know why, but tears started to stream down my face. I wiped them away and asked the questions that I knew I had to ask. "If

196

it's not you wanting something when you want it, then why are you telling me this just a few months before I get married? What took you so long to say something? If you feel so strongly about this, why are you keeping up the façade of a happily married wife and mother?"

I waited a few seconds to hear her respond, but I didn't get an answer. *No answer. I didn't know why I'd expected anything different.*

"Hello?" I asked, after impatiently waiting for her to say something.

"Sorry, I had to put the phone down. The hospital brass was walking by. Now what were you asking?" I was about to ask again when she cut me off. "Never mind, I'll have to call you when I get off. Better yet, we'll talk face to face. I'll be there at your place at four. Love ya."

"Teniyah, wait." But before I had a chance to say anything else, she'd hung up and I had less than three hours to get myself ready to finally call it quits.

4:10 PM

I began pacing around the house twenty minutes 'til four and once the digital clock read four o'clock; I looked outside my bedroom window at least twice every minute after. When she finally pulled into a parking spot it was already ten after which barely gave us an hour to talk. There were a lot of things that needed to be said and I wasn't sure if an hour was long enough to recover from it all.

When her familiar knock ran across my door, the butterflies I'd managed to suppress returned with a vengeance and managed to eat away at what little courage I did have. I rubbed my sweaty palms together to lose some of the moisture, checked the thermometer in the kitchen to make sure the AC was on and answered the door.

She walked in, still wearing her scrubs, yet smelling more like an exotic flower nursery than a hospital. She barely acknowledged me and casually walked past me as I closed the door behind her.

"Laela," she said stoically.

"Why are you the one acting like you have an attitude? You're the one who invited yourself over here!"

She sat down on the sofa, turned on the television and shook her head. "I'm just returning the favor."

"I get it, Teniyah. I haven't called. You don't seem to understand that I have a husband-to-be to take care of here. I am planning our future. That won't change."

"No, Lae, *you* don't get it. I haven't done anything to you. You're the one who's abandoned me. I haven't gotten a single call-- not one, since you've been back home. And then you have the nerve to say I'm selfish? What's selfish is the fact that you keep trying to be the perfect fiancée when all you're really doing is trying to hide what you really are. That's selfish."

I stormed past Teniyah and stood between her and the TV. "I'm selfish? Really?! Let me tell you about yourself. You complain that I'm trying to be something that I'm not, but the reality is that you're mad at me for not being what you are! There isn't a middle of the road with you, only absolutes. When we're out, you don't just ask for my free time, Niya, you practically demand it! It's like you want us to get caught! Is that what you really want? Is your life that bad that you'd like to see mine ruined too?"

"Why do you have to be so difficult? I love you and you love me, right? What about that is so hard to understand?"

"I can't love you like I love Quinton, Niya! I won't. It's not fair to him." As the tears began to fall, I knew I had to get this out before I allowed her to speak.

"I can't be what you want! I can't love you like that! You're not a man!" I felt the lump growing in my throat, but I managed to say what needed to be said.

She smirked, and even though she refused to show it, I could see how upset she was about what I'd said.

"You're right. It's not fair. Quinton's cool people and everything we've done, including how we feel about each other, is wrong to him. So, you wanna keep your man, I get it. What does this mean for us?"

I opened my mouth to speak, but when nothing came out, I ran to my bedroom and fell face-first into a pillow.

After a few minutes, Niya sat next to me and slowly ran her fingers across my back. I lifted my head from the pillow and turned just in time to see her warming smile.

I lifted up from the bed and softly kissed her top lip, slowly moving to her bottom one as our tongues grew reacquainted. As soon as she tried to withdraw, I knew she would try to assert her dominance, so I grabbed her scrub shirt and pulled her down with me as I leaned back onto my bed. No matter how badly I denied it, this is what I wanted – what my body craved.

It didn't take long before we'd both removed each other's tops. Her skin was so soft...I'd almost forgotten what it was like to be held by her. Though I loved Quinton's strong, rough hands, I didn't want to be manhandled now. I wanted to be caressed.

Niya kissed me all along my ribs, nibbling exactly where I told her to and careful not to move too fast. She'd just begun unfastening my bra when my cell phone rang.

Fuck.

I reached over to see that it was Quinton. Taking the chance to regain authority, she quickly unfastened my jeans and was pulling everything down when I answered.

"Hello baby."

"Hey, sexy, are you at the house?" he asked.

"No, I'm doing some running around."

"Okay. Well, I wanted to thank you for breakfast this morning."

"You're very welcome." I coughed, trying to mask the gasps as Niya's tongue tickled the insides of my thighs.

"I just wanted to tell you that I may be late coming home. We have some safety inspectors going over everything with a fine tooth comb and I have to be here for the audit."

I'd been rushing my sentences, but as Niya's tongue began exploring my forbidden region, I heard myself breathing heavily into my cell phone. "Well that's good news because I was going to be late coming-getting home. Maybe we can meet up somewhere after you get off?"

"Yeah, sure. Are you okay?" he asked.

"Yeah, I'm just, um, trying on some clothes in the fitting room."

"Now there's someplace we've never done it. I'm game if you are."

"We'll see. Fuck!" Niya had intentionally pushed my knees near my neck which left me wide open to do whatever she wanted.

"You sure you're okay?" he asked with such concern that I almost felt bad for what I was doing.

"I just fell over while trying to get into some jeans." With Niya's treachery, I continued to struggle with each word. "Hey, Babe, can--I call--you back?"

"Just be careful. I gotta go get something from Dre's house after work so leave me a message so that I know where to meet you. I love you."

"Love you, too." I barely had time to hang up when Niya knocked the phone from my hand. "What the hell was that all about? That was so fucking not cool, Niya. You could've gotten us in some deep shit!"

"If I wanted him to know I was eating you out I would've told him myself. That was fun."

"Dammit, Niya, that's it. I can't do this anymore." I began to sit up, but she forcefully pushed me back down.

"Lae, I'm sorry, but you want this as much as I do. You can put on a front all you want, but you love my tongue, especially when it's between your legs, don't you?" I clenched my jaws and frowned at her. She smiled and dragged her tongue over my clit. "Don't you?"

"Don't ask questions you already know the answer to."

"Don't you?" She asked a little more forcefully, her tongue now teasing the sides of my thighs.

"Yes," I whispered.

"Who does all this belong to?"

I didn't answer, so she smacked me on the side of my ass.

"Shit! That hurt!"

"I said who's is this?"

"It's Quinton's, but you're a good tenant."

She smacked me again.

"Will you stop doing that shit?" I asked, while trying to sound more demanding than pleading.

"This shit is mine, Lae, and it's just a matter of time before you realize it, too."

Smiling, she planted her face between my thighs. I loved her boldness and as I thought about the both of my lovers in between my legs, I pushed her tongue deeper inside of me. Her tongue was now perfectly placed, so I teased my clit until my toes curled, my body froze and I screamed as an orgasm erupted from my center.

Now damp with my love, Niya kissed me gently, grabbing my breasts and sucking on my nipples. But I knew it wouldn't be long before she was back to making demands.

"I'm not finished with you. Flip over. I want you on your knees."

I was exhausted, but I did as I did as I was ordered to. I touted my ass in the air, spread my legs, and relaxed my back as she ate me from behind. My body responded repeatedly as wave after wave of ecstasy came over me. Even if I'd wanted her to stop, the only words that fell out of my mouth were the curses of another oncoming orgasm.

7:05 PM

Our tryst ended a couple hours ago, but my body still tingled as I recounted the things we'd done. I texted Quinton to ask him where he wanted to meet. While I waited, Niya and I just talked.

For an hour, we talked about money, men, and manicures. As much as Simone and I talked about the same things, doing it with Niya was so much more fun. I didn't often compare the two, but the more time I spent with Niya, the more Simone seemed to be a drag.

Maybe I need to give her some time to take care of her own issues. God knows she has enough of them.

Simone was still my friend, but the longer I thought about it, the better it began to sound. Besides, I was tired of her Mike drama. For the longest time I'd never disguised the fact that I couldn't stand him, yet she still stuck around with some faint hope that he'd change. It suddenly seemed like such an asinine idea that any woman would wait around for a man when there were so many other options out there for her to explore.

Are you saying what I think you're saying?

"No. No, I'm not," I said aloud, forgetting that Niya was sitting next to me.

"Lae, what the hell are you talking about?"

"Sorry, I was just a little worried about Quinton. I don't know what's taking so long for him to call back."

"How many times have you called?"

"A couple, but they keep going to voicemail."

"Don't ever tell him I said this, but I was actually jealous of Quinton at Dre's Christmas party. Did you see some of those girls flirting with him? Even that obnoxious girl that showed her ass was cute."

I laughed. It found it strange that she'd ever be jealous of anyone. "You were jealous? I don't know why. Whenever the gorgeous Niya is around, all Quinton's friends' ever talk about is getting in your pants. Even Dre has said on more than one occasion how he'd like to break your back."

She continued on, completely ignoring what I'd just said. "What is that brother doing to have all those chickenheads swooning over him?"

"Why? Are you jealous about the fact that they are paying more attention to him or that he's paying less attention to you? Do you want those tricks swooning over you, too? Will that make you feel better? If that's what it is, just show them your tongue." I laughed again as she stuck it out and licked the side of my face.

"Seriously, Lae, I want to be the third person in your threesome." I quickly turned and looked at her with an instant frown. "What?"

"I want to be the third person in your threesome." She repeated exactly what I thought I'd heard, this time looking at me with one raised eyebrow.

"It'll never happen. First off, you're--you! Secondly, you're married. He's said more than once that he'll never go for it and I've asked him three times already. Why don't you just leave that idea alone?" For a second, I wasn't sure if I was trying to convince her or myself.

"Well then don't tell him it's me. Tell him that you found someone willing and we can go from there. Better yet, don't tell him at all. We can surprise him."

When she didn't smile, I knew she was serious. "Are you insane? Are you intentionally trying to break us up or is this one of your 'I want what I can't have' decisions?"

"Why are you so defensive, Lae? You're sleeping with the both of us now? Is it so bad that I'm curious as to why you're holding onto him?"

"Holding onto him?" I stood up from the sofa. "He's my fiancé and it's not him I'm holding onto--it's you. The only reason I called today is to tell you that I'm not doing this anymore. I'm not going to run back and forth between you two anymore."

Teniyah stood up, just to tower over me and show me that she wasn't about to let this go. "Like I said before Lae, you're selfish. It's okay for you to enjoy things when it benefits you, but as soon as someone disrupts the balance, you're Miss High and Mighty. If you were going to do a threesome anyway, why does it all of a sudden matter now? A month ago, you would've done it. Why are things so different now? You know what, I don't want an answer. Call me when you learn the difference between loving someone and fucking them."

Without waiting for a response, she shook her head and walked out the door.

For the next few minutes, I cursed her as I walked around the apartment. I sat down on the couch when I came to the realization that she was right. For as long as I'd known her, she'd never shown any inclination towards wanting Quinton. Even when they were around each other, it was always a competition between them, mostly for my attention. She was the best choice for both us whether I wanted to admit it or not.

I didn't entirely relish the idea of calling her and apologizing, but I did it anyway. Her phone rang a few times before she finally picked it up. "So have you come to your senses?" she asked.

"And hello to you, too."

"So what's it gonna be, Lae?"

"Fine, I'll see what I can do about the threesome, but that still doesn't change anything between us. Knowing how you feel--how we feel--I can't continue to carry on a relationship with you. Not like today anyway." I shivered as my mind wandered back to when her face was in between my thighs.

"So when is this elusive threesome going down?"

"His birthday is next month. That's as good a time as any."

"I'll be there with bells on. Maybe, bells will be the only thing I'll be wearing."

8:15 p.m.

Niya left an hour ago, but Quinton still hadn't gotten home. I nervously walked around the living room and wondered what the hell was taking him so long. With my type of karma I was surprised that he hadn't walked in on us. I called his cell and work phone several times after she left, but as soon as his voicemail message clicked on, I hung up.

My plan was to make love to him as soon as he came home, but Niya's visit curtailed that arrangement. I didn't know what I was going to tell him if he wanted some, but I hoped that he would be just as content with some head.

I grabbed some crackers and Quinton's card from the kitchen before I walked to the bedroom. Fatigued as hell and drained of every ounce of energy I had in my body, I shoved the crackers in my mouth two at a time to help replenish my strength while I watched a movie on Showtime, tossing his card on the bed next to me.

Where are you, Quinton? I asked myself, hoping that he'd suddenly walk through the door and I could satisfy him before my eventual collapse. I thought about making coffee, but I didn't have the taste for it. Besides, I'd heard somewhere that carbs help with energy after rigorous exercise.

After only a few minutes, I realized that the cracker therapy was a complete failure. I succumbed to my exhaustion as I fell asleep with the TV still on, cracker crumbs hanging halfway out of my mouth, and Quinton's Valentine's Day card lying on the pillow beside me.

Quinton

I left the apartment feeling like I had rocks in my stomach and was still feeling my insides being torn apart as I pulled into Dre's driveway. I jumped out of my car and ran up to his door banging furiously, hoping that he hadn't gone back to sleep after I called. He answered the door ten seconds later, but I knew he had taken his time in doing so. As soon as the door opened, I burst through and ran straight to his bathroom.

"Lae cooked you breakfast, I see."

"Eat shit!" I screamed back before running into the bathroom and slamming the door. I sat on the toilet and released the ferocity of my misdeeds. By letting Laela make breakfast, I had essentially allowed her to poison me and my body hated me for it.

"Didn't I tell you not to eat that girl's cooking? But no! You had to love her and therefore eat her poison! Now look at you! And I'll tell you what. If you get any of that shit anywhere but the inside of that bowl, we's gone have us a real problem!"

"Dre man, okay, I get it. Now can you leave me alone please?"
He walked away from the bathroom, spraying what I could only guess was deodorizer, making sure I heard him. "Poor thing, she received her father's talents at cooking; a true daddy's girl."

I came out of the bathroom feeling a great deal better than when I went in. Looking around the house for Dre, I found him in his bedroom in his most favorite position; on the phone. With all the smiling and whispering he was doing, I knew that he was most likely talkin' up his next conquest. I was about to let him know that it was time to go when he put up his index finger, a sign that he wanted me to hold off on talking.

"I'll see you tonight at your place, okay? Be naked when I get there." He smirked right before he hung up. "You ready to go?"

"I've been ready. Man, we need to leave now before we end up being there till midnight."

"Okay, let me throw on my jacket." I shook my head as he looked around his bedroom for a light jacket. It was a little cool outside, but even I knew that the jacket was pointless. In Houston it never stayed cool for long.

We both left the house and got into Dre's Cherry Red Escalade, a chromed out SUV that we affectionately termed "The Pussy-Wagon". If he was driving TPW, it meant there was some new ass on the horizon he had to impress. I didn't care about his phone conquests or riding around the city in his most treasured automobile. What I did care about was the line we were going to have to face at Mr. Larry's.

Between Mr. Larry, Mr. Duncan and Mr. Arturo, Mr. Larry's had the best trio of barbers in all of Houston. It was said that the three of them could put a fade in nose hair, but I'd never met anyone who was bold enough to test that theory.

Mr. Larry's was the premier barber shop in Houston and there wasn't a black kid in Houston, urban or suburban, who hadn't heard of him. His shop was in the heart of 5th Ward, in the oldest and one of the poorest neighborhoods in Houston. The plaza his shop was in was all but destroyed after an arsonist set fire to it right before Christmas a few years back, but even after the tragedy, his shop was untouched and he remained in the same place he'd been in for the last thirty years.

The shop didn't open until 8:30, but there was always a line before it opened, especially on days like today. It wasn't even 7:35 when we arrived, and we were already the ninth and tenth in line.

I sat in the truck and we listened to the radio for a few minutes before I looked out the window at all the other people waiting and wondered if they were playing hooky from work like I was. I was supposed to work today and chose not to. Today was Valentine's Day, the heaviest day of the year for us at EPD. With all the city-wide flower, chocolate, and package deliveries, it was the worst possible day to work. Through the years that we'd been together, I was always forced to work and when I got home, I was too tired to move. So this year, I took managerial privilege and called off.

I would've told Laela about my day off, but I wanted to do something unexpected for her besides pass out. This year I had everything I wanted to do all planned out and it all began with me getting a much needed haircut.

"What time do you think they'll get here?" I asked Dre. I needed to stay on my schedule if I wanted my plan to work.

"My guess is the time they usually get here; bout five after eight." He turned to me and smiled. "Quinton, I never told you how proud I am that you're getting married. I know that I bust your balls about Lae, but the truth is that I wanted you to get new pussy off your brain before you jumped the broom."

"Can we not talk about this? It was a bad decision and I feel like an alcoholic that fell off the wagon."

"At least you fell off the wagon drinking the stuff on the top shelf." He said, kissing his fingers.

I was glad to see that Mr. Larry and Mr. Arturo were walking towards the shop, laughing loudly at something the other had said. I pointed behind Dre's head and told him, "They're here." We both jumped out of the truck and patiently waited as they unlocked the steel curtain and finally opened the shop.

A following had built up in the twenty minutes we waited outside the shop. I didn't know an exact number, but there were roughly ten to twelve other people who were also waiting. Everyone knew that the shop only had eight available seats and with two people in the barber's chairs, Dre and I were the last one's to find a seat. The shop remained silent until Mr. Arturo turned on the old colored TV to the sports channel where they were showing basketball highlights from last night.

"You know what the worst thing about basketball is?" Mr. Larry looked at the row of waiting patrons as he spoke. "Those damn women basketball players. You gotta be manly as hell to want to play a man's sport. Like the other day I ran into one of them college players, what's her name, Tequanda Frazier and her "man", right? This niggra had tattoos all on his neck, muscles like a bodybuilder and when I accidentally bumped into them at the checkout line, this niggra turned around and I saw it was a shim! A goddamn woman, that looked like a damn man!"

Mr. Arturo shook his head. "Why is it that your old ass believes in every stereotype there is. Old as you are, you should know better, but you don't."

"I don't need nobody talking about me to my face, Turo. All I'm saying is that most of these women out here want to be with other women. Why you think they all coming out now. They doing it in Hollywood, in sports, hell they even marrying, if you can call it that."

I chimed in. "So what you're saying, Mr. Larry is that all women want to be with other women? I can't believe that for a second."

Dre was the next to speak. "You can't make generalizations based on opinion. I've dated a few basketball players and they certainly weren't attracted to other women. The truth is that when most men see a woman do something that he himself can't do, they think there has to be a reason. It used to be steroids, but now it's sexual preference. I mean really. Gay women, just like homosexual men, are born with the desire to be with the same sex. All that matters in the end is choice. Do you choose to live your life in what we call normalcy or do you choose to be an outcast by society's standards?"

Mr. Larry cut his clippers on and began cutting hair before he spoke up again. "Choice you say? That's what's wrong with y'all young folks today, too many choices. Y'all just don't know no better. You give up because it's easier to do than trying. Back in the day, we made marriages work because it was the right thing to do. We chose to stay together and make it work, which is why we stayed a community, stayed united. Back then a marriage was between a man and a woman. Sure there were queers out there, but even they knew marriage wasn't what you called a same sex partnership. It was called a union. Nowadays there's all sorts of terms for it; alternative lifestyle, gay, bi, open, swinging and what's the new one--metro sexual. Metro sexual? Please, that man is gay as a piccolo. Cheating is at an all time high and babies are being born out of wedlock and to only one parent. What happened to commitment?"

A man in a gray suit was the next to speak. "They call everything cheating nowadays. If you talk to a woman on the internet about sex, you're cheating. If you get caught watching flicks, you're cheating. If you flirt with someone around the damn office--you're cheating! My thoughts on this is that cheating is when you put forth the effort of being with someone else, knowing that you got someone at the house."

I looked down at the man in the gray suit as he gave the rest of us a smug smile. "Whoa, cheating is cheating, regardless if the other person knows it or not. You guys are thinking about the act and not the intent. Anytime you have the intent in your heart to sleep with someone else other than your spouse it's cheating. When people recite their vows, it says in the vow that they "will forsake all others." When did that stop meaning something? Why even get married if you're going to have an open relationship? Monogamy is the principle foundation of marriage and an open marriage defeats the purpose of what a marriage is and stands for."

Mr. Arturo nodded at me and added his point of view. "Y'all generation has forgotten what it means to be committed because of what they feel like they're missing. It's true that I haven't lost my wife to another man or woman for the twenty-seven years we've been married, but if you treat your woman like she should be treated, you wouldn't have to worry about those things. You gotta be pretty sad to lose a good woman to another man, or even worse, another woman cuz of what you continue to do wrong. That's jus' my belief."

The man in the suit pointed at me. "I gotta disagree, brother, with your views on open relationships. My wife and I have entertained a few extracurricular activities over the years, but that was to enhance the marriage, not take away from it. As people, especially black people, we're taught that all that shit is wrong, so we do it in secret. We don't talk about it and hope that other people don't find out. It's a part of life. It's out there and people do it. It's not just a *white* thing, it's an *everybody* thing. I mean my wife and I don't swing, but it doesn't hurt to have another woman in the bedroom from time to time."

"So let me ask you something," I interjected, "what if your woman wanted another man in the bedroom? Would it still be cool then?"

"Fuck no! Only my dick gets a starring role in my shit." Gray suit said and the barber shop roared with laughter.

"What a double standard! If it's wrong for another guy to join, what makes it right for another woman? If you weren't married, I'd say so what, but you made a promise before God to reject anyone who wasn't your wife. When did that become so trivial? Just because you can do it doesn't mean you should do it."

When Mr. Duncan walked in, the topic about open relationships seemed to fizzle and we instantly began talking about sports. Everyone in the shop knew that Mr. Duncan was a man of God and steadfast in his beliefs when it came to talking about fornicating or extra-marital activities. It was best to save that type of talk for either early in the morning, before he came or right after he left around four o'clock. If he heard us speaking about anything other than sports or movies, we'd be forced to sit in the front pew every night this week at his adult service. I sat quietly and watched TV while I waited for my haircut.

11:00 a.m.

We both left Mr. Larry's an hour later than we'd hoped, with a lot less hair on our heads and faces than when we came in; Dre's cut favored the taper and received a razor shave to maintain his baby-faced appearance, while I received a bald fade and a thinned out goatee.

"Damn, I look good, there is no denying that," Dre said as he looked at himself in his rear view mirror.

"Okay, Mr. Sexy, if you'd please drive us to get us fitted for our tuxedos, I'd be very appreciative."

"So are you gonna call any of them again?"

"Call who?"

"The big booty girl you were supposed to hook me up with and your Mrs. Good-pussy, Cheyenne. The way I see it, Valentine's Day is good a day as any to get a little fantasy side-action."

"Just let it go, Dre. That's not who I am and that's damn sure not who I want to be--again. It was a one-time thing, so can't we just leave it in the past?"

"Fine, I'll leave it in the past if you can answer one thing for me." I thought about not falling into his trap, but I didn't want to always be reminded of my infidelities, either. "What do you want to know?"

"How golden was Mrs. Old School's pussy?" He chuckled. "I mean, she had a brother hard on the phone. She sounds like a woman who knows her way around a pole. She turned yo' ass out, didn't she?"

Without saying a single word, I smiled.

12:05 p.m.

"Quinton, I was just thinking about you and I wanted to hear your voice, but you're not at work, so the voicemail was the next best thing. The last time we saw each other it was pretty intense and I wanted to know if there was an encore on the horizon. Call me..."

I sat in my car and listened to the voicemail Cheyenne left me. There was almost nothing more I wanted to do than to see her again, but I'd already fucked up once by sleeping with her. Risking what Lae and I shared for a married woman was just wrong. I just didn't know why it was so hard for me to resist her, though. What I needed to do was clear my head and pick up the flowers I'd bought for Laela, so I put my car in drive and headed downtown.

"Welcome. Do you have a pickup or would you like me to make an arrangement?" The lady at the counter asked in her Indian accent.
"Yes, I do, it's under James."
When she returned she had with her two dozen beautifully arranged red roses in a crystal vase.
"Is there anything else I can get for you?" she asked.

I was about to say no when I saw some yellow roses behind her. With all the talk of infidelity that we had this morning, I knew someone who was suffering worse than probably all of us combined. "Yes, how much for a dozen yellow roses?"

"Those are on sale for ten dollars."

I grabbed a card with a picture of the sun on it that sat on a rack by the register. "How much is it for this?"

"Go ahead and take it."

I wrote an uplifting message in the card that corresponded with the picture on the outside. I paid the $10, waved goodbye and walked back to my car with three dozen flowers. I sat the two dozen I bought for Lae on the passenger's side of my car, careful to keep them out of the sunlight and took the extra dozen with the card with me as I waited for the Metro.

With Simone's job practically down the street, I hopped on the Metro train and rode it down Main to her building. I was about to walk into the building when the smell of fresh bread and cookies deterred me. I walked across the street into a bakery and bought six warm chocolate chip cookies before entering her building.

I'd been to the building several times before, but I was usually with Lae who'd leave me in the car while she went to see Simone. I was about to walk to the security desk when I bumped into a goofy looking security guard.

"Excuse me," I said.

"Yes?" he asked, barely looking at me.

I looked for a nametag and found it right above his right breast pocket; C. Moore. "I'm looking for R.A. Gladden Investments."

"Sixth floor."

I walked past him and rode the elevator to the sixth floor. The office was impossible to miss. A gold Gladden Investments plaque adorned the left wall of the office space to my right, while random people constantly walked in and out the office doors, chatting away about work and sports, too wrapped up in their own existence to notice that I was carrying a dozen flowers as they callously bumped into me. I found out why they were so careless when I walked through the doors and saw several delivery men--none with my company, with huge bouquets, cramming the walkways with their large bundles.

I was about to ask someone where Simone's desk was when I saw her name plate sitting atop a dark wooden desk in the back corner of the front office. I walked over and verified it was actually her space by the pictures of Mike and MJ strewn across her desk. I shook my head. It still stupefied me that she would continue to keep his picture on her desk even though he'd put her and MJ through hell.

I waited by her desk for a few minutes to see if she'd show up, but when she didn't I laid the flowers with the card and three of the cookies on her desk before I took another elevator back down to the first floor and walked out through the turnstile on my way back to Main Street. The Metro came a few minutes later and I was at my car in another ten minutes.

4:20 p.m.

I'd spent the last 2 ½ hours driving around Houston, looking for the perfect gift I could give Laela before heading home. I wasn't sure what I wanted to get, but I knew that she'd like jewelry. Other than the engagement ring I'd put on her finger, I'd never bought her any type of jewelry, but she was going to be the first and only Mrs. Quinton James and I wanted to splurge a little.

Since I was already downtown, I drove to the Galleria and several other places, but it wasn't until I visited a jewelry shop on Westheimer that I saw exactly what I wanted to buy her. A sale on tennis bracelets caught my eye and when I walked out of the store, I'd bought her a white gold, one carat tennis bracelet that I knew she would love.

Driving home with the flowers and the tennis bracelet, I couldn't wait to see the expression on her face; nor could I wait to hear how jealous her friends would be, which could only add positive points to my already impeccable reputation. I smiled at how devious I could be.

At a red light I picked up my phone and dialed Lae's number. I wasn't sure if she was at the house, but if she was I didn't want her to expect me home on time. I knew that when I walked through the door earlier than I said I would, the surprised look on her face would be priceless. I rolled up my windows and cut on the AC so that she couldn't hear the traffic, took a deep breath, and prepared to lie my ass off.

"Hello, baby," she greeted.

After some brief small talk, I told her I loved her and was ready to hang up when I heard a loud thud and a voice on the other end.

"...that was so fucking not cool, Niya. You could've gotten us ..."

Gotten us what? Did she have a present for me that she didn't want me to know about? Curious to find out what they were planning, I pushed the mute button and listened.

The next voice belonged to Teniyah. "If I wanted him...eating you out ...that was fun."

What the hell are they talking about? I pressed the phone tighter against my ear to hear them.

What the hell was going on?

"...I can't do this anymore..." Lae complained.

211

"... You want this as much as I do...front all you want...my tongue, especially when it's between your legs..." Teniyah said.

I pulled into the nearest parking lot and sat with the phone to my ear. My heart was pounding in my chest and I felt sicker than I had when I ate Lae's breakfast this morning.

I couldn't be hearing what I thought I'd heard. With my free hand, I rubbed my temple and kept my ear to the phone.

"...you already know the answer..." she said.

"Fuck!" I yelled into the phone. "Fuck!" I sped out of the driveway and began racing home with the phone still pressed against my ear.

The fantasies of Lae sleeping with another woman suddenly infuriated me. I couldn't believe that she was betraying me and here I was, sitting in the car with flowers and a gift and listening to everything as it happened. Even with the air conditioner was on full blast, I could feel the warmth growing in my car from the fury I felt and I gripped the steering wheel as tightly as I could. I looked around at all the people smiling as they walked to their cars and felt nothing but malice. Questions poured through my brain, but I didn't have answers for any of them, though I knew who would. How long have they been fucking? *How long has this shit been going on behind my back? Why didn't I fucking see it before? Exercising my ass--they've probably been fucking all this time!*

As much as I despised Laela for cheating on me, the stale air was killing me as Niya's last question seemed to linger in Lae's head. My hands were so tightly wrapped around my steering wheel that I could feel my own nails digging into my palm, but all I could do was sit and listen.

"...does all this belong to?" Teniyah asked.

After a loud smack, I heard Lae shout. "Shit that hurt!"

"I said who's is this?" Niya demanded.

"It's Quinton's, but you're a good tenant."

Another loud smack. Lae was being punished for naming me, but the pain she felt was in no way measurable to the pain I felt.

"Will you stop doing that shit?" Lae pleaded.

"This shit is mine...you realize it too."

Not wanting to hear another word, I hung up the phone. All the excitement and anticipation I'd had through the entire day had instantly become anger, frustration and disappointment. As much as I tried to hold them back, tears began to fight their way down my face and as much as I tried to wipe them away, they wouldn't stop.

I began dialing Franklin's number so that we could both be at the apartment when they arrived, but then an uneasy question entered the back of my mind and wouldn't go away. As much as I wanted to hurt Lae, to blame her, to make her feel like I felt while listening to her fuck her best friend, I wasn't exactly innocent, either.

How much didn't I know about the woman I was supposed to marry? How much of a man was I really if I drove the only woman I'd ever proposed to into the arms of another woman?

This shit is crazy! When I went down on Laela, was she hoping it was Niya? Was the sex with her best friend better than ours? Why didn't she come to *me*? How could she do this to *me*?

I didn't care anymore. I put down my phone, turned the car back on and raced to the apartment. But no matter how fast I drove, I couldn't shake the feeling that I'd brought this on myself. Images of Niya tasting my fiancée ravaged my brain.

I was only a couple of minutes from our apartment when I realized I didn't want to go home. I didn't want to be where I was so easily replaced.

"...You're a good tenant," Laela's words rang through my head again. It hurt to know that as much as I'd given up to be with Lae, she'd given up on me to be with Teniyah.

I was at Highway 6 and Bellaire when I made a left onto Bellaire and drove towards I-59, away from the apartment. At the first red light, I called Cheyenne. If Lae could forget about me, then I could certainly forget about her, but when she didn't pick up her phone, I slammed my cell on the armrest several times before I threw it in the backseat.

With all this time I'd spent with Lae, I had no idea who she truly was. I wasn't ready to make sense of it all, so I drove to the only person who knew what I was going through. I didn't know if she could provide me with any solace, but at least she could understand.

If Teniyah and Laela fucking wanted each other, they could fucking have each other.

5:00 p.m.

I pulled into Mike and Simone's driveway, unsure if I should get out or not. I didn't see Mike's car, but as I looked upstairs, the lights were on and I knew someone would be home. I sat in the car for a few more minutes, regaining my composure before finally getting out and took the back steps up to the second floor of the duplex. When I made it to the top, I listened out for either Mike or Simone, but when I didn't hear anything, I sighed and softly knocked against the back door.

The door flew open and a seductive, smiling, and frontally nude Simone welcomed me home before realizing I wasn't Mike. She immediately closed her robe, but not before exposing herself and her newer, slender figure.

"Oh shit, Q!" she shrieked.

Still numb from anger, I didn't even make an attempt to cover my eyes. I'd already seen her and no amount of pretending was going to change that. I walked past her into the kitchen and sat down at the table.

"Lae is fucking cheating on me."

Still a little flustered, she quickly tied her robe together. She sat across from me. "What happened, Quinton?"

"I caught her, Monie! I fucking heard her on the phone! It was her and Niya and they were fuckin' each other!"

She grabbed my hand and stroked it a few times. "I know."

I jumped away from the table and looked at her.

"You know? How could you know about all this and keep it from me!" I yelled.

"Quinton, calm down, please." She stood up and walked over to me. "The reason I didn't say anything was because you asked me not to. God knows I wanted to tell you, I really did, but you're my friend and I respect what you told me. You're the one who asked me not to tell you."

I began to pace around the kitchen. "Fuck what I said, Monie! It's been going on for that long? They've been doing all this behind my back and you've known about it? What the fuck, Monie?"

She walked up to me so that she was barely a few inches from my face. "Don't blame me for this, Quinton!" She snapped. "I didn't agree with it and I told Lae to come clean! You're the one who told me you didn't want to know and I did exactly what you wanted me to! And for the record, I don't know how long it's been going on. Lae only told me a week ago-- right after she came home from Cleveland."

When I finally stopped pacing, I took a step away from Simone and sat down. "She threw it all away, Monie. We had something good and she just went and pissed on it."

As I began to feel the frustration all over again, I stood up to leave when she grabbed my hand.

"Quinton...stay."

I tried not to cry, but as Simone embraced me, I could feel my eyes welling up. I held her as tightly as I could, unwilling to let go.

At that moment, I admired Simone more than anyone else in the world. She was there when I needed her and even though I didn't tell her

214

about Mike's infidelity, she'd always believed in me, respected our friendship. No matter what I did wrong, I was always a good man to her.

Not ready to lose the human contact, we held each other a little longer. Without speaking, she took my hand and guided me towards the living room sofa.

As we sat down on the couch, barely inches apart, she innocently smiled at me and without thinking; I did something I knew I shouldn't have done.

I kissed her.

Simone

5:15 p.m.

I opened my mouth to receive him and as I did, the warmth from his kiss spread throughout my body. All of my fantasies about him had begun this way and he didn't disappoint. The feel of his lips pressed against mine made me feel like a new woman, but his kiss wasn't a kiss of love or passion--it was of angst. At that moment I understood what we both wanted--retribution.

Not wanting it to end with just the kiss, I stood up, pulling him away from the couch and as I did, allowed my robe to fall to the floor. He gently kissed me on the lips, then cupping my breasts; he teased my nipples with his tongue.

As he continued sucking and gently biting my nipples, I cooed and softly called his name. It wasn't until I couldn't stand it anymore that I grabbed his head, pulled it away from my breasts and tore away at his clothing: first his shirt, then his pants. I briefly admired the chiseled form before me before all of my attention was drawn towards the wonderful instrument he'd used to seduce Lae with so many times. I slid his boxers down his legs and as he stepped out of them, I kneeled before Quinton and took him into my mouth. It wasn't easy, but I relaxed my jaws and brought in as much as I could. I loved the way his dick felt inside of my mouth. As it grew to proportions that Mike could only dream of, I spit on it and slowly slid it down the back of my throat.

Even though I'd fantasized about doing it many times, taking him into my mouth was so arousing that I was almost ready to cum. After looking up and seeing his eyes roll into the back of his head, I knew that he was enjoying it as much as I was. Feeling emboldened, I placed his hands on the back of my neck and I grabbed his hips. Together, we pushed him as far as I could take him.

Continuing with our perfect rhythm of ebb and flow, it didn't take long before I felt the beginnings of his climax. Instead of me pulling him deeper, he took control, grabbing my hair and forcing himself deep down my throat. Knowing he was so close his orgasm, I played with my throbbing clit and only seconds before he finally cum did I release my own orgasm. I tried screaming, but as my throat was filling with his cum, I could only withdraw to keep from drowning. As I slowly pulled him out of my mouth, I dragged his dick along my tongue and felt his seed as it flowed down my chin.

Trying to stand, Quinton picked me up from the floor and with his legs still weakened from his climax; we staggered across the living room.

Whether he was about to collapse or I was too heavy for him, we stumbled over his clothes, running into a wall full of family photos. Although we didn't hit the wall hard, there was enough force between the both of us to knock down most of the pictures and puncture it. Oblivious to what we'd done, Quinton pinned me against the wall and slid himself into me.

With my back a little sore from the impact, I winced, but still wrapped my legs around Quinton as he pounded the both of us against the wall. With my arms around his neck and his hands supporting my waist, each thrust felt like a mini-orgasm. I could feel drywall crumbling down my back, and I screamed out his name as I craved every stroke of his dick inside of me.

Quinton punished me. He rammed himself deep inside of me, slamming my ass against the top of his legs and biting the side of my neck. He never spoke a word and every time I cried, he'd bite my neck a little harder. Countless times I climaxed and moaned out his name as I begged for mercy, but he seemed purposefully deaf to all of my cries.
Sweat was pouring from his face when he finally pulled me away from the giant hole we'd created in the wall. He carried me to my bedroom, slid himself into me as we began again. This time though, he was gentle with me. Taking his time, he pulled my legs up with his mighty arms and hit the deepest recesses of me. I was being manhandled and with almost every other stroke, another climax was on the horizon.

As the unrelenting explosions rippled through my body I briefly thought about Mike walking in and finding us. I imagined the anger and disgust on his face and I smiled. I honestly didn't care if he walked in right now; I wouldn't give up my Quinton for anything he had to offer. He needed to see for himself how a real man was supposed to make love to his wife and that real man was about to release another fucking orgasm.

When Quinton finally rose up, sweat dropped from his brow and illuminated his frame in the scarce light of my bedroom.

"Turn over."

I did as I was told.

Thank you, Laela. You're a fool to give all this man up.

After I'd assumed the position, he slapped me on my bare ass a few times before spreading my legs a little wider and pushing my face back down further into my pillows. Placing both hands on my hips, he again slid inside of me.

After about forty-five minutes of my perpetual orgasms, he was ready to cum again. Pushing deeper inside of me, he pressed his chest against my back and squeezed my throat.

My eyes rolled so far into my head that I feared they wouldn't come back down and at the moment of the most intense climax ever, Quinton came with me, releasing me from his grasp. With my throat now free, I screamed his name so loudly that I was sure my neighbors heard everything.

But I didn't care.

I collapsed into my pillows, my body trembling like I was overcoming hypothermia and each time Quinton breathed on me, I shivered a little more. As the fruits of our labor ran down my thighs, I smiled. He'd climaxed inside of me and more than anything, I wanted him to.

Oh God, this is exactly how I dreamed it would be.

7:30 p.m.

We were just out of the shower when I sat down on the couch. I was still nude, hoping for an encore, but as he picked up his clothes from the floor in silence, I put back on the same robe I wore when Quinton entered the apartment-- the same robe I'd let fall twice in front of him-- the same robe that would be there when this happened again.

When he sat down next to me, I placed my hands on top of his and noticed how distant he looked.

"Quinton, are you okay?"

"We shouldn't have done this," he quickly answered, sliding his pants up his legs.

I shook my head. "Why? What did we do that was so wrong? On a day like today, we were both alone because we were betrayed by the people we loved. Quinton, we just needed to be consoled-- and that's all it was."

"There's a big difference between consoling and fucking, Monie. What we did was fuck and it doesn't change the fact that the people we're with cheated on us! You're my best friend's wife and my fiancée's Maid of Honor! How is what we did any different from what they did?"

"Because, Quinton," I wrapped my fingers inside of his, "we did it because of them. If Mike was here, with his wife on Valentine's Day, and Lae wasn't with Teniyah-- this would've never happened. "

"That doesn't make it right."

"It makes it *fair.*"

"Fair? When you opened that door, you were half-naked and waiting for Mike. It wasn't about fairness, Monie. It was just coincidence and circumstances."

I pointed to the yellow roses that sat on top of my dining room table. "The only reason I was going to sleep with him was because he brought me those. I wanted to forgive him, even if it was just for today, but as you can see, he never showed up."

He looked at me and smirked. "Simone, that wasn't Mike. I put those on your desk, with some cookies and a card. I realized what you guys were going through and I wanted to brighten up your day."

"I didn't know! I'm so sorry, Quinton! The card didn't have a name on it and I just assumed it was Mike."

"No, it was me."

He really *is* the perfect man.

I leaned over and kissed him on the forehead. "Then the right person got what he deserved."

"So what now?"

"Look, I've never felt the way you made me feel tonight. I know that it's probably wrong to tell you this, but I'm glad it happened. I don't know where this is supposed to go, but you've always known that I cared about you. You're a good man and what we did tonight isn't going to make me think different about you. I just wish that Mike could be half the man you are."

"And Lae could learn a lot from you," he said softly.

My smile was so wide that I thought I may never have a straight face again. "Thank you." I said, sheepishly. I was still sore, but with just that one sentence, I was ready for him to be inside of me again.

"I should be thanking you. I didn't know what I was going to do, but with you here, I was able to let off some steam. I guess we could say that what we did was really tit-for-tat."

Tit-for-tat? Is that all I was? Was that all we did? But you said Lae could learn from me!

"So are you going to say something to Laela about what you heard?"

"No. After what just happened here, I won't say anything if you don't," he said, while putting on his shirt.

"So what's going to happen if she sleeps with Raven again?"

I watched him cover his sexy chest with the shirt I'd thrown to the floor earlier. "Look, Monie, I love Lae and no matter how much I wanted to hate her today for doing what she did, I'm not innocent either. I helped open the door to all of this, but if what she did with Niya gets it out of her system, then what we did will get it out of mine. I'm not giving her a free pass to do it again, but telling her I know would also mean telling her about what happened here. I don't want to lose the best thing I've ever had, especially when we're supposed to be getting married this summer."

"Well, she won't hear a word from me, but she'd better not do this to you again." I said, giving him a feigned 'hope everything works out' smile.

I didn't care if Laela knew what we'd done. Hell, I wished Mike would've walked in, but if this is what Quinton wanted, then I'd go with it-- for now. Because when Lae messed up again, and she would, Quinton would run to me and return to my bed.

Quinton

8:30 p.m.

I was halfway home when it all sank in. For most of the drive, everything seemed surreal. I wanted to believe that I hadn't just slept with Simone, but the remnants of rough sex still lingered below. An overwhelming feeling of disgust began taking over me, not only because of what Lae had done, but because of what I also had done in retaliation. I slept with--no, fucked--one of my best friends' wives and though I felt bad being with her, fucking her without any remorse was exactly what I needed to make me feel like a man again.

219

I heard her as she pleaded for mercy, but as I envisioned Lae's face supplanted over hers, neither of them deserved it. As unforgiving as I was, Simone took it and asked for more until I was too tired to give it. I tried to break her, but she'd broken me and I loved the way she tightened around me every time she had an orgasm....

Shit, you're doing it again! Get her out of you mind!

Fucking Simone was therapeutic, but it wouldn't happen again. It couldn't. The both of us had our own problems to deal with and sleeping with each other wasn't going to solve anything. If Lae found out about what we'd done...

"We have a clean slate."

I picked up my phone to call Simone to make sure she was okay, but as I opened the banged up cell I found that Lae had called several times while Simone and I were together.

Talk about irony.

I walked into my apartment thirty minutes later, bracelet in hand, and the only sounds in the whole house were that of the bedroom TV. I walked down the hallway to our room and saw Lae sprawled across the bed with half-eaten crackers littering the spread. I wanted to forgive her so badly that it hurt, but my heart was broken and I didn't need the bracelet on her arm reminding me out what we both had done to each other. I quietly slid it as far as it could go into the back of my sock drawer. The drawer squeaked several times as I tried to remain inaudible, but she never moved a muscle.

Eating pussy is hard work, I guess.

I took a deep breath and walked back to the living room. As soon as I turned on the TV to the sports channel, I crashed.

CHAPTER 15

Laela

February 25th (Saturday)

As the sun crept from behind the clouds and slowly warmed what little flesh I'd exposed, the day was finally beginning to turn into what the weatherman had predicted.

"I think I should tell him."

"Tell who, what?" Niya curiously asked.

I looked at Teniyah, who drove like a maniac, but was dressed like a diva: in a creme pants suit, with matching sun hat and black heels. We were only supposed to be going to the Galleria for our final fittings, so when she picked me up from the apartment, all I had on was jeans and a t-shirt. Instead of waiting for me to change, she allowed me to put on my sandals and dragged me to her car.

"I think I should tell Q about us," I said.

Looking at me, Niya almost ran over a family crossing the street and swerved her Cavalier out of the way just in time to miss them. As if completely oblivious to what had just happened, she returned her glare towards me. "Now why would you do some crazy shit like that?"

I looked through the back window just in time to see a young Asian man giving us the middle finger. "I think Quinton knows something. We didn't do *anything* on Valentine's Day and he's acting funny."

"So what? He's on his man period, big deal! Girl, if I was getting regular dick like you, I could hold out between sessions. Do you remember my drought?"

"How do you always manage to turn my problems into your drama?"

She smiled and rubbed my shoulder. "It's a gift. Now get out, we've got shopping to do."

She grabbed my hand and pulled me into the crowd that headed towards Neiman Marcus entrance of the Galleria. The sun was out and although it wasn't warm yet, the heat from Niya's hand made me uncomfortable. As I looked around and saw people who noticed us holding hands, I immediately pulled my hand from her grasp.

When Niya realized what I'd done, she disapprovingly shook her head and we entered the store.

Once the crowd had scattered and we passed several ladies offering perfume samples, Niya turned to me. "What's the deal, Lae?"

"I'm not holding your hand!"

She shrugged. "I didn't know it was such a big deal to you. We're women. I don't think anyone will care if they see us holding hands."

"Jesus Niya, you're married and I'm engaged! Hell, the reason we're at the mall in to make alterations to my wedding dress! Besides, there's a big difference between holding a hand and holding your hand. People at the job are already talking and I just don't want to give them any more to say."

"No one from the job is here and I don't think it's that big of a deal. But if you want to act homophobic, then by all means, you should indulge."

Rather than argue with her, I walked fast enough so that I didn't have to see her ridiculous smirk. It wasn't long before I found myself thinking of Quinton and why he'd seemed so distant. I pulled my cell phone out of my purse to call him when Niya grabbed my shoulder.

"With all this heat in between us," she leaned into my ear and softly whispered, "maybe we should get some ice cream to cool things down."

Our walk to the food court didn't usually take long, but we were stopped several times as Niya flirted with practically every man that walked up to her.

"Why don't you just tell them you're married so that we don't have to keep stopping?"

"Do you really think I'm wearing this to be ignored?" she replied and winked at me.

As we finally made our way into the bridal shop, several small Mexican women, most of whom were sizing us while the rest just chatted between themselves, immediately surrounded us. We'd made it to the front counter when Mrs. Rodriguez, a woman I'd met several times stepped from behind the white counter and nodded at me.

"Miss Booker and Mrs. Oliver, here for your fittings?" she asked in only a slightly Spanish accent. I returned her nod, but Niya shouted, "Si!"

After spending about forty-five minutes in the bridal store, we were gathering new measurements during our fittings, with me half naked and completely insecure about those last few pounds I needed to lose. My gown looked beautiful on me and Teniyah was ogling at my naked frame as I stepped out of the dress.

"So have you talked to Quinton about our ménage yet?"

"It's not that easy, Niya. He's been a little... temperamental and I don't think right now is the best time."

"There'll never be a best time for you. Just blurt it out and tell him that if he wants to do a threesome, then I'm your last hope."

I nervously looked around the boutique. "Let's get out of here, first."

After dressing we walked back into the mall.

"I can't do that."

"Why?" she asked, stopping in the middle of all the shopping traffic and raising her eyebrow at me.

"Because, I'm the one who wanted to do it in the first place. He's only doing it because I want to try it before we get married. That's why."

"That does tend to put a cramp in my strong arm policy. Oh well," she shrugged, "it's still about a month before it goes down. I'll be there regardless, so you might want to tell him why I'll be naked on y'alls bed."

We talked and walked around the mall for almost an hour before finally finding our way to Victoria's Secret. By that time, Niya had already purchased several purses and shoes for her children, while the only thing I wanted was a watch for Quinton. I knew that he probably wouldn't wear it, but I bought it regardless.

I was watching Niya fawn over some of the teddies when I looked over and saw Simone looking over the sheer lingerie. I thought about calling out her name, but knowing how she and Niya felt about each other, I snuck over to her and tapped her on the shoulder.

She looked up and when she saw me, instantly became flustered.

"Laela, what are you doing here?"

I looked her over and almost didn't recognize her. She had on a pair of tight fitting jeans and a white tank top that her breasts would probably fall out if she leaned over. Yet, it wasn't just what she wore; she seemed like an entirely different person. Along with having her weight loss, her hair was done, and she was positively glowing.

"Oh my God, girl," I squealed, "I almost didn't know who you were!"

"I just kept to my New Years' resolution," she said modestly. "All this stuff is old. I'm just wearing an old pair of jeans and Mike's wife-beater."

I didn't want to tell her, but I was a little jealous. She'd always been shaped like a stick, but after MJ, everything had grown. Now that she'd lost some weight, she had hips and boobs that I could only dream of.

"You look good, girl, and you seem really happy. Did you finally come here to get your dress fitting?"

She smiled. "Sort of. I plan to lose more of this baby weight, so I just wanted to get a temporary measurement for a few weeks. I just stopped by here because I wanted to buy something nice."

"So if it wasn't the dress, what really brought you out today? You finally had enough of Mike and MJ?"

She folded her arms and her brow furrowed. "No Lae, I'm here for myself. Is it that hard to believe that I'm just out shopping because I want to and not because I'm running away?"

"Simone, I-- I'm sorry," I stuttered, "I didn't mean it that way. You're just usually a homebody unless you're trying to get away. I didn't mean for it to offend you."

She nodded. "It's okay. You're right. Mike's back at home and we just pass by each other most of the time without speaking." She looked at me and shook her head. "But I have met someone else. He was a secret admirer."

"Is it the same mystery person who bought you the flowers for Valentine's Day?"

"I didn't think you were listening, but yeah, it's him."

"So he's the person that has you making all these changes? You lose some weight, smile while you talk and sneak out to buy sexy lingerie for a guy you haven't met?"

She closed her eyes and took in a deep breath. "Lae, I've already met him. We've even spent some time together and," she paused, "I did some things to him that I swore I'd never do."

"Jesus Christ, Simone! Where did you guys hook up? Where was Mike when all this went down?"

"He came over to my house and things just took off from there." A smile that I hadn't seen in years crept across her face as she recalled the things her mystery man had done to her. She didn't leave a single detail out and I found myself slightly aroused by what had transpired between them. "Lae, he gave me the first orgasms I'd ever had."

"Who *is* this guy? By the way you tell the story; I've really got to meet him!"

"Maybe one day you will..."

Simone abruptly stopped speaking and when I turned around, Niya was behind me.

"So what are you two ladies talking about?"
I returned my focus to Simone and watched as a scowl crept across her face. "Hello, Raven."

Teniyah smirked, but it wasn't a smile.

As I stood between them, both donning unrelenting glares and barely a couple of feet away from each other, I could feel the tension. I immediately turned my attention towards the taller of the two. "Hey Niya, can I talk to Simone for a sec?"

After a few seconds, Teniyah released Simone from her steely glare, shrugged and walked away.

"So, I know why you're here, Lae. Looking for something to spice things up in the bedroom-- with her?"

"That's a low blow, Simone. I didn't tell you so that you could throw it in my face."

She crossed her arms, pushing her breasts almost over the top of her shirt. "I can't believe what you're doing to Quinton. Are you two still...?"

"No, we're not. We're just here because of me. I was just going to buy something to surprise Quinton with."

With her hands on her hips, she looked at me disapprovingly. "You should tell him the truth about you two, Laela. It's not right. What you've done behind his back is wrong."

"So does that mean you're going to tell Mike what you did a couple of days ago, Monie? We're in the same boat."

"Call it whatever you like, but what I did to Mike is tit-for-tat," she said matter-or-factly. "What exactly has Quinton done to deserve what you did to him? You slept with your best friend, how would you feel if he did the same?"

"Somehow I don't think that a broken heart will drive him into Dre's arms," I said, covering my mouth to keep myself from laughing. Simone didn't even feign a smile.

"You know what I mean, Lae. Quinton's a good guy and you're fucking it up while sleeping with that tramp over there. Just because her marriage is already screwed doesn't mean that she should be able to drag you down with her."

I grabbed Simone's elbow and pulled her to the back of the store where no one could hear what we were talking about.

"Monie, you need to relax," but her arms were still tightly folded and her glare was as harsh as ever. "Look, it was a one- time thing and it won't happen again, okay? If I tell Quinton, then it'll be when I know he's ready to take it. Right now just isn't that time."

"As a person with some experience with getting cheated on, it'll come back and bite you in the ass when you least expect it. I'm just saying that if he hears it from you, it may lessen the blow than if he hears it from someone else."

I suspiciously looked at Simone to see if she was suggesting that she'd tell, but I didn't really get that from her. "Fine, I'll tell him. But like I said, it won't be today."

It was certainly time to change topics. "I miss you. Why don't you come out with me and Niya?"

As two nervous twenty-somethings passed by her, she finally dropped her arms and leaned against one the lingerie racks. "No thanks. Three's a crowd and I don't want to be where only fifty-percent of the people want me there."

I knew I should've given up on the aspect of the two of them being friends a long time ago, but I didn't want them bickering, either. "Look, it's just lunch. I'll make sure she's on her best behavior. C'mon Monie, I don't want this between you guys. As a peace offering, I'll buy you that sheer cami set over there so that you can show it off to your new man."

The smile returned. "Where are you guys going?"

"I'm going to kill you for inviting her."

Niya wasn't happy, but the lunch between us wasn't that bad. Niya was on her best behavior, Simone called Teniyah by her name and I was enjoying the fact that both my best friends were at least acting civil.

We'd left the galleria, and were heading back down Westheimer to the highway.

"You had fun. Admit it."

"You bought her lunch, why couldn't you buy mine?"

"You selfish whore! The only thing you had to pay for was the drink because the manager had a crush on you!"

"He was cute, too--for a white guy."

Between the watch, Simone's lingerie and our lunch, I was out a few hundred dollars. Still, it was all worth it.

As Niya continued swerving through the highway traffic at speeds I didn't dare go, she managed to interlock her arm inside of mine.

"So are you going to tell Quinton?"

"I'm not sure. I want to tell him... but I don't want to lose him."

"You know I love you, so I'm going to speak from the heart. Simone's life is garbage, so she just wants someone to join in on her misery. You, Laela, have a good thing going and why should a little tryst mess that up? If you want to ease your guilty conscience, convince Quinton to do the threesome with the both of us. That way, you can mess around on him in front of him; he'll love it and won't be the wiser!"

"How it is that you turn my problems into your problems again?" I asked, as I reclaimed my arm from hers.

"It's a gift."

"Quinton, are you here?" I yelled as I sat the gift I'd bought him and my keys down on the counter.

"I'm in the bedroom."

I walked to the bedroom, hoping to surprise him when I found him playing video games. "Are you playing against Tank?"

"No, this time I'm playing against Janette." At the mention of her name, I dropped the watch box and as I scrambled to pick it up, Quinton continued.

"I would show her mercy, but she talks as much shit as your brother does. So, did you have fun while you were out?"

"I bought this for you." I handed him the watch and was sorely disappointed when he showed no reaction and placed the box at his side.

"Thank you," he said dryly.

"Don't you at least want to open it up?"

He turned towards me with a curious expression on his face. "I'll wear it tonight. So what else did you do while you were out?"

"Niya and I met up with Monie and went out to lunch." When I leaned over to try to kiss him, he offered me his cheek. "What? Why can't I get a real kiss?"

"Because I don't know where your mouth has been," he answered nonchalantly.

He knows something!

"What do you mean? You know where my mouth has been! It's been on you!"

"I can smell guacamole and sour cream on your breath," he said, frowning. "You know I hate that stuff."

"Fine, I'll brush my teeth." I trudged over to the sink as after brushing my teeth, returned for a second attempt. This time, I didn't miss. "So anything happen while I was gone?"

"Dre's having another party tonight and he wants us to come."

"What's the theme this time?"

"It's a tribute to the eighties. But knowing Dre, it's probably going to be a hurl-fest, an orgy, or like the Happy Merry, an amalgamation of the two."

"You're still thinking about that kiss at the Happy Merry?" I asked, hoping that he was.

"It's crossed my mind a lot in the last few days."

I sat down next to him on the bed and ran my fingers down the back of his neck. "Quinton, the wedding is only a few months away and I don't think we're going to get a threesome before that time. Why don't we try someone we already know and that we're familiar with?"

"Lae, if that's your way of suggesting Teniyah, again-- then fine. If you don't feel like there's another option then I'll back down on one of my rules this once."

That was much easier than I'd thought it'd be.

"Can we do it on your birthday then?" I asked, still stroking his neck.

"My birthday isn't until next month. Why wait 'til then?"

"Because I want it to be the best birthday present you'll ever have."

Besides, I got a good look at Simone today and if she can look that good in one month, then so can I.

We arrived fashionably late at Dre's house, hoping that a few people would be there, but when we arrived, the party was already in full swing. Forced to park down the street, we passed several multi-colored mullets and dripping jheri curls en route to the front door.

228

Music blared out from Dre's open door and Quinton walked in looking like an extra from Miami Vice: wearing a cream blazer and matching pants, a pink t-shirt, loafers, oversized sunglasses and a cross hanging from his left ear.

My ensemble took a little more thought. I wore an oversized, neon yellow t-shirt, that exposed my left shoulder, biker shorts underneath a stonewashed mini-skirt, thick yellow earrings, banana pumps and a yellow headband that held down my Whitney Houston wig. I felt like a clown with all the make-up I had on, but the blue eye shadow I wore was still tasteful and the blush on my cheeks wasn't too over the top.

As I stood in Dre's entryway, I swore that we had somehow fallen into an eighties flashback. Everywhere I looked, there were remnants of the decade: colored hair and Mohawks, huge plastic bracelets and leg warmers, neon and pastel colored clothing, and even a streaking white man wearing a presidential mask.

In each corner of the room, away from the crowds, were three flat screen televisions; each on its own stand and playing a different 80's movie. I was familiar with 'Weird Science', but not with the other two.

"This is crazy!" I shouted to Quinton, but he was laughing at the mysterious streaker who whisked by us.

Dre had clearly outdone himself with this party. Streamers hung from his vaulted ceilings, laser lights mirrored around the room by several disco balls, and a disk jockey that only played 80's songs. I even found myself singing some of them as we looked for the host while slowly moving through the crowd.

It wasn't long before we found Dre in the kitchen getting cozy with a white lady whom I'd never seen before. Upon seeing Quinton, she waved frantically at him and as Dre patted her on the behind, she stood up and disappeared into the crowd.

"Should I ask how you know her?" I shouted into his ear.

"Not unless you want to hear about the Dre Shake."

"I'll pass."

"Glad you could make it!" Dre bellowed. "I honestly didn't think Quinton had it in him to come out dressed like that! What are you, Crockett or Tubbs?" he asked, laughing.

"And you're one to talk!" Quinton shouted back. "You look crazy as hell!"

Quinton was right as Dre's outfit looked completely ridiculous. As soon as I saw him, I had to pinch my lips to keep from laughing hysterically. Along with some ripped blue jeans, he wore a netted, neon green muscle shirt that stopped at his abs, a matching green headband that held his jheri curl wig in place, the thickest gold rope chain I'd ever seen, and topped all that off with red Chuck Taylor's.

"Andre Townes, what on earth is wrong with you?" I shouted, but I couldn't even hear myself over the music.

"I like what I'm wearing. It's what hip-hop artists wore when the music was pure and conscious. I am making a statement."

"And that statement is screaming 'Hey I'm gay'!" Quinton shouted.

"See now why ya gotta play a brother? I put this thing together in less than a day and all you have are insults? Okay, Boy James, I see how it is. You're always tryin' to hate on the Sexy. But never fear, as always, I have a few surprises still to be sprung."

"You're not going to drag Teniyah out with more mistletoe, are you?" I asked, trying not to smile.

"Sweetheart, the aphrodisiac of the eighties was gold. And by that estimation," he grabbed the rope around his neck, "your girl has no choice but to ravage my body."

"You're a sick man," I added.

"I can live with that." He turned and picked up a boom box from off the counter. As soon as he put it on his left shoulder, he leaned over and whispered into my ear. "A little bird told me you guys are looking for a third individual for some... new opportunities. If you really want to party like that, there are several rooms upstairs for my special guests. Just tell Block, Quinton knows him, to let you through."

"So Quinton told you?" I whispered back.

"All I'm saying is that there are some clean, willing participants for you guys to indulge with. Now if you'll excuse me, someone has to spike the punch again. Radio Raheim is now leaving the building! Damn I'm sexy!"

After Dre had disappeared into the crowd, I looked at Quinton. "So you told him?

"Told him about what?"

"You know what I'm talking about, Quinton." I shouted in his ear. "You told him about the threesome? Out of all the people you could tell, you told *him*?"

"You told Niya and I told Dre. I don't see what the problem is. What did he tell you?"

"He didn't say anything." I said, trying to smile. "So, this is a party. What do you wanna do first?"

He shrugged his shoulders. "Let's dance."

After dancing for about half an hour with not only Quinton, but with several men who looked like Boy George or boasted either a jheri curl, Mohawk, mullet, or something in between, I was near the front door when I watched as Mike walked in. He looked surprisingly nice as he strutted in wearing a red pinstripe suit, red gators, and a matching fedora with a peacock feather relaxing on the side, but I noticed he was without Simone.

I walked over to him and as he outstretched his arms to greet me, I thought about knocking them down, but instead accepted his embrace. "What's up, pimps-a-lot?"

"Ain't shit, baby girl, ain't shit." He brushed his nose with his left thumb. "Why, are you trying to get in my stable?" I gave him a menacing look. "Ooh, you're a feisty one," he joked.

"So where's Simone?" I asked.

"She told me that she'd meet me here. She said she had some more shopping to do, like we could afford it."

I gritted my teeth and prepared for a return to stab-happiness when Simone walked in. I honestly didn't recognize her until Mike walked up to her and kissed her on the cheek. She frowned at the sentiment, but nevertheless looked fantastic.

She walked down the few stairs from the foyer, grabbing everyone's attention with her black body dress that accentuated curves I didn't even know she had, and smiled at me. I was too much in awe to wave and I stood there looking dumbfounded. To complete the ensemble she also wore an onyx necklace with matching earrings and black stilettos. I wasn't even sure she was decade appropriate until I saw the shoulder pads on the sleeves of her dress. The DJ seemed to notice too because at the moment Simone strode is, his record skipped.

She walked over towards me, still smiling and with Mike in tow. "Hey girl," I said, but she looked right through me as if she were looking for someone.

"Sorry, Lae, I was just a little surprised by everything Dre had done. Did you know that there's a naked Reagan running down the street?"

"Simone," I shrieked, "you look wonderful!"

She spun around, revealing the entire dress to me. "Thanks. The dress was my mom's and my aunt kept it for all these years." She turned towards Mike and asked him to get her something to drink before returning her attention towards me. "So is this what the last party was like?"

"I'm pretty sure there are more people here." As I absorbed how amazing she looked, I noticed something missing from her skintight dress. "Are you wearing panties? I don't see a line."

"Yes, I'm wearing them. I have a really small thong that's slowly finding its way into uncharted territory."

"You're wearing a thong? That's not very eighties, you know."

"And neither are grandma draws. I flipped a coin and thongs won." As if eager to change the topic of conversation, she asked, "Where's Quinton? He decided not to come?"

"Yeah, he's here." I pointed out to the crowd. "He's somewhere out there dancing. So I guess you and Mike had your outfits planned out. He came as a pimp and you came as a Madame."

"Yeah, it was something like that at first, but he left me because he got tired of waiting."

"Does that mean you two are back together?" I asked as we walked down the few remaining steps into the living room.

She shrugged and let out a small laugh. "I don't know, Lae. I slept with him earlier this week because he is my husband, but I'm not into trying to make this relationship work out anymore. I'm focused on someone else. The only reason Mike is all over me now is because I lost some of the baby weight, but I just don't have the time to be dealing with him anymore."

While Simone and I talked, several men lined up next to her. "I think you have some invitations." I said, but Mike had already found his way back with drinks.

"So Lae, where's Quinton?"

"He's probably still out there dancing," but when I turned to where I'd last seen him, he wasn't there.

"Well, I came here to get my boogie on and that's what I plan to do." As if on cue, the crowd parted for her. She walked past me, intentionally ignoring Mike in the process, but he still followed her around like a lost puppy.

When I found Quinton, he was dancing with a girl who looked just like the Material Girl Madonna. "Did you see what Simone was wearing?" I asked incredulously.

"Am I blind? The music practically stopped when she walked in. She looks nice, I guess." He rolled his eyes and shrugged.

"You guess?" I was about to ask Quinton what he meant when a vaguely familiar voice called my name.

"Hello, Lae and Quinton. How is my favorite engaged couple?"

I turned around and saw Franklin, the biggest geek I'd seen at the party so far. He wore rainbow suspenders over a button up shirt, a pocket protector, taped glasses, floods, and penny loafers with an actual penny in the slot. He was as how I'd always imagined him in this decade.

"Franklin! It's good to see you!" I squealed. As a looked him up and down, I could only think of one thing. "I see you let Niya dress you!"

"What makes you think that?" he asked.

"It's just a guess."

"Yeah, she picked out most of it, but I already had the suspenders and these old glasses." He admitted while shrugging.

"So where is the wife? She left you to dance with one of the jocks?" I mused.

"I guess you could say that. She's talking to Dre and lobbying for his ghetto blaster."

"His ghetto blaster? I thought people like us from the burbs didn't use that kind of language!" I laughed.

"Well, you know that when you hang around Niya long enough, you tend to take on some of her personality."

"Tell me about it," I mumbled under my breath. "So is she dressed like you or is she being Niya?"

"Lae, this is your best friend we're talking about. Shouldn't you already know the answer to that? I'm gonna grab some punch if you wanna go look for her."

It couldn't have been easier to spot her in the crowd if someone had given me directions. She was in the middle of the dancing mob of people in Dre's living room and she just happened to be the only woman that stood over six feet tall, wearing a skin tight dress that stopped barely below her hips and a Tina Turner wig. With Dre's radio steadfast on her shoulder, I tried not to laugh, but it was almost impossible not to. When she saw me coming, she put down the radio and hugged me like she hadn't seen me in years. With the few extra inches the heels added on her, I found my face nestled in her breasts, though I didn't think it was too farfetched that she might have planned it that way.

"Hey, girl!" she shouted while continuing to dance, "Did you know that I'm your private dancer? I'll do what you want me to do. You know that means I'm not wearing panties, right?"

Without diverting any attention towards her antics, I stood on the tips of my toes and whispered into her ear. "Quinton said yes. He'll do it."

"Did he, now? So are we still waiting for his birthday or am I sensing sometime sooner?"

233

I thought back to what Dre had told me earlier in the night. "There are some rooms upstairs that Dre told me about. He said that they're private and if we wanted to do something...special, then we should check them out."

I immediately saw a spark in Niya's eyes and after returning Dre's boom box, she quickly grabbed my hand and pulled me through the crowd. As we approached the stairs, we didn't see any security guards, but as we began sneaking up the stairs, a huge man appeared at the top with his arms folded.

"Who the hell is that?" Niya yelled.

I didn't say a word until we made it to the top of the stairs. We whispered in each other's ear, much to Niya's chagrin, and after smirking at Niya he let us through.

"What did you say to him?"

I smiled. "I told him his name and that Dre invited us up here."

"So why was he smiling at me?"

"Don't worry about that. He asked if we were both for Dre and I already let him know that you were my bitch."

She shook her head. "So the lies continue."

In the long hallway that Block protected were five closed doors, two of them on each side with one directly at the end of the hall. With the exception of the one at the hall, there was a dim red bulb above the other doors, but only three of the four were lit. As we carefully tiptoed towards the first door on our right, Niya clung to my shoulders and I could feel her breathing on the back of my neck.

"You're making me nervous," I whispered.

"Shut up and just open the door!"

As I latched onto the door, I turned towards a lurking Niya, hoping that she'd stop me. Instead she nodded and as she leaned on top of me, we peeked through the door. Fully lit, in the room there were six people. Four of them were women, all of whom were kneeling in front of an expansive coffee table doing lines of what I supposed was cocaine. Both men held two glasses of champagne and were laughing jovially at the women, all of whom immediately began to smile after their heads shot upwards. I softly closed the door and Niya and I crept towards the next door on the left.

"I don't think that that's my kind of party."

"Who knew that Dre got down like that, too?" Niya asked and I shrugged.

Before we even reached the second door, we heard the moans of pleasure emanating through it. This time Niya stepped in front of me and

234

opened the door wide enough for the both of us to be seen. The same red bulb used outside the door was the only source of light in this room, but that's all that was needed. This was the room Dre told me about.

Both Niya and I took a step in, but almost no one in the room took notice to us, obviously engaged in their own sexual fantasy. On the bed in front of us was a 'perfect triangle'. Two women were facing each other, softly kissing, while the gentleman under them has his face buried in the thighs of one and his penis in the thighs of the other. Though I could barely hear him, their moans were the unmistakable sounds of pleasure.

"That's going to be us," she whispered, but my attention wasn't on Niya. I was wet at having seen them and turned away from them to slow down my racing heart.

I leisurely looked around the room and as Niya left to close the door, I saw several couples, some switching partners, moaning and scratching. Others were begging and pleading for more as they were pounded mercilessly by their lovers. Though barely lit with candles, I witnessed two women making love in the darkest corner of the room.

Niya kissed me on the back of my neck, then my shoulders. I turned around and allowed her lips to brush mine. I inhaled her breath and tasted the wine she drunk, allowing her tongue entry.

Since Valentine's Day, I'd tried pushing thoughts of us together to the back of my mind. Because of my guilty conscience, my only focus had been on Quinton, but as her lips fell to my neck and then my shoulder, the urge to fuck her again was returning. As she ran her tongue along my shoulder, I slowly inched her dress upwards, smiling when I realized that she told me the truth.

"You're not wearing panties," I whispered.

"I'm still you're private dancer, right?"

With her now exposed, I knelt in front of her and as she ran her hands through my wig, I teased her with the tip of my tongue. No longer listening to the other curses, Niya had joined the chorus.

I loved the way she straddled my face and with each successive swear, I grew more aroused. I was almost ready to join the rest of the room and throw my clothes to the side when someone tapped me on my shoulder.

I opened my eyes, realizing what I was doing. I was suddenly too mortified to turn around. I'd forgotten that I was at Dre's party and I'd finally been caught. I stood up.

"You dames want some company?"

I exhaled. It wasn't Quinton. I couldn't believe that I'd done something as insane as this and still, hadn't been caught.

I pulled away from Niya and as I did so, the man who spoke was behind me and his penis poked me in the ass. Disgusted, I turned around and frowned at him, realizing that I shouldn't have ever come in this room.

"I'm sorry. I'm not ready for this." I rushed past Niya and into the hallway. The cold air from the hallway was like a smack in the face and as I began to close the door behind me, Niya followed me out, still pulling down her dress.

"What's going on, Lae?"

"The guy in there poked me with his...you know, his thing!"

"It wasn't that big. I'm sure you could take it."

"It's not always about jokes, Teniyah. I mean Quinton finally agreed to this and the last thing I need right now is him catching me-- and you-- in and orgy!"

"Why don't we just skip the last door with the light and go to the one at the end of the hall? We can talk there."

I nodded and as we made our way to the room, all I could think about was how I freaked out when another man's penis had touched me. Perhaps it was a sign that I shouldn't go through with the ménage, but as I thought about the 'perfect triangle' I'd seen, those doubts quickly dissipated.

Once we opened the door to the room at the end of the hall, a small floor lamp was the only source of illumination, barely lighting a few feet around us. When Niya flipped the light switch, the lamp shut off and the entire room became visible.

Niya and I stared in awe at the amount of detail given to what we could only guess was Andre's bedroom. Everything in the room, from the enormous bed and bookshelf to the wood floors was made from the same beautiful dark wood. Several small pictures of Quinton and I were scattered about the room, but I only realized the true extent of Dre's narcissism when I viewed about a half dozen large portraits of him posing in different suits and a large mural on the adjacent wall of him practically nude.

I stayed in the doorway, but Niya quickly ran towards his bed, which looked like it was made up of two king sized beds put together, and fell into the comforter with a picture of Dre's face. Still in her Tina Turner wig, she rolled over and admired herself in the mirrors that were perfectly centered above the bed. "I could get used to this kind of living. What exactly does Andre do to have such an ego?"

I looked curiously at his mural and shrugged. "I honestly couldn't tell you, but there is certainly no love loss of himself."

Niya rolled over on top of the comforter and after pressing her breasts into his face, she flipped over to blow kisses at her reflection. "I don't think I've ever met a man who'd willingly be spread eagle for a mural of himself--in his own bedroom," she said. "I do like his boldness, though. I even like the hundred dollar bill that covers his little thang-thang."

I tried to keep from laughing, but it was a futile attempt as we both giggled like school girls who'd both seen their first naked picture. Suddenly, what happened inside the last room didn't seem so important.

"I'm sure Dre wouldn't appreciate you calling his 'thang-thang' little."

"I know," she said still laughing, "but that painting is still sexy as hell. I want one of those, but they don't have to cover me up."

"Girl, you need help. A lot of it," I said, still trying hard not to laugh at her foolishness.

"Do I?" she asked, now imitating Dre's mural pose before flipping over onto her stomach and thrusting her hips against Dre's comforter.

"You are so nasty!" I laughed out, covering my mouth with both hands due to Niya's antics.

I was sure that she hadn't heard a word I'd said as she repeatedly yelled, "Yeah, you like that good coochie, don't you?"

I finally closed the door and walked towards the bed as her feigned screams of pleasure grew increasingly louder. Hoping that Niya would stop before someone walked in and caught her acting like a complete fool, I took off my shoe and threw it at her, hitting her in the leg.

"Ow!" she shouted, laughing. "Okay, I see you're a little jealous!"

"You're grinding against the face of Dre's comforter. If you'd like to continue, please just let me know when you're finished."

"Don't be such a prude, Lae. If I knew Dre got down like this, I would've seduced him years ago. Still, he's missing one thing in here..."

She stopped, looked around the room and smiled. "There aren't any pictures of me." When she finally turned her attention towards me, she showed the same mischievous look that had always gotten the both of us into trouble. "Please tell me that he'll let us borrow this room for our threesome. It's perfect."

After sitting down on the edge of the bed, I looked around the room at all the various pictures of Dre before lying on the comforter that

Niya had just molested. "Somehow, I think that this room is all about Dre. I don't think he would want us cumming all over his precious face."

"Speak for yourself."

Niya crawled to the top of the bed where the pillows were, while I laid on the bed and let my thoughts wander to Simone and how good she looked in her dress. She seemed so happy. I closed my eyes briefly, letting the vibrations from the downstairs music soothe me, when Niya kissed me on the forehead.

"A penny for your thoughts?" she asked, looking down at me.

"One of the thoughts I have is that I wish you'd stop doing that. I already told you that I'm not doing that again. I mean—we almost got caught up, *again,* two doors down."

She kissed me again. This time on my nose and was going for my lips when I turned my head to the side, away from her.

"Fine, but that means I'll have to turn my affections elsewhere."

"Perhaps your husband is a good choice?" I suggested.

"Nope, that's way too predictable. Maybe I'll sneak Quinton up here and give him a preview."

I turned away from her and folded my arms, but Niya followed me. Again she perched herself so closely that our lips were almost touching and again I could inhale her breath. "That's not funny." I whispered.

"What happened in that room got me a little hot and bothered. Since we're going to do it anyway, why not now?" she whispered back to me, her wig hair falling into my face.

"Is anyone in here?" Quinton asked as he walked through the door, causing Niya to quickly fall onto the bed and me to abruptly sit up. For a few seconds, I remained perfectly still, hoping to magically disappear, but when I didn't, I just stared awkwardly at Quinton. My heart began beating so rapidly that I swore that everyone in the room could hear it. Looking at me, he asked, "Simone told me that she saw you and Niya come up here? What are you guys doing in here? I didn't think Dre's room was one of the party areas."

I managed a smile, but Niya was the first to speak up. "We saw the other rooms and it was a bit much for us, but this isn't a private party if that's what you're implying, Quinton. Actually, we were talking about you." She patted the bed and motioned for Quinton to come over.

He never took his gaze away from me as he slowly walked over to us and sat down next to me. He just looked at me with an uncertainty that I'd never seen before.

238

I wanted to tell him that we weren't doing anything, which was the truth, but all I could do was look into his eyes. He'd seen us. We were close enough to kiss and no matter how much I tried to deny it, all that mattered was what it appeared to be.

Seeing the blank stare on my face, Teniyah quickly rolled off from the bed, immediately sat on his lap and softly kissed his lips. During their kiss, his eyes remained open and I caught a glimpse of his puzzled look. Then he returned his attention to her and as she returned for a second attempt, he parted his lips for her. There, right in front of me, they tenderly kissed each other as if they had done it all before.

The heat of jealousy poured throughout my body as I watched them respond to each other with a kiss so perfect that it could've been rehearsed. I wanted to pull them apart, but I couldn't. After what I'd just done, I at least owed this much to him.

Once Niya had released Quinton from her Siren's grip, she asked, "So what made you finally agree?"

He looked at me with a sadness that I couldn't quite explain and as I quietly sat next to his right shoulder, he said, "Because I want Lae to be happy."

"That is maybe the most arousing thing I've ever heard you say, Quinton." Niya leaned over and kissed me on my nose and as her lips touched mine, I could almost taste Quinton on them.

Once she pulled away from me, I wanted to bring her back. I wanted to taste her lips over again to remove the sting of seeing Quinton kissing her, but after I opened my eyes I knew that I couldn't.

Instead, I leaned over and softly kissed my man, hoping that he would reward me as he had rewarded her and he didn't disappoint. I felt the same intensity kissing him that I'd always felt since our first kiss three years ago.

As our lips finally separated and the world around us seemed to reappear, he frowned at me. I was about to ask him what was wrong when I realized that I still had the taste of Niya on my lips from earlier. As if she already knew, Teniyah mischievously smiled at me and adding to my horror, Dre burst in.

"I'll be damned! I set up rooms, specifically for this shit and you find my room!"

I looked up, dumbfounded and embarrassed.

"Since everyone's in the 'gettin' some' mood, how can I be down?"

Niya quickly jumped up from Quinton's lap and began fixing her Tina wig, then sat next to me as I covered my face in shame.

"Dammit Dre, how long have you been there?" Quinton asked, standing up and meeting Dre before he reached the bed.

"Just long enough to see you and Niya, then Niya and Lae, and then you and Lae. Dawg, after seeing that shit, I may never go flaccid again. I know y'all don't want me in it, I can just be a goddamn voyeur, but don't let me miss this!"

"I'm so embarrassed!" I loudly whispered to Niya.

"For what?" she asked. "That's Andre and you know he won't say anything to Franklin."

With Quinton in tow, Dre walked over to his bookshelf, picked up a remote and as the bookshelf slid out the way, revealed a hidden camera.

"You were recording us!" I managed to squeal.

"Not really," Dre said smugly, as he handed Quinton a disc. "You were recording yourselves. When you cut on the light and walked in, it automatically started recording. What the hell can I say? I'm a freak."
Without another word to either of us, Quinton grabbed the disc from Dre and they both walked out into the hallway.

"What happens when he looks at that disc, Niya?" I loudly whispered.

"Nothing happens, Lae. We didn't do shit! Let him watch it a million times, nothing happened!"

She was right, nothing happened. Inside Dre's bedroom, I'd resisted Niya, but only because of what happened in the other room. Had we snuck into Dre's room first, I'm sure the disc would have incriminated us.

"So, are we going to your apartment tonight or what?" she asked nonchalantly.

"What if he doesn't want to do it anymore?" I retorted.

"After all that, I doubt that he'd back away." She seductively sucked on her bottom lip. "Your fiancé is a helluva kisser."

I cringed and headed towards the door. "You just don't give up, do you?" I said. We started walking back down the long hallway of Dre's special party favors.

"Why should I? You want this as badly as I do, but you're too scared to say it. So what's the plan now? Is it still going down on his birthday or do I have to ditch Franklin tonight?" Ignoring her persistence, I started down the stairs. She grabbed my arm and whispered in my ear. "Can you at least get Quinton to make me a copy?"

I went searching through the house for Quinton and when I found him, he and Simone were sitting next to each other on a love seat in Dre's den, laughing about something that I'd probably just missed.

Before Quinton had a chance to say anything to me, I quickly sat on the opposite side of him, barely fitting in.

"So Simone, where has your husband gone? I haven't seen him since you guys came in together."

She shrugged.

Feeling a little uneasy, I turned to Quinton and asked, "Can I talk to you for a sec?"

Quinton nodded and before we had a chance to stand up, Simone excused herself.

"I didn't kiss her Quinton."

"I never said that you did."

"You know how she gets when she's a little overly flirtatious and has had a few drinks. She already told me that she wanted to do something with us tonight and she was lobbying for her cause."

"Lae, I believe you. Can we talk about something else, please?"

I didn't want to start an argument though I could hear the agitation in his voice. "What are you going to do with that disc?"

"I've already gotten rid of it. The last thing I want is Franklin finding out about all of this. It's bad enough that I said yes, but having evidence is not something I'm willing to deal with right now," he said taking a sip of wine.

I gave him as much of a smile as I could muster. "Quinton, I love you and if you don't want to go through with it, you don't have to."

"Do you still want to do it?"

I wished he hadn't asked me that question. I wanted him to tell me that he didn't want it and that I was the only woman he wanted, but he hadn't. He left it up to me and as much as I loved him, I lusted for one last time with Teniyah. I wanted to finish what had started in the room upstairs.

"Sure... why not?"

"His birthday is so far away. How about we give him a teaser and then the full thing then?" Niya asked, dancing next to me.

Quinton and I left the den together, but when he didn't feel like dancing, I found my way onto the floor and Niya found her way to me.

"Why won't you let it go?" I asked, not masking my annoyance.

"Look, I just talked to Quinton and he said he'll go through with it if you still want to. Don't you still want to?"

I folded my arms. "Where is he then?"

"The last time I saw him he was talking to Simone. By the way, what the hell is she wearing?"

A white man with cups of punch walked past and I quickly grabbed one of the plastic cups from his grasp. After entirely gulping it, I asked, "Why can't you try it my way for once?"

"Fine," she said, but she was already rolling her eyes. "Anyway, now that I'm about to rock the both of your worlds, have you seen your girl Simone? Why is she dressed like she's high priced when she can't even afford to pay her own bills?"

"If you don't leave her alone, I'll cancel this whole thing."

"C'mon Lae, she's my outlet! Who else is that easy to make fun of and I know she talks about me behind my back!" She hung her lip out and I had to laugh at her pouting. "It's not funny, Lae, but I'll do it for you."

"Now was that so hard?" I asked, practically mocking her.

"Yes, and I hate you. This is just going to make me turning the both of you out that much more fun."

Only a few moments after I began dancing with her, a flock of curl-juice-dripping brothers came out of nowhere and began dancing with us to Kurtis Blow's 'Basketball'.

I looked around for Quinton, but with Niya dancing next to me and six other fellas trying to do the same, I figured I'd stay for a few songs before I went looking for him.

The DJ had just finished playing, 'Da Butt' when I finally got off the dance floor and went looking for Quinton. I looked all around the downstairs, but when I couldn't find him, I walked up the stairs in the middle of Dre's living room and thought about looking over the balcony to search for him when I caught him sitting together with Simone on a couch in the hallway.

As I walked up towards them, they stood up and walked towards me.

"Anyone ready to dance?" Simone asked.

For the next few hours, Quinton, Simone, and I danced with each other and varying partners, rehashing dances like the cabbage patch, Roger Rabbit, the snake, running man, and the robot while sweating to everything from N.W.A. to Guns N' Roses. Mike attempted to dance with Simone several times to which she offered a stiff arm until he finally left the party. After he left, I saw the smiling Simone I used to know come out and enjoy Dre's celebration of the eighties.

By the end of the night, my feet hurt and Simone was too drunk to drive. I offered to call her a cab, but Quinton volunteered to drop her off. Watching her stumble towards the car, a feeling of uneasiness swept over me as I thought about what secrets she might let go of in her drunken state.

During the whole ride home, no one spoke. I wanted to say something to Quinton about what hadn't happened between Niya and me, but with Simone still awake in the back seat, it just made sense to remain quiet.

After Quinton dropped me off at the apartment, I made sure that Simone saw me eyeing her when I stepped out of the car. I wasn't sure if she understood the message I was trying to send her, but after I gave Quinton a good night kiss, I saw her nod from the passenger's side.

Once in the apartment, I took off my heels, thinking about the threesome I'd agreed to. I knew I was just being selfish, not wanting to share Niya with Quinton, but I secretly enjoyed having a double life. With both of their dominant personalities, it was kind of fun having at least some semblance of power over them.

As I staggered down the hallway leading to my bedroom I wondered if Simone could keep her drunken mouth shut. She had a lot to talk to Q about at the party—they were together twice when I couldn't find him. Even though she was my friend, when Simone started drinking, secrets came out. The last thing I needed was her telling Quinton about what had already happened between Teniyah and me.

And what was *still* happening...

Tossing my wig on the dresser, I thought back to the fantasy room at Dre's party and the same feeling of lust I felt earlier began to envelope me. I closed my eyes and began to wonder how Quinton would react to the ménage.

What if Niya is better at pleasing him than me? What if Niya likes Quinton better than me? What if he likes her better? Would he tell me? What if they start fucking behind my back?

I opened my eyes and the lust I felt was gone. Instead, it was replaced by paranoia and doubt. The more I thought about it, the less I wanted to do it, but Quinton had agreed after all, I was the one who had bugged him about it for these last few months.

Taking off the rest of my eighties costume, I climbed into bed and let the wine finish it effects. The last thoughts I had were those of Niya, Quinton, the perfect triangle and our impending premarital ménage a trois.

CHAPTER 16

Quinton

<u>February 27th (Monday)</u>

My burger and fries had just arrived as I sat across from Andre. I was still dressed in my work clothes, but Dre's tailor made dark blue suit made me look more like his gopher than his best friend. And at the restaurant we were at, I was practically treated as such. I thought about breaking up the flirting that he was doing with the waitress, but instead I quietly sat and nibbled on my food.

It was a rarity that we went out on lunch together, but ever since I'd seen Lae and Niya about to kiss on Dre's bed, all I could think about was how much I'd given up. As much as I didn't want to believe that Lae would leave me for another person, a woman at that, the kiss that almost happened at Dre's party was proof that I had to start believing it.

"So dawg," he said, breaking the silence as the waitress walked away, "what's been up with you? You don't call, you don't write and I'm thinking I did something to get the cold shoulder."

"I've just got a lot to deal with--a lot on my mind, Dre. It's not you, it's me."

"If this is about what I saw you guys doing in my bedroom, don't worry about it. My lips are sealed."

"I'm not worried about that. I know you know how to keep secrets."

"So what is it then?" He continued flirting with the waitress, winking at her as she smiled at him. "So," he said returning his attention to me, "are you trying to break up with me? Do I have to make you my friend again, like I did in junior high?"

I smiled, which was something I hadn't done too much of lately. At home Laela and I were a perfect couple. I made love to her like she was the only woman I ever wanted, but secretly I fantasized about not only Cheyenne and Leslie, but also of Teniyah and Simone. I was good at playing the perfect fiancé: getting wedding invitations together and finalizing guest lists while pretending as if I didn't' know that my woman had cheated on me—possibly many times. But no matter how hard I tried, I couldn't forget. The possibility of my women with another woman—in a relationship, is something I could never get used to. This didn't feel like fun and games. Inside it was tearing me apart.

"So what's going on with you? Are you guys still following through with the threesome? Just thinking about that shit makes me hard." He shoved his mouth full of Chicken Alfredo while still trying to speak. "You're just lucky I was the one who was walking by and not Franklin."

"Dre, I fucked her."

There was a pause as he finished swallowing. "You fucked Niya already? The trifecta has been finalized? Q, tell me it was everything that I dreamed of! Tell me that the woman of my dreams if a goddamn tiger in the sack! C'mon brother, I need details!"

I solemnly looked at him before putting the few fries I had in my hand back down on the plate. "It wasn't Niya."

He put down his fork and tossed his napkin to the side before taking a sip of his red wine. "Well then tell me who! Did you get down with the fantasy fuck, Cheyenne again?"

"No." I said dryly. A look of curiosity spread across Dre's face.

"Then will you finally tell me about this person with whom you have cavorted with? Damn, I'm tired of guessing already!"

"I...I slept with Simone."

He coughed loudly and appeared as if he were choking. "Please tell me that there's a stripper out there with the name Simone!" When I didn't confirm his story, he continued. "Simone? The Simone Hall, Simone? Mike Hall's wife Simone?" he loudly whispered as he stood up and sat in the chair next to me. "Quinton, how the hell did this happen?"

"Lae cheated on me, man. And of all the fucking days to do it on, she chose Valentine's Day."

"So who is this dude that she messed around with? Did she meet him at work or something? Let me know who it is and we will kick his

246

ass right now!" But when I looked Dre in his eyes, he understood. "It was Niya, wasn't it?"

I nodded.

"Holy shit Q," he whispered. "This is some Spanish telenovela type shit. So what happened? How did you end up with Simone?"

It seemed like a lifetime ago that it had all happened, but as I told him the story, I was reminded that it had only been two weeks. Dre listened intently as I recalled the phone conversation all the way up to me leaving Mike and Simone's apartment.

"So the only people that know about Niya and Lae are you and Simone?"

"Yes."

He let go of a sarcastic chuckle. "So this threesome that you, Niya and Lae are planning is just about revenge for you, right Quinton?"

"When they asked me at first, all I wanted was revenge, but now I don't know."

"What the hell do you mean *you don't know?*"

"I mean I don't know! Damn, it's not like I started this shit anyway!"

"So do you want to call off the wedding or what?" he asked. "You at least need to make a decision about that."

"If I can make this work, than I want it to work. I want to marry Lae, but I don't want to have someone lurking in the shadows ready to take my spot-- especially not another goddamn woman."

"Then why don't you tell Lae that you know?"

"Because goddammit, I want to know why! What's so fuckin' special about Niya that she was able to seduce my fiancée?"

I'd finally said it. The answer that Dre wanted to hear and the answer I didn't want anyone else to know.

The threesome was just a cover.

I just wanted a crack at Teniyah.

"So," he said, "is that your final answer?"

"I just wanna know why, man. Everyday I'm around Niya, it's like all these people want to be with her. I just didn't think that Lae was going to be one of them. I don't know if I'm the only person on this planet who didn't want to fuck her before, but now I need to know what she has that I don't."

"Sounds like revenge to me," he said, crossing his arms.

"Fine, call it whatever you want. You can call it another one of my fantasy fucks for all I care, but I have to know. What makes Teniyah Oliver so goddamn special that people have to sleep with her?"

"And you're jealous of her, too? This would actually make a great porno. You should really let me put a camera in the room when this goes down." I glared at Dre, but that didn't stop him from talking. "So then, if this is going to happen and you're staying with Lae, what are you going to do about Simone? She's still the maid-of-honor and she may not want to give you up."

He was right. I hadn't actually thought about that and I just figured that the whole Mike and Simone situation would work itself out. "What is this-- an inquisition?"

"Answer the question, Quinton. If you don't want this to blow back in your face, you'll make sure that every angle is covered."

"I don't feel like doing this shit right now."

"Quinton, you're already knee deep in shit. Don't sink in any further by feeling sorry for yourself."

"What the hell, Dre! You were the one who told me to jump her bones! It's not like you didn't play a part in all of this! Fuck! Why did I even think telling you would help the situation? First you tell me to bang her and then you backtrack and jump down my throat for doing it! What the hell?"

"Are you done ranting yet?"

I took in a deep breath. "Yes."

"I feel like forgiveness is in order. I forgive you for listening to me. Lae needs to forgive you for reciprocity and you need to forgive her and get your ass hitched."

"So what am I supposed to do? Tell her about Simone and hope she forgives me?"

"And about Cheyenne. According to my scorecard, you've fucked around twice and she's only done it once."

I looked at him in disbelief. "You said a fantasy fuck doesn't count! Shouldn't the score be one to one then?"

"Well, by that logic, the score is one to zero." He stood up and walked behind me, grabbing my shoulders. "Your fantasy was Cheyenne, hers was Niya. So you're still the bad guy."

"So what if they did it more than just a couple times? Simone told me about one other time—before I heard them on the phone."

"You got proof?"

I looked over my shoulder at him. "Hello? Does your bedroom ring a bell?"

He smiled. "In fact, it does bring fond memories. If only I could've gotten there earlier. Do you still have that disc-- for posterity, you know.

Now that I think about it, what exactly did the video show before I got there?"

I thought about the disc that I'd taken from Dre--the same disc that I'd quietly hidden when I told Lae that it had been destroyed. The one I still have yet to watch for fear that I may not be able to live with what I might see.

"I threw it away," I lied. "I didn't want it getting back to Franklin."

"There you go again, ruining my fantasy," he said, walking back to his seat. "So the Simone thing, how sure are you that it won't get back to Lae?"

"Shit, I don't know. She calls me at work like twice a day since the whole thing went down. It's basically innocent talk, but I'll have to talk to her." The more I thought about what I'd done with Simone, the more nauseous I became. Unable to eat and almost out of time for lunch, I stood up from the table. "I gotta go."

"Before you go," Dre began, "perhaps you could at least reconsider having a camera in your room for your rendezvous with Lae and Niya." As I walked away, trying to ignore him, he shouted, "I'll even sweeten the pot by giving you TPW for a week!"

If Dre was willing to let me drive the pussy wagon, then he meant business.

I was still a little agitated from my lunchtime conversation with Dre when I returned to work. Out of all the people in the world, I figured coming out to Dre would be easy-- he knew me well enough to understand what I was going through, but he was just as judgmental as he always claimed I was.

I made it to my office without any one of the many people rushing past bumping into me, but as soon as I kicked my foot up on the desk to relax, Carmen burst into my office, startling me and causing me to fall backwards onto the floor.

"Quinton, I'm glad I caught you," she said, as she walked over to me, completely ignoring that I was on the floor. "I need you to run something out for me."

I pushed myself up from the floor, but remained seated at my desk. "I just got in from lunch, Carmen. Why didn't you ask me to run the package before then?"

"Because it just came across my desk, smartass. I'd do it if I had the time, but I don't and you do. So you can to take it out."

I wanted to scream, but I began to doubt that it would help me feel any differently. "What's the address?"

"It's in Spring. It may take you a while to do this run, so you can have the rest of the day off after you do it. Does that work for you?" After I nodded, she tossed the package onto my desk and I was out the door. I hadn't planned to work anyway, but at least this way I didn't have anyone walking in my office to complain about it.

During the entire ride, I thought about the things that Dre and I said to each other. If anyone could understand vengeance, I knew he could, but I was surprised when he gave me a lecture about doing the right thing. I mean, out of all the times for him to give me a lecture, he does it after I've already done something he suggested. I had to laugh at the irony.

Thirty minutes after I left the station, I was pulling into the driveway of a beautiful North Houston home. The two-story house was made of a light-colored brick and tall shrubbery helped to hide most of the first floor.

I parked under a fifty-foot elm tree in front of the house and cautiously avoided the tulips that out lined the perfectly manicured lawn. I grabbed the small box and signature record from the passenger's side and stepped out into the warm sun.

When I finally made it up the walkway, I hoped that someone had already seen me approaching, but when no one came, I rang the bell instead of pounding on the dark oak door.

Without warning, the door opened and the woman before me wore nothing but a baby blue business shirt and a loose fitting red tie. As I gawked at her perfect body, remembering how good it felt to be inside her once before, she simply smiled. She grabbed my hand, kissed it softly and led me inside of her house.

"I thought I'd get you to come out here one day."

I'd been set up.

I held both my clipboard and the small box so tightly in my free hand that I knew I was crushing whatever I was supposed to deliver. I hadn't seen her since the night she spent at my apartment, but she was more amazing than what I last remembered. The memories of that night flooded my head once again, but I reminded myself that I hadn't come here for her. I'd come to drop off this package and go home.

"Cheyenne," I began, "I just need for you to, um, to sign for this... um, package. I have brought this here--for you to sign--so that I can get back to work."

250

She let go of my hand, turned and smiled at my uneasiness. We were only in the living room, but by the way I began to sweat, it felt like were in the shower again. I could see her pinned against the wall and begging me for more.

"What are you thinking about, Quinton?"

Awakened from my daydream, I remembered how badly I wanted her and consequently how she'd left me. "I can't stay here. If I do, we both know what will happen."

"We've already seen each other naked, we have chemistry, and the sex between us is pretty good. I don't see you staying here for a little while as a major problem. It sounds to me like you're just trying to avoid me."

I inhaled deeply. She wasn't lying. I'd intentionally been trying to avoid her. I didn't return her calls or emails, and even now I couldn't bring myself to look her in the eye. Instead, I focused on the box in my hand.

"I'm not avoiding you. You avoided me. Everything about that night was perfect and when I woke up, you'd already snuck out. You made me feel like the only thing that I was missing was you leaving money on the nightstand. Now, if you just sign here, I'll be on my way back to the station."

She took the box from me, casually tossed it away, and then knocked my clipboard out of my hands and onto the floor. She pushed me down onto her cream leather couch and straddled me.

"You're so easy to read. No matter how much bullshit you talk, I know you liked cumming in me as much as I liked cumming on you."

Without my permission, she began to unbutton my pants.

"Cheyenne..."

"I'll take care of you, daddy."

I finally brought myself to look into her beautiful brown eyes. I wanted to be angry with her, to stop her and let her know how wrong she'd been, but I didn't. I couldn't. As she undressed me, tossing my clothes to the side, all of my reservations were thrown to the side with them.

I didn't like being the only naked person in the room, but with Cheyenne, it seemed like I was the only person who mattered. Like a queen to her king, she knelt in front of me and guided me into her mouth, where she took almost all of me before withdrawing. Cheyenne took her time, moving slowly while taking me in, as if I were the only person on the planet she made love to. As I filled her mouth, her seductive gazes brought the memories of the guilty pleasures we'd shared at my place. Flashbacks from the shower--the hot water pouring down our backs, my pushing inside of her as I pinned her against the wall, her climax as she dug her nails into my flesh--all rushed to the forefront of my thoughts, reminding me of how badly I wanted this woman. How desperately I wanted to be inside this woman again.

I wanted to grab her, to take control, but I couldn't. She wouldn't let me. I loved that she took over; that she was relentless in her pursuit of me and when the time came, she grabbed the reigns and took what she wanted.

I loved her dominance.

When she stood up, she was wearing one less article of clothing. The tie remained on the floor and as her shirt openly swayed, revealing her breasts, I grabbed her shirt and pulled it off. Even in the sunlight, her figure was flawless.

She didn't waste time. Holding my manhood perfectly upright, she easily slid onto it. Being inside of her was more intense than I'd remembered and as she rocked her hips against mine, I tightly held her against me. She took her time riding me, yet her body responded to mine as if we'd been together for years. She was warm and wet, firm and focused, innovative and insatiable.

With our eyes locked in a perpetual gaze, I didn't dare look away nor did I have any great desire to speak. No matter how great the sensation grew, I refused to show any emotion for fear that it would break our rhythm.

Staring at her steely gaze for so long, I saw the moment her façade finally broke and her once paced breathing became more chaotic. Her steady rhythm dissipated with her breathing and her slow ride became a rapid bounce. Soon after, soft moans began emanating, but she never took her eyes away from mine.

It's time.

I grabbed her waist and forced her to ride faster than she was willing to. As her nails dug into my flesh, I never stopped thrusting my hips.

"I'm cumming, baby."

I heard her proclamation and said nothing. I went faster and deeper, pulling her closer to me while thrusting harder and harder.

I didn't want to cum, but my body didn't care. I climaxed inside of her, but I refused to stop thrusting. I couldn't when she was so close. I was almost ready to give into her when she softly bit into my shoulder and I felt her warmth spreading across my thighs.

For a few minutes afterwards, we didn't move. As I listened to the sound of her breathing, I wondered why she had such a profound effect on me. I'd had sex numerous times with countless women and I could resist them all. Yet, when Cheyenne wanted it, I wanted it. I felt like an obedient puppy.

I thought about finally resisting the hold she had on me, and I became emboldened. I needed to focus on Lae and get back to where we were before all the drama had occurred. It was time for me to start doing the right thing. Besides, I was Quinton James and no woman deserved *this* kind of power over me.

I was ready to stand up and end this affair for good, when Cheyenne whispered in my ear.

"I think I'm ready to take you upstairs now."

Quietly, I followed her up the stairs.

I left Cheyenne's house feeling like I'd run a marathon. For an older woman, she had incredible stamina and my dick actually ached from over usage.

As she watched me leave, I fought off the urge to honk at her and just waved while driving off. All I could think about was how much of a pussy I was for not leaving when I said I would.

I was halfway home when I remembered the reason I'd gotten off early. I called Simone and after we agreed to meet at her house, I turned around and headed back downtown.

I took my time walking up her steps, replaying what happened the last time I was here. Me inside of her thighs...the couch, the walls, her bed-- if they could speak, we'd both be single. When I took my final step, I was ready to knock on the door when Simone pulled the door open.

Instead of me catching her off guard, this time she'd surprised me. My eyes examined her body, slowly processing how beautiful she became with all the weight she lost. The heat returned as I noticed that she was only wearing the top of a black camisole set.

She grabbed both my hands and slid them under her shirt, moaning as my hands began massaging her breasts. For a few moments, we stood in the doorway as the beginnings of foreplay took hold of us.

"See how wet you make me," she whispered before guiding my right hand further south. As my fingers entered her, I could feel her warmth pulsating around them. I pulled away from her, but as I did, she took my fingers and softly sucked on the tips of each one.

"Simone," I began, but she placed her finger on top of my mouth and proceeded to unzip my pants. I jumped away from her, partly because I was still in pain from being with Cheyenne. I was wrong for having ever come here.

"Dammit Simone, I didn't come over here for this shit! I'm not doing this anymore. I can't."

She sat on the opposite side of the couch and pulled a pillow over herself. "I don't understand Quinton. Did I do something wrong? I did this all for you. I didn't mean to offend you. I'll put the shorts on and we can make love however you want."

"It's not that, Monie. I came here to tell you that we can't be friends like this. You're Mike's wife and I'm about to be Lae's husband. You know that this is wrong as much as I do."

"So how is what they're doing right? Mike's still cheating on me and Lae is still cheating on you! How the hell is what we're doing any more wrong than what they're doing?" Irritated, frustrated, she held the pillow even closer.

I moved closer to her. "This isn't what either of us should be doing right now. Too many people could get hurt by this and you know it, too. Mike is one of my groomsmen; you're Laela's Matron of Honor, Monie! We can't be together like this anymore."

"So all I am to you is some little whore to suck your dick when you think Lae is cheating on you? After Dre's party, you were so willing to come to me for support and ready to shove it down my throat, but when I want something fucking romantic for us, you push me away! Like I did something wrong when all this time Lae has been treating you like crap and you accept it? How dare you side with her, Quinton! How dare you grow a goddamn conscience now! You owe me! You got what you wanted and if I can't have tonight-- I'll tell Lae."

Enraged, I reached out and grabbed Simone by her neck. After seeing her face and how much sadness I'd caused, I was too embarrassed for words. I let go of her and began to walk towards the door. Rushing past me, Simone made a dash for the door and blocked me from leaving.

"Let me go, Simone."

"I'm sorry, Quinton, I'll never yell at you again. Just stay." Tears began to drop from her reddened eyes. "Please don't leave like this."

"Simone, please move."

"Quinton, I swear to God that I won't ever say anything to Laela! We don't even have to do anything. Just stay with me--please!"

"Simone, I'm not going to ask you again. Please move."

"Why are you doing this Quinton?" She begged. "Wasn't what we had good? Didn't I treat you like a man? Didn't it feel good to be inside of me?"

With each question, more tears poured from her eyes, but I wasn't in the mood for compassion. "Nothing was ever going to become of this, Simone! We fucked! It's not anything more than that so leave it the fuck alone! Jesus Christ! Why are you hanging onto this so hard?"

"Because I don't have shit else, Quinton!" She yelled so loudly that I was sure her neighbors heard. "Lae has fucking *everything* and she fucking shits on it! We had a friendship and she sold me out for Teniyah! She had you and she sold *you* out for Teniyah! Everywhere Niya goes, Lae follows! That doesn't make time for anything or anyone else Quinton! What the hell do you think she's gonna do when she gets tired of you? It's only a matter of time before she ends up back in her bed! You just don't want to see it!"

I didn't want to argue with Simone. I pulled her away from the door and walked to my car as she continued to shout, "I'll always be here for you, Quinton! I'll never tell! *I love you!*"

Without looking back, I started up the car and started home as quickly as I could.

With Laela still at the hospital by the time I made it home, I threw my keys on the counter and slid the disc into the bedroom DVD player. I turned the power on and off several times before I finally worked up the nerve to play the disc, and as I stood in front of the TV watching my fiancée and Teniyah, I realized that I was practically shaking.

Nothing happened.

Teniyah moved in on Lae, kissed her even, and Laela turned away.

You didn't watch the DVD earlier so that you could cheat without remorse.

Cheyenne, Simone. I'd had my way with them. And I'd gained nothing from it. But now, my future with Laela was at risk. There were too many fuckin' secrets. I sat down on the bed, upset and deflated wondering how the hell I was ever going to make this right.

CHAPTER 17

Simone

<u>March 9th (Thursday)</u>

I'd already called in sick everyday this week, hoping that Quinton would stop by. He didn't usually call before he came by and I didn't want to miss him when he did. I'd left him at least a dozen messages to tell him where I'd be this week and I had yet to hear from him.

I knew he was angry with me, but I could explain it to him if only he would let me. If only he would call back, I could find a way to make it right, but he hadn't called. Almost two weeks had gone by and I hadn't heard a word from him, which meant one thing--it had to be Lae who was keeping us apart. She was always the one who got what she wanted. I knew that it could only be her who kept Quinton so busy that he couldn't call.

Mike had already taken MJ to my aunt's, but since he left, I hadn't even gotten out of bed. I hadn't worked out since Quinton left but my body still hurt. It hurt to move, to breathe, even thinking hurt. As I clutched my pillow a little tighter, I could still smell him on it.

Why wouldn't he come back? Why wouldn't he allow me to make him happy? Why couldn't he just give us another day together?

And suddenly the answer came to me. I was married and Quinton was too honorable to continue sleeping with a married woman! If I wanted Quinton, I was going to have to finally let go of Mike.

I'd began rifling through the yellow pages and called almost two dozen divorce lawyers before I wrote the names down of the five who were the closest. After a few calls, my life with Quinton was going to be helped out by a man named John Sparks.

I called the number and didn't waste any time telling him what I wanted. He didn't waste any time setting up an appointment and though my hair was disheveled from a week's lack of care, I threw on a scarf. Within an hour, I'd already left the house and headed for his office.

Quinton and I had only been intimate twice; once on Valentine's Day and again after Dre's 80's party, but I secretly hoped both times that Mike would've caught us. I didn't know if it was due to either my bad luck or his awful timing, but I didn't have any more time left for him to find out. Now I had to take things into my own hands.

Since Mike had returned from his whore's house a little more than a week ago, we hardly spoke. I didn't mind since we remained argument free, but whenever I asked him where he stayed, he'd always answer with the same lie: "I was at my mama's house." As much as I detested him and his lies, he was still my husband, I was still his wife and we were married, if only for the time being. I was sick of my miserable marriage to Michael Hall.

Soon, I was finally going to become the former Mrs. Hall.

When I arrived at Mr. Sparks' office, which wasn't too far from my job, the entrance to his office was open and I anxiously hurried inside.

To describe his sanctuary as a small business was an understatement. To me it looked more like an efficiency that was somehow turned into a lawyer's office. I turned around to walk out and look at the address again when a voice shouted from the back. "Mrs. Hall?"

"Miss Johnson," I replied a little quicker than I should have. If I was going to go through with the divorce, I knew I'd better get used to using my maiden name.

"Oh, I'm sorry. I had an appointment scheduled for someone else." He sounded a little excited that someone other than his appointment had walked in. "And what can I do for you, Miss Johnson?"

"I am Mrs. Hall, but I don't want to keep using my husband's last name. If I'm going to get divorced, I might as well go back to my old name."

He nodded. "I understand completely. Come in."

I walked into the cramped office and without the sun in my eyes; I was able to finally see him. He wasn't an incredibly handsome black man, at least not like Quinton, but he was much better looking than he'd sounded on the phone. Strangely enough he stood in front of a small desk and I could see that he was about my height, but fifty pounds heavier.

I walked in and seated myself in the small blue chair that sat across from his desk. Both the tattered cloth on the chair and peeling wood from his desk were in desperate need of junking, but he was cheap and that was more important to me than his decor.

"So Miss--Johnson, we spoke on the phone about price. It's evident you want a divorce, but by law I have to ask you several questions about you and your spouse, okay?" I nodded. "Okay, what's the reason for this separation?"

"We're like two different people. He's been unfaithful, dishonest, disrespectful, and I don't want to raise my son in that type of environment."

"So you do have children?" I nodded as he continued to write down everything I said in a form of shorthand, a skill I knew a great deal about.

"Do you think your husband is violent?"

"He can be. He's never hit me or anything like that, but he is very temperamental."

For the next forty-five minutes, Mr. Sparks asked me questions about my family, our life together, and even things I hadn't considered like our incomes versus our assets and liabilities, my depression and peoples' perceptions of me, the difference between a divorce and a petition for divorce, and educated me on what a temporary restraining order is and why it's necessary. By the time he finished, I found out that there was more to the divorce process than I would've ever believed.

"Look, Miss Johnson, I know you want your divorce finalized ASAP, but the truth is that it takes at least sixty days to get it finished and that's the best case scenario. Since you have children, custody is always an issue and that might drag it out much longer than necessary. My suggestion for you and your situation is to get a contested divorce. That way if he, your husband, chooses not to sign the divorce papers, the court will still dissolve the marriage for you. It's more expensive and takes more court time, but it keeps you from re-filing and re-paying should he reject the uncontested divorce."

"I always figured it'd be like it was in the movies or TV. You walk in, get a divorce, and walk out."

He laughed. "Yeah, most people think like that, but divorces are a process. And that process is more like a marathon than a sprint."

"Thank you for your help, Mr. Sparks." As I shook his hand, his left hand appeared from out of his pocket and I didn't see a wedding band on it.

"So should I begin the paperwork?" he asked, eyes pleading with me like a child's in a candy store.

I reached in my purse and pulled out the check with the amount he said he'd need as a down payment already written on it.

"Please do."

All that was left for me to do now was tell Mike. As I thought about Quinton finally recognizing how serious I was, a sort of calmness enveloped me. The one thing that I did know was that no matter how tranquil things were now, Mike still had to be told and he wasn't going to like what I had to say.

It was almost eight o' clock when I heard Mike's boots stomping up the stairway. Since he hadn't come home for most of the week, probably spending it with his whore, I'd guessed correctly when I said he'd be home tonight.

Because of how Mike could get when he lost his temper, I already left MJ at my aunt's house, lying to her when I told her we wanted to spend some quiet time together. The last thing I wanted was to deal with my son while his father was on one of his curse filled rants.

I involuntarily held my breath as he fiddled with the lock, a part of me hoping that it was Quinton, but I knew the sound of Mike's entrance all too well. As soon as the door opened, he looked at me as I stared at him, then walked past me into the living room and began watching TV.

I took in several deep breaths and calmed myself down. I'd already planned this out and I knew what I was going to say. "How was work?"

"I worked and now I'm home. How come dinner isn't ready?" he asked, frowning. He never treated me as if my day was important.

"It's not ready because all this week, you haven't even come home. You spend so much time at your whore's house that you're lucky I even stay here!" I blurted out.

In just a few seconds my plan had already been thrown out the window. Before I had a chance to even apologize, Mike came rushing into the kitchen-- his dark face contorted and fists clenched. As soon as he made it to me, he gave me a crooked smile.

"Maybe if I had something to eat, I would stay here more often. Maybe if I had a wife who went to work instead of calling off from her job all fucking week, I would stay here more often. Maybe if I had a wife who gave me some pussy every once in a while I'd stay here more often!" He was so close to me that I felt him spitting on me as he yelled.

"Mike, I..."

"You know what Monie, fuck you. I don't even know why I fucking came over here cuz you ain't shit."

As he walked towards the door, the only thing I could think about was him telling me how worthless I was. I could feel my body warming from anger as his words reverberated through me.

"Maybe if I had a man without such a tiny dick, I would make love to him! Maybe if I had a man who knew how to take care of his family, maybe I would work! Maybe if I had a man, a real man, I wouldn't have to divorce his sorry ass!"

Even though it wasn't supposed to come out like that, it had. With all the anger I had coursing through me, I didn't care how he felt anymore.

He slowly turned around and as soon as his eyes met mine, he never broke his evil gaze. "What the fuck did you say to me?"

"I said that if you were a real man I wouldn't have to divorce your ass!"

He punched the kitchen wall, leaving a small crater beside the light switch. I jumped back as he did, finally coming to the realization that the punch was meant for me and not the wall. I began taking a few steps back, but after he pulled his bruised hand from the hole, he came rushing towards me. I turned around to run, but he caught the back of my t-shirt and clutched it with both hands. He held me so tight that I could barely breathe and I began reaching for anything to make him stop.

"What the fuck did you say to me? You telling me I'm not a *real* fucking man? Is that what you said to me?" With each question his grip tightened.

"You're choking me!" I managed to get out and as soon as he heard me, he let me go and I fell onto the floor trying to catch my breath. Without another word, Mike walked past me and headed for the bedroom. I immediately stood up and ran to the kitchen drawer. I quickly pulled out the biggest knife we had and walked towards the bedroom after him. I held the knife behind my back, hoping that he would dare attack me again.

"What the fuck do you want, Monie? You need to get out of my face right now!"

As he threw clothes into a garbage bag, I mustered up all the courage I could as I looked into his eyes, which now seemed like the eyes of a crazy man. "Yes, I want to divorce you, Michael Hall. Yes. Does that answer your question?"

"You must be fucking joking, right? Right!?!" he screamed. "You wouldn't be shit without me! I fucking married you even though I knew you wasn't shit! MJ probably ain't my fuckin kid either, sorry ass bitch! Yeah, I heard all about you messing around before we got married, but I still fucking married yo ass! I'm thinking you might've even fucked Lae, but I can't even get a goddamn threesome? That's probably why that bitch hates me so much, cuz I took her pussy away from her!"

"I ain't sleep with nobody before we was married, Mike, and I wish you'd get that through your fucking head! You wanna know why I don't wanna do a threesome with you? It's because you were never man enough to handle one woman. Maybe if you cared enough about your family to see how they were doing, you could've gotten one! You talk about me not being shit; you ain't shit!" I screamed back.

"Well, maybe if you knew how to treat a man I'd stick around. You fucking suck dick like you just chewed on a bag of rocks! At least Starr can make me feel like a real man and she lets me do it anyway I want to, not like my wife, who lies in the bed like a dead fish."

"The man I got now doesn't feel that way!" Mike looked up at me and glared.

Gotcha!

"Yeah, that's right! He loves the way I ride him and I let him fuck me anytime he wants! I've had more orgasms with him in one night than I've had with you in six fucking years! How you like that shit? And I swallowed whenever he wanted me to. So when you kiss me, you taste him!"

I'd never seen Mike move as swiftly as he did. In one quick motion, he went from being across the room to having his hand around my throat. I quickly brought my knife from around my back, slicing his shirt open and catching a little of his protruding gut.

"What the fuck Monie? You stabbed me!"

"I barely cut you, but if you grab me again, I swear to God Mike, I'll kill you."

261

He saw how serious I was and backed away from me. "You think that shit is funny, bitch? You fucked another man and you think that I won't find him! You really think that sucking another man's dick get's you some sort of pathetic revenge?" He laughed as he threw off his shirt and saw the knife hadn't gotten deep enough to cause any real damage.

"You know what, Monie? Sleeping with another man makes you a hoe! A hoe, Simone! You hear that? Your used up pussy ain't worth shit to me anyway."

I tried not to cry, but I couldn't hold it back. "Fuck you, Mike. You never were a man and you'll never be a man! Why did you even come here? Your slut ain't here! You came back to hurt me, but I don't care! Don't you get it! I'm in love with someone other than my husband. I'm in love with someone else who on his worst day is still ten times the man you could ever hope to be. You can leave, but you can never call yourself a man the way you put your hands on me!" I shouted, as he put a towel around himself to stop the bleeding.

He laughed in the sarcastic way that only he could laugh. "You're so pathetic, you know that? You think Starr was the only person I've been with? Nope, she ain't. She's just the last in a long line of people I've been fucking since we've been married."

The way he'd spoken so callously to me was beginning to make my blood boil and I'd never been so infuriated with anyone in my entire life. The biggest migraine I'd ever had was beginning to settle itself in the front of my skull, but through the pounding, I remained rigid with my knife.

"You know what the funny thing is, Simone?" he asked, filling his bag with clothes. "It's that your stupid ass never even knew. You only suspected when I stopped giving a damn and really didn't care anymore about covering my tracks. For a while I thought about MJ and raising him in a family, but then I had to come home to you. You--the only person who could *never* satisfy me. Everybody else knew how to take care of a man, but not you. I fucked so many people that I just stopped wearing condoms altogether because I didn't care anymore. You think yo new man likes the way you fuck? He's just using you for a nut, like everyone else has."

"You--don't fucking--know--me!" I shouted, trying to fight back the migraine. I was so angry with him that I began searching for things I could throw at him, but the only things I could grab were shoes. I hurled every shoe I could at him, but he just sidestepped with ease and laughed.

"Oh, so now you're throwing shit? That's good because there's more I wanna say and I think you'll want to hear this."

"Fuck you, Mike!" I screamed. "I knew you were fucking around, but you never even suspected I was with another man. We made love all over the house and in the bedroom more times than I can count. Whenever you came home, and laid your head down on your pillow, you slept in his nut or whatever I wasn't able to swallow. How you like nut on your face, Mike? How you like the seed of a real man on your cheek? Too bad you couldn't absorb that shit and learn something from how a real man does it!"

He began walking over to me again and I was so scared that even with the knife in my hand, I could feel myself shaking. As he walked past me and towards the kitchen with his bag, he turned around and spoke. "You know what, Simone? I was actually gonna wait until I got the results, but you know what, I don't give a fuck anymore. I don't even give a fuck if you die and I hope to hell you do. You ain't shit and since you wanna kiss me with someone else's fuckin' nut on your lips, and sleep with another motherfucker in my bed..." He paused and I could see his fists clench. Something in me told me he was coming to kill me, but I would've never guessed how until he began speaking again.

"The both of you can die together and rot in hell for all I care. While I was out there, fucking the world, Starr is HIV positive. I didn't want to come home until I knew, but I needed clothes. But since you fucked me and your new boyfriend, all three of us might be carriers. Ain't life fucking funny?"

"You did what?!!!!!" I screamed, but the shock from what he said made my voice barely audible. I thought of Quinton, then Lae and began to cry. *"How, how could you do this, you fuckin' piece of shit!* Why did you do that, Michael? Did you ever think that with both of us dead, who would take care of MJ?"

"My parents will take care of him; away from you and your fucked up aunt. Goodbye and good riddance, you fuckin' ho."

"Your parents will never have my son and neither will you!" I searched for anything to hurt Michael with. Trembling with rage and fear—my eyes bloodshot from crying, I lunged at him. But before I had a chance to stab him, I suddenly felt dizzy.

"Mike!" I called out, but before I had a chance to reach him, I fell into a blissful darkness.

When I awoke, the sky was a beautiful shade of midnight blue and the stars lit up the night with such magnificence that I was in awe for a few seconds until I realized I was not inside my house. Then, I noticed that emergency lights were flashing everywhere and people were staring at me as I tried to look around. I made several attempts to move my arms and legs, but they resisted and felt more like bricks. I knew something was wrong because in addition to my immobility, I could barely utter a word out.

"Where am I?" I knew I said it, but somehow the words barely escaped my mouth and so I tried again. "Where am I?"

Suddenly a police officer stood over me. "Mrs. Hall?" He looked off in the distance and asked another person how long I'd been up before he returned his attention to me. "Mrs. Hall, I'm here to inform you that you're under arrest for assault and attempted murder."

Hearing the last few words of the officer's sentence awoke me completely from my daze, but as I tried to move to dispute the officer, I saw why I couldn't move any of my extremities. I was tied down to a stretcher on the way to an awaiting ambulance.

"What did I do?" I cried, but the officer continued reading me my Miranda rights without any regard for my questions.

"What the fuck happened?"

I laid my head back onto the bed and looked around in horror as dozens of people, including my neighbors watched as I was wheeled into the back of the ambulance. "What the fuck happened!" I screamed at the top of my lungs as they closed the door, and I was forced to stare at the ceiling of an ambulance instead of the night sky. As the doors closed, tears poured from my eyes and I'd never wanted to see my son more in my life.

"Where's my son! I want MJ! Why won't anyone answer my fucking questions?"

Then the ambulance door closed me off from all the pandemonium happening on my street and from the rest of the world. Even with the policeman and emergency worker on each side of me, I was once again, alone.

CHAPTER 18

Laela

<u>March 10th (Friday)</u>

When the phone rang, I thought it was all part of my dream. For the last few nights all I dreamt about was Niya going down on me while Quinton was fucking her, but this was the first time that I'd ever heard any phones ringing during our fantasy threesome.

When I finally realized that the phone wasn't part of the dream, I picked it up and Mike was already shouting unintelligibly into my ear.

"Slow down Mike! Simone did what to you? And she's where?"

Hearing my distress, Quinton woke up and sat next to me in the bed. I turned the speaker on so we could hear. We listened as Mike retold the story of what had transpired between him and Simone earlier in the night.

"Are you still bleeding?" Quinton asked.

"Hell yeah I'm still bleeding! I'm going to need stitches on both my arms. I asked the paramedic to call you and she's the one holding the phone to my goddamn face!"

"What did you do to her Mike for her to do this to you?" I asked, trying to fight back the tears. For as long as I'd known Simone, she'd never been violent. I knew that Mike would've had to do something to her to make her try and stab him.

"You know what Laela, only you would say some shit like that. I'm the one fucking bleeding to death and you think that I caused this!

You might not wanna believe this Lae, but that bitch was crazy. She was taking all sorts of happy pills to keep her normal, but I guess they stopped working. Matter of fact, I don't know why I'm even talking to you! Put Quinton back on the phone!"

I handed Quinton the phone and as soon as he cut the speakerphone off, I began to pace around the apartment. The Simone I knew would never intentionally hurt another living thing and yet she went on a knife wielding spree? It didn't make sense. It had to be something that Mike had done to her. I was so angry with what he'd done to get Simone thrown in jail that I started crying.

As soon as Quinton hung up, he stood up and began walking around the room and looking for his clothes.

"Where are you going?" I asked, wiping away the steady stream of tears.

"I'm going to the hospital to make sure Mike's okay."

"But we need to bail Simone out!"

"Lae, she just cut up her husband! Maybe what she needs is to sit in jail so that she can chill the fuck out! Mike is the person on the receiving end of that asswhooping, so I'm going to make sure that he's okay before I worry about her!"

"Well then, I'm coming with you."

Without waiting to hear his response, I threw on some jeans and a t-shirt and within five minutes we were on our way.

By the time we made it to the hospital, Mike was still waiting in emergency room. He sat away from the rest of the crowd and I saw that both his arms were wrapped in gauze from the wrist to almost his elbow.

As Quinton made his way over, Mike noticed us and gave us a head nod. Still pissed at him for what I knew he had brought on himself, I took my time walking over.

"You look like shit."

"Thanks Quinton, I really needed those words of encouragement."

"What I meant to say was have they seen you yet?"

"Yeah, they gave me some stitches and wrapped them in bandages. I was just waiting for you to come get me." He looked at me with a slight look of disdain, but I did nothing to hide my disgust.

Quinton helped him to his feet. "Say whatever it is that you wanna say, Lae. Let's get this shit over with."

"What did you do to her, Mike?" I asked through clenched teeth.

He laughed like I'd said something funny. "You know what the funny thing is Lae, you always side with her. You always side with her.

This time, she was wrong. She told me she wanted a divorce, I told her I didn't give a shit. Then she told me she was fucking her new man." When I didn't give him a surprised look, he shook his head. "So you knew, too?"

"Turnabout is fair play, Mike. You had your fling, she had hers. So what did you do after you found out? Did you slap her around a few times? Did you choke her? What did you do to make her grab a knife?"

"Why don't we just head to the car?" Quinton asked. "It doesn't make sense for us to fight in a hospital in the middle of the night."

As we walked out of the emergency room and towards Quinton's car, Mike began to whisper in Quinton's ear.

"If you got something to say Mike, then say it."

"Fine then, Lae. If you wanna know what really set your girl off, then here it is. When I told her I wanted the divorce too, her ass went crazy. I told her she wasn't shit, she wasn't ever going to be shit and that I had the real thing, so I didn't need her. After that, she grabbed the knife and tried to kill me."

I was speechless and I couldn't shake the feeling that had I paid more attention to Simone when she needed me, this could've all been avoided. I knew she had problems with depression, but I was a nurse and I completely missed all the signs she'd shown. I actually believed she was happier now, especially with her new man, but as I looked at Mike, I could see that I was wrong.

"I hope the bitch fucking rots in jail."

Without thinking, I lunged at Mike, hitting him on the arm that was most heavily bandaged before Quinton pulled me away from him. As Mike cradled his arm, blood slowly began seeping through the gauze.

"What the fuck are you doing, Lae?" Quinton shouted and rushed to Mike's side. He tossed me the keys. "Stay in the fucking car!"

I opened the door and started the car. I didn't give a shit about Mike or Quinton for protecting him. I was going to get Simone out of jail and make this right.

"So did you get her out?"

The sun was just peeking over the horizon and I was so tired that my head began to hurt. I didn't know what hurt more, the fact that I failed Simone or that I had to apologize to Mike, but the rest of the night went without another incident. We'd just dropped Mike off at his mother's house and we were on our way back home when Quinton asked me about Simone.

"No," I said, turning to briefly look at him while I drove. "They wanted to keep her in the psych ward for observation. Why did you run to Mike after I hit him?"

"Lae, he'd just been stabbed and you attacked him. What the hell was I supposed to do? You weren't bleeding and he was. Just so you know; it damn sure wasn't because I liked him more, but he'd just gotten out of the hospital and you put him back in."

"Fine, but did you know where I went?"

"Lae, I know you. You're blaming yourself for what happened and no matter how hard you try; it's not your fault."

"I know it's not my fault, but I don't want Mike in the wedding. I don't even want him near my wedding. I can talk to my parents and we could do the wedding up north."

"Fine, but I need a new groomsman and you're going to need a new maid of honor. Also, your parents are going to have to buy tickets for my whole family to go up north."

I'd forgotten that Simone was the maid of honor and because Mike refused to let the whole issue go, I knew Simone was out. With the wedding a little more than three months away, I could still find a replacement.

"I can ask Teniyah to take over. I'll have one less bridesmaid, you'll have one less groomsman and everything will even out."

"Why *not* ask Niya a.k.a. Superwoman? I mean damn, she's already helping us with everything else." I smiled because I knew what he meant, but Quinton didn't even feign a smile.

"Lae, how long have you known about Simone messing around?"

I forgot that Quinton hadn't known. With all the time they'd spent together talking at the party I figured she would've told him, but she probably thought he might've told Mike. "She mentioned it to me a few weeks ago. She never told me his name or anything like that. All she said was that he was special." I began to cry as I reminisced about our talk in the lingerie store. "She-- um, she didn't tell me anything about him other than he rocked her world."

Quinton brushed the tears away from my eyes with the sleeves from his sweatshirt. "Mike wants me to talk to Simone. He wants me to find out who this guy is."

"You're not going to help him!" I asked in disbelief. He grabbed and tightly held my free hand. "No. Mike won't get any answers from me."

By the time Niya had arrived, Quinton had already gone to work and I was busy stuffing envelopes with wedding invitations. When I opened the door, she walked in with her usual flamboyant flair, wearing sunglasses, a bikini top and shorts cut from old pants-- neither article of clothing covering much of her assets. She kissed me on the cheek and invited herself into my apartment.

"And hello to you, too." I said, as I closed the door. I invited her over because I needed help with the invitations, but the way she was dressed, I might've thought that I invited her to the beach.

She sat down on the couch and looked over all the invitations that hadn't been put into envelopes. "This is a lot of work for one woman. Where is your maid of honor? Shouldn't she be helping you with all this?"

"Cut the BS Niya." I said, while sitting down next to her. "Who told you?"

"Well, I was talking to Quinton this morning about the nasty things I was going to make him do on his birthday when he told me about Mike and Simone. It was such a horribly tragic and violent story, but now that the position is open, you don't even have to ask. I accept!"

The fact the she volunteered to accept the position didn't bother me as much as hearing her tell me that she called Quinton and they were talking about sex. "So he called you?"

"No, I called him. I figured he'd be at work and that we could have some privacy."

"What did you need privacy for?"

She turned and began to laugh. "Lae, you're jealous!"

"I'm not jealous!" I returned my attention to the envelopes, accidentally ripping the first one.

"Look, Lae, I've been thinking a lot about this threesome thing. I've even been watching some of Franklin's videos to get an idea of what to do, but if you just want me all for yourself, then that's tough. I really want to do this."

"It's not that I'm jealous," I replied, still stuffing the envelopes, "but what am I supposed to do when the only thing I dream about is another woman with my man? For the last few nights, it's all I've been able to think about. It's like I'm watching the both of you, and God help me, it really turns me on."

When I saw her wide grin from the corner of my eye, I continued, "I can't believe that I just told you that."

269

"Would you feel better if I told you that I've actually gotten off watching Franklin's videos? I sit back and imagine it's us instead of them."

"Do you really?" I asked sheepishly.

"Nope, I just wanted you to feel better."

She'd done it again and I always found myself falling into her traps. "So are you doing this so you can add Quinton to your trophy wall or are you doing it because you want to enjoy screwing me in front of him?"

"It's neither of those. I'm helping all of us fulfill a fantasy. If I like it, then maybe we can set up something else before you guys get married--perhaps even afterwards."

"And if we don't?"

"You will. If I'm a part of it, you will."

"Well, Maid of Honor, since you're so confident, you can start your pleasure duties by sealing those R.S.V.P. envelopes and I'll do the invitations."

"I love it when you take charge."

When Quinton finally arrived from work, Niya and I were looking online for her new dress. Niya stood up and greeted him with a soft kiss on his lips and a hard smack on the butt as soon as Quinton walked into the living room,

"I likes it when they have a big booty," she said.

I looked away, trying not to smile at Niya's crazy antics and buried my face in the laptop screen. It wasn't until Quinton bent over and gave me such a passionate kiss that my toes began to tingle that I closed the top and looked at him.

"What was that for?" I asked when he finally pulled away.

"I just wanted you to know who I belong to."

I blushed. "Another kiss like that and I may have to take you in the back."

Niya began walking towards the bedroom and when we didn't follow she turned towards us.

"What are you guys waiting for? I'm down for this right now!"

I returned my attention to Quinton. "Have you heard from Simone...or Mike?"

Quinton sat next to me on the couch and Niya perched herself on the other side. "I haven't heard from Simone, but Mike is focused on finding out who Simone slept with. I tried to get him to drop it, but he refuses to let it go."

"Simone was sleeping with someone on the side? Perhaps she's not at all like I thought she was." We both raised our eyebrows at Niya and she shrugged it off. "Anyways," she continued, "now that it's just us here, you can tell me about the kinky things you guys like to do."

Quinton opened his mouth, but I was the one who spoke. "You're the one watching all the videos. Why don't you surprise us?"

"I think I will," she replied with her devilish grin.

CHAPTER 19

Quinton

<u>Wednesday (March 23rd)</u>

In the last few weeks I received so many phone calls that I was ready to sell my cell. Every person who called had their own agenda and it seemed like I was more caught up in their worlds than I was in taking care of my own.

Dre called to bug me about filming the threesome. Lae would call about needing my help to finalize the wedding plans. Cheyenne called for sex, Teniyah usually called to talk dirty, which wasn't all that bad and Mike called for answers about the mystery man--who I already knew was me. The only people I didn't indulge were Cheyenne and Mike, both wanting something I wasn't willing to give them.

At least when Simone was blowing up my phone, which seemed so long ago, the only thing she wanted was attention. Even after she was put into a mental health facility a little more than a week ago, I seemed to be the only person she wanted to talk to. We never talked about much, except about how she was doing, but Lae and Mike both wanted every detail I could muster. The only detail I ever gave them was that she didn't remember much of anything.

I was on my way out of the office for the day when my cell phone rang. It was Mike...again. I answered, already agitated that this was his third call today. "This better be something important. I'm tired of you calling my phone and asking the same damn question."

"I got Simone's cell phone bill in the mail today. I've been through every number she called and only a couple of them haven't answered. The only people that she called a lot were you and Lae."

"Maybe she used the house phone. It makes sense that she didn't want his number on her cell."

"Yeah, that does make sense. Have you talked to her today? Did she tell you anything about him? Did she give you some fuckin' initials or something we can use?"

I knew he wasn't going to let this go easily, but I had no idea that he'd become obsessed with the idea of finding...me.

"Mike, you fucked around and she fucked around. She's locked up in a padded room, but you seem to be the one ready to join her. Let it go."

"I can't, Q. I slept with her after this dude nutted all inside her and I can't get past that. I just want to know if this dude knew she had a husband."

"And if he did?" I asked.

"Well then I'm goin' to fuck him up."

"Goodbye, Mike."

"Whoa, whoa, whoa, slow down Quinton. So Lae really doesn't want me in the wedding, huh? Have you even tried to get me back in, man?"

"Look Mike, there's nothing outside of an act of God that can get you back in her good graces. She doesn't even want to see your face in the crowd."

"But Quinton, you're supposed to be my boy and I want to see you jump the broom." He paused and then acquiesced. "Fine, maybe in three months, she'll change her mind. Anyway, hit me up when you hear from Simone."

"Don't I always?"

As I hung up the phone, I noticed the overcast and began to jog towards the car. I could see flashes of lightning in the distance, and I could feel the wind picking up as I rushed faster towards the car. But on a day like today, I wasn't ever going to move fast enough. Just as I reached the door the Camry, the skies opened up and the downpour had soaked my back as I bent over to load my extra work into the car. Once I was in the car all I could do was laugh at what was amounting to a shitty day.

I was halfway home when traffic came to a halt. My windshield wipers were moving as fast as they possibly could, yet with the sky as black as a coal mine and with all the rain coming down, I could barely see ten feet in front of me. I turned on the radio and began to listen to some music when my phone lit up. I reached over to see who it was and saw that Teniyah had left a text message. I quickly put the phone back down and focused my attention on the road.

Because traffic wasn't moving, I could've responded to Niya's text, but her texts were simply invitations to trouble. Truthfully, I enjoyed a little harmless flirting, but lately every time we'd flirt I always walked away feeling as if I'd already cheated on Lae. As relentless as Niya was, I finally began to understand what she'd put Lae through. I laughed at myself, I had to. For the longest time I honestly believed that Lae and Niya were in love when the truth was that Lae had finally conceded to a woman who didn't understand the meaning of the word "no".

The rain was beginning to lighten up when my phone chirped for the second time. I thought it might be Niya calling to curse me for not having returned her text right away, but instead it was Dre. Even though I didn't feel like talking to him for the third time today, I answered anyway.

"What, Dre?"

"Dawg, if you're about to do this threesome, then your ass needs to be in the gym with me."

"I think you care more about this threesome than I do."

"And I think you're right. Look man, if I'm going to get a good angle on you, you've got to look good for the camera."

I sighed. "How did I know we were going to talk about this for the third time today?"

"I'm transparent Quinton. If I think it, you know it. Like a week from now, you'll be able to masturbate for years because of the nasty things y'all about to do. Just thinking about that shit gets me going!"

"Dre, I'm hanging up now."

"Okay, wait! I'm thinking I need someone to spot me at the gym and you might as well be the one. C'mon Quinton, it's not like you shouldn't look good for this momentous occasion."

"Traffic is bad out here. I'll be there in thirty."

I stopped at the house to pick up some shorts and a t-shirt and about an hour later, I was in the gym.

As usual when I walked in, Dre was chatting with the same Hispanic personal trainer who didn't give him a second look. When he saw me walk over towards the weights, he rushed over to meet me.

"I'm breaking her down, Q. She's definitely going to be in my bed before the year is up."

I dropped my sports bag by the free weights. "It's March."

"Which means I still have time!"

"Why don't you just spot me?"

I hadn't been in the gym since after Christmas when he bought the both of us memberships, but it felt good to do something other than sit at the house. With every repetition, I could feel the stress of Mike, the wedding and the impending threesome slipping away. It also helped that Dre was mostly preoccupied with all the tanned, toned and half-naked, sweating women around the room.

We worked out for about an hour when Dre finally broke down and asked, "Aren't you glad the Simone thing worked itself out? I didn't think she'd go crazy, but she can't tell Lae shit from the cuckoo farm."

I placed the free weights back on the bars and sat next to Dre at the rowing machine. "She's in a mental health facility, but yeah, I am kind of glad that it happened that way. When she calls, she lets me know how sorry she is."

"So she's sorry about what she did to Mike?"

"Hell naw!" Though I didn't mean to shout, people in the gym turned around at my exclamation. I waved to let everyone know I was okay and leaned over to whisper to Dre. "She always says how she blacked out, but that she wished she would've killed his ass."

"Damn, what did that brother due to deserve her wrath?" He looked puzzled.

"She won't tell me. She says she may let me know in a few weeks, but not right now."

Dre stood up and walked a few feet over to my bag. "You mind if I grab a towel?" When I shrugged, he reached in, pulled out a towel and my phone along with it. As he was wiping the sweat from his brow, he tossed the phone to me. "You got a text, dawg."

I looked at my phone and saw it was the same message from Teniyah that I'd previously ignored. "This is just from Teniyah. I don't know what's wrong with this woman. Every time we talk, she's talking about what she wants to do and what she wants to try. She's actually scaring me with some of the shit she's already suggested."

"Like what? Is she going to wear a strap on and turn my fantasy into something nightmarish?" He shivered slightly and I laughed at his repulsion.

"Somehow I don't see it quite going down like that, but the way she talks, she's certainly not going to be the third wheel." He looked at my phone for the second time and then looked at me. "What do you want, Dre?"

"You know that's from Teniyah's sexy ass, right? You might as well open it. Perhaps I can get a glimpse of the freaky shit you're talking about and save you from the big, bad Amazon."

I mouthed 'asshole' towards Dre, but he'd already stood up and was looking over my back. When I opened the message, we both discovered that it wasn't a text at all. It was a video.

It began with a dark screen and as Jodeci's 'Freak 'n You' began to play, a wonderful pair of breasts emerged from obscurity. After a few seconds of focusing on her bare chest, she began to pan down and in doing so, caused Dre to accidentally fall onto my shoulder, hoping he could catch one last look.

As the music continued to play and camera slowly descended, the flawlessness of Niya's form was revealed. From her bare breasts to her midriff, there wasn't a single article of clothing. She was naked and there wasn't a single doubt in my mind about that.

The video continued until it dropped just below her hips. I felt myself becoming increasing more aroused when it abruptly ended.

For about thirty seconds afterwards, Dre and I remained fixated at the screenshot of her waistline until he shouted, "Play that shit again!" And like two high school teenagers, I was more than happy to oblige.

After a play through of about five times, I'd already had my fill, but Dre continued watching. I began to work out using the rowing machine and it wasn't until his phone began to chime that he looked away from mine.

"Quinton, I just want you to know how much I fucking love you, man! This is, by far, the best present I've ever had!"

I smiled and continued to row. "Glad to--see you're--happy. Your phone--is ringing."

"Don't worry about that. That's just me sending your video to my phone. Oh my God, Quinton, this video may just keep me from ever having another woman."

No sooner than he began to watch the video on his phone, it rang and he quickly answered. I listened to him as he began to fumble over words and nod hysterically as if the person on the other end could see him. When he hung up, he immediately jumped up and ran towards the exit. In a matter of seconds, he covered the length of the gym and was out the door before I could even ask who he'd spoken to.

I reached into my bag and pulled out my phone and called him. "Who was that?" I asked when he finally picked up.

"Quinton, who the hell do you think it was? Like I'd ever just up and leave you for any phone call."

"You would! And you *have!*"

"Yeah, but that's in the past." He chuckled. "Teniyah called and she wants to meet up at my house. She digs the way I throw parties and she wants to mash brains-- and hopefully some hips-- to see what we can do for the bachelorette party."

I sighed. "You see one video of her tits and now you're at her back and call? I thought I raised you better."

"You haven't. Now, if you'll excuse me, I gotta get to the house as fast as I possibly can."

I worked out for another hour after Dre left and as I made my way to the car, I played the video once more.

When I arrived home, Lae stood over a boiling pot on the stove. I laid my stuff on the counter and smiled at my beautiful fiancée. Still thinking about the video, I softly kissed her lips and sniffed from the pot what smelled like chili. Ready to curse myself for not stopping to pick up some Chinese like I'd planned, I gave her another small peck when I saw that she was following a recipe.

"You must've had a good day."

"It was certainly a long one," I said while walking towards the living room.

"Have you heard from Simone?"

"Not since the last time. Mike's still hounding for answers about her mystery man. Personally, I don't think the guy exists. I just think it was Simone's way of getting back at Mike for cheating."

When Laela didn't answer, I walked into our bedroom and was about to take a shower when Lae shouted for me. I ran to the front, with my towel barely covering me, to see what was wrong when I found her holding my phone.

"Quinton, what the hell is this?"

I looked at her and then at the phone. "It's a cell phone." I said nonchalantly, just then remembering that I'd left Teniyah's message on the screen.

"You always have to be the smartass! What the fuck are you and Niya doing behind my back, Quinton? I saw the video!" She tossed the phone on the couch. "Women don't send videos like that unless they mean something!"

I wrapped my towel around me and inched my way towards Lae. "I haven't done anything with her, Lae! You know how your girl is and I guess she sent me that to be flirtatious! I didn't ask for that, she just sent it!"

"C'mon Quinton, I'm not stupid! First Simone completely blows me off! And I figure that's okay because she's mad at me for not being around! Then when Dre had his 80's party, you volunteer to drive her home and you take forever to do that! And to top all that off, when she gets locked away and starts talking, she only calls you and suddenly Niya just happens to send you videos of her tits! Am I supposed to believe that these are just coincidences? Be honest, Quinton, are you messing around on me?"

I did the only thing I could do. I lied. "When you went to Cleveland, Simone didn't have anyone to talk to and so she talked to me. She's hurt Lae because she thinks Niya has replaced her and that you have a love for Teniyah that you'll never have for her. You want to know why it took so long to drive her home. She was sick as a dog and I didn't want her drunken ass throwing up in my car! So I drove a little slower to help her with her motion sickness! As for Niya, she's your friend! Why don't you tell me why she does the things she does? She flirts with you and that's okay. She flirts with me and it's like a goddamn national emergency! Why don't you call her and ask her why she did it?"

She picked up my phone. "You know what, you're right. I'll call her." As soon as the phone began to ring, Laela put it on speakerphone so that I could hear as well.

When Niya picked up she was the first to speak. "Hey sexy, I'm at Dre's but I guess you're still reeling over the message I sent. Are you calling because you want to see the lower half?"

My fiancée was as red as I'd ever seen her and she was squeezing my phone so hard that I could hear it begin to crack.

"Teniyah! What the fuck! You nasty ass whore! The fucking threesome is off!" She threw the phone to the floor. Tears streamed down her face as she stormed past me and into the bedroom, slamming the door.

Fuck!

CHAPTER 20
Happy Birthday!

Quinton

12:00 a.m.

I already knew who it was, after hearing the knock at the apartment door. Wearing only a t-shirt and basketball shorts, I opened the door and allowed Dre to sneak in. After peeking around to make sure that Lae wasn't in sight, he walked through the door and fell onto the couch.

Traditionally, every year on my birthday, Dre would give me a handful of money and we'd spend it getting the most vicarious dances from our favorite strip club across town. This year our plans had to be put on hold. Because of the video, I'd been apologizing to Lae so often that Dre and I hardly spoke.

"You still planned on going out or just getting off of work?" I asked after seeing that he was wearing one of his more expensive suits.

"I'm sure I'm not the only one who knows that today is your birthday. You know where we're supposed to be right about now?"

"I can't go."

"So, I take it she's still mad?" he asked while looking for the remote.

"Dre, she canceled the threesome and she hasn't spoken to Teniyah in a week. On top of that, I have to give her my phone every night so she can make sure that she hasn't called me."

"But she has called you. I know because she calls me and tells me. I don't ever think I've seen Niya upset, but she seems pretty distressed. I was thinking I could get some 'I'm so sad' pussy, but she won't even come back to the house."

"As always, you're concern for me is overwhelming."

"I do what I can."

"Anyway," I added, ignoring his sarcasm, "all she says when she talks to me is to tell Lae that she's sorry, but even if I say Niya's name... let's just say that happy words don't come out. So I just delete her number."

Dre settled on SportsCenter before tossing the remote and turning towards me. "So you're really going to buck tradition? The way I see it, this is the perfect time to go. I mean damn, wifey ain't here, you're already in trouble, and it's your birthday."

"I don't think I should risk getting in more trouble right now and neither should you." I said, while sitting down on the other side of the couch.

"I don't get why she's mad at me too?"

"You sent the video to yourself. Well, she thinks that I was so in love with it that I had to send it to you, too. So that puts us both in the doghouse. That's why I'm going to stay in this year."

"Damn you're whipped," he chuckled out and when he stood up to leave, he just shook his head. I didn't follow him as he opened the front door for fear that I might go with him. Before closing the door, Dre turned back and asked, "How the hell are you gonna be in trouble on your birthday?"

6:45 a.m.

I awoke feeling like everything that happened during the past week was a bad dream, but when the hangover didn't immediately follow, disappointment settled in.

With Lae still at work, I stretched out in the bed and quietly wished that I'd deleted that video. But since I hadn't, I just had to live with the idea that I was the one who screwed up what I hoped was the best birthday present any man could ever receive. I made my way to the bathroom where I quickly showered and brushed my teeth.

My father always told me that there were two times black people weren't supposed to work: holidays and birthdays. Because Dre and I usually brought in my birthday covered in half-naked women, it was a good credo, but today didn't seem like a birthday at all.

"Happy birthday to me," I mumbled as I glanced at myself in the bathroom mirror.

As I left the bathroom, the house phone rang and I debated answering. After the third ring, curiosity won out and I picked up the phone with a gruff sounding, "Hello?"

"What's up, b-day boy? You know I had to be the first to call and say it! I didn't want anyone to steal my thunder!" It was Dre, again, and he shouted each sentence into the telephone like I'd lost my hearing aide.

"Can you tone it down a little? I'm still half sleep."

"You need to wake your ass up and come with me to get some breakfast!"

"Where do you want to go? I'll meet you there."

"I'm already outside your apartment."

I walked over to my bedroom window and saw Dre on his cell, standing next to his car, waving at me. "I'll be down in five."

"So what you're telling me is that things aren't looking good for the ménage." I nodded and Dre shoved his mouth full of grits.

We went to an IHOP down the street from the apartment. I've heard that loud colors help bring about positive attitudes, but the building's bright exterior did nothing for my soured mood. We'd already ordered breakfast and I explained to him everything that had transpired between Lae and me the past week.

As I watched Dre shovel down his breakfast, I just played with my bacon and toast, making them do somersaults on my plate.

"Look, Quinton, I know you're a little upset about how things played out. I really do get it. But I did have to flirt with that extremely big girl to get you a birthday hook up, so at least you can pretend to eat."

"This wasn't how it was supposed to be."

"Are you mad now that you can't get your revenge? You can be so damn petty. You need to get past this little revenge thing you got going."

For the first time all day, I smiled. "After last week, I kinda understand the pressure that Niya puts on people to get what she wants. The innuendo, flirty remarks and naked pics...I mean damn! She lays it on pretty thick. But when I watched that disc you made and Lae turned Niya down at the party, I had more love and respect for Laela than I ever have. Hell, I don't even know if I could say 'no' to Teniyah."

Dre almost choked on his coffee. "So you had the fucking disc and you watched it? Then you lied to me and told me you threw it away?" He pushed his chair away from the table. "I don't even know if we can be friends anymore."

"Well then erase the videos of Niya's tits and we can be done with each other."

Without even thinking about it, he brought his chair back to the table. "You would really take my video? Do you really understand how much I love this video? We may have to fight if you want me to erase this."

I laughed and Dre soon began to laugh with me. "I was just so focused on doing this that it actually feels like less of a birthday now."

"It's still your birthday. I know a lot of people and I think you're the only man I know who could still pull this birthday thing off. You need to stop thinking like a fiancé and get back to thinking like the old Quinton."

"I don't get you. We've both had threesomes before, so why are you so hard up for me to follow through with this one?"

He looked at me like I'd just said something stupid. "You already know that Teniyah is my perfect woman! She's college educated, fine as hell, a freak in every sense of the word and she's willing to eat pussy! They don't make them better than her--with the exception of Lae." I smiled sarcastically as he continued. "The way I see it, if you can get the draws, then I can get them. Even if you don't see it, both Lae and Niya want this threesome to go down, but they're women-- neither wants the other to know."

"Well, oh wise one, infuse me with your wisdom," I mused. "Enlighten me so that I may bring my partners to the precipice of nirvana." Grinning, I bowed my head in front of Dre. "I am your humble apprentice."

"Well, I'll re-educate you, young grasshopper, but first we must eat."

Laela

8:00 a.m.

When I walked through the apartment door from a long night at the hospital, I half expected Quinton to be making breakfast. I knew it was his birthday and that I should've been making it for him, but with the night I'd had I could barely walk straight.

Quickly eyeballing the living room, I was greeted with nothing but silence. I yelled out his name, hoping he was somewhere within earshot, but when he didn't come, I began to look around the apartment. I quickly walked to the bedroom to see that the bed looked like it hadn't been slept in and that the room was as spotless as Quinton had left it last night.

I didn't know whether to be mildly upset or all out pissed. Quinton made a promise to me and apparently his promises didn't carry as much weight as I thought they had.

During the last week, he went overboard with trying to make me happy; bringing me flowers, cleaning the house and even going so far as to tell me that he wouldn't go to the strip club on his birthday. But with the apartment still in the same shape as it'd been when I left, it meant that he'd gone and hadn't come home.

Fucking Quinton.

Still, it wasn't all Quinton's fault, though I allowed him to shoulder most of the blame. I usually never carried grudges and I hated being angry all the damn time, but it was a culmination of everyone and everything lately.

Niya was supposed to be my best friend in the world. On more than one occasion she told me she loved me--but as soon as I opened the door for a three way her attention shifted. During the last month, I played second fiddle to her obsession with seducing Quinton. How could she do that to me? How could she tell me that she loved me and then treat me like a throwaway rag doll once a new toy came along? I always knew that anything that Niya wanted, she usually got, but I never believed she'd ever throw me to the wayside until a few days ago. When I saw the video, it confirmed that I'd been left out the loop and that Quinton was her new prey.

Fucking Teniyah.

Then, there was Simone. I knew I wasn't there for her as often as I should've been, but she wouldn't even speak to me. I told her to stay away from Mike, even to divorce him, but she didn't listen to me and somehow she ended up in the mental hospital because of him. Why didn't she listen to me? Why didn't she want to talk to me? The fact that she only called Quinton compounded the problem. Why was he the only one privy to what went down and why was he keeping what she said to him from me? What did he know that I didn't? I've known her so much longer than Quinton has, hell I introduced them! Why would she forsake all of our years of friendship and confide in him? Did she even know that he was helping Mike find out who she'd been fucking?

Fucking Simone.

I didn't want to be mad at any of them, but Quinton had stolen my friends, Niya was some oversexed kitten after my man, and Simone didn't even trust me anymore. I didn't know what I could've possibly done to alienate everyone, but the more I thought about it, the worse I felt.

Still standing in the bedroom, I reached into my pocket, pulled out my phone and called Quinton. He picked up on the first ring.

"Hello?"

"Where are you? You told me that you weren't going to go with Dre and this place looks like no one has been here. Why the hell did you lie to me, Quinton? Why couldn't you just tell me the truth?"

"Happy birthday, Quinton? I'm glad that you cleaned the house, Quinton? Are you out eating breakfast with Dre, Quinton? I'd be happy to join you guys. Aren't those the questions you could be asking? I don't know what brought on the interrogation, Lae, but I didn't go out. I kept my word. Dre and I are having breakfast down the street. Thanks for the birthday wishes."

Without waiting for an apology, he hung up. I just stared at my phone, tears welling in my eyes. I'd never been so upset and humiliated. I should've called to wish him a happy birthday, but I was so wrapped up in vilifying him that I hadn't even made the effort. I wiped the tears away from my eyes and called him again. He picked up on the first ring and before he had a chance to say a word, I spoke. "Quinton, I am so sorry. For the last week you've gone out of your way to just keep things civil and all I've done is treated you like shit. You deserve better than how I've treated you and I am so, so sorry for the way I've been acting. I don't want to think that the person I've been recently is the person you will marry and I promise that I won't act like this again. Can you forgive me?"

His silence was all that I needed to confirm that he hated me.

"Quinton, are you there?"

"Yes, I'm here."

"Well, I wanted to tell you happy birthday, but I see you don't want to talk to me right now. Just call me whenever you want to talk." I was about to hang up when he called out my name. "Yes?" I asked curiously, hoping that he'd tell me that all was forgiven.

"Thank you for the 'happy birthday'. Unless you want to join us, I'll be home soon."

"Do you forgive me?"

There was another small bout of silence before he answered. "I'll be home soon."

He hung up and the pain of his silence resonated throughout me. In the course of two weeks, I'd alienated almost everyone I cared about and I had no idea in the world how to get make any of it right.

Frustrated, I picked up my phone and made one more phone call.

Michael

1:45 p.m.

I needed to know who Simone had fucked and sitting around waiting for Quinton wasn't getting me the answers I needed. I wanted to celebrate Q's birthday with him, but some things were just more important and this was one of those things.

As I walked around the house, my arm still in a sling from what Simone's crazy ass had done, I knew that I still had to talk to her. I needed to know what she knew. I had to find out a name or else I was gonna go fuckin' loony. Was it someone I knew? Was it someone who knew me? Was it someone who even existed? Since she'd told me, I'd been waking up at all hours of the night, sweating and out of breath. Even though I hated my wife, I was still consumed with thoughts and dreams of Simone sleeping with the other man.

In the dream everything was so real. No matter how hard I tried, each time I saw them, I couldn't stop them as I watched him fucking her on *my* bed. I ran towards them as fast as I could, but it was like my foot was glued to the floor. Everything seemed to move in slow motion and even when I called out to her, I was muted by the sounds of their pleasure. As I ran towards her, she never looked in my direction, but I could smell her hair spray, her perfume, and even her essence. Yet when I looked at him, his face was darkened and all I could see were his teeth-- teeth that blinded me like headlights. He continued to smile at me and she continued to ride, while I remained unnoticed by her.

They moved Simone to a specialized facility, right outside of Dallas, which was almost four hours away. I tried calling several times, but she wouldn't accept my calls and had put me on a block list. That bitch had actually put me on the block list! If I was going to get the answers I needed, then I needed to confront Simone with a proposition-- one I knew that she would never turn down.

I picked up the phone and dialed a number that was all too familiar to me. "I need you to take me somewhere."

"I'm tired of driving your ass around, Michael. Why don't you call one of your friends?"

"Think about it and you'd know that there are two reasons I can't call them, Starr. Today is Quinton's birthday and I'm sure Andre has some huge ass party planned for him. The second is that I don't want any of them to know where I'm going."

"Where are you going?"

"I need to see my wife. I have some things I need to ask her."

"See, now I'm not taking your ass nowhere. That bitch tried to stab you to death and you're going to see her! Fuck you, Mike! You can kiss my natural black ass!"

"Starr, calm the hell down. I'm going to ask her where the divorce papers are. I tried to call, but they won't let me talk to her. If I go up there, they can't stop her husband from seeing her. All I want to do is find out what she did with the papers so that I can sign them."

"Don't be bullshitting me, Mike. You know how sensitive I am about that."

"I'm not bullshitting you, Starr. Now, will you take me--please?"

"Fine, I'll be over there in twenty minutes."

She hung up and I began reading through the divorce papers for the tenth time since I'd gotten them more than two weeks ago, cursing Simone as I read each word.

I hadn't realized it, but when Starr honked the horn, twenty minutes had passed and I was still tightly gripping the papers. When I heard the car pull into the driveway, I hid the papers in my jacket and walked down the front stairs as fast as I could. "What the fuck took you so long?" I shouted and raised my one good arm as I walked towards the car.

Seeing that I was upset, Starr pulled her blue Corsica out of the driveway and began driving away.

"Come back!" I yelled. "I'm sorry!"

The brake lights came on and I had to quickly walk an additional fifty to get to the car. She unlocked the passenger side door and as soon as I sat down, she began yelling in my ear. "It's almost a four hour drive from here to Dallas, Mike. If I'm going to be in the car with you for the next damn day, we are not starting out with an attitude. I'm doing this for you because we're in love and you need to find out where those papers are so that you can divorce that crazy bitch. Okay?"

I used my left arm to close the door and looked out the window. "Fine, whatever."

"Well, then give me a kiss to show me that you're serious." She leaned over and puckered her lips.

As angry as I was, I had to calm myself down because I needed this ride. The dreams weren't allowing me to sleep and I didn't know how long it was going to be before I could start driving myself with this damn sling on. I turned to her and gently kissed her lips. "Are you happy now?"

"That'll do, but it'll only get you halfway. You owe me a little more for the ride back."

"Whatever," I said and glanced towards the house Simone and I had shared since we were married.

I despised the feeling of nostalgia that was growing inside of me as we drove away from the house. The way she betrayed me by sleeping with another man was unforgivable. I abhorred the way she was, the way she is, and anything that I ever felt for her. As Starr turned onto 45 North, I knew there was only one thing in the world that I wanted from Simone, God help her if she didn't give it to me.

Quinton

2:30 p.m.

I hated to admit it, but Dre was right about Laela. All it took was a little guilt for her to become the complete opposite of who she'd been for the last week.

When I got home, she apologized so profusely that I began to believe she was going to call Niya. We talked until almost noon and though she conceded on almost everything, whenever I brought up Niya's name, she'd change the subject.

Even though she wanted me to go with Dre to the strip club, it was already too late. It was already Thursday afternoon and I wasn't so desperate as to get drunk and horny in the middle of the day. Besides, I had to meet Dre at my parent's house so that I could share at least some of my day with them.

While Lae slept, I snuck out of the house and made a quick fifteen minute drive to see my parents. When I pulled into the driveway, there were already a few additional cars parked on the street outside of their house. I stepped out of the car and could smell the food through the cool March air.

The front door was unlocked as I made my way inside the house. As I walked into the empty dining area, I closed my eyes to inhale all the delicious scents when everyone jumped out and screamed, "Happy Birthday!"

Startled, I jumped back and saw my parents at the front of the crowd laughing. I looked around the room as saw that it was filled with family, friends, and some of my parent's neighbors. Still laughing, Dre marched up to me and grabbed my wrist, measuring my pulse.
When I knocked his hand away he yelled towards the crowd, "Is there are doctor in the house!"

I walked over to my parents and hugged them. My mother kissed me on the forehead and fiercely squeezed me while whispering, "Happy Birthday, Quinton."

For about an hour I laughed with my family about old times and danced with some of my little cousins. It wasn't until I saw Dre alone in the kitchen, eating some of my birthday cake, that I was able to speak to him.

"Things didn't work out like we thought they would."

"What do you mean *we*? That plan was all you. I just cosigned in case it worked. It didn't-- so no threesome for you."

"You're such an ass. Whenever I come to you with a problem, you're all gung-ho when it works out, but if it fails, you don't want any part of it. What the hell am I supposed to do now?"

"Wait a second, Quinton, I don't give bad advice; you just may hear it the wrong way. Reasonable deniability allows me to keep a perfect record when it comes to giving advice. In your case, it was your plan. I just listened and agreed. I hate to be the bearer of bad news, but if it didn't work today, maybe it'll work in a week or month from now."

Dre turned his attention from me towards a beautiful brown-skinned, top-heavy girl who was approaching us and smiling at him. I quickly noticed that she was Mr. Williams' daughter, Alicia, and I stood between the both of them.

"Alicia?" I asked.

"Happy Birthday, Quinton! I just heard that you're getting married! Congratulations!" As we hugged, I made sure Dre noticed as she pressed her breasts against me.

"You're still seventeen, right?" I asked as our embrace ended. "I'll be eighteen in the summer," she replied.

"Then don't let me catch you talking to none of these perverts." I turned her around and shooed her out the kitchen.

"That was some foul shit to do, Quinton."

I smiled. "I also do some freelance cock-blocking if you're interested."

"Is this my payback for being an ass?"

"Yes."

"I'll just find her later, you know."

"Yeah like ten years later, and she won't be alone by then."

He stood and began walking out of the kitchen. "Well, at least we can look forward to your bachelor party."

"Right about now, I think that may be all the excitement I'll have these next few months."

Michael

6:00 p.m.

Due to Starr's lead foot, we made it to Dallas a few minutes after six; an hour before visiting time was over. After putting some gas in the car, we pulled into the parking lot a few minutes later.

The building didn't look anything like I thought it would. I half expected it to be up on a hill, dark clouds flashing behind it, with a long winding drive that had tombstones on both sides of it. But instead it was a two story building with a very short sidewalk, a flat roof and a single pair of glass doors.

I stepped out of the car and turned to Starr to speak, but she already knew what I was about to say.

"Yes, Mike, I'll stay here until you're finished."

Damn, why can't all women be like that?

The sun was setting as Starr pulled off and the glare from the glass doors briefly blinded me. With my hands over my eyes, I walked through the first pair of glass doors. When I walked through the second set, a white guy the size of Paul Bunyan looked up at me from behind more glass as he remained seated at his security desk. I didn't see a badge, so I knew he wasn't DPD, but I still grabbed my sling to let him know that I wasn't a threat.

289

He remained seated behind the glass, but still gave me an unpleasant glance. "Is there someone you're here to see, sir?" he asked, with his obvious country boy twang.

"Yes, I'm here to see Simone Hall. She's my wife," I answered.

"Is she expecting you?"

"No, I wanted this to be a surprise."

He raised his eyebrow as he looked at my sling and then returned his unsympathetic gaze to me. "You're the one she stabbed, right?"

"Can I see my wife please?" I asked, growing impatient with his demeanor and intrusion.

Without asking another question, he picked up the phone and said several things before he put the phone down.

"She doesn't want to see you."

I took in a deep breath and calmed myself. During the entire ride up here, I'd been preparing myself for this scenario. I knew she didn't want to see me, but I also knew that I had something she wanted. "Sir, can you tell her that I came up here to bring her the divorce papers. I want to get her out of my life as soon as possible."

"She already said she doesn't want to see you, sir. If you don't remove yourself from the premises, I'll be happy to escort you."

I could begin to feel my blood boil, but getting angry with him wasn't going to get me what I wanted. I reached into my jacket and pulled out the divorce papers, pressing them against the glass so the security guard could see for himself. "Please, just tell her that I have the divorce papers if she wants them. If she doesn't take them now then she can file them again whenever she gets out." I rolled then up and put them back inside of my jacket.

Sensing the urgency in my voice, he picked up the phone and called again, but this time when he hung up, he pressed the door buzzer and allowed me to walk through the an old metal security door. As soon as I was through, he rotated his chair towards me. "Mr. Hall, this facility closes at 7:30 p.m. sharp. I will escort you to the visiting room where you will stay for the duration of your visit. If the patient is abused in any way, I will not hesitate to stomp your crippled ass. Am I understood?" When I sneered at him, he stood up and walked his 6'10" frame over and reiterated what he'd just said. "Am I understood—sir?"

He put such a heavy accent on the last 'sir' that when he spoke, spit flew out of his mouth and onto my face. I thought about spitting back and taking my chances, even with only one good arm, but today was not that day. I just gritted my teeth when I responded. "Fine."

He escorted me to a room without a door that only consisted of two couches, a small coffee table, and wallpaper with an infinite number of butterflies on it. I sat down on one of the couches, and he told me that she would be along before he left.

After ten minutes of waiting, Simone finally appeared. She entered wearing grey sweatpants and a blue hospital gown that upon closer inspection wasn't made from cloth, but paper. As I looked more closely at her during her labored walk, she didn't appear healthy at all. With her hands dangling at her side, barely outside of the reach of the gown, she looked weaker than I'd ever seen her. She somehow seemed paler, if that was possible for a black person, her skin seemed to hang from her bones, and her hair was so disheveled that it appeared as if it hadn't seen a comb in months. She was so far removed from the Simone who'd lost all the baby weight that I hardly recognized her.

"Hello, Simone," I said, hoping to start things off on a pleasant note.

"Where are the papers?" she asked, impatiently. I pulled the roll of papers out once again and tried to smooth them on the coffee table as she stood by the doorway.

"I've signed them and I'm ready to give them to you."

She rolled her eyes and attempted a fake laugh, but only ended up coughing instead. "And to what do I owe this charity, Mike? The only time you do the shit you're supposed to do is if you've got some hidden motive. So what is it this time? You want your name back? Take it. Or perhaps you're about to be re-married and you want me to think that you're doing me a favor? It could be both of those, but knowing you, it's something like you wanting full custody of MJ and you want me to give up my parental rights?"

"I just want one thing from you Simone and it's neither one of those. In fact, I'm willing to do whatever it takes for us to come to some sort of agreement."

"Too bad you couldn't be like that when we were actually married or we might've made it work," she said sarcastically. "So, did you get your A.I.D.S. cleared up or are you still out there infecting unsuspecting women?"

"I don't have A.I.D.S. or H.I.V., Monie. I may have been exposed, but the test came back and I'm clean."

"Well, Mike, I'm not clean. I've had so many drugs shoved down my throat here that I don't even know what day it is anymore. Hell, most of the time I don't even know my own name, but thanks to you, I've been blood tested as well. See, I was hoping that you had some news for me because I've got news for you, too."

My heart stood still for a second and as rampant thoughts floated through my head, for the life of me I couldn't figure what she could have possibly had that I might've given her. But the more I thought about it, the more in dawned on me that he could've given her something and she passed it along to me.

"What the hell is that supposed to mean?"

"What do you want it to mean, Mike? I know you're thinking about all types of shit in that little brain of yours." She walked around the room twice, as if trying to taunt me not only with her words, but also her presence.

I looked up at her as she walked behind me and she just smiled, but it wasn't the Simone smile I'd grown used to during the last few years. There was something definitely more cynical about it, but I was tired of playing games with her. I balled up my fists and pounded on the coffee table, sending some of the papers flying onto the floor. I bent over to pick them up.

"Quit the bullshit, Simone, and just come out with it! What the fuck are you trying to tell me? Spit it out, goddammit!"

"You wanna know, Mike? I mean, *really* wanna know?"

"Quit this shit and tell me."

She was going to tell me! She was finally going to let me know the name of the motherfucker she's been fuckin'!

She stopped circling the room and walked over from the doorway. To further irritate me, she said nothing as she sat on the couch adjacent to me, but before I had a chance to curse her, she did something unexpected. As soon as she sat back onto the couch, she covered her face with her hands and suddenly burst into tears.

"That shit ain't gonna work with me no more, Simone." I began to twiddle my thumbs. It was supposed to help me calm down, but it wasn't working at all and I was growing increasingly frustrated with Simone and her outdated stall tactics.

She pulled her face out of her hands and for the first time I could see her bloodshot eyes. "Mike, I'm pregnant. I took a blood test once they brought me here and I found out I was pregnant. They had this depressed woman cocktail all ready for me, but now they just have me on Zoloft. I guess it's supposed to be one of the only drugs that won't have the baby deformed when it comes."

I was so caught off guard by the news that I just fell back into the couch. A mixture of emotions flooded through me and as I looked over at

Simone, I honestly didn't know what to feel. I didn't love her anymore, but once again we were about to be bound together for the start of another new life.

"Fuck me! What the hell do you mean you're pregnant? How far along are you?"

I don't want to go through this shit again-- not with her! Her ass is gonna get an abortion and I'll make that one of my demands if she wants me to sign these goddamn papers!

"What makes you think it's yours?" she asked defensively. "You act like you've been a father before! You've never been a father, Mike, you've just been around. You have a son, but you ain't never even been worthy of having a namesake. You're a sad and pathetic man who needs to be sterilized so that you can't ever fuck up another child's life. I hope to God that you ain't the father of this one! Maybe then I can be around something that hasn't been tainted by you."

And then it all dawned on me and I couldn't have been more disgusted. "You let that motherfucker up inside of you without a condom? So what, you letting everyone on the block hit my shit? Is that what it is? You're the neighborhood fuckin' play toy?" The level of my anger increased with every word and I knew that I wasn't going to be able to hold back if she said yes; even if she said it to simply spite me.

As if on cue, Paul Bunyan appeared in the doorway. He looked at Simone as she rained tears, then at me. "Is everything alright in here?" He asked while still eyeing me.

I inadvertently rubbed my sling as Simone answered his question. "Yeah, we're cool, Jacob," she replied, still sobbing and adding an additional sniffle.

"Alright, I'll be within a holler if you need me," he said without batting an eyelash and slowly backed out of the doorway while hanging onto his nightstick.

As soon as he was gone, I continued with my verbal barrage against Simone. "You fucking nasty ass ho! I can't believe I even laid down with yo' nasty ass. You're going to hell for this one and I hope you fucking burn for this shit."

"Cut the shit, Mike. You sit here and dog me, then act like you were the perfect husband and that you ain't never did nothing wrong! How the hell do you get exposed to H.I.V if you always stayed protected? Oh, yeah, perfect husband, how is that bitch Starr these days? Are you still fucking her or have you taken a vow of chastity for these last few weeks? You can't imagine how happy I am not waking up with your fat

293

ass next to me. Oh, yeah, you were the perfect husband. The best part of you being my husband is when I was fucking..."

I'd taken as much as I was going to take from her. If she wanted the gloves off, I could certainly accommodate her. "Fucking who, Simone? What's his name? Or are you getting shy now that there's no knife in your hands? You're big and bad with a knife, but we both know you ain't shit without it. You can talk about me being a bad husband, but let's talk about your pathetic wife skills. Popping pills, now that's a quality that all wives should have! Terrible cooking 101, you and your fucked up aunt could be the damn teachers of the year in that shit! And you have never been a mother to MJ! Running around the city with another man, fucking around at a job that you obviously sucked at, and stabbing your husband--yeah, that's gonna get you the mother of the fucking year award! Who's gonna be your next man? Charles Manson? In fact, how many times were you his whore before he went back to his *real* woman?"

"Fuck you! Get out of here, you bastard!" she screamed and launched herself at me. One of her nails caught me on my cheeks and I could feel the raw pain as she ripped the flesh away from the side of my face.

I tried to cover up, but the sling prevented me from stopping her blows. "Oh, I'm a whore! Who was the one who started all this shit in the first place? If you would've kept your dick in your pants, none of this would've ever happened! I fucking hate you! I hate you!"

Suddenly Jacob rushed in and pulled her away from me. She was still screaming as he began to lead her away.

"Wait!" I shouted loud enough for Jacob to turn towards me and for Simone to quiet her screaming fit. I remained silent for a few seconds as I regained my composure and stood up. "How do I even know MJ's mine? How do I know you ain't been fuckin this dude since before we were married?"

She spit at me, but she was too far away for it to even reach.

"Fuck you, Mike! Why do you even care anymore? You brought the fucking divorce papers, so what do you want, Mike? What the fuck do you want so that you can leave me alone for the rest of our lives?"

"I want his name. I want the name of that son-of-a-bitch who might be this baby's father!"

"Or what? Are you gonna rip up the papers? So what! You'll be hurting yourself more than you hurt me! I'm stuck here and I'm not going nowhere! But when I get out, I can have proof of your fucking around and I'll gain custody of MJ. Once I get him, you'll never see him again!"

She didn't laugh, but the cynical smile began to creep across her face again and I knew that she was laughing inside, where I couldn't hear her. She was laughing at *me* and she was the one in the fucking crazy house!

I felt the onset of rage coursing through me and I found my fists turning hard as boulders, but as soon as I became aware, I opened them and released the tension that flowed through them. As much as I wanted to hit her and make myself feel right for doing it, I didn't care that I wouldn't ever see MJ again when Simone got out and the more I thought about it, the more it made sense that I wasn't the one to take care of him. I hated the thought of being a father again and I didn't want the responsibility or the headache that came along with it.

I glanced at my watch and freaked when I realized that I only had ten minutes to get what I needed from Simone. We'd spent so much time arguing that I was about to miss my window of opportunity.

"Simone, I will give you anything you want. You want custody? Fine, it's done. I'm not ready to be a father. I'll let your aunt have him until you get out. You want out of here? I won't press charges. It'll be like this never happened. You need money? I'll pay double the fuckin' child support. I will give you these papers I have right now and I'll find some way to pay for the divorce if you just tell me his fuckin' name. That's all I want is a name. Just give me his name and I'll do it all."

She looked up at me with the saddest face I'd ever seen on her. "I can't do that, Mike. It's done and it's not important anymore. Let it go."

I began gnashing my teeth and I knew I was losing her. If conceding wasn't going to work, then threats certainly would. "Fuck it then. I will rip up these fucking papers right now and I won't pay shit for child support! I'll move out of town tonight with MJ so that you'll never see him again! Is that what you want, Simone? You never want to see him again!"

"Do what you have to do, Mike, I won't tell. I can't tell. You only want a name so that you can hurt him like you hurt me. It's always about you making yourself feel like a man. Whether you know him or not, you're going to go looking for him and hurt him like you do with everything in your life. That's all you're good for, Michael--bringing pain into everyone's life."

She nodded at Jacob and as he glared at me, he remained where he stood. As she began walking towards the door, I knew this would be my last chance. I couldn't let her leave, not without a name.

I ran past the guard and grabbed her shoulder with my good hand. "You never want to see your child again and for what? For what! For some dick? You would sell out your own flesh and blood for some fucking dick! You fucking ho'!" Just as I was about to slap her, Jacob flew out of nowhere. I never even saw him as he grabbed me, threw me against the wall and intentionally punched me in my bad arm.

I screamed from the pain, but I kept my eye on Simone as she watched Jacob punch me. With every bit of breath I had left, I screamed out at Simone, "Why are you protecting a man who doesn't even love you enough to come see you? He don't love you, Monie!"

As Jacob punched me in the stomach and everything I'd eaten came rushing to the surface, Simone screamed out, "I can't!"

Jacob held me on the ground and went to work on me in the hallway, but all I could see was Simone watching and crying. Then without any warning, all sound seemed to disappear as Jacob punched me in my ear. I could still see Simone crying, but her begging for Jacob to stop the onslaught fell on deaf ears--both of ours.

Simone ran up to Jacob and tried to pull him off, but Jacob held her back. With only one eye open, I turned to Simone and said the only thing

I could because I knew Jacob was about to kill me. "I love you, Simone." I wasn't sure that anything actually came out of my mouth since I was newly deaf, but she must've heard exactly what I said.

She ran over to Jacob once again and screamed at him. I have no idea what she said, but he stopped and took a few steps away from me as Simone rushed over and mouthed something to me.

"I can't hear," I mouthed out.

She ran to the desk and brought back a pen and pad and wrote on it. When she was finished, I read it with my left eye after a flurry of punches to the face from Jacob had shut my right. "Promise me two things. I want everything that you said you'd do in writing right now. Then, I want you to sign it."

"Fine," I said. I could taste the blood from my lip as I spoke.

"Secondly, you have to promise that you won't go after the guy and that you won't touch him ever!" She included a place for me to sign my name at the bottom. I knew I couldn't agree that I wouldn't touch him when the whole reason I came up here was to do just that.

I shook my head. "I want one punch at that bastard." But just as I said 'punch', saliva mixed with a little blood flew onto the paper.

Simone jumped back and began to cry. "No," she mouthed back. "No deal."

Jacob came from behind Simone and dragged me through the hallway towards the metal door by the collar of my jacket. After hitting a buzzer on the side of the wall it opened automatically and I turned my head towards Simone, nodding as vigorously as I could.

She shoved the paper in my face and I signed it as best I could with my body in such extreme pain. I completely missed the line, but my signature was there.

Tears began pouring down her sullen face and she mimed a name that I knew couldn't be right. I didn't have to be a lip reader to know the name of the person she mouthed, but I couldn't believe it either as a wave of shock came over me.

It couldn't be.

It was. In a muffled sound I heard Simone shout, "I'm sorry, Mike, but it might be Quinton's baby!" Then, she turned and ran back into the facility without another word.

Jacob stood me up and threw me out of the front door face first. With only one arm to brace myself, my face hit the sidewalk not long after my hand gave out from the force of the impact. Starr rushed out of the car after seeing me kicked out and ran to help me up. I could feel blood pouring from my lip and with me still retching from Jacob's punch to my stomach it hurt to talk, but I did manage to say one thing as Starr carried me to the car.

"*Quinton.*"

I promised not to hurt him, I signed my name, but I didn't give a shit about her contract. That mothafucka was going to pay the same way I did.

With blood.

Quinton

6:30 p.m.

"I'm sorry I missed your birthday party, but when you come home, I promise that I'll make it up to you. I'll be waiting for you."

I listened to that message more than an hour ago, but I didn't have any inclination to go home. The way Lae spoke, I knew that she was suggesting sex, but I doubted that my heart was even going to be in it. Somehow my birthday felt more like I was going through the motions of being happy than actually enjoying it. I'd screwed up and the birthday present I was getting didn't seem to make up for the one I'd lost.

Both Dre and I sat quietly on my parent's patio chairs, drinking and watching everyone else have fun inside the house.

Dre smiled for a brief second and looked at me before he broke the silence. "Are you ever going to forgive Lae for cancelling the ménage?"

After all of the years together and all the bull, it was uncanny how often Dre knew exactly what I was thinking. The truth was that most of the time, I couldn't stand all the crazy shit he did, still he was the only one who could relate to the dumb shit I did.

"How could I not forgive her? She's my fiancée. If we're going to be married, the least I can do is respect her decisions."

He took a sip of his beer and sat back in his chair. "That's great if you want to put that shit in a card, but you were right on the verge. I'd be mad as hell, but then again, I'm not you. So tonight, when you get your birthday sex, are you gonna think about what you missed?"

"How can I *not* think about it? It's funny though. This whole night I felt like Lae owed me, but now I'm beginning to feel like I didn't deserve it anyway. Between Simone, Cheyenne and even Niya, I've done so many things wrong this year that I probably shouldn't have done the threesome anyway. At first it was all supposed to be about us and having fun, but I got jealous. I lost focus of it being about us."

"Well, she did sleep with Niya without telling you."

"And I allowed myself to be seduced by other women-- each more than once. Do I forgive Lae? Yes. I know about what she did, but she doesn't know about me. A bigger question is could she ever forgive me for what I did to her if she found out." I stood up and began to walk towards the patio door.

"I don't think it's a good idea to test that theory right now, Q. You did your dirt and she's done hers. Why don't you go home and make the last person you'll ever screw feel like she's the only one." I nodded and after letting my parents know how much I appreciated them, I jumped in the car and drove off.

On the way back home, I stopped twice; once for gas, then at a floral shop where I picked up a half dozen roses. It wasn't long before I'd made it back to the apartment and I sat in the parking lot for a few minutes contemplating how great of a woman I had at home.

I thought about calling her, but surprising her seemed like a much better idea. I ran up the stairs and I quietly inserted my key in the lock. I slowly opened the door, but when I looked inside, I couldn't believe what I saw.

Laela

When Quinton peeked inside the house, I was already waiting for him. I stood in the hallway by the door wearing a red satin bustier-- the same one I'd planned to wear on our wedding night. Standing beside me, more beautiful than I'd ever seen her, was Teniyah Oliver. In addition to her sheer, black lace camisole and a matching thong, she also wore five inch stripper heels, towering over Quinton and me.

We both walked towards him and as he stood frozen in the doorway, fixated on us, I closed the door behind him and Niya took the flowers.

Every light had been turned off. The scented candles Teniyah and I lit throughout the apartment set the scene. The aroma of strawberries and vanilla permeating the air was an aphrodisiac I welcomed. The more I inhaled the more aroused I became.

I took Quinton's hand and softly kissed it. "Welcome home." I whispered in his ear. "Glad you finally decided to show up."
"Why didn't you tell me?" He tried to sound relaxed, but even I saw the lust in his eyes.

As Niya sashayed in front of us, she kissed Quinton on the cheek and without a word took the flowers into kitchen. With Quinton's attention diverted, I snuck up behind him and put on a blindfold.

"People shouldn't always know what they're getting for their birthday."

While he and Dre were out eating breakfast, I called my best friend. I'd never gone more than a week without speaking to her and I felt so bad that I cried before even getting a word out. After she apologized numerous times, we both continued to cry while blurting out our regrets. It was then when I finally told her how I truly felt about her. She was my friend and she would always be my friend, but even though I was confused about my sexuality, I wouldn't be confused about who I loved. I loved Quinton.

After reassuring me that she was only flirting with him and that she had never wanted to take Quinton away from me, I asked her if she still wanted to do the threesome. With an emphatic yes, I asked her to be here before he got home from his party and to also wear something sexy. She didn't disappoint.

"Now let us take care of you," I said, as I took his hand and guided him towards our bedroom.

With him now comfortably on the bed, I turned on the CD player and slowly removed each article of clothing, leaving him only in his blue cotton boxers. With his erection now conspicuously revealed, I motioned for Niya to join us.

Closing the door behind her, she stepped out of her shoes, walked towards the bed and straddled Quinton. She winked at me while slowly mounting him. Gingerly kissing the top of his penis through his boxers, she worked her way upwards, leaving deep, red, lipstick kisses on his bare chest. When she made it to his chin, their bodies were tightly pressed against each other and she whispered, "Guess who?" When he smiled, she ran her tongue over his lips and tenderly kissed him, gently hanging onto his bottom lip as she pulled away.

Watching their bodies and lips touch, I braced myself for the inevitable hint of jealousy that would follow, but it never came. Crawling onto the bed behind Niya, I removed her cami, tossed it to the side and ran the tip of my tongue along her spine.

Moaning softly as I ran my fingernails along her arms, she began to shiver. I nibbled on her ear and whispered, "Go take off the rest and get the cuffs." She stood up from the bed and I was left alone with my fiancé.

I pulled his penis out from the slit in his boxers and placed it in my mouth. He reached for me, like I knew he would, but I was ready. I moved out of his reach as Niya returned, now fully nude. Straddling herself atop his chest, she grabbed his hands and handcuffed him to the bed post.

She loved being dominant and I liked seeing it. Smiling, she whispered to him loudly enough for me to hear. "Now we get to turn you out and you can't do a damn thing to stop us."

I smiled at Niya, and with him now restrained, I removed the last piece of clothing and teased his tip with my tongue before returning him into my mouth. I'd never felt more powerful and as I slid him down my throat, I was in control and I liked it.

As Niya turned towards me, still straddling Quinton, I couldn't help admiring how beautiful she was. From her perfect breasts to her hourglass form, everything about her was flawless. Even with my fiancé's penis still erect in my mouth, all I could think about was kissing her.

I closed my eyes and remembered the last time we made love. Like two women who had completely lost their minds, we ravaged each other. I clawed at her flesh and she bit on mine. Even when we kissed, she never closed her eyes as she sucked on my tongue. I'd bite her lip and she would easily bring me to another climax. She was always on top and always in control.

Trapped in the ecstasy of my daydreams, I was already sitting up, away from Quinton's throbbing dick when I felt my favorite fingers inside of me-- Niya's fingers. It felt so good to be seduced by them again. I was so wet, her rhythm seamless. She pulled me closer to her and bit my neck. I was starting to rock with her when I grabbed her arm, trying to make her stop, but I couldn't. She knew exactly how to please me.

Oh God, I missed this. I miss her.

My self-imposed exile from her had been so long that I'd forgotten how good she felt.

How good we felt.

"Shhh..." she mouthed to me and placed her finger over my lips, but I loudly gasped several times before I was able to pull her away. As I stood up from the bed, trying fiercely to take off my bustier, she moved towards Quinton and circled her dampened fingers around his lips before placing them in his mouth.

I watched him feast on my essence like a starving man and once she was sure he'd had enough, she perched herself over his face. "Stick out your fucking tongue," she demanded. He did as he was told and she rocked her hips over him, throwing back her head and closing her eyes while he ate her.

I enjoyed watching him please her. I knew Niya's one weakness was my tongue, but as I watched her quickly climax over Quinton's face, I wanted to be a part of it. I straddled Quinton and as I slid his dick inside of me, my gratification was instantaneous.

I rode Quinton as slowly as I could; focusing...trying to retain control, but even with him bound and blinded, he was hitting every spot. I was so wet and he was so--damn--hard.

I tried to focus on something other than my orgasm by looking at Niya, but hers was more imminent than mine. Quinton's tongue was now inside of her and as she softly bounced on his face, reciting every vowel, her legs began to shake uncontrollably. The more I looked at her, the weaker my resolve became.

I closed my eyes, hoping not to see her, but as she began to scream, to curse, to succumb, she pulled me over the cliff with her. I couldn't stop it. My body trembled until it finally conceded. I, too, began cursing, my body giving way to one of the most powerful orgasms I'd ever experienced. I loudly cried for mercy, but mercy was already too late. As Niya collapsed and Quinton's faced was soaked with her essence, mine continued. With each overwhelming wave, he thrust himself deeper inside--I screamed and came even more.

Depleted, I fell over, away from Quinton and looked at the damage I'd done. I cum so much that I'd soaked everything around his waist and also the bed sheets. When I saw what she'd done, cumming all over Quinton's face, I smiled. The perfect triangle I'd seen at Dre's party felt as perfect as it looked.

I was sure that Quinton had already known who came on his face, but that didn't stop him from sucking on his lips. He tasted Niya and was smiling while he did it. Aware of the present she'd left for him, Niya quickly crawled over and patted down Quinton's face with her underwear. Then, she wandered down to the other end of Quinton and took him into her mouth.

Still shaking and falling several times while trying to stand up, I took the handcuff key and freed my man from his bonds. Now free, but still unable to see, he stopped Niya until he'd slid under her. Now in sixty-nine, Niya enthusiastically engulfed Quinton as he hungrily ate her out again.

Blinded, Quinton went to work licking and gently sucking her clit, not knowing her climax was already unavoidable. Niya tried several times to pull away from Quinton, but he was relentless. He kept her legs locked and separated while he explored every part of her. From teasing her clit to sliding his tongue completely inside of her, there was nothing that Quinton wasn't willing to do to get her to cum again. She tried desperately to prevent it, but no matter how strong Niya's will was, she had to know she was beaten.

Competitive as ever, she swallowed as much of him as she could and when she'd gotten him wet enough, she'd take it out of her mouth and try to finish him off with her hand.

Even as I sat back and watched, I loved seeing them battle. Neither of them would ever yield because what they put on the line was much too valuable to surrender. With Niya, it was her ego. For as long as I'd known her, she swore no man could ever conquer her. As much as I talked about Quinton's sexual prowess over the years, I always suspected she wanted a chance to see for herself.

With Quinton, it was his reputation. For the three years we'd been together, I'd only recently met any of his exes and for good reason. They were all stunning, even crazy ass Leslie, and they all still wanted him in their beds. Quinton was a ladies' man and he was very good at what he did. There wasn't a doubt in my mind that tonight, he was determined to break her.

The blindfold, still secure around Quinton's eyes made it impossible for him to see, but he knew who he was eating out. With the both of them too stubborn to give in, I figured it was time to help out. I licked my fingers and slid them inside of Niya as Quinton teased her clit. I moved slowly, only speeding up when I felt her tightening around my fingers and bit her several times on her back.

I like a little pain with my pleasure.

With each "fuck" that Niya shouted, Quinton softly began to moan. I was usually so focused on getting Niya to climax that I never got to see him weaken, but now-- I was watching him. Even with his eyes covered, I could see him struggling to keep his orgasm at bay and witnessing it made me wet all over again.

With Niya's climax causing her to clamp her legs around Quinton's ears I doubt he heard her whisper his name, but it didn't matter. There wasn't any doubt about how close he was. I rushed to the other end of the bed where I found Niya bobbing furiously, even as she was still cumming.

I watched Quinton's toes curl and knew it was time. Taking him out of Niya's mouth, I stroked him until he exploded on my tongue. As cum poured into my mouth, Niya grabbed him and began licking on the tip. After the last traces of his seed spilled on her tongue, she kissed me. As our tongues playfully wrestled with each other, reuniting the essence that we'd both stolen from Quinton, I could only think of one thing:

I'm ready for more.

Quinton

I never expected it to happen.

As Niya and Lae stood up from the bed and headed towards what I guessed was the bathroom, I just stayed on my back and looked into the blindfold, remembering how surprised I was when I walked through the door.

In her red bustier, Lae was absolutely gorgeous. Her hair was wild, with some of it even falling over her face and the bustier accented every part of her that I'd taken for granted over the years. She had tits, curves and even an ass. The red was a perfect complement to her butterscotch skin, altogether looking like the embodiment of sin.

I was all ready to ravage Laela when I saw Teniyah standing next to her. Teniyah stood tall and absolutely gorgeous. Her darkened skin, braided hair and sexy eyes were all accentuated now that she wore next to nothing. Already taller than Lae, the heels she wore seemed to add another six inches making her taller than me as well. As she walked by, the combined effect of her toned legs and sweet smell almost made me want to attack her as well. If Lae was Sin, then Niya was definitely the Sin-of-men.

Then, I was blindfolded. The sound of the shower and girlish giggles brought me back to reality and I finally removed the blindfold to see that the only light in the room came from candles.

"Are you going to stay in the bed or shower with us?" Niya asked. I quickly jumped off the bed and joined them in the bathroom.

With only one candle lit in the bathroom, it still wasn't difficult to see what was happening in the bathtub. I pulled the curtain back to find that Niya was behind Lae, cupping her breasts and passionately kissing her shoulder and neck. With their flesh pressed tightly against one another, Lae ran her fingers down Niya thighs and even before I stepped into the shower, I was horny again.

I stepped behind Niya and pressed my burgeoning erection against her ass before sliding it in between her thighs. She was still wet from cum and an inadvertent gasp from her was a confession that she still wanted me. I remained in between her thighs as I ran my hands along her arms and kissed the back of her neck.

As the shower ran and steam began to fill the bathroom, I watched intently as Niya's hands slipped further down Lae's body. Now fully erect, I was ready to enter Teniyah when I heard Lae softly moan. I pulled away from Teniyah and as I did, she spun Lae around so that now they were facing each other. Then she lightly kissed Lae's lips before sliding her fingers inside of her. Instinctively, Lae lifted her right leg and rested it on the edge of the tub while still kissing Niya. Taking another step back, I rested against the back wall of the shower, giving Niya more room to explore Laela. With more space to move, Niya released Lae from her grasp, kissed her down her belly and with water pouring over the both of them, knelt down to taste Laela.

Watching it as it happened more arousing than I could've imagined. A voyeur now, I closed my eyes and pictured the same thing happening more than a month ago. I remembered the hurt and pain I felt, but when I re-opened my eyes, I hadn't retained either of those emotions. Seeing them now, I couldn't even recall why I even ran to Simone.

I should've come *home*.

As Lae arched her back, water cascaded down her breasts and poured all over Niya. Pulling Lae even closer, hungrily sucking on her neck like she didn't want to let her go, what I watched between the two of them almost seemed like poetry.

Looking at me briefly before Niya began to finger her, Lae whispered, "Fuck Niya, I'm about to cum." She'd warned Teniyah, but Niya remain fixated, her intensity slowly turning to passion-- never breaking rhythm while eating my woman. I watched Lae and she ran her hands through Niya's hair and dug into the flesh on her back, signaling her release had come. Smiling, Niya stood up and Lae collapsed under the running water.

Seizing the opportunity of Niya being distracted, I lifted her leg, perched it on the side of the bathtub and entered her.

"Shit. Quinton," she whispered, slightly arching forward so she could receive me.

In the flickering light of the bathroom candle, an epiphany occurred. For so long I wondered why men like Dre relentlessly pursued her and why Franklin was so whipped and I finally understood. As Niya tightened around me, it was like her body welcomed me back every time I withdrew. Being inside of her was so warm, so inviting, so fucking-- perfect. It was such paradise, that for a few seconds, I remained still, wondering if I was deluding myself, but I wasn't.

From out of the darkness, a pair of hands grabbed my hips and returned me to heaven. "Don't stop when you're so close, Daddy," Niya said.

I held onto her hips and pushed in as I kissed her shoulders. For so long I'd wanted this. I wanted to be inside of her because of what she'd done to me-- because of what they both had done to me. I'd told Dre earlier that it wasn't about retribution, but I needed to be angry. I wanted to be angry. I grabbed Niya by her hair and pushed myself as deeply into her as I could. I wanted her to know now and forever why Lae had chosen me, but with every stroke, my manufactured resentment subsided. With every stroke, I didn't want to stop.

Oh my God, she's going to win. She's going to beat me.

After just a few strokes I was ready to yield to Teniyah when she pushed me away and stumbled out the shower.

"I think you've just given Teniyah her first orgasm." Lae said, from the other side of the tub.

"I guess that means I win."

"Why, are you finished for the night?"

I nearly was. "No, but isn't the birthday boy supposed to get a wish? I've been blindfolded and showered, when is it my turn to create the fantasy?"

"I'm not stopping you. Tonight, we can do whatever you want."

I quickly pinned Lae under the showerhead. It'd been a few weeks since the last time we made love, but Lae was always a perfect fit. I started off slowly, causing her to rise and drop against the shower tile, but as she unflinchingly glared into my eyes--she was challenging me.

I liked a challenge and after releasing her from the wall, I scooped her legs up from the bathtub floor. With her thighs now being supported by my forearms, she wrapped her arms around my neck as I plunged deeper inside of her. Our bodies slapped together so loudly that I could barely hear her screaming curses even though her mouth was next to my ear.

With the water hammering against my back and sweat obscuring my vision, I was relentless. As her ass slapped against my thighs and as she dug her fingernails into my back, I continued to pound my dick inside of her. Only when she screamed, "Fuck!" did I cede. Fuck was exactly what we'd done and what brought her second orgasm running down my leg.

"I'm not finished," I said, letting her down. I smirked as I watched her step out of the shower. She was still beautiful though her hairdo had been sweated out from the water and steam and her thighs still trembling from her climax.

I usually had a rule when it came to kissing women, even Lae. I wouldn't do it if she went down on me and didn't brush her teeth. I knew that she still had a taste from each of us on her lips, but that didn't stop me from passionately kissing her. Surprised, she smiled as she held me and we kissed.

After turning off the shower and drying off, we both stepped out of the bathroom looking for Niya, finding her sprawled across the bed.

"Don't tell me you're already tired." I said, slapping her on her ass.

"I'm not tired, just recuperating."

"Recuperating from the mighty orgasm I've heard so much about? Who would've ever thought it possible--the mighty Niya, slain by a mortal?" I loved to antagonize her and I was going to hold onto this one for years to come.

"Don't act like you weren't close, Quinton. I could feel you ready to give. Today, I just gave in a little sooner than I usually do."

I frowned. "I don't get you, Niya. If you liked it and you came, fine. I don't see why it's so hard for you to just say it."

"Fine, I'll play along. I *allowed* you to give me an orgasm," she said, still on her stomach, unwilling to turn over.

I lied on the bed next to her and whispered in her ear. "So how was it? *Was it everything you dreamed of?*" I added, trying not to smile, but before she even attempted to answer, I began nibbling on her earlobe.

"Yes," she whispered back with her eyes closed.

"I still want it, daddy. I'm still wet."

Still lying on the bed, I moved behind her, parted her legs and slowly entered her--still perfect. She was still wet, still warm and as I pushed deeper inside of her, she even began to grab the sheets while calling for me. Teniyah Oliver had finally been broken.

I laid on her back, knowing that I would cum, praying that I could hold out. With every thrust into her, her body hugged me as I pulled away.

"I'm coming, daddy."

As warmth and wetness flowed, she clenched so tightly that I couldn't move--my only saving grace. When her body finished convulsing, I kissed her down her spine.

"See, now don't you want to know what you taste like?" I asked.

"That depends."

"On what?"

"On how much I can get you to cum."

I crawled to the top of the bed and she flipped over, allowing Lae to get in between her soaked thighs.

"Make me."

Laela

I'd tried to appear nervous before going down on Niya, but with both Quinton and Niya's attention focused on each other, it didn't seem to matter. I didn't know whether I should act like an amateur to pacify Quinton, or like an expert who knew how to please Niya. Instead of guessing, I just closed my eyes and hoped that I was able to do a little of both.

307

I licked the inside of her thighs, tasting the excess cum that she'd expelled. Still, being with them and doing this was better than I ever dreamed it would be.

Maybe this doesn't have to end?

It *didn't* have to end. I wasn't sure if Quinton was ready for this type of relationship, but I knew that after everything that happened tonight, Niya would most certainly be on board with me.

I worked my way upward from her thighs, tasting inside of her before tickling her clit. I secretly opened one eye to see if they had stopped the stare contest, but they hadn't. Niya, her eyes fixated on Quinton's, pulled him in and out of her mouth and soon had him licking on the tips of her nipples.

He seemed to take instruction well as he went from licking to biting, palming her breasts with his hands. With Quinton playing with her breasts, she began to gyrate her hips to the rhythm of my tongue. I closed my eyes and began to play with myself, remembering how it felt to have Niya's tongue between my thighs.

The memories and images quickly made me wet again. I could feel my clit slowly growing between my fingers when suddenly, I felt Quinton slowly enter me.

I was pretty adept at handling Quinton, but his dick felt so much larger than usual. I gasped, losing my rhythm with both myself and Niya, and fell face first into the sheets.

Quinton quickly picked me up and returned my face to between Niya's thighs. "Make her cum, baby. Keep eating that shit until she comes."

Surprised at Quinton's authority, I was even more aroused. I did as I was commanded, holding onto her thighs while eating her as Quinton rammed me from behind. I held off for almost an entire minute, but as soon as I felt her climax spilling into my mouth, I immediately released my orgasm.

With the both of us screaming at the same time, Quinton backed away and began to laugh.

He hadn't cum and I knew what I had to do. I crawled to the top of the bed and whispered in Niya's ear. "Would you let him cum inside you?" She smiled and happily nodded.

"Well then, make him."

As if reading my thoughts, Niya moved herself in between my thighs. Then placing her ass high in the air, she wagged it as she went down on me. Knowing what she wanted, Quinton stood behind her and slid himself inside.

I saw the strained expression on Quinton's face both times that he was inside of Niya. I knew what he liked, but he knew my body too well. Niya was new and I could tell how much he enjoyed her.

I almost didn't feel Niya's tongue as I watched Quinton struggle. When he kept his eyes closed, I knew he was trying to think of something other than Niya and though she tried to focus on me, I could see the contorted look on her face as well.

"Stick out your tongue." I demanded and she did as instructed. I grabbed her head and slowly drug it across my tingling clit. I could feel her struggling to hold back, but when I whispered for her to let it go, she got on all fours a rocked her body against Quinton's. He immediately opened his eyes and when he looked at me, I nodded, giving him my permission.

He grabbed the underside of Niya's chin, pulling her closer to him as their bodies slapped against one another. Quinton, with short, forceful strokes, grabbed her neck tighter and I watched him pound against Niya as he prepared for finality.

Niya's eyes seemed to roll into the back of her skull as Quinton began to cry out her name. She too screamed out his name and as another forceful climax overtook her, she trembled like I'd never seen her before.

With several long, deep strokes, Quinton spilled his seed inside of her as they shouted in unison.

I snuggled up next to Quinton and kissed him on the back of the neck.

"You did good, baby."

As beads of sweat decorated his brow, he loudly exhaled, "Thank you," before collapsing onto the bed.

"Happy Birthday," Niya shouted, clearly out of breath.

We all laughed.

After it was all over, we cuddled in bed and talked openly about what had just happened. I was in between them, Niya's breasts against mine, Quinton's flaccid dick still poking me on the ass, but I didn't mind.

"So how did you guys like it?" I asked, curious to see what they thought.

I watched Niya smile and then lift her head up to see if Quinton was sleep. When she saw that he was awake, she shrugged and spoke anyway. "Lae, forgive me for saying this, but if we'd done this sooner, it would've already been a weekly thing."

"What makes you so sure that I would've agreed to that?" Quinton asked. "I was blindfolded for part of this and as arousing as that was, I didn't get to see half of what I was supposed to."

"Next time we won't blindfold you then." Niya said, sticking her tongue out for my benefit.

"So why did you let me cum inside of you, Niya?" Quinton turned to me. "Why did you let me?"

Niya and I both looked at each other and though I knew I should answer first, I let her answer.

"Quinton, Franklin and I are basically over, I told Lae that earlier. Next week the kids and I will be moving out. It's been a while since we had sex and I wanted it to happen. As much as we fight between each other, you really--you put it down tonight and I wanted it. It's been so long since a man has gotten me horny enough to swallow his load...and then that orgasm in the shower. Lae asked me to, but I really wanted you to nut inside of me anyway." She looked at me. "I hope that doesn't make you mad."

When I shook my head to let her know that I wasn't upset, I looked at Quinton and answered.

"I let it happen because I knew I wasn't going to get you to cum quickly. This was your birthday and your surprise and I wanted you to be happy. Truthfully, I was aroused as hell when it happened."

"So how does it feel to go down on another woman?" Quinton asked me.

"It doesn't feel like anything, I guess. It didn't taste like anything bad, she didn't smell funny and it doesn't force you to breathe through your nose." I said, smiling.

"So when can we do this again?" Niya asked, completely devoid of tact. The both of us looked at Quinton for his confirmation or disapproval.

"Why are y'all looking at me?" he asked with a raised eyebrow.

Niya leaned over me and softly kissed him before answering seductively, "You're the daddy. If you want to, we all want to. If you don't, we don't."

Quinton smiled. I knew he liked the way that sounded. "We'll talk. I don't really think we should be doing this after we're married and especially not with a married woman."

"So, what you're saying is we can do this until we get married? Then, when she gets her divorce after we get married, we can do this as much as we want?" I interjected.

Quinton looked at me like he was surprised at what I'd suggested. He finally smiled and said, "I'm just saying that if anyone else finds out about this, I don't know either of you."

"So we can..." I was interrupted by a loud banging at the front door.

"Who the hell is that at this time of night?" Niya asked nervously. Quinton turned towards Niya. "Where does Franklin think you are? Where did you tell him you'd be?"

"He thinks I'm at work and I'm covered. He always calls my cell because I told him we can't use the floor phones for personal use."

"Quinton, just go see who it is," I said, and ushered him out of the bed.

The banging at the door continued while Quinton threw on some jeans and a t-shirt. After telling Niya to stay in the bedroom, I grabbed a softball bat, put on a robe and followed Quinton.

The candles around the living room were burned to the core and I was straining to see my way to the front door. After peeking through the peephole, Quinton turned towards me. "It's Mike," he whispered. "Maybe if we don't say anything he'll go home. He's probably drunk."

"Quinton! Open up, man! I need to talk to you!"

Quinton

Everything in me told me not to say anything, but even as Lae looked scornfully at me, he was still my friend.

"Mike, go home! It's too late right now! We'll talk about it in the morning!"

"I can't Quinton!" he yelled. "I can't fucking let this go, man! I think that the guy Simone has been messing with is at her job-- some punk ass security guard! If you not gone help me kick his ass, then I'm goin' to prison because I killed his ass! Don't nobody go behind Mike Hall's back, goddammit! No--fuckin'-- body!"

I knew Mike was obsessed with finding out who it was that had slept with Simone, but I didn't think he'd go as far as murder. If I told Mike who it really was, I'd be stopping him from murdering an innocent man, but then I'd be in his crosshairs. Not only that, but Lae, the marriage, and the life we built might be over, too. I was caught and the only thing I could do was talk Mike down off the ledge.

I looked at Lae. "Why don't you go in the back? I'll take care of this."

Lae glared at me for a moment, but she'd heard everything too and even she was unsure of how far Mike could really go. "Set him straight and then get him out of here, Quinton."

I nodded and as soon as Lae had gotten to the bedroom, I began to open up the door. Suddenly Mike bulled in, knocking me into the divider that separated the kitchen and living room. Before I even had a chance to get up, Mike jumped on top of me. Easily sixty pounds heavier than I, my arms were pinned under him as a flurry of punches connected with my face. With each punch, I felt the depth of his fury. I tried to move—to speak, but each time I opened my mouth, I was greeted with another fist to the face. I could hear Lae screaming, but I was trapped as he continued to pound on me.

Struggling underneath his heavy frame, it was getting harder to see and I could begin to taste my own blood. Everything was becoming blurry and I knew I was about to pass out when Mike fell over and both Lae and Teniyah pulled me from under him.

I saw Lae yelling and the utter horror on Niya's face as they stood over me, but I could barely hear what was happening. It wasn't until Lae screamed in a muffled voice, "What the fuck is wrong with you?!"

"Quinton, are you alright?" Lae screamed, then walked a few feet over to a curled up Mike and shouted, "Get the fuck out of my house!" She smacked him with the softball bat. Mike slowly stood up, looking at Lae with her bat, then at me. Without warning, he launched himself at me a second time. I tried to move out of the way, but I was too slow and his fist caught me in the side of the face.

He hit me twice more in my exposed ribs before Lae hit him in the back, swinging like she wanted to kill him. Teniyah was already dialing 911 when Lae helped me up and I sat on the couch.

"Get out of here Mike or I swear to God I'll kill you before the police get here!" Lae yelled.

"Not before I say what I need to say, goddammit!" Mike yelled back. He eyed me angrily, but even though I had never laid a hand on him, he looked like he'd just gotten the ass whoopin' of his life. Both of his eyes were swollen, his right one nearly closed, his lip and shirt were covered with blood and his once white sling barely held any part of his arm, yet still dangled clumsily around his neck. He smiled menacingly at me.

"Quinton...you mothafucka. I wanted you to find out who fucked Simone and you knew the whole goddamn time."

Lae turned towards me with a puzzled look on her face. "What is he talking about, Quinton?"

Mike laughed. "Oh, he hasn't told you either, *Lae?*" And that's when he saw Teniyah. She was wearing one of my robes and now he knew what had happened here tonight. "What--the--fuck? This shit just gets better by the goddamn minute! Does Franklin know what you've been doing in your free time, Niya?" He turned towards me again. "You just don't fuckin' quit, do you?"

"Mike just go home," I pleaded. "The police are on their way and you're already dealing with enough shit."

Even though Lae kept the bat up, ready to attack, he turned towards her. "It's just like Quinton to help out, isn't it? I mean, damn, you wanted to marry him and he asked you. Niya wanted to fuck and I'm sure he helped with that too! I guess there's nothing Quinton wouldn't do for his friends--or your friends either, Laela."

Lae glanced at me before putting down the bat. "Is he saying what I think he's saying, Quinton?"

Before I had a chance to respond, Mike jumped in. "This whole time I suspected it was you, but I thought 'Quinton's my friend, I know he wouldn't do that shit.' The whole ride here, I thought about killin' yo' ass. I swear that I was only a breath from doing it too! She cried for you! She fucking cried when she told me! That night she went to jail, she was so fucking smug when she talked about you. 'He's the best. He's a real man', but I fixed her ass. I told her Starr was H.I.V. positive and that she might be too!"

As he began to laugh, a fear unlike any I'd ever felt surged through me. Though barely able to see, I stood up and grabbed the bat away from Lae. As he continued laughing, I held the bat in both hands and before he could stop me, I slammed the barrel across his throat.

He's fucked up everything!

I slept with Simone without a condom and if he'd passed it to her, there was a chance that she'd passed it to me. This meant that...

I stood up from Mike and threw away the bat. I wanted to turn towards Laela, to face her, but how could I? Mike told and now everyone in the apartment knew. As Mike coughed and gagged, all I could do was slump my shoulders.

"So-- you're the goddamn man she was screwing, Quinton?" When I didn't respond, she screamed.

"Answer me, goddammit!"

I turned and faced her, watching as tears poured down her cheeks. It hurt knowing that what I'd done had put them there, but she wasn't the only one that had been wronged. "Let me explain." I took several steps towards her and reached out to grab her hand. Instead of taking my hand, she cringed as she pulled away from me and then took a step back.

"What the hell are you backing away for?"

"We all have to get tested. We all have to go to the hospital and get tested tomorrow!" I tried to reach for her a second time, this time she didn't back away, she screamed. "Don't fucking touch me! I can't deal with this right now, shit! I just can't. She went crazy because of you! I can't believe it was you! All along it was you that slept with my best friend!"

"You didn't seem to mind when he was banging Niya. She's your friend, too, isn't she?" Mike chortled.

I'd had enough of Mike and his comments. Still struggling to see, I grabbed him by the sling around his neck and dragged his fat ass towards the door. I'd never even entertained the thought of killing someone else, but Mike had me damn near that point.

While I dragged him to the front door, he began laughing. I opened up the door and was ready to throw him out when he shouted at Lae, "She's pregnant, too!"

Oh God.

I let go of Mike and turned towards Lae who was already throwing the bat at us. I moved just in time for it to miss me and leave a small hole in the wall next to the door, but Lae didn't stop there. She grabbed anything that she could throw, including the lit candles, and cursed me. I looked over at a horrified Niya, who shook her head and ran towards the bedroom.

I ran quickly out of the apartment and closed the door, leaving Mike to fend for himself. The sounds of breaking glass, aerosol cans, electronic equipment and shoes pelted against the door for a couple of minutes before the ruckus stopped.

I was about to walk back in when a very tall woman ran towards the apartment, her heels sounding more like cleats as she approached. When she finally stopped in front of me, she was about a three inches taller than me and I saw that it wasn't a woman at all, but a man dressed in drag.

"Is everything all right?" he asked, sounding out of breath. When I didn't answer, he looked at me like he had an attitude. "Well, is Mike okay?"

"Is Mike okay? Who the fuck do you think started all this? If it hadn't been for goddamn Mike...Who the hell are you?"

He threw his head back, rolling his neck and looking at me as if I had been indignant in asking. "Little man, I am Starr."

I couldn't believe what I was hearing. "*You're* Starr?"

"Why, do you know another Starry Heavens?" But before I had a chance to respond, he stuck his hand in my face and replied, "I didn't think so."

I threw my head in my hands. My birthday was almost over and this was supposed to be the happiest night of my life, but instead it had turned to shit. Lae and Niya had found out about Simone, a pregnant Simone, who was possibly carrying my child and fuckin' Mike was gay.

When I opened up the front door, Lae wasn't anywhere in sight, but Mike was still where I left him. He was curled up in a ball and under a bunch of shit that Lae had thrown at the door. Starr rushed past me inside the door to see if Mike was alright, but I didn't care. I kicked him as hard as I could in the leg.

"Dammit!" he yelled. "What the fuck did you..." He stopped talking when he turned over and saw Starr. "I told you to stay yo' ass in the car!"

"I would've, but I left to get a smoke! Next thing I know, I hear all this arguing and yelling, so I knew you had to be a part of it! Excuse me for taking care of yo' miserable ass!"

After Starr helped Mike up, I didn't hesitate to grab him by his sling. "Now get out." I mumbled through gritted teeth.

"I don't have H.I.V., Quinton. Simone ain't got it either, but she is pregnant and I hope to God it's your baby." Without another word Mike and Starr left the apartment. After I closed the door, I went looking for Laela and found her crying on Niya's shoulder. I tried to sit down next to her, but Niya quickly pulled Lae towards her and away from me.

"I don't think she wants to see you right now. Maybe you should spend the night with Dre."

"No, dammit, I need to talk to my fiancée."

"You can't say shit to me Quinton!" Lae blurted out. "You fucked my friend and then I find out after all we did tonight? I trusted you, Quinton. Everything that happened tonight was because I trusted you, but now I feel-- I feel so fucking nasty."

I was tired of playing the villain. "Don't try that shit with me, you fucking caused all this! You were already fucking Niya way before I even got the chance!"

Lae looked at me with a malice that I'd never seen from her before. "So you knew?"

I hadn't meant to tell her I knew, but the cat was already out of the bag. "If it weren't for you, none of this shit would've happened in the first place. I didn't want to fucking sleep with Simone--but you betrayed me! You betrayed us!"

"So this is all *my* fault? I drove you to fuck Simone?" She laughed sarcastically. "You just can't be wrong, can you? I was curious, Quinton! I mean we were going to fucking do it anyway!"

"Yeah, but you did it behind my back, Lae! You didn't include me! You didn't ask me! You didn't even want me there! How the hell am I supposed to react when you didn't even want me to be a part of it?"

The women simply looked at each other, grasping each other's hands as if I weren't even there.

"So if you knew about what happened all this time, why didn't you say anything? Was it because you were so bent on revenge that you had to fuck the girl who screwed your fiancée?" Lae asked, not even looking at me when she spoke.

"I don't know. At first, it was jealousy, then it became revenge, but it didn't end that way. I love you Laela and I wanted what you wanted. I didn't do this tonight for me-- I did it for you. You wanted it and so I wanted it to happen, too."

When she didn't respond, I bit my lip and walked towards the closet to get a jacket when Lae spoke again. "Why did you do it Quinton? How could you hurt me like that?"

And that's when I lost it. "How could I hurt you? You fucking took everything from me! You made me feel like I wasn't worth a goddamn thing! Everything we have is in your name and I gave you the only thing I had to give! I gave you my goddamn heart and you fucking threw it away for her, Lae! I heard you on the phone! You left on your phone and I heard you fucking! And I heard you loving it! You wanna know why I slept with Simone? Because she wanted me when you when you were already fucking her!" I said, pointing to Niya and turned my attention to her. "What else was I supposed to do? I could've come home, but you two were busy!"

Feelings of anger, frustration and betrayal coursed through me and before I knew it, tears were falling from my eyes. I quickly turned away so that I could wipe them from my eyes. I thought that telling her I knew would absolve me from feeling guilty, but instead I felt sick to my stomach. I found myself wishing that I'd left.

This time Teniyah spoke up. "So why did you stick around? If you knew about us and everything we did, why stay?"

"Because more than anything, I wanted to forgive her. When I proposed, I meant it. I love Lae so much that I forgave the *both* of you. Why is it so hard for her to do the same?"

"You slept with my best friend! You exposed us to H.I.V.! She's having your child! How the hell am I supposed to forgive you and you're having a baby by another woman?"

"Mike made most of that shit up and you would've known that had you stayed out there."

"Is she pregnant?

"Yes."

She began to cry and my heart began to break all over again.

"Out of all the people to choose, why *her*?"

"I thought that I wanted revenge. I wanted to make you feel like I felt. You picked a friend, so I did the same."

"Do you love her Quinton?" Lae asked.

"I never have. I love you. It was never about *love*, Laela--"

She shook her head. "That's the difference between you and me, Quinton. I can only make love to people I'm *in love* with." She smiled slightly at Teniyah. "For the last three months, I've been trying to give her excuses why we can't be together. Quinton, being with her again tonight has taught me a lot about myself."

My heart stopped. They didn't just have sex, they had a relationship. They'd done it all behind my back and I was the fool for not having seen it. "You've been sleeping together *all this time*?"

"Yes," Niya said. "I really love her, Quinton, and she loves me."

"I didn't mean for it to go this way, Quinton, I really didn't. But I can't keep lying about who I am. I'm bisexual and I've been trying to deny it, but I can't. Right now, I need to learn a little more about myself." She looked at the floor. "What I'm saying is that--I'm not ready to get married right now."

Now I was angry. "What the fuck do you mean you can't marry me? Mike said he doesn't have H.I.V.! He even said he's not sure who the father is! Don't do me like this, Lae! I forgave you! Why are you just throwing three years away?"

"What happened tonight was just the final push." Laela closed her eyes as Niya began to rub her back. "I talked it over with Niya and I think you should move in with Dre for now. I need some time to sort this out."

"So where the hell is Niya going to stay?" When they both looked at each other, I knew. "So her and the kids were supposed to stay here all along? You were already kicking me out?"

317

"They were supposed to stay here until she found a place! You fucked up Quinton! Don't try to put this on anyone else, but you!"

"So you're really giving up on us for her?" I already felt the lump in my throat overwhelming me. This time I couldn't hide the tears as they fell.

"I'm not giving up anyone for anyone. She makes me happy and the more I deny it, the harder it will be for all of us. I'm sorry that I can't be the person you want me to be."

"You can't be who you want to be? I've been replaced and to add to my fucking humiliation, it's by another woman. You don't know what it's like to love someone and then have the taste of another woman on their lips when you kiss them, but you still try to love them!"

She stood up from the bed of softly kissed me on my lips, a goodbye kiss. "Yes, I do."

I wanted to fight and argue or do anything that would keep me here longer, but no matter how much a tried to stay, I wasn't wanted anymore.

"So the kiss at Dre's Christmas party, that's what started it off, huh?"

When Niya nodded, I grabbed my jacket from the closet-- the only thing that I still owned that I was sure I'd bought-- and walked through the demolished living room. I picked up my cell phone and both women followed me to the front door. I turned to Lae, who was crying like a baby, before I opened it.

"You were always the one."

With tears pouring down her eyes she placed her ring in my hand. I quickly opened the door and slammed it behind me.

As soon as I made it to the car, it began to rain.

"It fucking figures," I muttered as I pulled my cell phone from my pocket and called Dre. I was glad that he picked up on the second ring.

"I'm staying with you for a while."

"What the hell happened?" He asked while yawning. I looked up at Lae's apartment and saw the bedroom light turn on. I tightly clutched on the ring she'd put in my hand and tried to keep from crying, but I couldn't.

"Quinton, what's wrong?"

My faced burned as tears fell over the open cuts. "She left me, man. She found out about Simone and she left me."

"Damn. Why don't you just go to her and talk? I mean you guys are supposed to be getting married, right? Why don't you just stay there until y'all talk?"

As the clouds opened up and the rain began to pour, I watched as the light in our bedroom came on and went off. "She picked Teniyah, man. She said that she was fooling herself with me and that she wants to be with Teniyah. She even gave me the goddamn ring back."

Still silent, I could tell that Dre was as shocked as I was.

"I'll see you when you get here," he finally said, and I slid the phone back into my pocket.

When I opened the door and sat in the car, I was soaked. I turned on the car and warmed myself up as I thought about what the hell I was supposed to do next.

My heart felt so heavy that it hurt to breathe.

How the hell could she put this all on me?

She even carried on a relationship with Teniyah behind my back for months. But between Simone and Cheyenne, I wasn't completely innocent either. We'd both messed up, but why was I the only one paying for it?

I didn't know how, but I was going to make it right. She was supposed to be my wife, not shack up and play house with Teniyah. I'd already run away once before and it cost me my future with Lae.

This isn't over.

I slammed my hands down on the wheel before turning off the car and stepping back out into the night. Like a man possessed, I ran through the rain, back up the stairs and pounded on our apartment door.

I'm not going to quit.

I am going to get my woman back.

Valentine

New York City

"Damn baby, you keep fuckin' with me like this, and you might just see a grown ass man cry."

She slowly licked the underside of my shaft, kissed me at the very tip of my manhood and put just enough tongue on it to make me shiver. "So, you'd cry for me, Antoine? I didn't think men like you cried for much."

She was right. Even though I'd only spent three days with this woman, I couldn't stop myself from acting like a goddamn fool whenever she was around me. *What the fuck is wrong with you, man? Show her why they call you the Rock Hound.*

I'd come too far and I wasn't about to become a bitch now, not when I was so close. I was Antoine "Rock Hound" Davis and it was time that she knew this, too. "Perhaps *cry* is a strong word. See, you got me wearing this damn blindfold and I'm not really feeling it right now because I can't see shit. But I do know that if my dick is anywhere near your mouth, you can't take what I say seriously."

She wrapped her hands around my dick like it was a microphone and softly whispered into it. "You mean like this?"

I cringed but there wasn't a damn thing I could do about it, she had me trapped. "Stop doing that shit! If you're just going to tease me, then you got to go."

"What are you willing to do for me?" she asked, before licking the tip a second time.

"What the hell do you mean what else am I willing to do?" I pulled against my arm and leg restraints but I was securely tied to both ends of the bed. "You think I would let some *other* chick do this shit?"

She laughed and I loved it when she did. "I think I've made you wait long enough. It's time for daddy to cum."

She made her way up to me and softly slid her clit across the tip of my nose before asking, "Can you smell it, baby?"

"I can smell it."

"Does it smell good to you?"

I loved the way both she and her pussy smelled. I didn't care if other men had been here before me; all that mattered was that she was with me now. "I wanna taste it. Can I taste it, ma?"

"I want you to taste it, daddy."

I could feel her heat next to my face, calling me. I wanted nothing more than to grab her and press her against my face, but with the handcuffs still restraining me, it was a losing battle. I cursed her several times for doing this to me, but as soon as she pressed her clit against my lips, I ate like a hungry man.

She softly rocked her hips across my face and my tongue followed her every motion. Several times I pushed my tongue inside of her, but as I felt her clit growing against my tongue, I began to suck on it.

"Don't do that," she whispered, but as she clamped her legs against the side of my head, I knew I was near.

I continued to suck on her until she yelled out my name and spilled in my mouth.

When her body finished trembling, she stood up and stepped off my bed. "I know you not gone leave me hangin' like this, right?" I heard her moving around, but when she didn't answer, I tugged at the restraints again.

"Right?" I was getting pissed off.

"Don't get so mad, baby. I just had to get something." She straddled my erection and I became a little more agitated when she slid the condom on.

"What the fuck is this?"

"You know what? I don't have time for this shit. I'm gone." She stepped off the bed and I could hear her heading towards the door.

Still chained to the bed, I wasn't about to let her leave and let anyone catch me like this. "Whoa, you need to just chill the fuck out. I just thought that since this was the third date and all-- that we could get past this."

"You know I can't do that." Even though I couldn't see her, she sounded almost upset.

"I said if anything like that ever happened that I'd take care of you, didn't I? Hell, I told you I'd take care of you after the first night, so why is you trippin'? I got you, ma. Whatever you want, I got you. Don't take that lightly."

I could hear her walking back towards the bed where my erection was still waiting for her. "The condom stays on."

"Alright, but after this is all done, I really wanna talk to you."

But before I had a chance to say anything else, she grabbed hold of me and slid me inside of her. I gasped, trying to prepare myself for how good she felt, but she'd moved too quickly for me to prepare. As she rode me, her body grinding against me, her warmth permeating the condom, I tried desperately to stave off my orgasm-- but I couldn't. We were only thirty seconds in and I could feel my body giving way. I hated how she did this to me, but I loved the way she did it.

I didn't know whether she saw my toes curling or because I allowed and extra 'fuck' to escape my mouth, but she quickly switched from grinding to riding. With our flesh slapping against one another's, I felt more like I was in Madison Square Gardens receiving applause than in my bedroom getting my brains screwed out.

"Talk to me, ma. Tell me you love this dick."

She dug her nails into my chest before reaching up and grabbing my neck. With one hand on my chest and the other firmly grasped on the front of my neck, she began to squeeze.

"What--the--fuck--are you--doing?" I asked, barely able to get it out because of how hard she began to squeeze.

"I'm almost there, baby. You got me there."

With her so close I didn't want to say anything, but even in complete darkness, I was beginning to black out. "Get it--ma. *Please* fuckin' get it," I yelped, hoping that she got hers before I passed out.

"I love your dick, daddy. I love it. You love this pussy, right?" she whispered. Her smoky voice was exactly what I needed to push me over the edge.

"Fuck you," I whined with her hand still tightly grasped around my neck. "Fuck you!"

"I'm coming baby," she said, and that was all it took.

We both came, but that didn't stop me from cursing this woman and what she'd done to me. As soon as I began to relax, she pulled me out of her, removed the condom and sucked up any remaining seed. As several shockwaves ripped through my body, a single tear began to form in my eye and I thanked God that I still had on a blindfold.

When she finished, she left me in the room. My neck hurt like hell and wanted to choke the hell out of her ass, but I just simply yelled, "Yo' ass better be coming back!" With her gone, I was forced to listen to the sounds of my own breathing and inhale the wonderful scent that she'd left on my nose and tongue.

That woman was so fucking perfect that it hurt not to be around her. I'd just met her three days ago, through Angelica's Service and already I was ready to give up all this shit for her. Hell, I had been afraid she was white for the first couple of days, but she had always sworn she wasn't. Still, she was light as hell and those hazel eyes were so clear that I felt like I could see her soul. Because she was built like a sister, I really didn't give a damn. Truthfully, she was everything that I'd ever wanted in a wife: smart, sexy, well toned, and the pussy was so damn good that she could keep my wallet.

This wasn't the first time I used Angelica's Escorting Service, but she had certainly went out of her way this time. Shit, for the thousand an hour I was paying, the service should've always been this good.

There were two problems I had though. The first was that she didn't know what I did, almost no one did and if she found out, how long would she stick around? I mean, I made good money, but traffickers always did.

From drugs to stolen cars, I could have anything shipped anywhere in the world, but for the last few months, I'd been trafficking kids. Goddamn kids from other countries were being shipped in to me and suddenly, I found myself up to my ass in Slovaks and Eastern Europeans. It made me sick to my stomach, but I just needed this last deal and I'd be set for life.

That brought me to my second problem, my *wife*. She didn't know what I did, but I suspect that she didn't care. We weren't together out of love, at least not anymore, we were together because we had to be. She was a marriage guru and when we were married, I was legit. Now that I'm not as legal as I used to be, divorce would be very bad for her business, which she seems to do really well from.

Shit, if it wasn't for her terrible business sense, I wouldn't have had to hustle. But that was the past and this woman that just screwed my brains out was certainly my future.

"I'm back."

The sound of her sexy southern drawl brought me out of my daydream and back to the present. "What took you so long and when can I get these damn chains off? My shit is starting to hurt."

"I still have a surprise for you."

"And what kind of surprise is it? You came, I came-- you wouldn't happen to have a friend with you? Because I think I can squeeze out one more if you brought a friend."

"I had to make a call and it doesn't seem as if my friend will be coming."

"That sounds fucked up, but I still need to be untied. This shit is really starting to hurt my rotator's cuff."

"You never answered my question." she asked as she stroked my flaccid dick and ran something extremely cold down the center of my chest.

She brought ice. This bitch is freaky! I think I'm in love!

"And what question is that?"

"What are you willing to do for me?"

I pulled on my restraints, hoping that she would let me go. This was getting tiresome. "I answered that already, but if you want to know more, then fine. Look, I'm really digging you, Val."

"I'm digging you too, Antoine, but would you die for me?"

"Die for you? Hell naw! I mean I don't even know the real you. What's your real name? I know it can't be Valentine, right? That's just your trickin' name, right? I mean who the fuck names their kid after a holiday?" When she didn't answer, I continued. "I mean I see a future for us. I know you don't wanna be an escort for the rest of your life and I wanna be able to take care of you. That's real shit."

Suddenly there was silence and she stopped stroking me. "That's so sad to hear."

"What do you mean? Why is it sad to hear?" And that's when I smelled something strange.

"You smell something funny? Do you smell smoke?"

"You know something, I do. See, I had this gun in my hand and I was just going to shoot you, but I can't do that anymore. My benefactor wants you to suffer just a little bit more."

"What the fuck did you do?" I yelled, struggling to break free of the bonds she'd placed me in, but they wouldn't let go. "Val, let me go. This shit ain't funny."

"To answer your question, yes, my name is Valentine and the sad thing is that this is goodbye Antoine. I'll always remember-- your tongue."

She gently placed tape over my mouth as I flailed around on my bed, trying to break free.

"It's time for me to go, but I just wanted you to know that your house is on fire. Maybe we can hook up next lifetime, but in this one, you shouldn't have known that what is done in the dark comes to the light. Didn't you know selling kids was a *no-no*?" I heard her heels against the bedroom's wooden floor as she walked away from me when suddenly she stopped. "Just so you know, you weren't that great of a fuck, *Rock*

Hound. Maybe next time around, you'll get a bigger dick. And uh, your last ride was compliments of *Mrs. Davis.*"

Fuck you!

I wanted to scream out, but the tape was pressed so hard against my face that all she could hear was me murmuring. For several minutes, I tried to push my tongue against the tape and scream for help, but it was too strong. I wriggled around on my bed for what seemed like an eternity, but no matter how hard I fought, I knew this was about to be my tomb.

For the next few minutes, I panicked. I screamed, I wrestled, I cried, I cursed and fought against the handcuffs she'd put on my hands and feet and felt the steel cut into my skin. Even though I couldn't see the fire, I could smell the charred remains of my house and I could feel the heat from the flames moving closer to me. I fiercely yanked at my restraints one last time and I could hear the headboard cracking, but I was already too weak, gasping for my last breaths. I had inhaled too much smoke and the world was slowly darkening around me.

I am going to die.

As I felt the unbearable heat from the fire surround me, the last thought going through my mind was of me choking the life out of both my wife--and that fucking *Valentine.*